ST. CHRISTIE'S ISLAND

ST. CHRISTIE'S ISLAND

a novel by

ELLIE OSBORNE

Beach Street Press
Daytona Beach Shores, Florida

Published by Beach Street Press LLC.

BeachStreetPress@aol.com.
Osborne, Ellie. St. Christie's Island
ISBN: 978-0-9859734-1-4

Cover image/ BigStock. Cover: Graphic Design by
RallyPointConsulting@gmail.com

Interior layout: MrLasers.com

In memory of my parents

Catherine and John

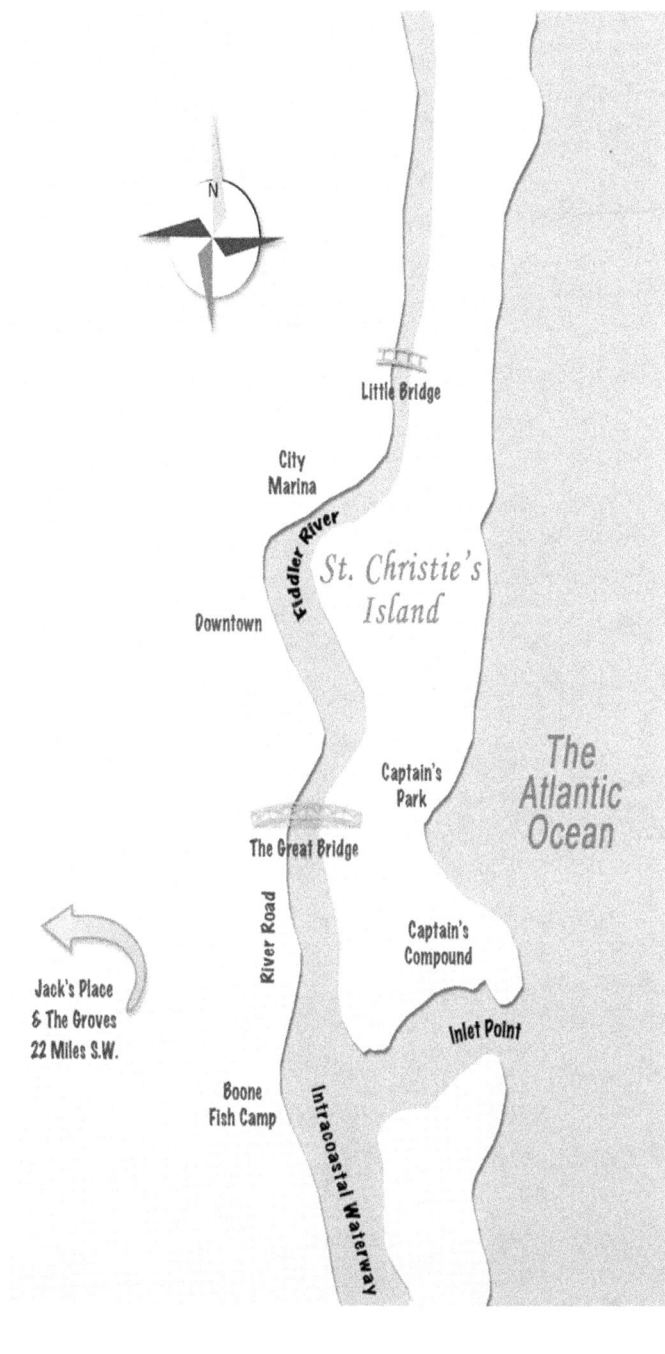

BOOK 1

CHAPTER 1

1977

ON A SUNNY NOVEMBER SATURDAY, Phoebe Moffitt was presiding over the general mayhem of the St. Christie's Island annual Music Festival and Pig Roast. Every year people complained, "For God's sake, pig roast! can't we call it something nicer?" Despite numerous attempts at re-naming, the task proved too daunting, and so, Pig Roast it was now in 1977, as it had been for twenty years before that – a weekend festival that took place at Captain's Park on the Atlantic oceanfront.

Phoebe, a woman of sixty-five, had for ten years been widowed by a Mr. Thadeus Moffitt. In this, Mr. Moffitt was entirely blameless, but among some, his demise had provoked considerable dismay – the reason being that few had expected Phoebe to achieve the status of respectable wife, never mind the rank of rich widow. Hence, some thought an impropriety had been committed, but couldn't be proved. Spearheading a successful roast was Phoebe's way of paying everyone back, in more ways than one.

Among Phoebe's helpers were Grace and Parker Quinn, who had arrived early together with their daughter, Ainsley. Parker was tending one of several fire pits, smoking in the distance, while Grace stocked cold beer into tin washtubs that reflected the rays of the rising sun. She was also in charge of making the gravy, her specialty.

Most islanders would agree that at seventeen, Ainsley was an unmistakable blend of both Parker and Grace, with her mother's wide-set eyes and wry humor, her father's slanting smile and dauntless optimism.

1

"The worst of everything," as Grace would say.

Ainsley and her best friend, Beth, were in the pavilion, Ainsley walking between the tables, rearranging gifts for the silent auction, and energetically directing her committee of two with nods of approval and disapproval. They were also awaiting the arrival of the town's favorite race car driver, Billy Fiske. It was a short wait. Soon the familiar red roadster was backing into its reserved spot, and a few minutes later, Billy stepped out, and into the center of a gathering circle – compact and medium in height, sandy blond hair set in motion by the ocean breeze. He was neither on time nor late. Billy had come early! showing right off how much they all meant to him. The circle grew as Billy moved toward them, surrounded by eager virgins, moms, and the racing groupies people called Pit Lizards.

"Look at those girls," said Ainsley, resentful of their nipple-hugging T-shirts, their spiky sandals. In contrast, she considered her own outfit – the committee's jean skirt and baggy yellow top emblazoned with the directive: Pig Out! in purple letters.

Some may have thought that Billy lacked a predatory edge, but wiser onlookers knew that daughters were on the endangered list and wives, too. Someone was overheard saying, "Circle the wagons, men." Nobody cares though. Race car fever grips the crowd, and the sunny mother of all stock car races, the Daytona 500, is just two months away. An epidemic of adulation and hope is about to break out for the hometown boy.

A volunteer guided Billy toward a tent where all the naked lust had gathered, a booth set up for autograph signings, a new way this year to raise money for charity. Ainsley watched as teenage girls like her crowded in. Of course this was not the kind of itch seen on the infield at the speedway. After all, right over there, men were tending to the fire pits, and moms were more concerned about burning biscuits than burning desire.

Ever since she had first laid eyes on Billy, Ainsley had been filled with romantic imaginings. He was twenty-five, grew up in North Carolina, had raced half his life and slowly climbed up, with some people saying he could be the driver of his generation.

Watching Billy from a distance, Ainsley's confidence waned, despite her arsenal of highly-praised skills: She could captain a boat, navigate by the heavens, grow eight-inch sunflowers, and bake the tastiest of corn breads. And, because she was slim and taller than most girls, people insisted she took after her mother, even though she was not the beauty that Grace had been. Nonetheless, this assumption, and her much-remarked upon auburn hair and blue eyes, ringed as they were with indigo, made up for most other defects. Men turned to look as she passed, men in a fever with so many half-dressed beach-ready girls to admire, men who looked to be on the verge of barking and howling in the hot sun.

Ainsley's successes were small but multiplying, and this very evening, she had a date with Charlie Portman, a boy she had set her sights on before Billy had entered her orbit. More important, she had recently been elected Speed Weeks Queen, just as her mother had once been, an honor conferred annually to commemorate Halifax County's history in stock car racing.

Few outsiders had ever heard the name Halifax County. Of its main cities, Daytona Beach stole most of the attention, and Ormond Beach, the rest. Amid this bright constellation, St. Christie's Island was barely visible. The only remaining spot of reflected local glamour was racing, promising as it did a compelling mix of death and sex.

Billy had lately purchased a place on the River Road, just up from the rented cottage where Ainsley's family lived. How many times had she walked by his house in the hope of being noticed? And how many, to pet his puppy, being careful not to look directly at Billy, right over there, working on his car? Too many to count.

Billy was now busy signing his name and initials on photographs, ball caps, and even on girls' wrists and arms when Beth rushed up. "We better get in line."

"I'm not going to wait there like some kid."

"I am," and Beth left to join the end of the line. When she finally reached the head of it and stood next to his table, Billy looked up and smiled before leaning in to continue signing.

3

Beth ran back to Ainsley, fanning herself with Billy's picture. "I got one for you, too," she said, separating it from her own and passing it to Ainsley, asking, "Why didn't you go meet him?"

"Because." Her reason? Why would she be a mere fan? After all, she had been elected Speed Weeks Queen, and didn't that make her equal in status to Billy? Or almost? In the pavilion, the musicians had played several sets, but all the while – about an hour more – Ainsley's eyes had never left Billy, who now – so soon? seemed to be gathering up his things, even though the pig roast was barely underway, the tantalizing smell of roast pork just beginning to waft through the park. Off to the side, a Pit Lizard was also watching, a girl who looked to be in her early twenties: tousled brown hair, a crocheted bra inadequate for its task, legs shifting beneath a sarong skirt tied below her belly. The set ended, and the girl began moving toward Billy, and he toward her, and the girl was slipping her hand around Billy's waist, hitching a finger on his belt loop and he was putting his hand on her hip, like he had done it before.

At a distance, Jack Henderson was hauling wood chips to the fire pit, the burlap sacks tossed over his shoulder, when the small drama on the beach caught his notice: Billy Fiske walking with a pretty girl and Ainsley Quinn with her eyes locked on him. Like many Islanders, Jack had long been an Ainsley-watcher, partly because he owned citrus groves adjacent to the Quinns's. At twenty-six, he was tall and fit, but most people thought him a little older, maybe because of Vietnam.

Like a patient cat, Ainsley stood quiet and observing, an intense look in her eyes, apparent even at a distance. Not like her, thought Jack. Despite her beauty, she was an underdog socially and economically and people tended to root for her. The summer sun had raised the copper in her auburn hair, moving in the breeze, the same shade Jack had seen in sepia photos of the Captain's late wife, her grandmother. No one could fault any part of her, and although separately her features might not be perfect, combined, they made a picture that most passers-by seemed to find pleasing. If she had cared to do it, he thought, or had known how, she might have become one of those girls who fill men's fantasies. Many young girls had that power, at least briefly, but luckily for men, most didn't know it.

Ainsley's eyes stayed fixed on Billy as he and the girl maneuvered toward his car. Before going around to his side, he kissed her on the mouth. They were laughing and he kissed her again after getting in the car and driving off, one hand on her shoulder. Ainsley stood watching. A small breeze rattled the photograph she still carried; she looked at it and then slowly began tearing it down the middle, past Billy's short-cropped hair, past his hazel eyes, his nose, past the lips that had just been pressed against that girl's, and she continued tearing, until Billy and his scrawled dedication "To my friend, Ainsley," were in a hundred pieces, scattered by the wind across the sand.

"Don't you know there's a fine for littering?"

His voice startled her, but without turning, she knew it was Jack Henderson.

"Billy Fiske seems to have got your Irish up."

"Not at all, but I didn't know I was being spied on."

"If you knew, it wouldn't be spying, would it?"

"Beth gave me that picture. She knew I didn't want it."

"Just as well," he said, smoothing things over, "to leave a few men for the other girls."

She forced a sweet smile and turned away, leaving Jack with his good intentions as she hurried across the littered dune, stomping on as many torn-up bits of Billy as she could.

CHAPTER 2

NOVEMBER WAS AN IDEAL FESTIVAL time in St. Christie's, and the early afternoon lull found Ainsley and her friends in the pavilion enjoying all the things that were absent – sudden summer showers, mosquitoes, lubber grasshoppers big as toads, and northern snowbirds, with their sharp, quick ways of speaking.

The girls, mostly high school seniors, were keeping an eye on the boys, tossing a Frisbee on the beach not fifty feet in front of them: Tupper, whom they thought the most athletic, Bear the best looking, and Charlie the smartest. Grace had stopped for a moment to watch too, and to remind her daughter that she was scheduled to work at three o'clock. Watching Grace head back to the beverage kiosk, Ainsley felt a moment's anxiety, stemming from a belief that both her parents required constant monitoring and defending. Their family history and goings-on were well known: her mother's sculptures and her shocking opinions; her father's citrus experiments. Both were reliable sources of town amusement.

Ainsley felt a nudge. "Remember," said Beth, "I still need to find earrings."

"I'm supposed to work soon with my grandfather."

"It won't take long. I want to go back to Trudy's," an artists' consignment shop at the edge of the park.

"It's expensive," warned Ainsley.

"I'm a patron of the arts."

The shop was one of eight, set in a one-story stucco building with Bahama shutters. "You girls need some help?" It was the same lived-in looking woman who had waited on Beth before, Trudy herself. As a struggling shop keeper, Trudy was a good example of the local code of everyone being more-or-less equal. The idea worked well in a town where people brushed elbows whether they wanted to or not, and where no one owned up to being more than comfortable anyway. "Ten percent off for locals today." Beth wasted no time making a purchase.

As they walked back to the pavilion, Beth's new earrings swinging jauntily, Ainsley wondered, would Billy like such earrings? Would Charlie? Years before, when boys had begun to seriously capture her notice, she had posed a similar question to her mother: "What do boys really like?" thinking her mother might be well-versed in such matters.

"They're not peas in a pod," Grace had said. "So why try to figure out what boys like? Let them figure out what *you* like. Just be yourself, and boys will find you; they're good at that."

Her mother was no help. "If they find *me*, maybe I won't like *them*. I want to do the finding."

"Of course you do. It's a lot of work making yourself likeable to someone. That's why I never tried."

It was almost time now for Ainsley's shift, helping her grandfather sell soft drinks and beer. He was her mother's father, and was called Captain by almost everyone in St. Christie's, a name he had encouraged for so many decades that few had ever known him as Frank O'Rourke. With his shrimping business, a hand-built 20-slip marina, and a modest inland citrus grove, "I learned to squeeze out a little living," was his way of telling it. With this, and the piece of land he'd grown up on, he'd been able to raise Grace "almost comfortable."

Ainsley was looking forward to spending time with him that afternoon, and as she approached the beverage kiosk, she saw that he was already there, but not alone. Phoebe was helping too, and so was Jack Henderson, who better not say anything.

CHAPTER 3

THAT NIGHT, AINSLEY'S DATE WITH Charlie Portman had turned into a foursome at the drive-in movie. The credits rolled past and the last notes of the theme song crackled over the tinny speaker as he slowly backed his father's new Buick out of its slot, the black fenders gleaming under the field lights. Ainsley was saying, "That is the last movie we are ever going to let you pick."

From the back seat, Tupper complained, "Would you film critics please drive to the inlet?" his first words in a long while, followed by a girl's laugh.

"Sorry," said Charlie, lying, "but I have to get us and you straight home." The girl cracked her gum in explosive complaints, Tupper groaned in disappointment, and they both disappeared from view again.

Later, Charlie and Ainsley drove back to the inlet alone, just as she had imagined it. Would he kiss her right away, taking up from earlier, and maybe something more? A sloping ramp led to the deserted beach, and a low tide let Charlie park close to the water. With the windows down, the sound of the surf accompanied an Allman Brothers tape, the hometown boys singing their hit song, "Crazy Love."

He turned the engine off and moved closer, his cheek next to hers, his spicy scent touched by a trace of salty mist seeping inside. Leaning in to kiss her, he smoothed her hair and by chance loosened the satin ribbon tied there. It released an auburn tumble, which he grasped to draw her nearer. It seemed to Ainsley as if time had slowed and she was floating on a wave of new sensations, like a swimmer buoyed easily on, without effort. It wasn't long before his hands were skimming over her shoulders, then her waist, and she was drawn into the unknown, swept along as he freed her sweater from its anchoring skirt. When she didn't object, he touched the bare skin there, then higher up, and a feeling, starting small, began to rise deep inside.

Having allowed this last she relaxed, indecision and apprehension behind her, leaving only a growing warmth in its wake, and a gentle current rising.

He whispered her name, and the thrill of it made it seem as though a door had sprung open, with every secret worth knowing lying just beyond, if only he would take her there. As if reading her thoughts, he lifted her sweater, another barrier fallen. Cradling her head, he lowered her onto the seat, his body pressing gently at first, then more insistently, making a claim with his weight alone, and it was clear they were nearing a precipice, a place from which retreat would soon be impossible. If only they could stay exactly as they were, making no other advancement at all, but simply remaining in that exhilarating sphere of anticipation. But clearly that was not possible, and knowing it and then fearing it, she stopped kissing him, raised her arms and pressed her palms against his chest, pushing him away, but he was propped on elbows on either side of her and she felt helpless.

"Don't be scared," his voice reassuring, but as she tried to move away, the velvet upholstery gripped and pinned her in place, and she must have looked afraid, because Charlie stopped kissing her and then drew back. Everything went still for what seemed a long time, and then she sat up and rested her feet safely on the floor again, disappointed not in him but in herself. Resigned, he told her how much he cared about her, and those reassuring words were all she needed to hear before relaxing into his arms again, and "Crazy Love" was playing for the second time.

They were moving together, sliding against one another, fully dressed but it didn't matter, and a feeling she had never known set every nerve free… cascading… holding… and slowly letting go. Their warm exhalations condensed on the cool glass, transforming the windows into a sheltering cloud, and they couldn't stop kissing or touching, until finally they drew apart for just a moment, before falling back into each others' arms, murmuring and sighing in Mr. Portman's new Buick.

CHAPTER 4

TO ANYONE WHO CARED TO notice, it was evident on the second day of the festival, that friendship across class and economic lines was the town norm. Everyone knew that Parker Quinn could dig a perfect fire pit for a 125-pound pig every time. Tupper's father made the best hog marinade, with honey and orange juice and hot pepper flakes in liberal amounts. In fact, Phoebe knew someone who could perform every needed task: from turning black-jack oak into the best charcoal, to transporting the old folks, to hauling chairs and tables. Some friends could be counted on to tell a good joke, play the harmonica, or turn up looking so good that's all that was required.

The social divide in St. Christie's had been mainly bridged except in that quarter occupied by Lady DeWitt, her clan and her admirers. Lady, in this case, was not a royal title, but a given name which served as an adequate substitute. She was seen by many, and by herself, as Grace's rival. Both were in their early forties and known for their beauty, but there, the similarities ended. While Grace and Parker had little that money could buy, Lady and her husband, Clay, had everything, and the highest social rank possible in such a place. As Lady had learned, the social hierarchy in a small town was as treacherous as in Charleston, or maybe Philadelphia, for all she knew. A Southern lady in every sense, she was petite, with straight blonde hair, brown eyes and a dramatic way of presenting herself, as seen in the sheer, salmon-colored dress she wore that day. Clay never understood how a woman so good looking could never give him a hard-on he didn't have to work for.

Now Lady was presiding over a long table set beneath a bougainvillea arbor in hot-pink bloom. Her daughter Tessie, a junior in high school, had Lady's coloring and features, but the way they were put together had come out all wrong.

"Why don't you go join your girlfriends?" asked Lady.

The girl glanced over at her schoolmates. "They're not my friends. They just want to watch those stupid boys."

Lady favored them all with her signature sigh. "You are likely to marry one of those stupid boys," she said, then thought: *If you're lucky.* The family had been waiting years for Tessie to grow either clever or pretty and hope was running out on both scores. This feeling of receding hope for Tessie swept over Lady, overwhelming her patience. She looked up, just in time to see a cloud of smoke drifting their way. "Lord!" She pushed back, knocking over several glasses of tea, and promptly berated the glasses.

A boy rushed in with a towel. "Sorry! They just tossed wet wood chips into the fire to make some smoke, Ma'am."

"I thought it was more dead citrus trees burning up. I'm going to smell like a fire pit!" She glanced over to where a pig was resting inside a wire basket, attached to a motorized pulley. Every thirty minutes for the past nine hours, someone had rotated it over the hot coals. It was one of several, being started at intervals. People had gathered to watch as the basket was raised, inhaling the fragrant aroma and crowding in for the first glimpse of crisp, roasted pork. Thick streams of honey-laced juices poured from slashes where the skin had been scored and the fat caramelized to a dark brown.

"Easy," whispered Parker, as they set the basket down. It took three men to wrestle it onto a makeshift plank, set up on a picnic table.

"Get that thermometer over here," said Phoebe. Confident the timing was right, Parker untied the pig's front and back legs, then removed the block of wood propping open its mouth and the foil protecting the ears and curly tail. "One hundred sixty-five degrees," announced Phoebe. "More than done!"

At her table, Lady turned impatiently to Tessie. "Where did your father and brother go? She fanned the air as a bee approached her fresh glass of sweet tea.

"Bear's on the beach. Dad's over talking to Mrs. Quinn and them," said Tessie, hoping to upset her mother further. Being a disappointment to her parents sparked a vigilant, if furtive,

11

need to retaliate. Lady threw down her napkin, stood shakily in her high heels, and with a careful gait tip-toed across the lawn, but seeing her husband and Grace together, Lady frowned, hesitating in mid-stride.

Clay was forty-five, not as tall as he wanted to be, with a full head of gray hair and a muscular body he took pride in. He stood with one foot raised onto a bench, setting him apart in some way from the others. His once-prosperous family had fallen for a while on hard times, but football had been his ticket to college. In his senior year, he had met Lady at a sorority party, wrangled a holiday invitation to her parents' home in Charleston, and the rest was easy. "I had a classy sounding name," was what he liked to tell Lady, "a good throwing arm and so I fucked my way to the bottom, right Honey?" And he liked to brag that nobody had ever bested him in a business deal "I got timber, I got ferns, I got groves, and I got everybody in Halifax County by the balls and scared shitless. What more can a man want?"

Lady was mid-step when Grace turned, and having been noticed, Lady continued on. She was a woman with a bit of college education, gifted in how to run a house, set a table and chair a committee, but at times, Clay DeWitt made no secret that he could not stand the sight or sound of her. Arriving at her destination she said, "My! I hope I am not intrudin'," When she was excited or agitated, which were identical states of being, Lady was overcome with a deep, Southern accent.

"No. The fun is about to begin," said Grace. "Parker has been appointed the carving expert."

"Lord help us!" said Lady. "The same as he's the citrus expert?"

"Shut up," said Clay, and he turned to join the men.

"I don't know why he's rushing off," said Lady. "It needs a half-hour's rest." She patted Grace's arm. "Don't mind what I said. You always were touchy." Then she added, "Just don't tell me you're making that pig gravy again."

Grace blanched. "Fine. I won't tell you."

Lady shook her head as if in despair, but then, noticing that her husband was again stationary and in shouting range, she called out, waving her glass, "I need a refill, Clay honey." Several people turned, but Clay seemed not to have heard. Lady flushed and turned back to Grace. "As I was sayin'—that gravy! Seems they ask for it, so's not to hurt your feelin's."

"Then I should tend to it so people can do their good deed." She left Lady standing there alone, her high heels sinking into the sand.

At the outdoor wood stove, Grace added parsley, onions and celery to the simmering stock of chopped heart and liver. She glanced over at Parker and the others who were threading strips of pork fat on skewers to make more crackling. Lady's barbs aimed at her were bad enough, but she resented those intended for Parker more, since they bore some truth. Parker's citrus experiments, trying to develop a more freeze-resistant orange, set people to shaking their heads. To find and introduce a valuable new citrus hybrid could take a breeder's entire lifetime, and last winter's freeze had taken a toll.

The men, several growers among them, were laughing now, pulling crackling off the skewers, shaking and licking their burning fingers as if they hadn't a care in the world, not that Parker would ever let on he did, either. The way men kept things hidden and kept on going in the face of disasters, was a quality Grace admired.

Men had the harder path in life, she thought, with so much expected of them, so much to live up to publicly. Women didn't have to be good at sports, go off to war or prove they were brave; they weren't judged by how much money they earned, what kind of social status they provided for their families; and they didn't have to worry about erections or being good in bed, because it seemed men thought kindly about most women, when it came to having one in bed. If a woman was reasonably neat, good around the house and with the children, she was generally considered a success. But standards for men were different, and men's paths were laid out from the time they were little, with everybody pretending they had choices they really didn't. Of course, men did have their penises, and Grace couldn't help but smile at the way men thought about them, some even giving them names, for God's sake. So maybe being a man had compensations a woman just didn't understand.

Grace lifted the lid on the kettle and breathed in. Was Lady right about Parker, and right about the gravy too? Steam clouded her sunglasses and she couldn't see a thing.

CHAPTER 5

GRACE PARKED IN FRONT OF the high school. Ainsley would be surprised to see her, but maybe not pleased. Still tired from the weekend festival, she leaned back, wanting to take her mind off Parker, who was going to get an earful from her later on.

The school looked just as it had when Grace went there, but everything was different now: students caught up in the '70's revolution and all its symbols – love beads, noxious incense, tie-dye and macramé. Not to mention weed. But thank God for the macramé craze. Her own hangings sold well, although the rage for it was fading.

The school bell, loud enough to be heard a half-block away, was ringing, and she sat up as the heavy glass doors opened and the first of the students surged down the steep, stone steps. The principal followed close behind.

"Don't run!" he called. He hadn't changed much since he and Grace had been classmates. Still awkward, still kind, he waved to Grace and she waved back. "You're not supposed to park there, Mrs. Quinn." He wagged his finger. "You know that!"

"Sorry!" She caught sight of Ainsley and beeped the horn. The principal shook his head and so did Ainsley, whose face fell when she saw her mother waiting. Grace told herself she'd imagined it. They drove home not talking much, but even after they arrived at their cottage, Ainsley was still complaining. "You know I don't want you to pick me up, and you always park in front when you know you're supposed to park in the back where the other parents do."

"So I can hide the car? I was only parked there a few minutes," but her daughter didn't answer, just went inside the house, with Grace following after her, still trying to make her point. "Is it such a big thing?"

"Yes. You could have been here, doing what you said you'd do."

Lately it was always something. "And what's that?"

"My emblem." Ainsley held up a shirt. "You said you'd sew my emblem on last week. I don't want to go to Castalians anymore anyway, and they'll be here any minute to pick me up."

"Get my sewing box." Her daughter's voice had Grace's low timbre, but today, all she heard was the complaint. Ainsley came with the kit, banged it on the table and stood in her slip, watching. Grace smoothed the shirt on her lap, placed the Castalian Literary Society badge with its pompous embroidery on top, and began sewing. Why was she always out of step?

"...Mom! hurry."

"Be quiet; you should be doing this, not me."

"You're better at it than I am."

"Not after today I'm not. Next time, join a sewing club." Ainsley hunched her shoulders and expelled a judgmental groan. "Tessie's mom would never do this."

Grace bit her lip. Why must she always be compared to Lady? "Tessie's mom doesn't work. Tessie's mom doesn't sew the damn things on, either. The maid does."

"Why can't we be like normal people?"

"Normal?" The needle pricked her finger, and she put it to her lips. "I suppose we'd all be happier if we had someone following us around picking our panties up off the floor." A drop of blood from her finger landed on her lap. "I don't have time to sew this right now," she said, and started pulling at the threads holding the badge.

"Stop it, Mom!" Ainsley yanked at the shirt. Grace pushed her arm away, but as she did, the badge ripped free, and they both stared at the hole, and then a car was honking.

"They're here." Grace held the shirt out at arm's length.

"I'm not going!"

"For me, okay?" The horn sounded again. Grace pushed her daughter toward the door, watching as she walked down the asphalt driveway, buttoning the shirt, her back straight. The car door opened and light fell on three smiling girls as they welcomed their fellow literary enthusiast. Grace closed the door and leaned against it, feeling ashamed. What was wrong with her? It was Parker. Something was up with him.

Grace, once the prettiest girl on the island, still turned heads at forty-three, even though some said she'd missed her destiny of making important art or marrying up. "She could have had anyone she wanted," they said, shaking their heads, and most of the men silently included themselves in that assessment. Instead, Grace O'Rourke had married Parker Quinn. Most said he was lucky, but the feeling was, he sometimes had a hard time of it. Yet, his light-hearted personality and his tall, wiry frame seemed to complement her just right.

"It can't be easy living with an artist," they'd say, and that word "artist" was so alien that little else need be added. In both looks and attitude, Grace was the woman no one understood: her long, brown hair flowing-free at her age! her long skirts decorated with mirrors that got sat on, for God's sake. But it was her classic face, free of makeup, with its oval shape and generous mouth that people could not forget, nor the sharp remarks that sometimes came from those pretty lips. ("The dumb Irish! The sex-crazed church." And chauvinist men, whom she described as having "cocks the size of my thumb." and then holding her thumb up.) Only an Irish Catholic could get away with it, and not always.

Two hours later, she was standing on the front porch, watching for the girls' car. Quickly, she snuffed out her cigarette, stood up and smiled at Ainsley as she came up the steps. It was Parker she was mad it, not her daughter. Ainsley walked past without looking up. "You've been smoking." That judgmental tone. Grace caught her by the arm and pulled her back. Ainsley looked away, but when Grace took a chance and folded her in her arms, she allowed it. "I'm sorry," she said, smoothing her daughter's hair. "I don't know what got into me, being so upset over nothing." Ainsley stiffened.

"Please."

Ainsley rocked back on her heels and let out a long breath. "It's okay, Mom. I know how hard you work." She patted her mother's back, and Grace felt her body go slack. "I hope the other girls didn't give you a bad time about the rip."

"They didn't." Then Ainsley pulled back, lifted her shirt and poked a finger through the hole from the inside out, wagging it at her mother. "I said I asked you to add some macramé, and you were just getting started."

"You did?"

"Now they'll all be wanting macramé." She turned and darted from the room, calling over her shoulder, "but don't forget to do it, Mom!"

⚬⚭

Later, when the setting sun was shooting pink streamers from the horizon. Ainsley was standing at the window watching for her father. "He's late."

"A little."

The stove was cold. Usually, the table was set when Parker arrived, and Grace had dinner under way. Her mother always said, "Set the table first, because it gives people hope, and if the dinner isn't much, light some candles."

"What's wrong?" asked Ainsley. Her mother was pretending to read in the fading light, and Ainsley hoped she wasn't still upset about the shirt.

"Nothing's wrong. Everything's going to be fine." It was their favorite family expression. They said it at funerals. They said it when freezes threatened the groves. They said it in the face of bill collectors and whispers.

"It's not that bad, is it?"

"No, it's worse."

"Mom!"

"Kidding."

Candlelight was flaring in the cottage windows when Parker's pickup rumbled and sighed to a stop outside. The tinny door slammed and his boots crunched on the gravel driveway. From outside he called, "How's my girls?" to pave the way for his entrance, a trial balloon of sorts. Stepping inside, he surveyed the dim cottage. "I see the old Florida Power and Light boys were here." Ainsley had already guessed why her mother hadn't fixed dinner, why they were in candlelight. They weren't celebrating and it wasn't the first time their power had been shut off.

He kissed Grace on the cheek. "I'll take care of this tomorrow," but reading his wife's doubts, he added, "Davis will cut us a check on next week's shipment, I promise."

Grace turned away. "Hey!" said Parker, laying his hand on her shoulder. "Don't want my girl mad at me. C'mon, none of that." He raised his eyebrows in hope, and she gave him a rueful smile, enough for the moment. "Now let's get going here," he said, rubbing his hands together. "You're cracker girls. You know what to do." Parker's great, great grandfather had been a cracker, driving his cattle on the open Florida range to the crack of a whip. Neither the word, nor his pride in it, had diminished. Parker lit charcoal in the grill while Grace filled the kerosene lamps kept in case of hurricanes, and Ainsley rinsed the dusty globes. He took charge of the chicken, brushing on barbecue sauce and laying the skewered onions and tomatoes along the sides. He looked at Grace. "It's gonna get better, real quick. I promise." The sauce hissed as it fell onto the hot coals, and the fragrance of spice pierced the cool night air.

They sat quietly around the kitchen table, candles guttering, as Parker told them about an irrigation system he was installing, another of the odd jobs he took to keep the family going. As the lamp wicks blackened and grew long, the soft light made Ainsley's eyes feel so heavy that when Grace reminded her of the time, she went upstairs without lingering, drifting into a half-sleep, until her parents' voices awakened her.

"It's not fair, especially to Ainsley." Her mother sounded both persuasive and angry. "I want her to have a nice home and some of the things other girls have."

"Don't go using Ainsley to make me feel bad," said Parker, followed by a sound of dishes rattling as his fist banged the kitchen table. Parker had always admired that in St. Christie's, people high and low were mostly respected and treated the same. It didn't matter what, or how much anyone had, they didn't feel judged or looked down on. Yet he admitted that in recent years, this universal acceptance had begun to wane, a change deeply felt and lamented, even by those who were more than comfortable, and maybe most by the young people it sorely affected.

Grace said, "Why do you insist on hanging onto all that grove land, instead of selling some of it? We'd never miss it."

"Because we don't have to. Those in trouble are the ones with big payments who bought in late," he told her. "Not us."

She wasn't listening. "It's selfish, and you just keep fooling with those damn citrus experiments year after year!"

He took a good breath. "That's what you call it? Fooling?"

"Nothing ever comes of it! You don't know how it hurts me to say it." Tears sprang up, and she brushed them with the back of her hand. "I'm sick of it, Parker – driving that old heap, people feeling pity, dropping off their old clothes!"

"Damn them!" He banged the table again. "Don't they know we've got enough old clothes of our *own?*" He looked at her, grinning, the creases around his eyes deepening, but she refused to laugh.

"I guess they don't," punishing him. Now they were quiet and Ainsley turned over, their voices dropping off to a whisper as her eyes closed.

Downstairs, Grace blew out the candles, stubs now sitting in soft pools of wax. Every time they were almost out of debt, there'd been another problem or freeze, another loan, but she had no intention of backing down this time. Troubled by her lingering mood, Parker said, "If you want me to sell some land, I will," an unprecedented concession.

She seemed to think it over. "I just want to get out of this place," and her arm made a sweeping motion that took in everything from the cracked ceiling to the worn linoleum floor. "We could have both – the groves and a new house too." Parker shook his head, knowing what was coming next. "How many times has the Captain offered us land at the compound? I want to build a house there, near his," but her husband turned away. "Why do you get to decide everything? I'm sick of it!"

Why wouldn't she be sick of it? What was he trying to prove. and to whom? To the town, his dead parents? Were his citrus experiments really for them?

"Look at this!" She scraped back from the table, and from deep in a kitchen drawer dug out a dog-eared calendar with the first day of each month circled in black.

"What is it?"

She slammed it on the table. "My secret. I've been calculating the days, the years of payments on our loans. They're almost paid, and after twenty years I want something too, whether you sell some land or accept the Captain's offer," an ultimatum.

Instead of selling off acreage when business went bad, Parker had often taken more loans to keep going. "The doctors and lawyers are getting out of citrus," he would say, "but the real growers are hanging on." Loans, and what they would be used for, were a topic they'd argued over many times. He picked up the calendar. "I wish I'd known." He rose slowly from the table and walked out onto the porch, letting the screen door slam, a hollow sound in the still night. Even the bull frogs had been hushed by the cold. His wife's garden shoes sat empty on the porch – as if she had just stepped out of them and vanished.

CHAPTER 6

EVER SINCE OPENING HER EYES that morning, Grace had lived under the cloud of Parker's impending surprise, a threat from two weeks earlier, when the electricity had been shut off. In her view, and Parker's too, a good surprise didn't exist, but at least she'd been warned there would be three extra people for dinner: the Captain, Phoebe and Jack Henderson. It was late afternoon, everything was ready, and she and Ainsley were in the backyard, Ainsley weeding while Grace painted a clay wind chime someone had ordered for a wedding gift.

"Mom?…" Something odd in Ainsley's voice made Grace stop working.

"Remember before… when you promised we'd move out of here?"

Grace wiped her paintbrush clean while considering her answer. "I remember," she said, "but it wasn't a true promise." She felt ashamed that her own complaints were being echoed by Ainsley. "It was more like a wish."

"It's because of Dad and his groves!" daring her mother to deny it.

Grace drew on her cigarette and expelled a long stream of smoke. "That's not fair. You know we've had loans – almost paid off, thank God."

"And why did you ask Jack Henderson tonight?"

Grace cocked her head in a chiding way. "Jack has been a good friend, and your father invited him, I didn't."

"Why?"

"It's a surprise!" Grace laughed. "And another thing – criticizing your father is my job."

Ainsley was about to object, but just then her grandfather and Phoebe came through the gate. The Captain never arrived empty-handed. "This is for you," he said, handing a sack to Grace. "The shrimp you wanted, and some pompano, too."

"Pompano! I hadn't expected anything so grand."

"A *good* surprise?" Ainsley taunted.

"Be quiet, and make yourself useful." Phoebe and the Captain went on ahead; the Captain held the screen door for Phoebe, and stooped as he crossed the threshold, as if thinking himself too tall for the frame, which he clearly was not.

While Grace washed the lettuce, Ainsley set six places. "The good dishes," Grace had told her. Pink ginger lilies had been arranged in one of Grace's handmade bowls, and at each setting, tiny candles rested on glossy magnolia leaves set afloat in bowls of water.

"I think I'll help by getting out of the way," said the Captain. "Come keep me company, Phoebe." He put his arm around her waist, and led her to the covered porch where, in a few minutes, they'd both by dozing in the old wicker rockers.

Everything for dinner was ready when they heard Parker's truck, followed by another, which they assumed to be Jack Henderson's. By the time the men reached the porch, Phoebe and the Captain were already on their feet waiting, as Parker hopped down from the cab and stopped to collect a box from the back, glancing up and smiling. "The way you're all lined up there, it looks like Masterpiece Theater, except I think you misplaced your mansion." He loped up the steps, followed by Jack , who handed a quart jar of home-raised orange blossom honey to Grace. "For your sweet tooth." Both men must have stopped to shower at Jack's, because they were wearing ironed, short-sleeved shirts, and their hair was still damp. Ainsley appraised Jack. Some people thought he was good looking, with his dark hair and blue eyes, but she wasn't sure. From working outdoors, he seemed strong enough, but if you watched closely, you saw he limped a little, and even though he was twenty-six, he seemed older.

Ainsley poured iced tea, sweetened with Jack's honey and added mint, just picked. "You look real grown up," said Jack, a strange observation since he saw her all the time.

"I do?" frowning at him.

"I meant you look nice." The only thing she could think to do was shrug her shoulders and turn away, still smarting from when he saw her rip up Billy's photograph. And she didn't like being told she was grown up either, because it seemed to imply something not said, and she didn't want men thinking about her that way or in *any* way, although Jack never did that. Tonight she did look older, though, maybe twenty? in a yellow dress and wedges that made her almost as tall as she wished she were.

The fact that Jack Henderson had helped her family with his college-learned citrus ideas, and pitched in when they needed help, magnified her resentment of him: the indignation of the indebted. Besides that, he was unlucky, and she had once overheard someone warning of the possible contagion of the ill-starred. Jack had been married, she knew, but a drunk driver had killed his family, and when he was only four, his parents had died in an arson fire, still unsolved. After the fire, an uncle ran the groves, and Jack had been raised by him and his aunt, who didn't have children of their own. Now they were gone, too.

"Time to sit down," called Grace, untying her apron. Beneath it, a white dress set off the tan she always had from working outdoors. Even though the table was in the kitchen, Ainsley thought it looked like something in a magazine – plates shining, napkins folded like accordions and standing in stemmed glasses. Jack pulled out a chair for her mother, and Ainsley disliked him all over again. Her father would never show off like that, and she hated it when men paid attention to her mother. But then the Captain did the same for Phoebe, and her father for her. But Jack had started it.

Grace had wrapped the pompano in six heart-shaped buttered papers and sprinkled each fillet with parsley, salt and pepper. The paper sealed in the flavor, she said, but let the bundles breathe as they baked. Now the packages lay open like presents, steaming on their plates. "Never had this before," said Jack approvingly. On top of each fillet, Grace had placed a slice of lemon and a row of overlapping shrimp, now curled and pink. "You've got the touch," said the Captain. "It's like a celebration."

"It *is* a celebration," said Parker, and they lifted their heads. His color rose. "I didn't mean to make a big thing of it," he said, but quickly reconsidered. "It *is* a big thing." He nodded at Jack for confirmation.

Jack had lived through many of the same problems with his groves that the Quinns had. After Vietnam and college, he'd come home with new ways of doing things and had turned a decrepit grove into a good business. Even Parker, at first skeptical, had adopted Jack's methods of fighting freezes with close-planting and micro-sprinklers.

Grace's head tilted expectantly. "What is it, Parker?"

"I've got good news," he said. "It looks like our ship has come in!" They stared back with blank faces. "Or… our orange crate has come in!" he said. There was an in-take of breath around the table.

"What do you *mean*, Dad?" They all leaned in.

"You know, I've been at this citrus experimenting for a long time."

"Yes, Dad."

"Well, I got started in the experimental part by accident, as you know." The Captain nodded. In his view, accidents often had a lot to recommend them.

"*I've* never heard the details," said Phoebe.

"Dad, hurry up." Her father loved telling the story.

"I want to hear it," said Phoebe, ignoring Ainsley's impatient stare.

"Okay," said Parker. "Right after the freeze of 1966, the one that almost put us under, Ainsley here almost got herself killed, which was a very lucky thing." He winked at his daughter.

"Parker, I don't think you're telling it right," said Grace, teasing.

He raised his eyebrows. "Okay then, you tell it, Jack."

"I'm not much good at stories, but since you're not, either, I'll try." He took a sip of water and began: "It was January 31, eleven years ago…"

"I thought ten," said Parker.

"Eleven. Anyway, that freeze hit hard two nights in a row, taking the fruit."

Parker jumped in. "All I'm thinking is, it will take five to seven years for new re-sets to be in production. And maybe three for damaged trees to come back."

"I remember," said the Captain.

"Of course, Phoebe," continued Parker, "no two freezes are alike, but a week later, the freeze comes back again. We're sure the trees are lost."

"And me," said Jack, "I'm in high school looking to make some money, and Parker offers me fifteen a day to run the dozer and shove his dead trees over. Of course the money was 'way too good to pass up…" A glance at Parker. "So there I was, working that dozer, dead trees, hundreds of acres of them. Not just ours, everybody's."

"Wait," said Parker. "Don't forget I was there, too, with Ainsley, watching all this go on, re-living every minute of what had happened to my folks."

"Anyway," said Jack, "I'm knocking the trees over, boom – boom! and all a sudden I look down, and there's Ainsley, running right in front of the dozer, waving her skinny arms and yelling for me to stop! She was about seven then, but from where I'm sitting, she looks two-feet tall, in her shorts and flip-flops." He raised his eyebrows at her. "I didn't think I could stop. I braked, and the damn thing kept going."

"He was swearing at me, but I couldn't move."

"Somehow, the dozer stopped in time," said Jack. "I just missed her." He could still picture Ainsley in front of the dozer, protecting a little tree.

"It turned out," said Parker, "that Ainsley's tree had survived both freezes and nobody had noticed. That one tree had made it through everything. It gave me hope."

"I didn't know." said Phoebe, "not the whole story, I mean."

Citrus development was on-going in Florida. The state had a stake in it and supported research through the universities. A few people also worked independently on citrus breeding, with dozens of different objectives: to develop oranges with fewer seeds, oranges that were easier peeling, later ripening, sweeter – and resistant to freeze. Parker's parents had lost most of their trees to freeze, and developing a hardier citrus that could survive a few extras degrees of cold, a few extra hours of freezing temperatures, had become his obsession.

"That tree was a survivor," said Parker. "Ever since that day, all these years, I've been budding and cross-breeding that tree and those seedlings. I've given it plenty of trials God knows."

"You've given us plenty of trials, too," said Grace.

"We want to know about our orange crate coming in," Ainsley insisted.

"Sure," and turning to Phoebe he said, "I was convinced we had something." He left the table, and from the bundles he'd carried in, he lifted two bottles of orange juice. "Jack's Leola squeezed this up for us," he said, and then he went around the table, pouring juice for each of them. "Here's to the Quinn Perfect," he said, raising his glass. They all joined him, and then everything got too quiet.

Parker stood up. "I told you I had a surprise," he stammered. "I've got the backing," and he looked at Jack. "Financing, from the bank! I'm re-planting twenty acres in the Quinn right away, and before you know it, we'll have a full-blown nursery just for the Quinn and in time, we'll be taking orders from every grower in Florida."

"When, Dad?" Ainsley envisioned herself rich, the Orange Princess. A welcome reversal, since her aspirations were usually at odds with her circumstances.

"Backing?" repeated Grace. "Financing?"

"I know, it's a surprise, but this is a sure thing," said Parker, "Of course it's experimental, but Jack here believes in it, and he's going to give two blocks over to it. That clinched the deal at the bank." The Captain looked worried.

Grace said, "Why would someone take a chance when you've always said it would need 20 or 25 years to prove it, to introduce it?"

Ainsley's jaw dropped. In twenty years, she would be middle-aged, half dead. Seeing her stricken expression, Parker

27

quickly made a more encouraging estimate: "Not that long, no. I've been proving it for ten years already. The trees are bearing fruit." He reached across the table to take his wife's hand. "And you helped. With your nagging."

"I did?"

"A little nagging spurs a man on," said Parker, "and I didn't mean to spring it on you, but you're with me, right?"

Grace grimaced. "Do I have a choice?"

"I'm with you," said the Captain. "Put me down for one block. Wouldn't want to miss getting in on the ground floor of an experimental sure thing."

"Wait!" said Parker. "There's something else." He dragged one of his bags over to the table, and out of it, pulled a flat, brightly wrapped package and handed it to Grace.

She looked at it suspiciously, weighing it in her open palm. "If this is what I think it is, I'm going to make you suffer." She tore part of the wrapping away and her guess proved right. "A calendar!" Grace pushed her chair back, stood up and started hitting Parker over the head with it, until the colorful, glossy wrapping paper was in pieces on the floor.

Parker said, "A *five-year* calendar! It's special!" He had ducked his head and lifted his elbows to protect himself. "Stop! Grace, this loan is for you, too. You're getting your new house first, Grace! It's part of the package." All at once, the room went quiet, and Grace was sitting in Parker's lap, her arms around his neck, holding back tears. Parker raised his arms in the air telling them, "Everybody loves calendars!"

CHAPTER 7

WITH A NEW LOAN AND money in the bank, Parker wasted no time. Within weeks, sketches for their house had claimed a semi-permanent place on the kitchen table. Bulldozers had leveled and scraped the plot of land they had bought on the river, despite the Captain's complaints. "I don't know why you didn't build at the compound," he said. "Plenty of room there, and free."

"We didn't want to have to chaperone you and Phoebe," Parker told him. For years, he'd been wondering what was holding the Captain back, since it was obvious to everyone that he and Phoebe would be good together, and happy, too. "We don't want to spoil a good thing," was what the Captain answered.

One morning, soon after the blueprints had been settled on, Parker announced they were having a picnic at their new house. "It's nothing but a pile of sand," protested Grace, but he insisted, and standing in the kitchen in front of the open refrigerator, he began tossing food into the cooler and singing that song her father liked, "Stand by Me," making up the words, dancing and bumping hips.

When they reached the site, Ainsley grabbed the cooler and ran ahead. When she turned around, she saw her father lay his hand on her mother's shoulder, looking in that moment like the boy she had seen in the black-and-white yearbook photo, full of youth and hope. And she saw something else that she'd ignored all these years – that he had sacrificed, too – that he hadn't been thinking only of what he wanted, but for so long had taken all the family burdens he could onto himself. The house meant as much to him as it did to her mother. How had he not let them see it?

At the site, orange-tipped posts had been hammered into the ground and blue twine tied from post to post outlined the perimeter. Grace stepped over the string and hugged each of them as they did the same, Ainsley first, then Parker, who handed her a sprig of blue chicory he had picked from the roadside. He took her hand and she kissed him on the lips.

As they walked from room to imaginary room, they placed beds and dressers and chairs in their minds' eye, hung pictures, put away sheets, towels and dishes. While Parker searched the radio for his favorite oldies station, Ainsley spread a picnic blanket that had belonged to Grandma Sarah, and then saw her mother lose the struggle to keep her eyes from welling up.

After months of anticipation, Speed Weeks events were about to begin, and part of Ainsley's happiness came from the thought of repeating her mother's role as Miss Speed Weeks. With Christmas vacation and her eighteenth birthday behind her, all she and her friends could think about were the events building to the Daytona 500 in February.

Racing and racing references were everywhere. In the town center, a bronze replica of the famous "Bluebird" race car was a reminder that in its heyday starting in the late 1890s, Halifax County had been a magnet for automobile pioneers as well as the country's rich and famous. But by the 1940s, Palm Beach had superseded it and residents of St. Christie's had never fully recovered from their disappointment, nor abandoned hopes for a second chance, or coming, as the case might be. Reflected glory was all they could claim.

Ainsley and her court would receive tickets to the race for themselves and their families, and invitations to the Speed Weeks dinner-dance with the drivers. On this evening, she, Beth and Vickie were at the Captain's compound fixing dinner, an overdue birthday promise from Ainsley. "This year," he told them, "I am definitely going to the races," and he slapped a scoop of cheese grits onto his plate for emphasis. When the new speedway opened in 1959, the Captain had stopped going, nostalgic for the time when races were run on the beach. "Wouldn't miss seeing my granddaughter standing there on that stage."

"You'd *better* not, Grandpa."

And then to Beth and Vickie: "I wouldn't miss seeing *you* girls, either."

"Good thing you added that," Beth said, "since I made the grits."

"Delicious," he told her. "And what about Billy Fiske? Everybody's saying this could be his year."

"I think so," said Beth. She picked up the newspaper, and Billy's hazel eyes were squinting into the sun from the front page of the sports section. In the photo, Billy was standing outside Island Motors with the dealer and three General Motors executives, looking displaced in their expensive navy blue suits. A breeze lifted Billy's thick, short-cropped hair and the sun blazed on his jacket. The sports writer said Billy could thread the needle like nobody else, the driver who seemed to have come from nowhere, yet he'd been racing for 10 years. "Billy Fiske," he wrote, "has the skill and nerve that show up once in a decade. He's due." Fans all over Halifax County were cheering for him, none more than Ainsley, despite that girl at the pig roast.

Chapter 8

As Parker had predicted, word of Jack Henderson's faith in the Quinn had made other growers anxious to follow his lead, but Parker was a long way from launching the Quinn in the wider marketplace. So many things could go wrong with a new hybrid and not show up right away. A variety might produce well only in alternate years, a common occurrence. Others developed an off-color or flavor, too much acid, not enough sugar, susceptible to disease. Everything had to be tested and documented before asking people to commit their livelihoods to it.

"That's why," he was saying to Ainsley, "citrus breeding of one strain can take a man's entire lifetime." She and her parents were sitting at the kitchen table waiting for Jack Henderson. Grace's old car was in the shop and Jack was driving Ainsley to the speedway to pick up passes and tickets for the Daytona 500. Grace had a financial ledger open before her. "You have to be a gambler to go into citrus breeding," she said.

"But every one of us thinks his work is going to amount to something," added Parker. He recalled how worried he had been about that one tree, the original Quinn – building a fence around it, waiting nervously for the weather to warm so he could begin propagating. Then, when the trees were slipping – growing again, with sap flowing, he'd harvested and budded 1,500 hardened-out bud eye leaves onto cold-hardy stock. The next year, there was a healthy new flush of leaves, and so it would go, year after year, everything taking money, and bringing in none.

Ainsley still hadn't accepted how long the breeding process took: seven or eight years after a mutation produces, then another seven years of watching to see if it yields well. "You keep watching," Parker was saying, "twenty-five altogether, at least."

"You should grow tomatoes, Dad. You could experiment with four crops in one year."

He dipped his head, looking at her over the top of his glasses. "Tomatoes and strawberries are for sissies."

He thought she understood by now that oranges were a noble challenge because of their size, their biology, and their long years of juvenility, years when they grew straight up, with long thorns and produced nothing. Over ten years' time, Parker had planted newly budded Quinns on high ground and low, testing in sandy soil and loam, and budded them onto a variety of root stocks. Historically, only one citrus mutation out of hundreds of thousands had ever proved to be worth anything in the long run.

"The modern red grapefruit took 50 years to develop," he said.

"Tomatoes," she told him.

Grace closed the ledger and put it aside. "The truth will out when we get hit with a few big freezes back-to-back." Parker's brow furrowed. "The Quinn isn't a big gamble." Reassuring himself now, and happy to end the conversation, which had taken a wrong turn, when they heard Jack drive up. Ainsley was dashing outside before Jack had a chance to park.

As they neared the track, signs of Speed Weeks were everywhere, with roadside hawkers selling souvenirs from flimsy tents set up overnight. Ol' Dixie and Confederate flags were flying, and the air was heady with the smell of grease, of cinnamon funnel cakes and deep-fried turkey legs. Traffic crept as drivers scouted parking spots, but nobody seemed to mind. Everyone understood that they had entered the land of speed and lust, of murderous racket and unrelenting expectation. From grizzled old-timers to eager girls like Ainsley, right down to the pre-pubies, everybody got it. No test for relevance was necessary – everything was good!

From a distance, the girders of the Racing Cathedral could be seen climbing high against a pale sky. Daytona International Speedway! Steel risers glinting, pennants flying, a spread of 480 acres, with an infield lake, an asphalt track 40 feet wide, turns banked at thirty-one degrees. Surrounding the track and

33

across the street, media vans, tents splashed with drivers' names, winning cars from races past, vendors selling every kind of anything, blended into a patchwork of color, noise, and desperate excitement.

The past two weeks of racing bliss, practice sessions, time trials and races, had only been a prelude to the Daytona 500, two days away! Traffic was in gridlock, keeping Jack trapped through two green lights. "Only real quiet time left is fall," he said.

"Not like the old days."

"Things disappearing every day that you thought would be here forever." Their sighs fused into one note and the car behind honked. "They plowed up the trees and planted shopping centers," he said. Gopher tortoises were disappearing, manatees, ospreys, and scrub jays too, and now, the last Florida panthers needed tunnels to safely cross the Tamiami Trail. They were moving again. A van filled with students passed them on the shoulder, kicking up stones, and from a GTO on their left, The Commodores were pounding out "Brick House."

"Hey, there's a tent for Billy Fiske," said Jack, inclining his head and looking at her. "You sorry you tore up that photo of him?"

"What photo?" she asked, and managed a smile. "Don't be silly." She clucked her tongue, but then, having no choice but to be a good sport, told him, "Beth still has his picture, and any time I want to, she lets me look at it," and he laughed. She could still picture Billy that day in the park, and then she grew quiet; they both did.

"Here at last," Jack said, and a guard waved them though to the ticket office. Practice sessions were going on and the smell of gasoline blanketed everything, a smell better than bacon! better than coffee! People walked with purposeful strides toward the gates and inched their cars forward to the infield tunnels. Soon, thought Ainsley, I'm going to be part of all this. Two more days.

The next morning, all Ainsley wanted to do was dream, but her father had other plans. Citrus canker had shown up again in South Florida, scaring everyone that it would spread north. The government could make them burn all their stock, shut down the nursery even. Because of the threat, Parker inspected his groves with increasing frequency, and had asked Ainsley to come along.

"I think they'll stop the canker before it gets up here," he told her. They parked at the edge of the grove and began walking in to meet Sam, a sometime jack-of-all-trades who worked in the groves and at the Captain's marina. Sam, a local boy who'd returned from Vietnam wounded and solitary, was in his late twenties and lived in one of the odd buildings that dotted the Captain's compound. The family had an understanding that Sam had a job and a place to stay whenever he wanted either one, and that he was apt to disappear for months at a time. His dark hair was always neatly combed, his beard trimmed, and his thrift-store clothing clean and military-neat; he was a close listener, but seldom had much to say.

They were on a sandy rise, Ainsley and Sam trailing behind her father, who was pointing out tasks to be done. "I want you to pay attention, Ainsley, so you can get involved some day. Girls can do anything now, you know."

She rolled her eyes at Sam. "We always could."

Parker supported women's lib, saying to anyone who would listen that objections to it were just a way for insecure men to control women. And he certainly approved of women burning their bras. He told Sam, "No use arguing when I have two women set against me." Grace had worked in vain for passage of the Equal Rights Amendment in Florida, but there had been more derision than support for it in St. Christie's. The men took Grace's opinions and used them against Parker. "Because they're a bunch of dumb little pricks," Grace would say, and Ainsley agreed. She had also taken up Grace's opinions about civil rights and also the church. Every church she knew of put women down, and tried to pass it off as respect. Worst of all, said her mother, were men who quoted only the parts of the Bible that suited them. "I don't believe in the Bible," Grace would say, and those men, and some women too, would go into fits. Her mother had dropped out of religion altogether. "I go direct," she said, something else for Ainsley to hide, or be proud of, she hadn't yet decided which.

They had walked about a half mile by then and Parker took a sweeping look at the groves, tipping his hat back and raising his tanned face to the sun. "In Florida, citrus practically grows itself," he said, "except for one or two cold nights a year." He threw his arm over Sam's shoulder. "And it's especially easy when you have a good man like this to help it along." The grove was in blossom, bees everywhere, although, because of their structure, the flowers were self-pollinating.

Planted in neat rows, the trees spread their limbs in round, symmetrical shapes that seldom needed attention. Their roots dug easily into the sandy loam, and the thick leaves shone in the morning light. These were Valencias, the primary Florida juice orange. Along with the flowers, there were fruits from the previous season still on the tree. From blossom to harvest, the cycle might last as long as fifteen, even eighteen months, all stages of the Valencia visible at once.

"The good thing about oranges is they're self-storing," Parker told her, as if reading her thoughts. He reached up and picked one. "The harvest window is wide, and the longer they sit in the sun, the sweeter they get." He picked another and tossed it to her. The skin was lightly scarred from breezes rubbing the branches together.

"I like to think of our oranges traveling all around the world," said Parker, "to places I'll never see." He had always held the notion he was doing something good. "Growing something useful is a fine thing to do with yourself," he told her now.

"Except Jack says the workers have it worse than ever."

"We're working to fix that, especially Jack," but he didn't tell her how unpopular Jack was becoming with some other growers. Satisfied that the trees were safe from canker for now, they left Sam and began walking back to the pickup, but there was something else Ainsley wanted to confirm: "Dad, you won't like this, but I want to know, are we comfortable yet?"

He shook his head. "What a question."

"Are we?"

"Getting there."

CHAPTER 9

BY 8 A.M. ON RACE day, every artery leading to Daytona International Speedway is packed with cars: I-95, I-4, I-75 and every feeder road, too. Today, only one destination matters, and only one event – the Daytona 500, the star of The Show, Cup Racing's top prize. This is "The One" for every racer who ever put on a fire suit and helmet, climbed inside sheet metal, sat on top of 110-octanes, and set his heart on rolling to victory under the checkered flag.

On S.R. 17/92 Lynyrd Skynyrd and "Sweet Home Alabama" is blasting, sending vibrations that thump three cars away. It's joyous! Nobody has wrecked. Yet. Nobody has died. Yet. Everyone can be a winner. Still. Fans lean out of car windows, ready-to-go: their tickets are stashed safe in back pockets; their beer-filled coolers, cameras, radios, their Cale ball caps are all set, along with their certainty that this is day, and this is the place of all places to be.

In his garage-area stall, Billy is ready, wrapped in calm as he goes over the check-list yet again with his Crew Chief, Wendell Jablonski. "Lookin' good," said Wendell, a man of few, but choice words. A U.S. Army veteran who had served in Korea, he brought both the discipline and camaraderie of the service to the job. Wendell's broad-shouldered frame, his height and size put almost every part of Billy's red Chevy within easy reach. His rosy face and quick athleticism didn't come close to revealing his forty-four years.

Under Billy's and Wendell's direction, the car's technical setup has been fine-tuned, tested and kept under wraps. Everything is ready to go, with as much insurance as anyone can have against bad luck: Car crews and pit crews are in their fire suits; the red Chevy is ablaze with sponsors' insignia, from the hood, to the smallest space on the roll pan and spoilers; and Billy is set to make his run with a car that can go the distance

The track infield, with its RVs, campers, vans, tents and jalopies is waking up, fans shaking off last night's party, ready for today's. It's early, but not too early for men to be yelling to passersby, "Show me your tits!" or for women to oblige them. Some campers have been there for a week of races and are doubtless wondering, Will this be the day of the "Big One," a wreck that sweeps up a dozen cars in a single, 150-mph swoop? No, it's too pretty and calm a day for that, with rosy streaks stretching through the palm trees, and a promising warmth in the low sun. Men, stripped to the waist, are having a moment of freedom, firing up grills for hotcakes and scrambled eggs with pepper sauce. Many woke up beyond wasted and are ready to do it all over again. Some are already stretched out on beat-up sofas and recliners hauled onto the roofs of their rides, drinking beer, hoping a girl will wander by, maybe smile. The comforts, and none of the discomforts, of home are everywhere and men are in their element, fulfilling their destinies of drinking, screwing, and taking another run at happy, remembered youth.

When the sun reaches it zenith, official ceremonies get underway: respectful music and song; local dignitaries each one having his moment; the introduction of the Miss Speed Weeks Queen and her Court; a prayer offered by the Rev. Hal Marchman; the anthem sung in one of those funky arrangements that doesn't quite work. It was then, during the anthem, with everyone on edge that the singing would go wrong, as it so often does with those musical improvisations, that Billy, sitting in his race car, caught sight of Ainsley on the speakers' platform. A white dress skimmed her figure, and a rhinestone crown, nested in a halo of auburn, caught the sun and seemed to wink at him. He then recognized her as the girl who used to walk by his house, stopping to pet Agnes but pretending not to notice him, working on his car ten feet away. Now she looked different. When she seemed to smile in his direction, he took it as a good luck omen, but then he turned his attention back to the track. His car sits in its starting position – the grid – every car in its assigned spot, Billy at position 12, ready.

So much pomp! patriotism! solemn Christian goodness! Finally, the military flyover, jet engines screaming, as if to prepare the crowd for the thunder to come – fans on their feet, 100,00 hearts filled with love and anticipation – and then those words everyone is waiting for:

"Gentlemen, start your engines!"

A cheer rises from the stands, a ground-swell from all four cardinal directions, but even that great noise fails to smother the ear-shattering, hypnotic buzz and clamor of forty-three race cars springing to life, ready to make a run at history. The pace car rolls out, the drivers follow, swerving, jumping, as if they're holding back wild horses, zigzagging to warm up the tires, picking up speed, the cars circle the oval: turn one... two... backstretch... turn three... four... approaching the line, running now at race speed. The pace car peels off onto pit road and all eyes turn to the flagman in his tower.

The green silk drops. A boom of voices from the stands.

That's Racin'!

The Daytona 500 is on, and for Billy, there has never been a day with so much desire or certainty. He feels the track through his feet, his legs – feels the thrust in his arms, and the mental hammer of second-by-second demands and decisions. In his subconscious, his father, Eddie Fiske, is there helping him as he always had, but you couldn't plan the unexpected.

Wendell is the new breed of college-educated garage geniuses, expert in automotive science and aerodynamics. He grew up in Hamtramck, Michigan, where his parents, and most of their friends all worked in the auto industry, first arriving in numbers when the Dodge Brothers opened a plant in 1914. By 1970, Hamtramck was 90 percent Polish, and hadn't changed much in the seven years since, except that GM had moved in, too, with its premier assembly plant for Cadillac and Buick. He grew up in a traditional Polish neighborhood, amid people who kept their houses immaculate, their gardens blooming, and their children striving. Growing up, Wendell's life centered around St. Florian's church, the yearly Strawberry Festival, and Paczki

Day – when every kitchen was fragrant with the scent of airy Polish jelly doughnuts being lifted golden from deep fryers.

Like so many other Hamtramck boys, Wendell loved automobiles, knew them, lived them, and after Korea, went to college, the first in his family, graduating with a degree in engineering that would help put him at the top of the stock-car racing circuit. He was a big man, a football linebacker in high school, with Slavic features, blond hair, transparent blue eyes, and a neck that seemed too broad for any shirt collar. Despite offers from a few big teams, he believed in Billy. Both are confident they can go all the way today.

Nearing the speedway's high bank, as drivers jockey for position, Billy sticks to his plan. On the first 50 laps, almost behind him now, he hooked onto the last of the Georgia-Gang freight-train, drafting and staying there. Later, he'd work his way up inside. Five-hundred miles, and 200 laps; he'd let fate and mechanical troubles take out a few of the front-runners, and after that, he'd be running flat-out, all out, all the time. His concentration stays fixed inside the track, on drivers almost airborne, racing inches away, and on the yahoos – pushing, bumping, trying to bully their way ahead.

He relaxes his shoulders, remembering his father's advice: "Just do your job the best you can." This race is for Eddie Fiske.

Half-way in, everyone seems to be competing for the number-two spot, trying to stay on Cale's bumper. Coming into Turn Four of the 98th lap, the car in second place spins out, going into a barrel roll along the fence. The car behind skates high and into the wall. Another does a hairpin, fishtails, barely avoids a T-bone, and slides onto the infield grass. Three top drivers out, but Billy is still safe as he drives onto pit road.

Fifteen seconds later, he's back on the track at number four, a draft train trailing behind, and Delroy Hazel coming on.

For Billy, only one thing is missing this day, his father. It was Eddie Fiske who had been there, advising him, giving all he could to help Billy do what mattered most to him. Standing at five-seven, Eddie seemed all muscle – able to handle any job in a garage, even hoist and place an engine on his own. After a ten-hour day at his garage, where he worked seven days a week, he would shower, put on a fresh shirt and come home to sit down to dinner with his wife and four children – fingernails scrubbed clean, out of respect.

More than any of his other children, Eddie understood Billy. After racing for years on dirt tracks himself, Eddie knew the excitement, and also what it was like to be helpless with obligations that couldn't be set aside. He had warned his son about making commitments that couldn't be broken, and Billy had listened hard and learned from it. It wasn't easy seeing his son, barely more than a child, working construction, doing whatever he could to make money to keep his car running. Eddie had helped build it, but skill and encouragement were all he could offer. Nobody ever imagined things for Billy the way Eddie had. In spirit, his father was there, beside Billy now.

With fifteen laps to go, Billy is ready to make his move, but then Hazel pulls inside. Billy feels the tension in his back, the Gs pulling his torso apart. Then it's ten laps, a four-car race, with Yarborough in the lead, Baker third, fighting hard against Benny Parsons, second. Everybody's blocking, trying to hold position. Billy fourth. Fans on their feet.

He concentrates on Baker, feels the wind pushing him. Almost home. Five laps… then four laps… three… two… and all the years fuse into this one moment.

"Billy! Billy!" The chant seeps into his subconscious as the white silk flag cracks in the wind, the final lap, 2.5 miles to go, and everything he has hoped for is waiting at the end of it. Billy maneuvers into position. Turn one… Turn two… the straightaway coming up, a half-lap remaining. He asks his car for every last push held in reserve. In the stands, fans stomp, scream. A four-car shootout.

Seconds to go. He pulls even with Baker, the thrust almost lifting him from the track. On the straightaway, a slingshot before heading into Turn 3, passes Baker, passes Parsons. Next up, Yarborough. Just enough track left to do it. The crowd bellowing, its cries sweeping through the palmettos… through the swamps… through the longleaf pines miles away.

Out of nowhere Hazel again.

And then came A Tap.

Not a big hit, A Tap. It could have been a lot harder, could have slammed Billy sideways into the wall, could have punched him into a roll. Billy feels the car jump beneath him, the Gs dragging at his chest, his gut, shaking everything loose inside. Just A Tap. Hazel is low, peeling sheet metal that flies in curls down to the apron, the infield, pale smoke billowing from his tires. Billy's car is shuddering, and behind him, not seeing it but knowing it, race cars are wailing in a storm, ready to explode against the wall, waiting for a shower of debris to rain down. Seconds to go.

Billy dives down, trading paint with somebody, and the driver trades punches with him. Hazel's strike had been Only A Tap. Still a chance? Somebody gets into Parsons, but he bumps him up the track.

And then it's over. Yarborough shoots over the stripe, then Parsons, then Baker. The checkered flag slaps in a figure 8. Billy Fiske finishes in the top ten of the Daytona 500.

He pulls his Chevy into the pit as Wendell, the crew, and a sea of people surge forward. "Next time, Billy." He goes through the window netting, Wendell, thumping him on his back. Next time.

CHAPTER 10

IT WAS ALL BILLY COULD do to play the good sport. Would he ever have as promising a chance at the 500 again? The post-race ceremonies began: the trophies, the speeches, while outside the grandstand, a crowd waited in the Victory Tent for the drivers to arrive. "Over here!" yelled a photographer as Billy shouldered his way through the fans and the hawkers, making their last-ditch efforts.

"Billy! Good job!" and Billy threw a thumbs-up. It didn't matter to them that he'd lost. He'd given them a good race. Reporters crowded in, and in the background, the girl with the auburn hair was looking in his direction. She was just as he remembered her from that morning. Not the good-luck omen he had imagined, though. Billy squeezed through the crowd, heading her way, as every eye followed him. When he was several feet away, and still holding his crash helmet tucked under his arm, he gave what some people would later describe as "a kind of a bow."

"Wanted to say hello," he told her. Then, noticing that her tiara had slipped to the side, and always self-assured with women, he reached up to adjust it. She shrank back a little and reached up too, but his hand was still there, and he gave her a smile. The band began playing again and Ainsley looked down, not sure what to do next. He extended his hand and she did the same, telling him her name. She looked relieved when he released her at last, telling her, "Don't leave, okay?" Ainsley nodded, as Billy stepped a few feet away, agreeing to one last round of photographs. Beth and Vickie huddled close, while from a distance Grace and Parker watched with the Captain, who looked concerned.

"That's it, people," she heard Billy say. "I'm going to have me a soda, and there's someone I need to talk to," nodding in Ainsley's direction. She flushed as heads again turned her way, watching as Billy strode to her side, threw his arm around her waist and pulled her close as flashbulbs popped.

Copies of The Island News were stacked on the counter in Grace and Parker's kitchen the next morning, and Grace was reading the lead story aloud. "I'm trying to read here," she told the Captain and Ainsley, who kept interrupting with comments and criticisms.

"Pour me a little more coffee while you're at it," said Parker. The press had been inspired to start calling Billy The Gentleman Racer because of the way he had taken his loss, especially after being recklessly tapped. Grace read aloud: "This is another step forward for Billy Fiske."

"Let's hear that part again about Miss Speed Weeks and her Court," said Ainsley.

"There *is* no such part," said Parker, "but that's a nice picture of you and Billy there, don't you think, Captain?"

"Very nice," he said, seeming to put as much enthusiasm into it as he could muster, studying the photograph of Billy smiling at Ainsley. "Your Ma says you're going out with him."

Ainsley could hardly remember a greater happiness, but now her grandfather's worried expression was about to spoil it. "You sound like I shouldn't. Don't you like him?"

Grace chimed in: "That's not the point. He's a grown-up man and you're a school girl." She looked at Parker. "What do you think,?"

"I worry some."

Ainsley said, "I've never given you cause."

"You're eighteen, you've barely had a chance," joked Parker.

CHAPTER 11

BILLY HAD MADE RESERVATIONS AT one of the few formal restaurants in St. Christie's, an Italian place called Firenze, which faced a lighted pond rimmed by a small orange grove in full fruit. Ainsley's friends ate there only with their parents on special occasions. She had worn a favorite knit dress in a pale blue, an outfit she had been saving, and Billy was wearing slacks, a white shirt and a navy sports coat, which Ainsley thought the perfect choice. People turned to look when they walked in, but were too polite to stare when the waiter called Billy by name.

They both ordered cannelloni and salad, and for dessert, Firenze's famous rum cake. Throughout dinner, his quiet ways inspired her trust, and the attentive way he listened made her hope he didn't find her boring. St. Christie's was not a late-night town, and it was only nine o'clock when they finished dinner. "Is there anything special you'd like to do now?" he asked.

"This was special." Dinner was all she had expected. He was helping her into her coat when she turned to face him, finally answering his question. "I don't know." He was different from anyone else she knew, and she thought guiltily about Charlie.

"We can go to a club," he suggested, "or I could show you the river from my place."

Weighing what that might mean, and delaying an answer, she said, "I know your place, up from us on the River Road."

"Exactly," he told her. "Is that a yes?" Ever since he was fourteen, women had always been available to him, but at twenty-six, being with a young girl was something he had no room for in his life. Not her or anyone, not being a driver and out of town thirty weeks a year, and he wondered what he was thinking. Just show her his place and then take her home. He wasn't a seducer of school girls, although he was certain that if they had been together right after the race, with all the adrenalin and emotion, he would have thought differently. Was she a virgin? Probably, or almost, anyway.

With that thought, he knew he hadn't decided anything after all, and she wasn't really a kid, she was eighteen, and he felt his good intentions dissolve. "So… my place?"

"Yes." Was she agreeing to more than a destination? Maybe, but having accepted, she felt a sense of relief. Indecision will kill you, her mother always said.

"If you're sure," putting the burden to her.

"I'm sure." With a reassuring look, he placed his index finger under her chin, tilted her head up and kissed her lightly on the lips. "Don't worry. I'm not plotting anything," disarming her as well as himself.

The small cottage where he lived was old and in need of repair, which Ainsley knew – unpainted cypress clapboard outside, and Old Florida inside, with floors of heart pine and beamed ceilings finished in bead-board. They came first through a tiny kitchen, where his puppy Agnes was waiting, then into a dining room with glass-front cabinets set below a wood counter, then finally into a small living room with a coquina fireplace and a wood mantel flanked by glass sconces.

"I wondered why you would live here, and now I know. It's nice."

"It could use some work, but it's got character, and the river." He took her hand and walked ahead, leading her to the rear of the house. "Another advantage is, I can work on my cars and nobody cares. In the suburbs, the neighbors wouldn't like it." At the back of the house was the only bedroom. He stopped at the threshold and kissed the side of her neck before pulling her tight against his body.

The bed looked freshly made, with a pale spread and two big pillows and she wondered if it had been planned that way for her. He led her there, lifting her just enough to set her on the edge, raising her legs onto the mattress and running his hands from her knees to ankles, till she had stretched out completely. The bed rocked as he sat next to her, bent down and kissed her again.

"How about some atmosphere?" A tape-deck was within arm's reach, and classical piano music she didn't recognize began playing. In answer to her surprised look, he explained: "My mother's doing. Let me fool with motors if I did my piano practice first, and then I came to like it."

From the kitchen, he brought two sodas in tall glasses packed to the brim with ice and clinking softly when he set them on the dark wood table next the bed. Ainsley lay self-conscious and rigid, and he sat beside her again, taking time to light the table-side candle and turn off the small lamp. When he placed his hands on her arms, goose bumps rose from the coldness of the drinks he'd carried. Gently he turned her head so that she was looking directly at him. "Nothing's going to happen that you don't want to happen." She sat up in his arms and felt the slight dampness of his shirt. That he was older inspired her trust, and in any case, she wouldn't go too far, at least not any farther than she had with Charlie.

Billy buried his face in her hair, cradling her head and lowered her into the pillows, kissing her, parting her lips. Then he took off his shoes and socks and her sandals and lay beside her, slipping an arm under her neck. With his bare feet, he clasped hers, and she could never have imagined the feeling kindled by such an innocent touch. She turned on her side, facing him as he circled her with one arm and pulled her close with the other. Already, his body seemed familiar, her shyness and fears fading, but then she thought about the girl in the park and wondered if she had been there with Billy too.

Shifting sideways, he placed both hands on her hips, drawing her close as he buried his face in her neck, whispering, "lavender," and then he pulled off his shirt, and brought her hand up to his chest; she felt the slow beat of his heart, traced his nipple with her finger as Billy lay back and drew her closer, kissed her lips, her earlobes. Her skirt was hiked up and she felt his trousers against her thighs.

"I'm going to take your top off."

It wasn't a question, but she nodded yes. Helping him, she slipped her arms from their sleeves, and they were both half sitting, facing each other, naked on top. With both hands, he cupped her breasts and kissed her in their center.

"You must drive the boys at school crazy."

"I don't think so." She wasn't a big girl after all, not like some.

He tilted his head, doubting. "Every man dreams of tits like yours. You know that, don't you?" He was closely watching her expression.

That word. She felt herself flush. "No."

"Tell me a story." Postponing things, letting everything build slowly maybe. "I want to know your most secret story."

"I can't."

"A story about you and your tits then."

That word again, a shock. She sighed, thinking.

"How old were you the first time you let somebody look?"

"Fourteen," she said, but was sorry the minute the word left her lips.

They lay back together on the pillows, his arm cradling her neck. "Tell me. We've got time."

Unsure, she studied him in the candlelight, thinking about boys, and men sometimes, and the way they looked at her or tried not to. One man in particular came to mind – the father of her classmate, Tupper. Billy's fingertips were lightly brushing her panties, down there, and she could hardly think. It had happened at a party four years ago at Tupper's house, and his father had asked Ainsley to help him bring things in from the garage. She thought it odd, with so many boys there, but went with him nonetheless. When they were inside, he closed the door to the house, took her hand and led her to a dark corner where he touched his forehead to hers, and not saying a word, held her by the shoulders and kissed her, his tongue touching her lips, a shocking first. It was obvious where Tupper's good looks came from, even though his father was in his early forties. He had taken charge of her, just the way he did with people all over town, and she didn't mind.

Then he had stopped kissing her, slid his hands underneath her top and said, "Let me look at you." Ainsley must have given a sign of consent. In the kitchen, somebody dropped a glass and everyone started laughing. She had stopped breathing for a minute, but then raised her arms a bit and Tupper's father lifted the sweat shirt she was wearing, slipped her arms out of the sleeves and pulled her straps down to her waist. He held her shirt up and she remembered the way he had looked at her, how that felt, and then he said he was going to touch her. She felt like a woman in some forbidden book, and remembered his hands, then his mouth, followed by the sound of more laughter in the kitchen, the fear of discovery, the thrill of it. Whenever she was at Tupper's house afterward, many times, Tupper's father never said anything to her except 'hello,' and for a long time, she wished he would. Could she tell Billy this? His hand was high on the inside of her thigh now. No, she couldn't tell him, didn't want to risk being sorry, even though she trusted him.

Billy lifted her onto her back, crouching over her. "So you were only fourteen when you learned you could rule the world."

"Not at all."

Then, just as if they had been together many times before, he removed his trousers; his white cotton briefs were drawn tight over his body. "Help me," he said, and guided her hands to the waistband as he slid them down onto his thighs, his penis only inches away. Ainsley pulled back; she had imagined this moment and had thought she was prepared for it.

"You're a virgin, aren't you?"

Nodding yes, she closed her eyes. It didn't matter, nothing did, except Billy and her feeling of thrilling recklessness. His mood grew serious, and he took her hand, placing it between them where he wanted it, just below her navel. "Just give us a minute and you'll be fine," he said. "We have all the time we need." He put his arms around her, holding her close and breathing in short, quick beats. She felt his penis pressing against her, almost as if it were a separate being, and then he moved away, lying naked on his side, letting her look at him, and his perfection reminded her of a painting she had once seen.

"Are you intact?"

She shook her head, not sure.

"It could hurt if you are."

"I don't care," she said, coming to a decision. A frail moon sliced though the window, sketching shadows and planes on his body, and he looked so strong and sure that it made anything they might do seem all right. She lifted herself onto one elbow, pushing gently against Billy till he was lying down, stretched out on his back. He took hold of her arms, pulling her on top, still in her skirt and panties, Billy naked beneath her, drawing her down, kissing her, his hands on her buttocks, moving her body gently.

"Take your skirt off." Finding her zipper, he pulled the skirt away, and the next thing she knew, Billy was straddling her, pinning her arms above her head, his penis touching her thin cotton panties, the only thing separating them. "Do you think we can still stop?" His lips were brushing hers as he whispered the question, his eyes narrowed. "We can," he told her, releasing her arms, but pulling her up, her naked breasts pressed against his chest.

"I want to," she whispered, and now it was Ainsley who was caught in a fever of wanting.

"Baby," he murmured, "okay." Kissing her lightly, he slid his thumb under the elastic band of her panties, pulled them down over her hips and off altogether, and they were lying on their sides naked, hips touching, legs locked, and she felt his hand there, between them, drawing small circles on her vulva. "Ease up," he said, and her whole body seemed to be flowing: he rolled on top, and everything she had imagined was happening: being naked and pressed head to toe with Billy, being possessed by him entirely.

Listening to his voice, soothing and soft, Ainsley found herself letting go, just the way he'd told her to. He sat up part way and opened her legs, taking time to look at her, stroking her, then bending to lightly kiss her there… "and now it *is* too late," he whispered, and she felt the naked heaviness of his body, the silky tip pressing against her labia, then inside, the sweet fullness of Billy overtaking her… and nothing could ever again be the same.

Chapter 12

AINSLEY SLID HER TRAY ALONG the chrome counter of the school cafeteria, looking for Beth and Vickie. The month since her night with Billy had been filled with a kind of loss she had never known, made worse by her determination to keep everything hidden. There had been not one word from him, and Ainsley's days of hoping and waiting could be no secret in the Quinn household or among her friends. Yet, when Grace had tried to talk to her, Ainsley's pride wouldn't allow it. Why had she been so trusting, letting herself think she meant something to him? She picked up her tray and saw Beth waving from a distant table, but as she was about to sit down, Bear DeWitt and his group unexpectedly joined them.

His sister Tessie slid into a nearby chair and, looking sly, she leaned in toward Ainsley. "How's your boyfriend Billy?" and all eyes turned in her direction.

With as much calm as she could muster, Ainsley said, "First, he's not my boyfriend, and second, he's probably out of town." Her only reports of Billy came from The Island News, and she was too embarrassed to be seen reading it, even at home. Now, in the momentary lull at the table, she searched for another topic.

"He did himself proud up in Talladega," said Bear, trying to smooth things over, but instead, bringing the subject back to life. His girlfriend Dance, the exotic class brain, shrugged knowingly. "That's not the only thing he's doing proud," frowning at Bear for seeming to take Ainsley's part.

Ainsley flushed. "…if you mean that picture in the paper…"

"Yes," said Dance, unable to mask her pleasure. "It must be so exciting for Billy, all those girls throwing themselves at him." The photo had been taken in another city and published in The Island News. In it, Billy had his arm around a tall, blonde girl who looked up at him smiling. Ainsley wondered, had that girl given in to Billy as easily as she had?

She smiled at Dance. "Posing for pictures is part of his work."

"Well," said Dance, her voice soft with triumph, "he certainly seems to enjoy his work!"

"For your information," said Vickie, jumping in, "it's part of his endorsements." When no one contradicted her, she said to Ainsley. "Let's go," and they fled out into the courtyard, Beth pausing to gather their sandwiches, food always a comfort in times of crisis.

"I wish I never had to see Tessie or Dance again," said Ainsley, especially Dance, who had always disliked her for some reason.

But Vickie, always direct, couldn't help asking what was on everyone's mind. "What *did* happen with Billy? He seemed to like you so much." No one, not even her best friends, could have guessed. "I don't know." Ainsley shook her head. "I never think about Billy at all," and her two friends didn't dare say a word.

Two weeks later, Billy was back, waiting across from the high school, looking up at the broad, steep stairs and columns, architecture meant to lend importance to the enterprise inside. Sometimes he wondered what it was like to be a part of something like that, the world of high school, which he hadn't known for very long. He hadn't meant to see Ainsley again, but here he was, his heart flying around in his chest. He'd apologize. What he had done was wrong.

The bell began ringing, classes dismissed, and soon afterward, Ainsley stepped through the glass doors and onto the granite landing where several students were sitting on a high ledge that ran along the side. As she approached, they made room for her, and it was then that Ainsley looked up. Billy knew he'd been noticed, and stood away from his car, nodding ever so slightly in her direction and wondering, How had he had let himself stay away so long?

For a moment, Ainsley forgot all the ways she had dreamed of punishing Billy, the things she would say. He was leaning against the hood of the roadster convertible he liked to drive on the island and was wearing jeans and a black T-shirt, the same kind of outfit she'd seen him wear when she used to walk by his house. But she ignored him now, stepping aside to say a few words to Charlie Portman before he rushed off to track – then surprising Charlie and herself by giving him a peck on the cheek before sitting down with the others, nerves jumping, waiting for Vickie and Beth. Thank God her mother wasn't there to surprise her too. Despite what her head was saying, her traitorous heart was telling her something else, and she felt like singing and throwing herself into Billy's arms. Beth and Vickie joined her and the three girls began walking in a direction opposite from the way Billy's car was facing. It was a few minutes before he caught up with them, driving slowly alongside before tapping his horn.

"Billy!" Vickie said, startled. "Ainsley, it's Billy!"

"Keep walking!"

"But…"

"Please!" Beth looked worried but said nothing.

"Ainsley!" Billy yelled, "get in. Don't do this."

"Go away!"

He kept this up, traffic building behind him, horns starting to honk, and then he pulled ahead, parked in the first open spot, about 100 feet up, got out and began loping back toward the girls. Ainsley was in the center, her hair loose and swinging, her short skirt rippling as she came toward him on high, wedge shoes. Maybe she'd cross the street to avoid him, he thought, but she didn't, and when they were close enough to talk without shouting, she stopped walking. They all did.

"What do you want?"

"A few minutes ."

"No," and turning to her friends said, "Let's go," but nobody moved.

Billy advanced toward her and took her books away before she knew what was happening. "Just get in the car." Beth, nervous now, took Ainsley by the arm. "Why not?" she asked.

"Because," and she started walking again.

"Get in," said Billy, following them.

"Apologize," tossed back over her shoulder.

"I will, and I do."

"Say it."

"I'm sorry."

A pause. "I can't believe you."

"Just hear me out." They were next to Billy's parked car.

"Do it, Ainsley," urged Beth, then turning to Billy: "Drop Vickie and me off last," and Ainsley couldn't help laughing; It was, after all, a two-seater. Billy took advantage of the moment, opened the car door and shut Ainsley inside. Vickie and Beth stood on the sidewalk watching as they drove away.

∽

Alone now, they were heading toward the island causeway, neither knowing what to say, but it was Ainsley who couldn't stay quiet. "Why didn't you call me?"

A long moment passed. "Because I've got a big, tough job to do, that's part of it."

"Nobody's job is that big." She tried to ignore all her stifled feelings, but the hurt rose again, overwhelming her. "I want to go home, Take me home!"

"I'm not taking you home." He pulled off the road into a parking lot and stopped the car. "I've done nothing but think about you," he said. "I'm sorry I didn't call. It was wrong."

She wanted to cry but whatever it took, she wouldn't shed one more tear over him now or ever.

"Forgive me."

"Why would I?" For an answer, he tugged her close and wrapped her in his arms, sweeping away everything of the past weeks. But it wasn't over; Ainsley knew that. They drove to the beach, a better place to sit and talk, but cars were backed up on the ramp. "There must be a shuttle launch," he said. Billy let the car creep ahead, looking for a place to park on the sand, but some cars were already leaving. He signaled a man carrying binoculars and folding chairs. "What's up?"

"Called off," he said, disappointed.

Billy made a tough-luck expression, and turned to Ainsley. "We'll stay a while, miss the traffic." They settled back into the leather seats and Billy bought two ice cream cones from a passing vendor. "Peace offering," he said, handing one to her. But instead of peace, she started everything up again. "I still don't understand."

"I said I was sorry. I've got lots on my mind when I'm out of town."

"Yes, I saw her picture."

At first he looked confused, but then quickly understood. "That was a publicity thing," waving it away as if it were a sand flea, and tilted her chin up the way he did, with one finger. "I told you one part about me, or us, and here's the other: I can't give you what you might be looking for – not now anyway." He grimaced. "But there's a problem; I want it too."

Slowly, the beach was coming alive, with music drifting out of the bars that lined the sand. Near the pier, tourists gathered in groups, or walked in twos holding hands. Ainsley steadied herself enough to ask, "Do you expect to see other girls?"

"Girls aren't an issue."

"You didn't answer."

"Having a steady girl when you're away almost every weekend is hard on everybody."

"Other drivers have girlfriends, wives and families too."

"So will I, when the time is right." After a long pause, he went on. "You don't have any idea what goes on out on the road, and neither do those wives and girlfriends."

She was holding her head in that dignified way that was her habit when she might feel defenseless. He said, "I'm going to tell you how it is with me, explain," weighing every word. "But I promise I didn't mean to take advantage of you; it wasn't like that."

"I'm sure of one thing."

"What's that?"

"I'm not going to like this," and they both laughed. "I need a cigarette," she said, patting his shirt pocket.

"No you don't."

"Sex is all right, but cigarettes are bad?"

"Exactly."

She rested her head on his shoulder, ready to listen.

"What matters to me," he said at last, "is racing. And the ladies? Sure, especially you, but racing is my first love."

"But…"

"Let me finish." He squeezed her hand. "When I was four years old, my daddy set me in a go-cart, and from that day on, it's been racing, and only racing." and he recalled his father's warnings about the way family and commitments can steal your dreams. "My dad was the best mechanic in Georgia pretty much, and a good man." Billy named his boyhood heroes: his father Eddie Fiske, A. J. Foyt, Rodger Ward and Fireball Roberts, in that order. "I knew one day I'd follow after them, or try to."

"Why does it have to be either racing or me, a choice?" hoping she didn't sound pathetic.

"Because that's what life is, choices, especially when your means are small and your ideas are big." What he was about to tell her would sound selfish, but it was honest. "If you're setting a hard goal, the first choice you have to make is for yourself. That might seem easy, but it's not."

"I know that."

He smoothed her hair back from her face. "You don't know; most people don't, until it's too late."

"I'm different."

"What's a girl like you know about the work, the years I put in? – and I'm not there yet."

"I'm not some girl who's never gone through anything." Her face flushed. "You don't know anything about me, either."

"Sorry, that wasn't fair." He leaned back, closing his eyes. "I quit school at fifteen. Every bad thing my mom's family had predicted when she married my dad seemed to be coming

57

true." Most people might say his parents had never seen or done anything grand, but he thought their lives had added up to something more than grand.

"And what happened?"

"I was a kid, had no idea what I was up against. Spent the next two years on every dirt track from New York to Florida, then three more on the Sportsman's Circuit." She'd never heard of it, he could tell. "That, darlin', is like Harvard undergraduate school for racing, but you still have a long way to go."

"I don't know why women are expected to cheer on the sidelines while men chase their dream," thinking now about her father. "I'm sure it wasn't all bad."

"It wasn't. I was doing what I wanted to."

"Like now."

"Like now." Purposely, he left out any hint of apology, and when he reached to touch her cheek, she pushed his hand away. "Keep going… I want to hear it."

"A lot of years, I had nothing at all. My dad helped me build my car and I was working every job I could find during the week, working on my car nights, racing weekends." By then, his dad was sick, and Billy was trying to help *him*, too. "That day in Daytona? The only thing missing was him. I love my Ma, but it was him who would've understood, right down to that tap I took at the end."

It was still early when Billy pulled up in front of her house, but the porch light was already on. Billy hadn't even suggested going back to his house. "I hope my mom doesn't come talk to me." The engine was still running. "Better go on in." She sat thinking, Didn't he know to ask her out, or tell her his plans? "Get going," he said, nudging her playfully. She jumped out of the car and slammed the door, hoping that Billy would run after her, make a million promises even if he couldn't keep them, but he didn't, and the sound of his car melted away.

CHAPTER 13

ALL THAT DISTRESS FOR NOTHING! Before Ainsley had even brushed her teeth the next morning, the phone had rung, and now she and Billy were having dinner at one of the town's favorite restaurants. They joined a small group waiting in the bar, sitting at a small table beneath a ceiling of gaudy stained-glass flowers. Because it was Saturday night, the diners were mostly couples, some older, but that didn't stop a few women from smiling at Billy and appraising her. Finally his name was called and they were seated in a booth.

A waitress set water glasses, announcing her name. "I'm Mindy." Her face lit up. "And *you* are Billy Fiske!"

"Yes, ma'am," and his eyes traveled over her skimpy outfit.

"I can't believe it," she said. "I was at the 500, and I said, If I ever get to meet Billy Fiske, it will be the best day of my life." Ainsley felt herself grow small and jealous. Billy must have sensed it, because he reached over and patted her hand. Like a puppy, she thought. They both decided on the skewered beef and noodles. "Help yourself to the salad bar."

When Mindy brought their orders, Billy picked up where they'd left off. "You go to all the races?"

"Wouldn't miss it," she said, and flashed a broad smile of pink gloss and pretty teeth. "Racin' gets my blood pumpin."

He shifted his glance to her scoop-neck T-shirt. "You got a real healthy pump."

"Well, now!" tossing her head as she turned to go.

Ainsley's face flushed. "Don't make a fool of me, Billy."

"Don't make something out of nothing, that's just me."

"Not when you're with me."

By the time their food came, the restaurant had emptied a bit, and they ate their dinners hardly talking. The girl returned, her makeup freshened. He seemed to be studying her: wild and curly hair restrained by combs, a shadow between her freckled breasts, legs in black mesh stockings. She asked, "Was everything all right?"

"Fine," they answered together.

"Is there anything else I can do for you?" Her pink tongue darted, and all the innuendo was directed at Billy. Ainsley bit her lip, hoping Billy would let it slide, and if he did, she would too. But he didn't. "What did you have in mind?" he asked, a knowing grin on his face. And Ainsley couldn't help thinking of all the women who had sat as she was sitting, being made fools and voyeurs. Leaning across the table, she told Billy: "*I'm* here, and you need to stop."

The girl and Billy stared at her.

All the misery of the past weeks seemed to crystallize in that moment, and Ainsley understood what Billy had been trying to tell her about himself and maybe his life. She had no place in it except on his terms. Conversation stopped at a nearby table, as the older couple stole covert glances. Ainsley slid to the outside edge of the booth, and the girl jumped back, startled. "I'm not going to sit here," said Ainsley, "and act deaf, dumb and polite when you two act trashy and mean at my expense."

"I didn't do anything," protested the girl.

"Calm down," said Billy, embarrassed.

"Shut up, Billy." She turned back to the girl. "This piece of work I'm with isn't even worth having," and then to Billy: "Don't think you can insult me and I'll sit quietly." The girl turned to leave, and Ainsley called after her, "When you bring the check, don't say one word."

A different girl brought it.

Ainsley insisted he take her home. They drove back in silence and he parked beneath a bay tree that hid them from view. "I'm sorry about tonight," he said.

"I gave you too much credit." All his words seemed empty now, and she knew she shouldn't trust him, shouldn't let herself care about him.

Billy touched her shoulder. "You're important to me."

"I expect more." Without a kiss or a backward glance, she opened the car door and ran into the house. This time, she'd make Billy do the suffering.

It didn't turn out that way. Days went by, and finally there was news: Billy had left town, not by himself but with a girl from the junior college, a part-time waitress. Ainsley felt her heart give way, but she kept her word: she wouldn't shed one more tear for Billy Fiske.

CHAPTER 14

FURTHER PROOF OF THE QUINN family's "getting there" had come a month earlier when Grace announced that she and Parker were going to a wedding in North Carolina, then spending a few days at a resort. A resort! The word was like something from a foreign language. Ainsley and the Captain were loading suitcases into the old Ford, newly waxed, its white paint gleaming in the sun.

"You take care now, hear?" admonished Parker.

"I'll see to it," said the Captain, winking at Ainsley.

"I'm sure," said Grace, frowning. She wore a pantsuit, a new kind of outfit for St. Christie's, and her hair was caught in a clasp at the back of her head. The Captain took their picture as they leaned against the trunk of the car; Grace blew kisses toward the camera, a mock celebrity.

"I guess we're set," said Parker.

"Hurry up," said Grace, "before some crisis comes along." He helped his wife into the car, and then went around to the driver's side, throwing yet another wave before heading down the road, beeping the horn, giving themselves a send-off. The Captain and Ainsley watched, their arms hitched around each others' waists, as Parker and Grace disappeared down the straight, flat road, heading toward the coastal highway.

The Quinns had rented a cottage on the beach at Cape Romain. "As if we don't get enough beach back home," said Grace.

"This is different. This is hundred dollar a day beach. No wonder I can't relax."

"Better rest up. You know I've mapped out lots of sightseeing on the way home." Grace had always dreamed of seeing the world, of spending days in Paris art museums, seeing Rome and sitting on the Spanish Steps eating gelato, but this was a start. They were side-by-side, cross-legged on the bed, maps and brochures spread out between them. The plan was to drive back through Charleston and Savannah to see the historic houses. In a noisy way, Parker began folding the maps and carelessly gathering up the brochures that Grace had collected in anticipation of their trip. She lifted her head, annoyed. "What are you doing?"

"If I was to agree to all this sightseeing, I'd have to be in a weakened condition." He flung himself back onto the pillows, his arms stretched open. "You know, weakened?"

"Is that so?" She continued reading.

"Definitely," and circling her waist from behind, he pulled her down beside him. Turning to him, she threw her arms around his neck and started kicking at the brochures, catapulting them into a pyramid on the floor.

They didn't see the old houses of Savannah. The sheriff would later call it a freak accident, a description that robbed it of meaning and dignity. They had been on Route 17 out of Charleston, south bound where it joined with I-95. From what the Highway Patrol would later put together, a horse-trailer carrying a stallion had been about a quarter-mile in front of Parker and Grace.

Easing the horse-trailer through a construction maze, the driver could not have anticipated what was to come. As he rounded a blind curve, traffic was stopped dead. The trailer-driver hit his brakes. Behind him, a four-door Chrysler sedan slammed into the trailer, tires screeching. The trailer crumpled. One moment the door was there, its heavy locks holding a chestnut stallion safe inside. The next, the doors flew open, the hinges dangling, and the horse was heaved onto the asphalt. Startled drivers slammed their brakes, lay on their horns, and closed their eyes against the sight of a horse lying bleeding in the middle of I-95. The horse's eyes were wide, his legs flailing. He tried to stand but fell back on the hot pavement. Finally he stood, blood

63

running from his head, onto his coat, which shone red in the sun. A sliver of white, like bone, twisted his shoulder into a curve.

"Oh, God!" screamed Grace. "No!" Cars seemed to be coming from all directions. And then the horse was crossing the highway, moving toward the median when a young couple and their baby, coming the opposite way, rounded the curve. Their car spun out, rolling over, propelling them across four lanes of traffic.

Time stopped. It wasn't just a saying. The on-coming car veered into the Quinns's path, and Parker had a faint awareness of Styrofoam coolers, maps and Oreo cookies creating a collage on the road to Savannah.

The days immediately following the accident closed in like a fog that never lifted – the mass at St. Mary's, the doctors, the phone calls, the cards, the visitors bearing warm, foil-covered casseroles.

"Casseroles are a lesson for us all to be more cautious drivers," said Parker. After two weeks, he was at home now, sitting up in a hospital-type bed, side-by-side with Grace's in their new living room. His and hers, as he described them. "I always wanted twin Corvettes or twin Boston Whalers, not twin beds," said Parker. He joked about the accident, but knew they were lucky to be alive. Their car had rolled over and been hit twice.

"I told you we weren't meant to travel," said Grace, looking over at Phoebe.

"I've stopped wishing for us to be like other people, Mom," said Ainsley.

"And it's too bad," said Grace, "we didn't build an infirmary in this new house." She had broken her collar bone, her arm and several ribs. Parker had a head injury, and they wondered still if he would regain sight in his left eye.

"One is all I need," he assured them. Parker's back, a persistent problem, was worse now.

"We always wanted to try drugs," said Grace, "but they're not nearly as much fun as I thought they'd be."

"Reality is for those who can't handle drugs," Parker told her. A favorite old joke. Grace laughed, but then clutched her side "No jokes! Oooh… my ribs!"

Because Parker didn't want Ainsley fussing and worrying, a nurse came in briefly each day, and of course there was Phoebe, who had been helping out from the start. The biggest change was that Ainsley would stay at the Captain's compound for a while, a decision she knew had been made to spare her, not themselves.

Among the couple's belongings, returned by the Highway Patrol a few days after the accident, were three rolls of film, just developed and being passed around. "Look at this. I sure was good looking two weeks ago," said Grace, whose face was still bruised. "You still are, darlin," said the Captain, handing the prints to Ainsley. The next photo showed Parker grilling hamburgers outside their Cape Romain cottage, and the next, Grace posing with her fishing rod and a small sea bass. Ainsley's eyes were brimming.

"Honey, don't worry," said Parker, noticing. "We're still the luckiest people in the world." Which finally pushed her over the edge.

Grace gave Parker a look that said, Now see what you've done! "Must you be so relentlessly cheerful? It's depressing."

"Things are beginning to sound normal now," said the Captain. He turned to Ainsley, picking up her suitcase. "Let's let them enjoy their squabbling in peace. Time for us to go before it's dark." He looked at Phoebe. "You're in charge now."

"Dad," said Grace. "I hope you won't be making a pest of yourself now that Phoebe's here." She looked at Phoebe. "He always at his best when you're around, so that's a plus."

"Grace, hush," said Phoebe. "Once children are adults, it's not right for them to torment their parents." Throughout her life, Phoebe had made an art of smoothing things over, of getting past every social pot hole, and had even made it fashionable to come from a poor family. For generations, the Boones had variously specialized in fishing, running rum and operating a grill at their fish camp, where Phoebe, from her early years, had cooked, served, and later, made a little spending money reading tarot cards .

Her looks may not have been classic, but boys were much less interested in classics than they were in Phoebe's long, reddish hair, swept up and held back from her round face with barrettes, or the way she dipped her chin and looked up at them with her light blue eyes. She wasn't tall, but her sixty-two inches had provided ample accommodation for boys' daydreams, especially since she wasn't considered a "nice" girl. How could a Boone be nice, when they were known for poaching crab traps, for drinking and brawling that made them frequent guests at the county jail? Now 65, Phoebe is almost the same height as then, her eyes are still blue, her hair still red in the sunlight. What's different now is that there's more to understand – the Phoebe she dared not reveal as a girl.

People still shook their heads in wonder over that day long ago when Mr. Thadeus Moffitt and his northern entourage of land speculators had stopped at the Boone Fish Camp run by Phoebe's clan. The visitors, dressed in their dark, three-piece suits and straw bowlers, sat beside the river at tables covered with yesterday's newspaper, which they read while waiting for their smoked mullet, crab legs and oysters. They thought it charming.

Over time, the story became embellished, but as recounted by various fish camp customers, from the time it took Phoebe to set the tall, frosty glasses in front of the group, until she emptied the tub of oysters out onto the newspaper in front of Mr. Moffitt, something amazing had happened. "The butter was melting in a sun-warmed dish," recalled one observer. "And that pyramid of oysters, dumped onto the newspapers was steaming! And Mr. Moffitt was steaming too, if you know what I mean!" When Mr. Moffitt looked up into her face, he didn't see just a server standing there. He saw a young woman with clear, rosy skin, and an intelligent demeanor – a woman he hoped was destined to be in his life, just like that! That was the story, and no tarot readings were involved.

To the chagrin of many, and the astonishment of all, Phoebe had been struck by the same clap of thunder, and to make matters worse, it happened that Mr. Moffitt was wealthy beyond all good taste and comfortableness. The couple married and spent years traveling in Europe, living in Mr. Moffitt's houses in Spain and Italy, but after he had died, ten years earlier, Phoebe returned to her old home – a world-traveler, fifty-five years old, and took up almost where she had left off, except people saw qualities in her that had somehow escaped them before. Thus, the legendary power of oysters gained ever greater renown, and the Moffitt incident would be blamed for the further decline of local oyster beds.

Now at the Quinns' home, Phoebe was determined to help Parker and Grace get well. She had set herself up in a spare room, had packed Ainsley's things for an extended stay with the Captain, and had everyone believing they were in good hands, which they were. She handed the Captain a loaf of banana bread wrapped in a cloth napkin and patted Ainsley on the shoulder. "Keep an eye on him," she called, as the two headed down the walk.

CHAPTER 15

THE CAPTAIN OPENED THE WEATHERED pine door of his house and held it for Ainsley, worried about all that had been put on her shoulders, foremost, her stricken parents and now this – being put out of her house on account of it. As soon as they'd stepped inside, she threw her arms around his neck. "I'll try not to be too much trouble," and he could hear Grace's smoky timbre in her breaking voice. "You go on up," he told her. "I'll be right there." He started for the kitchen, a diversion, to put Phoebe's bread away, fix two glasses of ice water, and catch his breath, taking his time about it, worrying about how Ainsley would get on staying there with him.

Slowly, he climbed the stairs to the top floor, where she had always slept when visiting. This time, her stay would be different. He stood at the threshold of the room, remembering his wife and their baby of so long ago. Grace's bedroom, and his own bedroom, long before that. The years had rushed by like a fast-moving river.

"When your great granddad built this place," he said, "we put up a roof of palmetto fans. I'd listen all night to the critters nested up there." The attic ran the length of the house, and had been an ideal place for a boy who liked to dream big. Funny, he thought, how people held that dreams died when you got old.

"I like the tin roof, Grandpa," interrupting his thought, "especially when it rains." His granddaughter, trying to comfort him, when he should be doing that for her. "Rain sounds like a hundred little cymbals," he told her. "I know." For a moment, as he watched Ainsley open one of the big dormer windows, he remembered his wife Sarah, whom he had seen in that very attitude so many times. Things should have been better between them: they had been so young, so unaware of what life had in store. The worst thing about getting old was the way your losses piled up.

The windows were situated to the east and west to capture the ocean and river breezes, which now billowed the thin white curtains he'd never had the heart to part with. He remembered the day Sarah had hung them, a day long before he'd given up his hopes for the two of them. She'd been an energetic kind of woman, always on the plump side, with blue, wide-set eyes and long, auburn hair – shining, looping and wild – her only vanity.

"I'm going to like being here with you," Ainsley said, bringing him back from his dream. "And being in Mom's old room."

"Your Ma was a big collector." The Captain remembered scouring the beach after storms, with Grace running ahead to get the best finds. Most of the early houses along that stretch, including theirs, had been built partly from salvage. Grace's old dresser was still crowded with mementoes, with shells, with photographs in rusty frames. He picked one up: Grace and Parker sitting on the front steps, innocent and untouched.

Over the next weeks, they were still feeling after-shocks from the accident. Parker and Grace were recuperating slowly, with more setbacks for Parker. A wheelchair had been brought in for use now and then, and his injured eye still hadn't recovered. Ainsley knew that even with Sam's help, the groves would suffer. Her grandfather refused to be anything but optimistic. "We still got my shrimp business and the marina," he said, "enough to stay up with the bills," almost.

After the accident, they'd bought an old pickup so Ainsley could run errands, and this day, the last of her trips had brought her to the River Road where her family had lived and where Billy had bought a place not so long ago. It was already dark, and she knew from the newspaper that he was on the road. How often he still came into her thoughts. On impulse, she parked the pickup near their old cottage and walked the still-broken sidewalk that used to send her tumbling on her skates. Warm lights spilled from the jalousie windows of the closed-in porch where her mother used to sit and read. Had it always been so cheerful and welcoming? If only she could turn back time, be here again, her parents healthy and happy.

She started to walk away, when a gleaming flash of metal caught her eye, and there in the driveway she saw a small foreign car, a strange blue thing that her parents would never have thought of owning. Even the yard was different. Her mother's flame vine had been cut back to earth, and over the garage, someone had hung a basketball hoop, a hoop in place of the orange-flowered vine that belonged there.

Then a dog barked inside the house. A young boy came to the window, shielding his eyes to look outside, and Ainsley backed away into the darkness. It was then that she saw the sign, put up between two newly-set posts. The Anderson Family. She leaned against a tree. Never would she see her mother and father in that place again, or lie in bed upstairs, listening to them murmuring or sparring in their young, hope-filled voices.

CHAPTER 16

THE CAPTAIN THOUGHT HE KNEW all about how to raise a girl. After all, he'd done it once, but he'd forgotten the parts about worry and self-doubt. When summer came, he would be away a week at a time, shrimping at night for hopper shrimp and brownies, forty miles at sea. Luckily, in spring he shrimped just offshore for white shrimp, and tied in at his marina every night, easing his concerns.

The name Captain was first given to him in jest, when he had been just twenty-two and a new husband. Every morning at dawn in all weather, he would head his 15-foot outboard into the river for the day's catch. He knew where the deep holes lay along the sand spits of the lagoon, knew how to coax crabs into his traps when he needed to, and could throw a casting net for hours on end.

Fishing had opened up his world. Although he considered himself under-schooled, he liked to read, an interest sparked by spending hours alone in a small boat and living on an island with few diversions. "Nothing high-toned" he assured people when they remarked on how many books he checked out of the library. Later, these same people would comment that his daughter had also been afflicted with books. What he lacked in formal education or opportunity, he had made up for by trying new little enterprises – selling honey, building oil-drum smokers, making smoked mullet – until he finally realized his dream of owning a shrimper, The Sarah, named for his late wife. He wished she were there to see her granddaughter.

Ainsley's senior year was nearly over, and when classes ended for the day, she tended the counter at the marina, then visited her parents in the evening. When the Captain returned with his daily catch, she read the detailed notes she had written, telling him everything that had happened during his absence and how she'd handled it. "Watch out," he warned, "or you'll turn into one of them C.E.O.s." At the marina, there was also an influx of older boys who had taken a sudden interest in fishing.

The marina shelves had never been so orderly, and he doubted he could find anything if he had to. His cash book had never been kept with more diligence, and she always had her weekly pay envelope ready, set aside for his okay. He pretended to check the numbers carefully, but had to fight an urge to double her pay. Weekends, she sometimes went shrimping with him. He had taught her how to handle the winches and set the nets, how to head and ice the shrimp, hard labor even for a man.

Over the years, she had learned to captain the boat, but despite her many pleadings, he had always taken over the wheel when passing between the river and the ocean, since Halifax Inlet was considered the most treacherous on the coast. This day, they were on the river, heading to the channel and out to sea for a full weekend of work, not just a day trip, Ainsley at the wheel, turning the boat into a fast-moving wave full of cross-currents. She glanced over and caught him watching.

He said, "You're quite the skipper."

"Let me prove it."

She never let up.

"I'm ready to take her through the inlet, Grandpa. You'll be so happy," she added, piling on a great helping of charm.

He would be so happy? Her reasoning escaped him, but after so many years and so many trips, she'd finally worn him out. Instead of taking the wheel, he took a breath, accepting her smile as his reward for such weakness. She wore her usual sailing outfit: baggy blue jeans, sneakers, and a red tee shirt, reminding him of Grace and of everyone he had ever loved.

"You know," he said, "there won't be much more time for shrimping and this kind of thing."

Her head swiveled around. "What do you mean?"

"I want you to enjoy this last bit of high school. You've been through a lot, but we're all okay, praise God." He was an optimist, the family curse. "Some day, you'll find work you like, and if you're lucky, a man with a good heart. You'll be happier than you can imagine, I promise."

"Like you, Grandpa, with Grandma Sarah."

A wrong assumption, but he let it go. His marriage to Sarah – well. If there was one thing you needed to get right, it was finding somebody you loved who loved you back. True happiness was rare without that, but he tried not to dwell on it.

Their marriage had started out hard. Frank and Sarah had had a son who died in infancy, and when no second pregnancy happened right away, they feared they'd never have another child. Thanks to the power of prayer and human collaboration, in time, Grace was born, and Sarah would later say they should have named her Patience or Mercy. Once Grace arrived, Sarah felt she had done God's will, having submitted over and over to His plan for procreation, and wondering why, in all His wisdom He had devised something so untidy, so gymnastic!

Thus, after the birth of their new baby, and except for rare concessions, Sarah's hierarchy of wifely duties began with motherhood, followed by cooking, cleaning, sewing and gardening – and what more could a reasonable husband expect?

The shrimper was passing the lighthouse now, with its clapboard out-buildings and a museum with a first-order Fresnel lens. Ainsley must have felt a need to ease his mind of worries because she turned to him and said, "I'm already happy now, Grandpa. We have everything we need." He loved her the same way he loved Grace, a fact that had taken him completely by surprise when he realized it long ago.

Piloting the shrimper through the inlet, Ainsley looked as if she was made to be right there at the helm. Usually there was time for a cup of coffee before the try-nets were brought up; then they could inspect the first haul, decide whether they were in a good spot or move somewhere else to try again. After that, shrimping was non-stop work. They and the two young hands now working below, would empty the catch on deck and sort out the shrimp, edible squid and fin fish from the trash fish. In fall, jelly balls crowded the nets, as much a nuisance as sharks and rays. Below deck, twenty tons of shaved ice stood heaped for packing. The crew would head the shrimp, ice them to a depth of four feet, and toss the heads and trash fish overboard, attracting an escort of scavenger sharks. Then it would be time to spread the nets and do it all over again.

Using block and tackle, the Captain and Ainsley set the nets free, always a big moment. He loved watching them fan so gracefully, the mast and outriggers like a sea-going angel with out-stretched wings. He rested his arm on Ainsley's shoulder and said the family prayer, "Everything's going to be fine."

∽⌾

"I'm almost good as new," Parker was saying. He was sitting up in his living room bed, and the Captain, Grace and Jack Henderson all nodded their agreement, but it was clear to Ainsley they had doubts.

"You will, Dad," glaring at the others for their lack of conviction. Of the two, Grace had made a better recovery from the accident, and although her ribs and collarbone still hurt, she wryly described herself as being "my old, very old self."

Jack had come by to settle the details of a plan they'd worked out for him to manage Parker's groves. "Just temporarily," Jack said, noticing Ainsley's cheerless expression. The groves would be secure, but once again, Ainsley resented him. Her father's pride must be hurt, having to turn to the much younger Jack once again, and having no choice. He's broken in body and spirit, she thought, even though he looked relieved for the first time since the accident.

"Your offer is more than generous," said Parker.

"I'll come out fine in the end," Jack assured him.

"You will," chimed Grace and the Captain, too loudly, and they all laughed, embarrassed as if they were crooked salesmen who'd just signed a deal with a poor widow.

"I want to help with the groves, Jack," said Ainsley, "I know all about citrus, everything."

Jack hesitated. "Everything? Good. I'll keep that in mind, but I guess you'll have your hands full now, with graduation and all." Coming to his feet, he wished her good luck.

He was dismissing her. "I like working," said Ainsley. "I have my own business, you know," a statement that surprised her as much as everyone else.

His eyebrows shot up. "A business?"

"You wouldn't be interested."

"I would be."

"...It has to do with – driftwood."

"Aaah," said Jack, nodding. "I heard about the rising market in driftwood." He picked up his papers. "Thanks for your offer, and if you need any help with the driftwood part, you let me know." He touched two fingers to his forehead, made his goodbyes and closed the door quietly behind himself. Boots, the yellow puppy who'd been waiting outside, followed him to his truck, barking.

"I don't know why you're so rude to Jack," said Grace. "He has been a good friend to us time and again."

"I'm never rude," said Ainsley, and they all managed not to laugh.

CHAPTER 17

MOST OF THE WINTER TOURISTS, the songbirds and northern yachts were gone, as the in-between season settled on St. Christie's Island. Too early for summer crowds or hurricanes still waiting in the wings, too late for spring breakers, and so, a seasonal pause tiptoed in.

For Ainsley, the last senior-year events filled the void as the Class of 1978 observed the rituals marking its ascent into the world. Tonight, photos from the senior prom at the King's Crown Inn would be archived in albums and memories. In St. Christie's itself, there had been no historic glory days to recall. No Grande Dame hotel, no Robert Trent Jones golf course or Rockefeller Christmas parties held on vast, sloping lawns. The King's Crown Inn was as close as they had ever come to elegance, their premier venue.

Despite that, many still hoped that good fortune would some day return to Halifax County and that St. Christie's would be at its zenith. Committees intermittently looked into the possibilities, but inevitably came to the same hopeless conclusions. For the present then, modest niceties were as much prosperity as anyone in St. Christie's was likely to aspire or admit to.

Ainsley and Beth were now preparing to make their entrances into the King's Crown Inn ballroom. Charlie Portman, the ever-hopeful candidate for Ainsley's attention, had come to her rescue, as Beth put it. Proms had not taken place in the school gymnasium for years, evidence, people said, that St. Christie's wasn't just a backwater town after all.

Instead of the covered-dish suppers of years past, the hotel was catering a dinner of chicken Kiev, potatoes Anna and roasted asparagus, choices that many would be sampling for the first time. When the committee had announced the menu, potatoes and asparagus, garnered unexpected criticism. "You call these treats?" but the committee had stood fast. The posse in charge of decorating won acclaim, however, for tables draped in ivory damask and centered with leatherleaf fern and pink camellias in crystal vases – and of course, above it all, a mirrored ball showering multi-colored lights on the dancers in their new shoes. With their last-minute etiquette lessons, the boys were dutifully holding doors, pulling out chairs, and standing whenever the girls left, or returned to the tables. If this was what it took to be gentlemen, they were up to the task!

This was a night to remember, whether your date made your heart spin or not – in the long run, more likely not. Everyone's clothes had been appraised and complimented. Beth wore a midnight-blue A-line dress with a slit high on her leg, and Ainsley, a white crepe with thin straps and a waltz-length skirt. Vickie's New York father, generous with money if not time, had sent a silvery dress with a designer's name inside, but at the table later, Vickie had leaned in and whispered to Ainsley: "I'll trade you my dessert and a car for your date," nodding in Charlie's direction. "Hands off," she whispered back, as Charlie took her hand and led her to the dance floor, pulling her in close. At moments like this, and there had been more than a few since Billy, Ainsley felt certain she would survive after all.

Tonight, everyone was standing on the doorstep to the future, and she imagined each of them holding a clean canvas, to be inscribed later with dates of weddings, births and other milestones. Their lives might appear to be similar now, but later, they would all be unique. What would the ordinary days between milestones be like, those days that would comprise their daily lives? Would Charlie become an attorney, fighting for the poor? Would Tupper find his path, would any of them? Her mother had told her that every life was a self portrait, a painting you added to every day without even realizing it. Up close, your painting might seem baffling, but seen over time and from a distance, it would tell a story that was completely clear. "Unfortunately," Grace had said, "every brush stroke represents a decision you made, some good, some not."

"I hope," Ainsley whispered to Charlie, "that all of our lives turn into amazing paintings."

"What do you mean by amazing?" he asked. "a Rothko, a Rockwell, a Picasso?

"You're making this complicated."

"I think it is."

She hoped her painting would show a life lived with purpose and maybe some bravery, with joy in it, too, and of course, love. "I guess," she told him, "I'll figure it all out in college."

Charlie pressed his cheek to hers. "We'll set Gainesville on fire."

"We will?" She had accepted a bid to the University of Florida, mainly for its citrus program.

"Nothing will make me happier," he said, "than being tormented by you for four more years," She was grateful Charlie had never said anything about the way she'd abandoned him for Billy. He raised his arm, let her pass under, then drew her in close again, but Ainsley sensed someone staring at them, and glancing up, saw that it was Vickie.

"So," he whispered, "what are you going to *be* when you grow up?"

Ainsley hesitated. "A party girl?" Charlie raised his eyebrows in hope, even knowing she didn't mean it, "College may exceed all my expectations."

"It'll be good to get away," she told him.

"Not away from me."

"Of course not." Away from the chance of running into Billy, or *not* running into him, but she couldn't say that.

Summer passed quickly, with Ainsley working for both her father and grandfather, wherever she was needed most, and soon, she and Beth were packing their suitcases for Gainesville.

After a month of college classes, of feeling near-terror of professors who called her "Miss Quinn," and still thinking of Billy sometimes, she found she liked rooming in a dormitory with Beth, and liked college more than she had hoped. On Fridays, students from St. Christie's met at Aquarius, a bar run by a married couple who were former U of F students. The pony-tailed man dressed in muscle shirts. The woman wore her graying hair long and straight, and dressed in faded bell-bottoms. Now a crowd was backed up along the sidewalk, and the smell of rancid beer escaped through the rough-paneled, open door. Elbowing through the line, Beth and Ainsley searched for their friends. Beth pointed to a far corner and they began making their way past redwood picnic tables filled with students. "Make room," said Beth, as they squeezed onto the hard bench seats being saved by their friends. "It's so stuffy and smelly here," Beth complained. "Why do we come?"

"Because," said Tupper, "this is the spot where opportunity knocks," and he tapped lightly on the scarred table and grabbed her hand.

She shoved him away. "I've known you forever. I want fresh blood."

Ainsley sometimes thought of Tupper as a lost boy, but such troubling thoughts – perhaps colored by what had happened between her and his father, quickly vanished when she remembered his many positive traits – his loyalty to friends, his good-heartedness. If something was missing from his life, Tupper was too proud to show it. The rest of the St. Christie's crowd – Charlie, Vickie, Karl, Anne, Leo and Bear DeWitt were arguing about the upcoming football game, when Beth noted Dance's unusual absence.

"She's studying," Bear said, shrugging.

"Well, in that case, come on over and sit by us," said Beth, her voice mockingly seductive. But when Bear rose, she and Ainsley broke into surprised laughter, watching him make his way to their side of the table. "Thank God we don't have to hear Dance whine about keeping her scholarship," someone said, but Bear seemed not to hear it, or chose not to, perhaps because, as some of them thought, he was as burdened by her scholarship as Dance was: an unwelcome encumbrance for someone as free-spirited as Bear. As he continued moving through the crowd, all eyes followed him.

Charlie, attempting to re-gain Ainsley's attention, tapped his glass: "Listen up, everybody. I want you to know that Ainsley here aced every one of her midterms." A small silence was soon broken by groans and boos.

"And you promised to be a party girl," he complained.

"I lied."

Bear had reached the other side of the table, where Ainsley was making room for him. "That's good enough," he said, climbing over the bench and squeezing between her and Beth.

"Stay away from my girl," warned Charlie jokingly, but Ainsley knew he half meant it.

"Lookin' good," said Beth, appraising Bear and squeezing his arm. "Dance oughtn't let you out loose. There's lots of bad girls around."

He didn't seem to know what to make of her remark, or of Ainsley's when she said, "We'll protect you," taking hold of his other arm and sliding closer to his side.

"I hope so," he said, reminding Ainsley of how much she had always liked his relentless earnestness. The owner brought their beers, fanning her heart as if she couldn't take the heat when she stood next to Bear. Women often reacted that way around him, but he seemed not to notice. After two rounds, Leo made the first move to leave, then Beth, who had an early exam, and by ones and twos everyone else, with Tupper being half-carried out between Karl and Charlie, who clearly hadn't planned to end his evening that way.

"I guess it's just you and me," said Bear.

"Looks like it," said Ainsley. She dreaded going back to the dorm and the usual Friday night card games and boyfriend critiques. They decided to get a pizza at a restaurant in a converted house just off campus. "I never trust places called ristorante," warned Ainsley.

"It's okay," he said. "You can trust me," and he took her by the elbow, steering her toward the double doors. He felt, for some reason, an easiness he hadn't known in a long time.

The noise level at Pizza Palazzio was worse than at the Aquarius. Hard rock music bounced off the carved plaster ceilings and stucco walls, painted with inept murals. Never had Tuscany looked so forlorn, he was sure. They placed their order and were in luck when a corner booth opened just as the pizza arrived on a battered aluminum pedestal – extra cheese and nothing else, the choice of both. A sign? he wondered, then felt silly thinking it.

"I know that band," said Ainsley, but Bear cupped his hand to his ear and shook his head. He couldn't hear a thing she was saying, and maybe he'd had too much beer, because he felt light-headed, and so much happier than he had lately. Ainsley leaned closer, so close he could feel her breath, smell her faint perfume, catching him off guard. Imagine, Ainsley Quinn having such an effect on him.

"You like their music?" he shouted.

"What?"

"Do you like the music?"

She shook her head and shrugged her shoulders, uncomprehending, then brought her lips close to his ear. "I can't hear you!" As she drew away smiling, Bear felt dazzled by the indigo blaze in her eyes, the high color in her cheeks. He leaned closer. He had known her all his life, and in a sense he had never noticed her until now. For the briefest moment, he paused before taking her hand and, on impulse, touched his lips to hers. She pulled back and looked at him surprised, and in a moment, she was kissing him back.

Chapter 18

THE DEWITT FAMILY HAD BEEN a presence in Florida since the 1910s, when Bear's great grandfather had swindled his partner out of hundreds of thousands of timber acres in Florida and Georgia. When DeWitt learned that his partner had killed himself over it, he was reported to have said, "It's the first thing that sonofabitch ever did that I approve of." DeWitts had been repeating the story ever since. By the time Bear's father, Clay, was in charge, the holdings included more forestry acres than ever, and a DeWitt conglomerate of lumber, pulp and paper mills.

What Clay could not forgive was that his grandfather controlled everyone from his grave. They lived lavishly, the DeWitts, but wills and trusts, investment bankers and executors held the reins. When his own father had died at a young age, Clay, then 18, understood the curse of having wealth you could never put your hands on, as out of reach as a virtuous married woman. Worse, he soon discovered that the DeWitt fortune existed on that very famous paper only, and that the badly-run companies were deeply in debt from over-expansion in bad times. Not many people had known it, except Lady DeWitt, and she, only after her marriage to Clay, when it was too late. Over time, Clay had managed to break the trusts and other restraints and to build a fortune all his own. After he was rich, "not wealthy, rich," he liked to look back and brag about how close he had been to going under. Clay loved having money, using it, controlling people with it, lording it over them. No point in deceiving himself that he had many true friends, or that his family would treat him with such deference if his circumstances were different. On all sides there was mutual contempt, but only he was in a position to show it. Lady, of course, had the last laugh, and he respected that.

Lady's family, the Forneaus were an old clan out of Charleston – rich, everyone said, and rich had had its charms with the DeWitt enterprises so in peril. Clay had wed in haste to save his businesses, and he was still repenting. Lady was as dull-witted a woman as he'd ever met, but haughty and striking, and despite his repeated promises to himself never to touch her again, he did, and often. God help her. That was her punishment for being stupid and for having produced a plain and charmless daughter, and then naming her Tessie, which Clay considered a homely and apt choice. To his way of thinking, a girl's primary job was to be attractive, and he often thought: That girl will never find a husband. No amount of money can spring *that* trap.

His son had been his only remaining hope. Bear. He'd been just a toddler when he got the name. They'd been up in the high country in North Carolina, along the Cherokee Trail, he and Lady, Bear, the nanny and his people from the company, looking at timber. Somehow they'd lost sight of the baby. They called him by his Christian name then, Mark. He'd wandered off from the cabin, and they had sent out search parties and dogs. For only the second time in his life, Clay DeWitt knew what it meant to suffer for love. They'd finally sighted him, standing there in his denim coveralls, but when they called out, the baby started to run away, thinking it was a game. He stumbled, and then they heard a low noise, a rumble. A sound guttural and deadly – and then movement, thrashing, and something advancing through the underbrush.

Then it came into view, a black bear about to cross the baby's path less than fifty feet away from the spot where he had fallen. He was laughing, as he tried to get up and the bear, standing there, seemed to be deciding something. It moved closer, and the baby looked up, transfixed. Clay, Lady and the others held their breaths. No one was armed. No one dared move.

The bear stood on its hind legs, five-feet tall, its light colored belly exposed, its forelegs high in the air. Then it dropped on all fours and took another step toward the baby, sniffing him, probing him with its paw, and the baby tipped over on his side, lying there quietly. Clay thought his heart would stop. The bear stood still for a moment, raising its head, his fur shining in the light slanting through the trees. Then it turned and walked back into the woods. They couldn't move.

"Bear!" said the baby, pointing after it.

"Bear!" they whispered, and Clay rushed forward and caught his son up in his arms, his body shaking with grateful sobs. That was the last time Clay DeWitt could remember feeling such love for his son, because soon after that, he and Lady began their tug-of-war over him, and Lady had won. Bile rose up in him when he saw Bear growing up in the image of his mother, good looking and soft, no toughness in him as far as Clay could see. Yet every now and then, he still pinned his hopes on him. For that, too, Clay made Bear suffer.

Bear and Dance had played their usual Saturday tennis match and were sitting on the grass critiquing the other players. Sweat glistened on Dance's olive skin, and her damp, dark hair spilled into ringlets on her forehead. Bear had played badly, distracted by thoughts of the night before and knowing he had betrayed Dance. Her trust only troubled him further.

"What do you think of Ainsley Quinn?" he blurted, and the question startled them both.

"Why do you ask?" She pulled a pale blue towel out of her bag.

He heard himself stammer. "Curious. That's all. She was at the Aquarius last night."

"Oh?"

Was her voice wary, he wondered? "Yeah. Big crowd," then adding for a measure of safety, "Everyone asked about you."

Pleased, she finished patting her face dry, and studied him. "Is Ainsley still mooning over Billy Fiske?"

"I don't think so. She seemed fine."

"I'm not surprised. Everything is so easy for her."

"Be fair," he said, sounding more defensive than he had intended.

Dance reconsidered. "Okay. She works hard." At last she had said something Bear wanted to hear. After leaving her at the library, he headed for the dorms; maybe he'd run into Ainsley.

Dance Hendrix watched as Bear crossed the campus lawn. They had little in common, and yet, he had her heart. Her family struggled, his was rich. She was ambitious and studious; he wanted to work on boats, be with friends and have his freedom. Sometimes he drove her crazy, and these last weeks, a feeling she couldn't put her finger on had become unsettling – perhaps it was just college – an obligation for Bear, more than an aspiration.

When her family had come to St. Christie's five years earlier, it was to make another new start. Her father had lost everything in his latest get-rich scheme of selling shares in a commuter airline. Before that it was coffee plantations in Costa Rica, and before that, she couldn't remember. They'd always lived high or low, more often low.

What Dance claimed to envy were people who lived in nice little houses, kept the same jobs and friends for a lifetime, and were indistinguishable from everyone else. However, in moments of truth, she admitted to wanting more for herself. She simply wished that her parents were those wished-for selfless and ordinary people, so she could more easily go on to be something else. Which she would. With her brains, looks and hard work, she had every confidence in the future, picturing an extraordinary and happy life with Bear. All the women in her family were fools for love, a long-standing tradition.

Looking back weeks later, Bear wondered why Dance hadn't been suspicious of him. All the signs of trouble had been there for her to read – the absences, his unexplainable moods, his professed need to spend time alone studying.

"What's going on?" she demanded at last. The sun shone brightly, but the November day was cold. A haze of early frost had turned the grass brittle brown, and dead leaves crunched under their feet as they walked along the concrete walk that crossed the campus. Despite the chill, she was wearing a thin sweatshirt with "U of F" imprinted on the front. Her demanding tone and the question took him by surprise.

"What's going on?" she repeated.

"What do you mean?"

Her eyes darkened. "I think you know." They stopped walking. Her small-boned frame stood only five-four, so that when she stamped the ground with a child-size sneaker, she only seemed more vulnerable. Bear reached out to touch her, to protect her from himself. She slapped his hand away. "Stop it!" and he quickly stepped back. "Something's going on, and I want to know what it is." The U of F logo crested and fell, like a small boat foundering.

She read the shame in his face, and dropped to her knees on the grass. He bent low, but couldn't touch her; he only wanted to run. "Everything I heard is true," she said at last, holding back tears, her voice shaking. "Behind my back... you've been going behind my back with Ainsley Quinn." She looked up, expecting his shocked denial.

But he couldn't bring himself to betray Ainsley too. One betrayal was enough. "I'm sorry" was all he could summon.

"Sorry!"

She stumbled to her feet, still choking back sobs. "Whether you're sorry now or not, you *will* be!" she cried, standing up straight, holding her books as if to protect herself, and she started to run, but stopped and turned back to face him. "Don't ever try to see me again! I know you will try, but I won't let you!" The wind caught her hair as she fled, leaving him with a sorrowful joy.

Over the following weeks, Bear and Ainsley were inseparable, meeting every morning for coffee, between classes whenever possible and at night to talk, to study together, to sleep together. It was as if all their childhood meetings, their teen parties, their almost daily encounters over the years had been leading them to what now seemed the inevitable. To outsiders, the romance appeared sudden, but to Bear and Ainsley, who had known each other over their entire lifetimes, it seemed ordained. At the Pizza Palazzio, he proposed to her, and they both said that of all the restaurants in the world, this would always be their favorite. In Bear's big water bed, Ainsley found a peace and refuge she had thought would never again be hers.

They decided to announce their engagement to both sides of the family together, at the same time and place, inviting their parents to a brunch on the first Saturday of their Christmas break. They had kept the engagement secret, knowing in their hearts the disapproval their parents would feel.

The Coquina Inn was one of the most loved in Halifax County, not far from St. Christie's, with keystone tile floors and French doors opening onto a broad oceanfront terrace. It had been built as a private home by one of the turn-of-the-century robber barons and to celebrate the season, was dressed in holiday splendor, with every nook, archway, mantel and column emblazoned with lights, garlands, swaths of silk ribbon and Palatka holly. The young couple was waiting near the front entrance, Ainsley in a winter-white sheath, Bear in a long-sleeved white shirt and navy blazer. When their parents arrived almost together, Ainsley saw at once that their plan had been a mistake, that she should have taken into account her mother's aversion to surprises of any kind. The two older couples stood in embarrassed confusion, clearly wanting to escape the hotel and each other. Once they were seated, Grace guessed why they'd been assembled there, and after the stammered Champagne toasts, the forced congratulations and the endless lunch, Grace tried to imagine the years that lay ahead for the Quinns and DeWitts, four people less than friends, yoked in the bonds of family.

When they were alone later at the Quinns's house, Grace told Ainsley, "You're not married yet. You really should think twice about getting mixed up with the DeWitts," adding hastily, "not that Bear isn't a nice young man, nothing against him."

"Mom, that's a terrible thing to say. What do you mean?"

"Lots of things. I don't want to get into it, but lots, from 'way back." She was chopping peppers and celery for dinner, filling up a frying pan that smoked and spat, and then she raised her voice, calling to her husband in the next room. "Parker, did you see the way Lady took over once the shock wore off, how she began planning absolutely everything?"

"Mom, it won't happen. Please stop."

"And did you notice," continued Grace, "how she had to bring up that their house would be more *suitable* for a shower?"

"At least you told her she wasn't allowed to give one," said Ainsley.

"She'll find a way, trust me," said Grace, and the cleaver fell as she attacked another defenseless pepper.

Chapter 19

St. Christie's was in a holiday mood, or in some cases, pretended to be. December 21, and just enough time to complete the shopping, the baking, the wrapping – and, for Jack Henderson, maybe time enough to convince himself that everything was just as he wanted it. He was sitting at the bar of the Gray Wolf and signaled for a refill.

Holy God, trying to count my blessings, he thought, maybe even make some up. What a dickhead. The bartender brought a bourbon rocks and a fresh napkin. Jack had driven in from his groves for some last-minute errands in St. Christie's and had promised Parker and Grace he'd stop by. Wished he hadn't. All he really wanted was to head home, throw a steak on the grill and hit the hay, maybe forget the steak.

In a booth behind him, a loud laugh made him glance into the bar mirror, wondering if it was somebody he knew. It wasn't. He'd been coming to the Gray Wolf for years and usually ran into friends, but not today. If you really wanted to feel depressed, this was the place, with its twinkling white lights, poinsettias claiming every tabletop, greenery coiling and dipping – but thank God, no Christmas carols, just Frank singing some oldies.

Someone approached and the next thing he knew, a skinny woman wearing a red Santa hat and black boots was throwing her arm across his shoulders and kissing him on the cheek.

"Hey, hon," she told him. "A good-looking guy like you needs to cheer up!" A pat on the shoulder, and she was gone.

Good looking? It was pretty dark in there. He glanced around as people do in such places, appraising his fellow human beings – a pretty sorry bunch overall – and wondered if there was anybody who would want to sleep with any of them, himself included. On second thought, not that he claimed to be an expert, most of them probably *were* getting slept with. He tossed back the last of his drink, placed a holiday-size tip on the bar, and wondered where the skinny girl in the Santa hat had gone.

The Quinns' new house was modest in size, but a far cry from the cottage on the River Road. As he walked up to the front door, Jack was picturing their old place, where no amount of paint or effort could hide the sloping porch, the curled roof tiles, the general look of defeat, no matter how much Grace had tried to make it better. But everything hadn't been left behind. A reminder of the old place was the door-knocker that had made such a stir the first Christmas it appeared – one of Grace's sculptures: a baby angel, asleep with his bronze head tilted on a wing, one hand resting on his penis. People wondered: Do I have to touch it to knock? The answer, of course, was yes. Jack had no sooner done so now than the door sprang open, and Grace was standing there smiling, phone in hand. She covered the receiver, and called into the house, "Parker, Jack's here!" Waving him inside, she finished her call with kissing noises before hanging up. "Merry Christmas, Jack." She leaned to hug him and her earrings clinked and swayed. Grace, who he'd heard was 44 now, had piled her dark hair into a loose bun that caught the light, and wore a long paisley skirt that barely brushed the lithe figure beneath. She led the way to the glassed-in porch.

"A little something for you," Jack said, handing her a package wrapped in silver paper. She kissed him on the cheek.

"Merry Christmas," said Parker, rising from a peeling leather club chair and lifting his glass mug toward Jack. "We're having hot buttered rum."

Grace told him, "I always feel obliged to make it this time of year, even though we don't really like it." On a tray, she had arranged cheese straws, crab claws and giant red radishes carved and chilled into flowers.

"Nice," said Jack, dipping one into sea salt.

"Grace likes to put on airs," said Parker, closing the book he'd been reading. "It's a hold-over from when that's all she *could* put on," tossing a smile her way.

Grace brought another mug, spiked with a cinnamon-stick swizzle, and they watched as she untied the bow on her present and folded the tissue back: "I was hoping for this," she told him, holding up one of the thick, beeswax candles. "Thank you, Jack. From your hives?"

He nodded. "I can't take credit for the candles themselves."

"I would," said Parker, joking. He was about the same age as his wife, but his face was etched from working in the groves, and his dark hair and short beard showed streaks of gray. He reached for the morning newspaper which had been set aside on the floor, and peered over his wire-rimmed glasses. "I suppose you read this," he said, holding up the paper.

"Every word."

"Says we're safe through Christmas, no freeze. I'm not going to worry if it kills me."

"Me either," said Jack, and they both laughed, stopping when Grace lifted a finger asking for quiet, and they listened as a car with a bad muffler idled outside; a door slammed, a horn beeped.

"Ainsley's home," said Parker.

The front door opened and Ainsley, wearing what looked like an ancient fur jacket, and loaded with plaid shopping bags, nudged the door closed with her hip and stuck her head into the room. "I'm home!"

"We know!" said Grace.

Raising her arms to show her purchases, Ainsley told them: "Presents to wrap…" and turned toward the stairs, a red skirt flashing above black tights. From the stairway, she turned back to call over her shoulder, "Merry Christmas, Jack."

Jack wished she'd taken time for something more, and said to Grace: "I hear congratulations are in order."

"Yes, you could say that."

After he finished his drink, they walked him outside, and Grace handed him packages wrapped in her hand-made paper.

Instinctively, they all looked up, studying the sky, listening to the wind. "See you tomorrow at the Posada," called Parker.

On the drive back to his groves, Jack couldn't escape the signs of Christmas all around him: houses and yards ablaze with red, blue and green lights; shoppers carrying packages to their cars; a man struggling to tie a Christmas tree to the roof of one of them; a bell-ringer hoping for last-minute good will. As far as Jack was concerned, if Christmas came every five years, that would be often enough. The few Christmases he'd had with Julia and their son were the happiest he'd ever known, but he had no memory at all of holidays with his parents; he'd been too young. Every year since the accident had taken Julia and Tommy away, he had tried to keep "What If" thoughts at bay, but just as now, he couldn't always do it. What If they were at home now, waiting for him? What If Julia were wearing that sweater with elves embroidered on the front? And What If the house smelled like anise because she had hauled out the old pizzelle iron and baked his favorite cookies? What If there were a bicycle loaded in the bed of his truck, and pearl earrings tucked into his pocket? And What If he found someone to love again some day?

CHAPTER 20

EVERY YEAR ON DECEMBER 22, the workers at Jack's and Parker's groves celebrated Christmas with a Mexican Posada at Jack's field house, a re-enactment of the journey to Bethlehem, followed by a traditional dinner.

"Why do I have to go?" complained Ainsley.

"Because," said Parker. "It's expected."

"I expected not to go," said Ainsley; "I'm not Mexican anymore."

Grace said, "I think you're better than this."

"I'm not."

"Pretend."

Seated in the truck with her parents, Ainsley was sullen, squashed and silent. They always arrived early to help Jack set up, and after taking her parents there, she would handle the last-minute errands, which Grace was still enumerating when they arrived: find a piñata, buy more small gifts for the children, and finally, stop at the Mexican grocery store for an order that would be ready for pick-up.

She asked, "Is that *all*?" calibrating the degree of sarcasm allowable without actually spoiling the Christmas mood. Grace shook her head. "Just do it," and gathered her things. Ainsley pulled away and headed into town, glancing back just as Jack Henderson came outside striding toward her parents and looking much too cheerful.

Jack's property had a large field house kitchen and dining room, as well as small cottages and a bunkhouse for the men. By that evening, the field house had been transformed, with candles lighting every window, the scent of sugar and cinnamon in the air, the tables set with white paper cloths and red poinsettias, which Leola, Jack's cook, called *nochebuena* flowers. Most of the workers had been in the groves from morning 'til late afternoon, and some were just arriving, showered and ready for the festivities ahead.

In a far corner, the Captain and Phoebe were drinking tequila layered with orange and red juices, a Tequila Sunrise. "We're going all out," said Jack, handing Ainsley a cola with an elaborate strawberry garnish. Coming from a distance outside, they heard singing and guitar music, and taking Ainsley's hand, he led her to the window to watch the Posada. The procession began with a dozen people carrying lighted candles, followed by Emilio and Irena Mendoza as Mary and Joseph, knocking at the first of several cottage doors seeking shelter: "*Yo les pido posada*," called Emilio, but was turned away each time. The group proceeded to the next door and the next, singing the song of the pilgrims, their breaths turning white in the cold air.

"I know how this turns out," said Ainsley.

"Shhh. Don't spoil it for me."

Finally, the group appealed at the door of the field house, where Leola welcomed them inside, and the party began. Everyone, including Ainsley and her family, was wearing a new red, white, or green sweatshirt, purchased the week before, and it seemed to Ainsley she had never seen such a festive-looking group in one place.

"By the way, fleece becomes you," Jack whispered, giving her arm a squeeze.

"The fleece was easy; finding the piñata wasn't."

In the center of the room, Emilio was raising his arms to get everyone's attention, and thanking those who had prepared the dinner. Over several days, the women had worked evenings to replicate a classic Posada feast of turkey in *mole* sauce, red rice, spinach tamales, *bollitos* instead of the usual tortillas, beans, fritters called *bunuelos*, and for dessert, flan, and flat Mexican pralines.

The boys had hung a banner, "*Feliz Navidad*," above the dance floor, and now Jose Feliciano was singing his trademark song. When it ended, someone tossed a homemade paper maché sombrero into the center of the floor. "We can't miss this," said Jack, pulling Ainsley into the circle forming for the Mexican Hat

Dance. Hands on hips, guitars humming: right-heel, left-heel, clap-clap. Where was Bear? Jack was wondering, but didn't want to ask. Maybe she hadn't invited him, and in any case, that was his own good fortune, someone to sort-of be with, if only for the evening.

Holding Ainsley's hand, he could feel the diamond of her engagement ring pressing into his palm. Now the dancers were skipping sideways, right… then left… two steps forward, arms up; two steps back, arms down… melting inside their fleece sweatshirts. When the music stopped, he held her for maybe an instant too long, but she didn't seem to notice. Out of breath, she told him, "Skipping becomes you," patted his arm in a goodbye way and set off to join Grace and Parker. A too-short dance.

By 8:30, the dining room tables had been cleared, adults stifling yawns, children asleep in their parents' arms, and Father Jimmy preparing for a final blessing and hymn… *"Noche de Paz, Noche de Amor,"* Silent Night… sung quietly by the exhausted people assembled there. Peace and rest, at least for tonight, thought Ainsley, and stars to light the way home. She placed her hand on her mother's shoulder. "I may still be part Mexican after all."

That night, a pale Florida moon hovered over Halifax County. Snug beneath their comforters, residents rested in anticipation of Christmas. When they woke, it would be December 23.

Ainsley lay in bed thinking of Christmas Eve, of seeing Bear and giving him his present, which had cost most of her savings – gold cufflinks inscribed with his initials. If everything went as hoped, she would be wearing a black velvet dress, a gift from her mother, and the week beyond would be filled with parties and romance. No sooner had that word come to mind than an image of Billy came with it. Did he know she was engaged? Did it matter? When at last she closed her eyes, the music of the Hat Dance rocked her to sleep.

In the Quinn house, Grace turned over abruptly in her sleep and cried out softly, "Oh, oh!" In her dream, she was taking a pumpkin pie from the oven, when suddenly the flimsy tin buckled and hot custard went flying, burning her arm, spattering the wall and floor – but she was in Lady's kitchen, not her own, and Lady was watching, sighing, handing her a mop. Again, an "Oh!" and Parker stirred and moved closer in the chilly room.

Across the river, the Captain was waking in his recliner, a lightweight throw pulled up to his chin and all the lights turned off, except the one over the stove. He'd have to apologize tomorrow to Phoebe, who had stopped in after the Posada, and she hadn't been sent home properly. Imagine falling asleep after such a pleasant evening, and with Phoebe looking so good in her red sweatshirt! Yes, she still had something, lots of somethings.

In the citrus groves southwest of St. Christie's, Jack Henderson was wide awake, lying in bed thinking back over the evening: little Lolo, Emilio, Ainsley. Before turning in, he had sorted through the day's mail and cards, one of them from Barbados, written in a hand he knew well, and he was beginning to feel a lot like Christmas.

On the morning of December 23, Jack woke, fixed a pot of coffee and opened the presents Grace had given him: a tin of dates stuffed with walnuts and dusted with sugar, another tin with spiced pecans, and the last, his favorite, homemade shortbread cookies, scored in pie-shaped wedges. He'd try to make them last. The card from Barbados was propped up next to the sugar bowl, a drawing of a steel drum band, and musical notes spelling out "Merry Xmas!" Unexpectedly, Ilse would be arriving today.

The newspaper had one of those year-end recaps that were always so popular because they reminded readers of all the year's disasters, while at the same time making them glad for a fresh start just around the corner.

The year MCMLXXV111, 1978:

The Great Blizzard of 1978 strikes the Ohio Valley…

Serial killer Ted Bundy is captured in Pensacola...

The Hillside Strangler claims his tenth and last victim...

Annie Hall wins an Oscar for Best Picture...

Hotel California wins a Grammy for best album...

Porn publisher Larry Flynt is shot and paralyzed...

Karl Wallenda of the Flying Wallendas dies after a fall...

The U. S. Senate votes to turn the Panama Canal over to Panama...

The Democratic Republic of Afghanistan is proclaimed...

The "Son of Sam" killer is sentenced to 365 years...

Garfield makes his comic strip debut...

In Yemen, the president is killed...

The U. S. Supreme Court bars quota systems in college admissions...

King Hussein marries 26-year-old Lisa Halaby, Queen Noor...

Pope Paul VI dies, succeeded by Pope John Paul I, who dies after 33 days...

The Camp David Accords are signed...

In fiction, the book "Elbow Room" wins a Pulitzer Prize...

Pope John Paul II becomes the first Polish pope

Millions demonstrate against the Shah in Tehran...

In Guyana, Jim Jones leads his cult in a murder-suicide of 918 people...

In San Francisco, George Moscone and Harvey Milk are assassinated...

Killer John Wayne Gacy is arrested in Chicago...

Mainland China introduces a One Child Policy...

The Play "Da" wins a Tony Award

China lifts the ban on works by Aristotle, Shakespeare and Dickens

The drama, The Gin Game, wins a Pulitzer Prize...

The Collected Poems of Howard Nemerov wins a National Book Award...

Carroll O' Connor and Jean Stapleton win Emmys for All in the Family

And Jack was feeling as if he had won something too, a Christmas gift from Ilse, and there would be no cool side of the bed to roll onto tonight.

BOOK II

CHAPTER 21

SOME MIGHT CALL IT A contest, others would describe it as a tug-of-war. Ainsley and Bear didn't know what to call the polite struggle being waged by their mothers over plans for their upcoming wedding – they were just happy to be out of the fray.

Safely away at college, they had left it to their mothers to attend to most of the details – five months to plan a June shower and an August wedding. At school, they saw each other every day, intermittently approving or modifying wedding suggestions, sketches and menus sent to them from home, as they were doing now in the campus union.

"Lucky we're here," Bear was saying as he looked over suggestions for the font on their wedding invitations.

"Let's have Arabic," said Ainsley, "it's so flowy and pretty, and nobody will notice any typos."

"Or Cyrillic, that's good too."

"Imagine playing referee between our mothers."

"I can't," he said, and set the papers aside.

In a few weeks, though, they'd be home for the summer and in the line of fire. Bear loved Lady but knew she wasn't above using her money and influence, just as his father did, to get her way. "I hope we'll all get along, that's all."

"And be one big, happy family?" she asked. They both laughed, but in fact Ainsley did worry about pleasing her future in-laws – Lady, so different from her own mother – and Clay, so critical and domineering with Bear that she felt concerned he would act that way with her as well. No matter how hard it was, she had resolved to stand up to him from the start.

"I'll be the perfect daughter-in-law," she assured Bear, "and you'll be the perfect son-in-law."

"I think I have the easier job."

By the end of May, with a year of college behind them, Bear and Ainsley were back in St. Christie's, immersed in wedding plans, which Ainsley and Grace were reviewing as they sat in the kitchen, Grace recounting what she considered some of Lady's outrageous and unaffordable ideas; after all, the Quinns were paying most of the bills.

"The worst part," Grace was saying, "was when Lady said, 'I know how bad off you are sometimes, and Clay and I will gladly take up some of the financial mess.'" Doing a perfect imitation.

"Mess?"

"Her exact word, and let me tell you, we will serve peanut butter and jelly sandwiches before I let her pay for anything she shouldn't."

"Mom, when did you get so Emily Post?"

"*I invented* Emily Post."

"Just think how close this is bringing you and Lady!" Ainsley chided.

"Close to bloody murder!"

Grace had been right about the shower: who would plan it and who would make the decisions. Parker had tried to smooth things over, using gentle, back-handed persuasion with his wife. "Let Lady have her day. God knows Tessie's never going to get a husband, so this is her only chance to show off."

A group of Lady's friends had issued the invitation, but the twilight shower was at the DeWitt home, a change of location at the last minute, the original hostess said, adding: "It is so kind of Lady to take this on for me," and Lady was clearly in charge of everything, from the food, to the music and favors, and of course the conversation, which centered on the DeWitt and Forneau ancestries, their wealth, influence and philanthropy.

Grace listened politely through the better part of the early evening, but when she suddenly felt like standing up and hurling dishes, (Spode), when she could no longer bear that buttery accent, or Lady's overbearing opinions, she crept upstairs hoping she wouldn't be missed. The hardest part had been watching Ainsley sit there so politely trying to agree, even approve, of everything. Perhaps upstairs she would lock herself in a bathroom and sneak a cigarette or find a bed and lie down for a minute. Or let out a scream.

The ladies' muffled voices traveled upward along the rosewood staircase, down the corridor to where she stood, at the threshold of the master bedroom, looking out past the furnishings and French doors, out to the balcony and a lighted garden beyond planted with heritage roses. She stepped into the room to better see them, but for a moment, all she really saw was the bed, an oversized four-poster with pineapple finials, symbols of warmth and hospitality. Is that how Lady welcomed Clay into bed, with warmth and hospitality? Pineapples were repeated in the carved headboard, heaped with banks of pillows. When passion took hold, did Clay wait patiently while Lady re-stacked them elsewhere? Did they have designer pillow fights? Outside, the moon hung by its points above the oak trees, as if at any moment it might let go, just as she might. Idly, she rested her hand on a bright object sitting on Lady's desk. It moved with her touch, a stabile.

She shouldn't be here. Lady felt a deep attachment to her possessions and would likely consider it intrusive. Despite that, everyone knew where and when she had purchased almost every object in her home and what it had cost ("Oh, I hate to say, but…"), and how the maid was instructed to care for each treasure. ("What a burden owning such pieces could be! Sigh.") Always the sigh. Idly Grace touched her fingers to her hair, swept up today to show off her neck and the pretty low back of her dress. But the dress, a pale green silk, had wrinkled across the front, and in the mirror, despite her slimness, Grace saw her body as too heavy, not that of the youthful Grace she still thought herself as being.

The hum of conversation downstairs seemed to have stopped. Grace breathed deeply, then heard Clay's laugh, followed again by conversation. Clay, the center of attention as usual, had arrived ahead of the other men, who would be along soon to have a piece of cake and look at the gifts before driving their wives home. Her head felt heavy from wine and tension. She studied the room: the unexpected canopy draped with gold silk, a Chinoiserie armoire, two chairs that seemed to be Louis XVI or something like it, a metal table between them, and this desk. The stabile still swayed, animated by the currents of air conditioning. This must be the Calder that Lady had told them about, the one she had just purchased at auction from Christie's. Strange, Calder's path, from engineer to toy maker to artist. Grace was charmed by the piece before her. Why was it that people like Clay and Lady were able to own art such as this?

It rested on a pronged foot of red metal. A pointed arm reached upward eighteen inches. Balanced on its arms were a large black disc on one side, smaller red and yellow spheres on the other. She lifted the sculpture, surprised by its weight, and ran her fingers over its smooth, cool surface. Startled, she heard footsteps and then a voice calling. "Grace? Are you up here?" Grace stiffened, turning toward Lady's voice and the light that cut a narrow path on the marble floor. She set the piece on the desk, it's arms swinging, and tried to still them.

"Grace?" Again she tried to quiet the arms, all pointing accusingly at her. She reached forward too quickly and the piece tottered on the polished cherrywood desk, then lost its footing. "Grace?" Nearer now. The sculpture tilted, and the base hit the edge of the wood, tumbling in an arc. Grace gasped as it spun, the body flailing, then flying in a way Calder never conceived. She reached out to take hold of it, and slipped to the marble floor, but catching the piece in time.

The door opened and the path of light widened. Lady stood silhouetted there, Clay behind her, his hand resting on her waist in that possessive way he had. Lady's eyes swept the room. As Grace struggled to her feet, Lady relieved her of the Calder and restored it to its rightful place. "Oh, Grace." The words carried with them Lady's disappointment in absolutely everything.

CHAPTER 22

TIME WAS RUNNING AT A different speed now, faster every day. Maybe they shouldn't have planned an August wedding, but it had seemed a good idea to be married before going back to college. Of course they could have waited until they had their degrees, which Grace had frequently suggested. "Or," urged Parker, "you could run off and elope, but you'd have to invite *us*, of course." The wedding was just two days away. After the shower, all the gifts had been moved from the DeWitt house to the Quinns' where they were on display, and eventually would be stored at the Captain's, where Bear and Ainsley planned to stay during breaks from college. "I think I see a few recycles here," said Phoebe, picking up a large bowl and turning it upside down to read the mark. She'd stopped by with the Captain to give Grace advice on her roses, Phoebe being the local expert, but it was lunch time, and they had been persuaded to stay. She set the bowl down, a bright tart amid clear crystals and sedate silver conservatives. "Recycling is a custom I approve, and one I practice a bit myself."

"It's called re-gifting," said Grace, "more generous-sounding."

Phoebe held up a gold-leafed compote. "Nice piece. What do you say, Ainsley?"

"Not exactly to my taste, Aunt Phoebe. It's pretty grand for a college apartment."

"I like that I'm still your honorary aunt."

"Of course you are." Today, nobody was dressed in high-compote style, this being one of the now rare occasions when everyone could relax. That would include Ainsley, outfitted today in a yellow off-shoulder blouse and jean shorts, and Grace, in a dress she often wore when working. And then there was Phoebe, in whom they could detect both the past and present in all of her aspects, including her appearance this day. After all, she'd started out a Boone, and such genes could not easily be suppressed. Some might comment: Those diamonds, so cumbersome! That bosom, still rising with such enthusiasm! That exhausting vigor! Such observations were heaped on a figure that stood no more than five-two, on tanned legs which were often on view – as they were now in shorts that ended well above the knee. All of those present today admired Phoebe in all of her many incarnations, then and now.

In those shower gifts sent by Bear's side, Ainsley could see Lady's hand, a way of saying indirectly: These are the things you must have to live the way I think you should live. a life different from that of Ainsley's friends and parents, and in Lady's view, better. But did she want a life of gold-leaf compotes? No, but she would put a good face on it for Bear's sake.

Grace had just finished arranging the table, which was set up on the back porch, when Jack arrived, backing his pickup close to the spot where Parker and the Captain were already seated. "A present for the bride," he called out, then hopped down from the cab and started wrestling one of several cardboard boxes from the truck bed. "Let me give you a hand," yelled Parker, but Jack waved him off. Stumbling under the weight of a leaking container, he eventually decided to balance it on the porch railing. "C'mon, have a look – wanted you to see them first," he told Ainsley, and opened the flaps to uncover branches laden with orange blossoms, layered between sheets of wet newspaper.

"Jack," said Ainsley, "no words will do." In moments, the air was fragrant, and it was clear why brides chose orange blossoms when they could.

"I cut them myself," he said. "There's more in the truck, from Parker's trees of course," taunting him, and Parker played along protesting, "That's next year's crop in there!"

Jack looked at Ainsley; "We wouldn't want these to go to waste, so if there's a hitch, like a no-show, you can put me on standby."

"It's nice having a backup," she told him, but knew if there were a standby, it would be Charlie who, as recently as two nights before, had pulled her aside at a party to make one last effort. They had been on the terrace talking, feeling the weight of something coming to an end, an almost love-affair that had gone on for so long. "Last chance." He'd said it lightly, but they both knew he was serious: it wasn't too late to back out if she had any doubts. For Charlie to propose such a thing was daring but not surprising since he had never made a secret of his feelings.

"I mean it." He'd grasped her upper arms, and she wished she could say something to make it easier for both of them. For a moment she thought he was about to embrace her, but he didn't. "I've never meant anything more than I do this," telling her so in a heartfelt yet calm way. "No commitments," he added quickly, "but if later it turns out that it's me you want, I know we'd be happy," and then after waiting for a moment, his expression changed and it was clear that he had accepted the answer she couldn't put into words. "Or at least *I* would be happy." He took a deep breath and dropped her arms. "I had to ask one more time. Couldn't live with myself if I didn't."

"Help yourselves," called Grace, breaking into Ainsley's thoughts as she set a basket of sweet rolls on the table. "The drinks are over there," pointing to a small bar setup. Grace was known for always putting something tempting on the table. "Crab claws just for you, Jack," she said, offering a tray ringed with parsley and centered by cups filled with mustard sauce. "Ainsley made the brownies."

"From scratch."

Looking at the faces around the table, Ainsley thought, the next time, and almost every time I sit here in the future, Bear will be here too. That idea had never before occurred to her. So many lives were changing so fast. Bear had even hinted that his groomsman, Nick, might make a good match for Beth. Romance was in the air, pollinating everything.

After the Captain had left to drive Phoebe home, and the others had gone to deliver orange branches to the florist, feelings of concern kept at bay swept over Grace, part having to do with Parker, using his wheelchair more and more; part with her father, who seemed so lonely lately; and most with her daughter, marrying into the DeWitt family. How would they cope with everything? She remembered her own early marriage, the wild, knocked-out crazy love that had helped her and Parker get past so much. She hoped Ainsley and Bear had that too, because even though passion fades, if it's there in the beginning, it comes back time and again, surprising you, just when you thought it might be gone for good.

The Captain decided to drive Phoebe home the long way, although such a way didn't actually exist in St. Christie's. "We'll take the scenic route," he told her, and then, stopping suddenly and on impulse, turned the car around and headed in the opposite direction from her home. "You're going the wrong way, Frank. Should I be worried?" Teasing, he hoped.

"Not unless you're threatened by chocolate-almond ice cream." Her favorite.

Jerry's? You're taking me to Jerry's?"

"A Dutch treat." Jerry's was the ice cream shop they went to when they were children, when having ice cream was something rare. Jerry Booten and his wife Henny made it themselves, and served it in homemade waffle cones. As kids, they used to stand in the window and watch as Henny mixed the batter, poured it onto her special waffle iron, and then shaped the waffles, while they were still warm, around a cone-shaped metal form. Now a third-generation of Bootens was in charge, and many looked just like their Dutch grandparents, spectacularly tall and blond, and the ice cream was still homemade.

Glancing at her now, her blue eyes framed by tiny lines, he still saw the Phoebe of long ago, and something about her made him recall one particular day, when Phoebe Boone had stood in front of Miss Harmon's English class, a girl dressed in a skirt washed too often and worn too many times, with knit stockings up to her knees and brown lace-up shoes that reached her ankles. He thought she was lovely then and lovely still.

They'd arrived at Jerry's, and the Captain came around to Phoebe's side to open the door. Inside the shop, everything was nearly the same as it had been fifty years earlier, even the marble-topped counter where they sat on high stools to order chocolate-almond ice cream cones.

"Remember Miss Harmon, the Rime of the Ancient Mariner?" he asked.

"How could I forget ?" It was eighth grade, and they had been told to learn by heart The Rime of the Ancient Mariner, to be recited at an assembly of several upper classes. For more than a week, Phoebe had read it over and over, practiced it out loud until her brothers were threatening mayhem. Something told her Miss Harmon would call on her, the way she often did when she suspected or perhaps hoped, that Phoebe was unprepared. Miss Harmon had made it clear she thought Phoebe inferior, coming as she did from the Boone clan. It was equally obvious, from the compliments and smiles given to Barbara Shiff and her friends, that Miss Harmon measured her pupils' worth by the health of their parents' bank accounts. More than once, Phoebe had been sent home to change into more acceptable clothes; more than once, she had been asked in front of everyone if she had food for lunch, or pennies to spare in collections for the poor. "Oh — some of you *are* the poor!" the teacher had once said, looking in Phoebe's direction.

Concerning Miss Harmon, Phoebe had made a correct guess. "Phoebe Boone," the teacher said that day, "please come forward and do us the honor of reciting Part One of the Rime of the Ancient Mariner." Miss Harmon bestowed her mocking smile, and then turned a knowing glance at her prize pupil seated in the front row of the small assembly room. Despite all her preparation, Phoebe sat in her chair paralyzed with fear, her mind empty.

"Well?" It was a long moment before Phoebe rose slowly and walked to the front of the room, head bent, her worn shoes squeaking, and setting the class laughing. "Maybe you'd rather go barefoot," said Miss Harmon, "but that wouldn't be fair to the rest of us, would it?" Looking out over the laughing students, she wagged her finger playfully: "Now, class," she cautioned, her delight barely contained.

When the laughter had died down, Phoebe looked at Miss Harmon, held the fear rising inside at bay, and then let her eyes sweep the room, briefly lighting on each of her schoolmates. She held her back straight, and began speaking in that clear voice the Captain could still recall.

❧

"The Rime of the Ancient Mariner, by Samuel Taylor Coleridge...
It is an ancient Mariner,
And he stoppeth one of three..." and continuing, with passion! with expression! to the very end...
"...God save thee, ancient Mariner!
From the fiends, that plague thee thus!
Why look'st thou so? – With my crossbow
I shot the Albatross."

❧

Then silence. Perfectly done through all twenty stanzas. Phoebe dropped her head, and some of her schoolmates came to their feet clapping, Frank among them.

The Captain still remembered that day, the poem, and the girl who had stood alone in her faded dress, her home haircut, her young girl's dignity. It was the first moment that he loved her.

CHAPTER 23

THE WEDDING WAS ONE THAT people would still talk about years later – Ainsley in a peau de soie gown which some remembered from Grace's marriage to Parker, with an illusion bodice and tight-fitted long sleeves; Bear in a morning coat and striped trousers, too handsome by far. And the ceremony at St. Mary's church, with three attendants each, and later, two-hundred guests, gathered back at the Captain's compound. At least Grace had had her say in that, and with everyone pitching in with food, flowers, tables and chairs, expenses had been kept as low as possible; Grace had designed and printed the invitations, and chosen the font.

The date had been selected to take advantage of a full moon, and now it shone on white canvas tents that had been set up on the Captain's lawns amid pink hibiscus Grace had helped plant years before, and in high bloom despite the heat. A band comprised of musician friends played in one of the tents, where couples danced on a wood floor that had been put down as easily as sod. Another tent held the bar, although waiters were circulating, pouring Champagne and delivering drinks. In a third tent, round tables for eight had been set up for dining, and others, on the lawn and patio, all covered with stiff white tablecloths, and set with gold-rimmed china and thin, lead crystal glasses that would later ring like bells when struck with knives. The table settings, lent by Lady. "I think she was afraid," Grace had said, "that we'd have paper plates."

Ainsley was standing in a quiet corner with her grandfather, her arm hooked through his, escaping for a moment from the party. Strains of "My Girl" were drifting by as she held his hand. "You're too good to me."

"I've been thinking of this a long time – a lot longer than you," he said. She knew he loved seeing her in her mother's dress, and with his own mother's gold locket at her throat. He touched it lightly. "Remember when you was wondering about the right man finding you, and you him?"

"I remember." She squeezed his hand. "And he was right here all along." The Captain was dressed in a cutaway coat, and though he had joked about how out-of-place he would feel, he looked to Ainsley as if he were meant to wear it: perfect on his erect frame, and a complement to his mane of white hair. He cleared his throat, signaling he had something to say and she looked at him expectantly.

"I waited till now to tell you about your wedding present, because I wanted to tell it just to you."

"This is my wedding present – it's all I want, having everyone here, in this place."

"I know, but there's something else. Placing a hand on her shoulder, he said, "I want you to have this house and some of the land here at the compound… part of my groves too."

The enormity of what he was saying was too much to absorb. "Grandpa, no. I couldn't let you do that. I won't."

"It's already done," he said, patting his jacket pocket, and withdrawing an envelope. In it was a deed that had been made weeks before; everything else would someday go to Grace. He was beaming, but Ainsley could hardly hold back her tears.

"Hey, none of that on your wedding day."

"Saying 'thank you' isn't enough, Grandpa."

"It's more than enough," fighting tears of his own.

"I love this place, and what I love most about it is you."

He patted her shoulder, gave her a gentle prod and put the envelope back in his jacket pocket. "I'll hold onto this for now, but you better get going. Someone seems to be looking for you." He inclined his head toward Bear, who was standing at a distance with his parents and Tessie, and looking relieved when he saw Ainsley walking toward them, holding out his arms as she neared.

Clay leaned in to give his new daughter-in-law a kiss on the cheek, then said, "I don't know what you want with him," nudging Bear. "I hope you have better luck shaping him up than I ever did."

Bear blanched, and Ainsley slipped her arm through his, pulling him close. "Don't worry, Clay. He's perfect just the way he is." and she kissed Bear on the mouth.

"If you say so," but he clearly resented even this gentle rebuke, and by instinct changed his tack rather than back off. "Son, get me a drink, will you?"

"Sure, Dad, but we have waiters. One'll be by in a minute."

"I want it now, not in a minute."

They all knew it wasn't a drink that Clay wanted. Bear's color rose. "Just wait a little, Dad," he said patiently.

Ainsley's breath caught. She gave Bear a little shove. "Go get it, Bear. Your Dad deserves a drink after all he's been through today. I'll come with you."

"Let him wait."

Ainsley put her hand on Clay's arm. "Behave yourself, Clay, or I'll have to stomp you to death and ruin my nice shoes."

Clay's eyebrows shot up, but instead of bellowing he let out a mean little laugh. Ainsley wondered where her courage had come from, and Bear's for that matter. She'd never spoken that way to an older person.

"Said like a true DeWitt." Having the last word.

Why did Clay treat his family that way? How could Bear have stood it all these years and yet grown up to be so forgiving and good? Clay waylaid a passing waiter and raised his glass in her direction, a kind of nasty tribute, but she and Bear were already fleeing to a corner where their friends were standing. "I'm sorry," Ainsley told him.

"Forget it. Someday *he'll* be sorry.

Dinner was announced, and Bear's groomsman led the guests to the dining tent, set at the end of a path lined with rose petals, courtesy of Phoebe, and lighted with luminarias. Ainsley, Beth, Vickie and Tessie, her third attendant, had gathered sand from the beach, filled the brown paper sacks, and placed candles inside them days before, but it had taken Sam an hour just to light them all. Pink and white roses and massed sprays of orange blossoms were grouped in pottery vases on each of the tables, which glowed with tiny candles set into silvery shells that

Ainsley and Grace had painted. At the buffet tables, arranged on two sides of the main tent, Leola, Jack's majordomo, was directing the waiters, who were replenishing platters filled with crab claws, shrimp, and spiny lobster. A chef wearing a white toque stood at one end slicing roast beef and barbecued pork, and at separate tables, salads and fruits had been arranged on banana leaves from Grace's yard. Sweets of every kind, from coconut cake to key lime pie, gifts from St. Christie's kitchens, stood in unaccustomed elegance under crystal domes.

"Now don't you pass up them sticky buns," Leola warned Ainsley. "They's your Grandma Kate's own receipt."

"And because you made them, Leola, I wouldn't miss them for anything." Ainsley filled a plate for herself and their friends, who were waiting at the bridal table, ready to harass them with fork clanking and embarrassing toasts. Jack Henderson had come up behind her. "Are all those sticky buns for you?"

"Of course. Now that I have a husband, I can let myself go."

"All those years spent perfecting your charms, planting false hopes like dollar weed, and you're going to chuck all that effort?"

"I am."

"Our loss is your sticky bun gain."

"Lucky, then, you weren't called on as my standby today."

"Was I lucky?" his question caught her off-guard, but then he grinned, took her plate of sticky buns and carried it to the bridal table. Returning to the buffet, he was joined by a woman wearing a one-shoulder dress and high-heel sandals, a woman close enough to Jack to let him take her hand and peck her on the lips. The same girl who had visited over Christmas.

As she looked from table to table, Ainsley wished she could stop the clock, to somehow imprint every moment in a way that would never fade from memory. Tonight, she and Bear were bound in new ways to the world, their families and each other. The enormity of it made her take his arm for reassurance.

"All this wonderful food!" said Beth interrupting Ainsley's thoughts. "and I'm too excited to eat." Waxy orange blossoms were pinned in her hair and trailed from silk ribbons at the front of her dress. She was lovely, but Ainsley knew she'd never believe it.

Nick, Bear's groomsman, looked up smiling. "Would you like to stretch a little?" Nick had worked briefly for the DeWitt company, where the two young men had become friends, and now Nick was at school in Gainesville. "I'd love a stretch," Beth said, letting him take her hand; Ainsley watched as they left the table, thinking Bear might be right about them.

They crossed the dirt road to the beach and climbed to the top of the dune, where the moon was laying a path of light. "Wait right there," said Beth, as she darted out of view to pull off her shoes and pantyhose. After a few moments, she was standing beside him again, and they walked toward the sea – the moon high in the sky, the sound of the falling waves growing louder, the music from the wedding fading. The water was warm where it lapped the sand and they kissed before returning to the dune. Nick folded his jacket into a pillow, and braced Beth's elbow as she let herself down onto the sand, feeling the faint warmth it still held. He lay beside her, propping his head in his hand. "I wanted to kiss you from the moment I saw you at the rehearsal."

Could that be true? "It's the wedding." Weddings always seemed brimming with sex, everyone celebrating the passion of the bride and groom, everyone remembering their own best days and nights.

"It's not just the wedding." He kissed her again and lay back in the sand beside her, cradling her head on his arm. "I think I could fall in love with you."

"That's the Champagne talking," but part of her hoped it was something more, because Nick was so attractive, and seemed to want to take control of her in the nicest way. "You don't even know me."

"We can fix that." He pulled her close, and she let him kiss her again. let him touch her breasts, her stomach, stopping short of where he could easily have gone. For a long while, they watched the lights of the shrimpers far out at sea, the glow of the waves breaking on shore. Then the breeze freshened and the air felt cool and damp. "I suppose we should go," said Beth. He put his jacket on her shoulders. "If I told Ainsley, would you mind?"

He kissed her forehead. "Of course not. I want to tell everyone." Then, as if to himself he said, "Two free spirits."

"Us?"

"Ainsley and Bear. I know him better than I do her, of course, but it's great that two free spirits, with so much in common, found each other."

"I wouldn't describe Ainsley that way, but yes, they have a lot in common."

"Now they have us in common."

So soon, did they?

∽

Parker had been determined, despite growing reliance on his wheelchair, to walk Ainsley down the aisle, which he had – "and at just the right, wedding pace," or so several people had remarked, and now he was about to undertake another challenge: the traditional father-daughter wedding dance. When he rose from his chair, Ainsley's first impulse was to go to him, but she forced herself to stand still while he walked slowly toward her, opening his arms, making it hard for everyone to keep their eyes from going damp. There was no secret how close they were, or how, from the time she was a baby, Parker loved taking his little girl with him wherever he went, showing her off, when many fathers might have been thinking of ways not to.

It was likely that just then, an old movie was playing in many of their memories: of Parker carrying Ainsley on his shoulders at the beach… teaching her to ride a bicycle… standing at her side for first communion… showing her how to drive a car… everything. They knew he'd also taught her other things, or tried to… to tell the truth when it was hard to do… to stand by someone in trouble… hold to principles… stay with things, persevere… give the benefit of the doubt… be kind… work hard… although she hadn't mastered all of these yet, and Parker would be the first to say, neither had he.

When he reached her side, he lifted her hand, and led her to the floor, a modest space but theirs alone where Parker, once the best dancer of all the men, managed to summon – from the Wedding Angel or someone – the presence and grace that had always been his. The small orchestra had already begun playing... "You are so beautiful to me..." when he placed his hand on his daughter's waist and they began dancing.

"I'm proud of you, *every* day," he told her, "even though I know all your faults."

"You couldn't possibly."

He had his own way of leading, and few noticed that he barely moved while guiding her into the twirls and turns he had taught her as a young girl. People remembered that, too.

"You must be thinking about your own wedding, Daddy."

"I am, and how lovely your mother looked in that same dress, just as you do."

When the dance ended, he kissed her cheek, whispering, "Be happy, darling."

CHAPTER 24

RACQUETBALL WAS A LIFESAVER, A college refuge. Bear had stayed later than usual at the court and was thinking, Marriage is good for my game, a bonus he hadn't foreseen. In the three months since their wedding, adjusting to the new expectation of reporting home, of always having to be accountable, hadn't become easier. He sat in the car staring at the place he and Ainsley's had rented, and dreaded going inside. It wasn't just the house, the downstairs of a duplex close to campus. By student standards, the old Victorian, with its mock tower, Greek Revival columns and sagging porch, was a notch above average. Still, he wondered what they were doing there. Ainsley had liked the idea of something homey, while he had preferred a small apartment, but seeing her disappointment, he had mustered as much enthusiasm for the place as he could.

Soon after their wedding day, he was ashamed to admit, an almost unbearable loss of freedom had taken hold, a feeling that had grown heavier every day since. He should be happy, he knew, yet Ainsley's plans for their life – no, her plans even for the day – overwhelmed him. What did he care about routines, or about college, for that matter? Monotony ruled their lives, suffocating him with endless repetition: classes, home, study. There seemed no relief and no escape. Being with Ainsley should make him happy, but words like "trapped" were always coming to mind. He hefted his gym bag and knew he would have to go inside. What choice was there?

When Ainsley finally began noticing his small absences, he wondered that it had taken her so long. Although he'd done nothing wrong, he felt uneasy, spied upon, when all he wanted was some freedom, not more questions. What was wrong? Was it her? Where did he go? Having to explain everything, account for each minute, discuss and compromise on the smallest decisions – the way he saw it, that was the total of his marriage.

As Ainsley cleared the dinner dishes, rinsing and piling them in the sink, Bear sat in the living room staring at the TV, not watching. The clatter stopped, and then she was there, seeming to hover over him. He looked up, attempting a smile.

"I need to turn this off," she said, and he didn't protest when the TV screen went black. It was some cartoon for God's sake. "And we need to talk." Those words threatened an interrogation, or God only knew what.

"I've got work to do."

"You weren't working."

"I'll *start* working if it will make this go away," he joked.

"You mean make *me* go away." Standing, he stretched his arms toward the ceiling, voicing an irritated sigh reminiscent of Lady's. "In a minute," he said, going to the kitchen for sodas before settling himself at the far end of the sofa. Squeezing into a corner, he made himself as small a target as possible.

"This is hard," said Ainsley. "We've been married three months and already, things have changed between us."

"Is that all? That's normal," he assured her. "Everybody says the first year is the hardest," followed by what he hoped was a confident smile.

"I never understood that. Why should it be hard?"

"It just is."

"This is still our honeymoon." She moved closer and took his hand, another thing he hated, the feeling that he had to let her do that any time she wanted. Forever.

"Is it me?"

"Of course not." Another lie.

For a moment she looked relieved. "What, then? Half the time I don't even know where you are." She hesitated, as if unsure whether it was safe to continue.

How could he tell her that he felt smothered? He couldn't. "This school business is not for me," he said finally, a believable excuse. "I've tried." As he had hoped, Ainsley seemed satisfied with his answer, but when she tried to comfort him, he wanted to bat her hand away, run out the door.

"I know you're not happy here, but what can we do? The school year's almost half up, and soon we'll have two years behind us."

If only he could tell her how he really felt, not about her, but about marriage itself, but that wasn't possible. "Sure, we'll finish up the year," he agreed. That was another thing he hadn't foreseen – Ainsley being so interested in her studies. Or the Captain giving her his groves, which now seemed less a burden to her than they had at first, and more of a burden to him.

"What do you mean finish the year?"

"Do we have to talk about this now?"

"You're scaring me."

Again, everything had to be discussed, wrangled, agreed upon. Freedom was a word that had little to do with him anymore.

"It's important to me that we graduate," she told him. "I'll do more. You don't have to do a thing, just go to class and study."

Would she ever understand the more she did, the more resentful he felt? Between her studies and her never-ending presence he felt as if she were squeezing the air right out of him.

Professor Duncan Price checked his watch. He'd better put his desk in order. The DeWitt girl was due any minute, and he'd promised her a tour of the citrus nursery. Too bad she was married, a juicy thing like that. He smiled to himself, always thinking in citrus metaphors. That's what happened after decades of such a singular preoccupation.

A light tap on the door. "Good morning, Professor." He looked up to see her leaning into the office, half-in, as if she couldn't make up her mind. Still, slim as she was, she seemed to be taking up the whole space. "Come in, come in!"

For more than 20 years, Duncan Price had been working to perfect an orange that would be juicy, unblemished and brightly colored, an orange that could compete with California navels. He was years away still, and perhaps would never reach his goal, but that was the citrus business, the beauty of it and the challenge.

He pushed back from the desk and stood up, buttoning his jacket, the one everyone complimented him on. "Mrs. DeWitt. I've been looking forward to showing you around and hearing more about your father's work – very impressive." Touching her elbow, he nodded toward the door. "This way," and led her to the adjacent greenhouse, pausing in the entrance, then slowly walking down each aisle, describing the procedures and the reasons for them. There were no secrets, just work, patience and a little luck, he told her.

"My father's work hasn't progressed much these past years, Professor. In fact, it has stopped."

"My dear, *you* can start it up again."

"I hope so."

"You'll need more determination than that."

"I know. I want to learn everything."

"My dear, you shall."

❧

What could she do to please the increasingly unknowable man she had married? Letters from the Captain arrived at least once a week, filled with news of St. Christie's and offering a few words of advice on everything from studies to making money go farther. Over and over she read his letters, but found no remedy for Bear's unhappiness, and now, her own. How could everything have changed so fast? Somehow they'd made it through the holidays in St. Christie's, and after returning to campus, Ainsley continued misreading her husband, attacking her studies and their home with new resolve, sparing Bear as much worry and work as possible, and strangely, it was she who found unexpected pleasure in her efforts.

"You're impossible!" she told him one night as he sat sullen and silent in front of the TV. "I never imagined my life like this."

"That makes two of us."

CHAPTER 25

JACK HAD CALLED. MORE PROBLEMS in the groves he'd told her, trouble with Clay and a few other growers, who were accusing him of causing labor problems. Coddling workers, they said. Jack wanted Ainsley's approval of the way he was running things for her.

It was March, finals were looming, but instead of settling things on the telephone, the groves were an excuse to go home. Bear had decided to stay on at school, happier than she'd seen him in weeks. Now, driving through downtown St. Christie's, she felt almost like a stranger; life had gone on without her. Like the Captain, she never arrived anywhere empty-handed and planned to stop at the bakery to pick up muffins for her father and peanut butter cookies for her grandfather. As she searched for a parking place on the street, she saw the little roadster she was always looking for in St. Christie's, parked up the street just outside the hardware store. And something shifted inside her.

If she were honest, the chance of seeing Billy, however briefly, was the exact thing she had hoped for from the moment she decided to come home. For a long time, she sat in her car, through several songs on the radio, waiting for him to come out of the store, but after a while, feeling conspicuous and embarrassed, decided to risk going into the bakery. When she came out, his car was gone, and she could not have predicted how disappointed she felt.

Grace was in the garden, her outdoor studio as she called it, when Ainsley pulled into the drive. She was kneeling in the grass hammering a piece of bronze as if to kill it, but when she saw Ainsley's car, she threw down the hammer and quickly came to her feet. Her face lit up in surprise, and then gathered into a frown as she lifted her arm to shield her eyes, perhaps to confirm it really was her daughter, home unannounced. Then she hurried to the car, looking puzzled.

"Sorry for the surprise." She turned away to avoid her mother's eyes. "I have to meet with Jack Henderson. Spur of the moment. He almost insisted."

Grace looked askance. "Too bad Bear couldn't come with you."

"I know," dodging the bait and her mother's implied question. It was probably enough not-said for Grace to draw her own conclusions. Ainsley was already climbing the porch steps when she called back, "I'll just put this in my old room," and then she was gone, and Grace was looking concerned, not for the first time since the wedding.

It seemed forever to Ainsley since she had slept in her old room, and now it served as a catch-all for household items too good to throw out and Grace's many books. Still, it was exactly where she wanted to be, not just with a room of her own, but one with a door and a lock. She kicked off her shoes and threw herself on the bed, not ready yet to answer her parents' inevitable questions about Bear and everything else, and wishing she'd asked Tupper for some weed. What would Jack think if he knew she'd used him as an excuse to come home?

Sun streamed into the room, filtered through the branches of a magnolia that had grown up to the second story, its white blossoms just emerging and touching the glass, a grandiflora that could reach sixty feet or more. At the window, drawing the curtains aside, she looked down at her mother, now back at work. As if sensing it, Grace stopped hammering and glanced up. Ainsley waved, then let the curtain fall back. It was good to be home, to feel like a girl again, almost carefree, but she couldn't linger; her mother was doubtless waiting for her to come down.

Grace was standing up, hands on hips, doing a backwards stretch when Ainsley joined her outside, looking at the pieces Grace had been working on. "You've never done anything like this before."

"Do you like them?"

"How could I not?" Four bronze sculptures were hanging from heavy cables attached to a nearby live oak, the bright metal in sharp contrast to the dark, deeply etched bark. Not bells, and

121

not chimes, either, the shapes were open and furled, as if the bronze were ribbon, floating, the longest, five feet from top to bottom

"Who are they for?"

"One of the new millionaires from New York. I warned him that his neighbors wouldn't appreciate hearing chimes this big, but he assured me that he has no neighbors near his estate. That's the word he used: estate."

Imagine, thought Ainsley, people using such a word to describe a place in St. Christie's, a vision of the awful future on their doorstep. Grace tapped the largest bell, which sang with a deep, pulsating note that reverberated in her bones. "I just re-heated so I can't stop," said Grace, who continued hammering, a large torch lying on the grass beside her, sweat pouring down her forehead beneath the wide-brimmed hat. Even red-faced and sooty you couldn't take your eyes away, thought Ainsley. "I wish you'd given me notice," said Grace, "but I don't know what I could have done about this, because I promised to deliver these pieces next Thursday."

"I understand. It's your work."

"You make it sound important," and she laughed self-consciously.

"Of course it is."

Grace shook her head. "No. There was a time when I expected more of myself than bells or chimes, or whatever fusion of something I have here." A small sardonic grin. "But that's what I make."

"You make art, Mom. You turn metal and clay and bamboo into art."

Her mother looked pleased, but never one to take a compliment easily, she turned away. "You think so?"

"Just because people in St. Christie's *like* it, doesn't mean it's not art."

Grace looked up, puzzled. "That's a joke, Mom. Laugh."

∾

"We've had a good bit of labor trouble from your daddy-in-law," Jack was saying. "I don't suppose you have any influence over him?" Late that afternoon, Ainsley had driven out to Jack's field house to meet with him, Emilio and Irena.

"I don't understand the problem," she said. I know we pay a little more, but is that it?" She looked from Jack to Emilio to Irena, who was sitting in a patio chair, observant and silent.

"No, Senora, it is more," said Emilio, standing up from the table. "Mr. Jack he has place for us to live, and safe. We have wells in the field to wash our self. We have…" smiling at her, "bathroom in the house."

"Anything else?"

Emilio's thoughts were running ahead of his English. Ainsley had heard stories of migrant workers' plight so often she was afraid she might have stopped listening a long time ago, but could not with Emilio standing right in front of her. He was a compact man in his late twenties, with the even features and straight black hair of his Aztec and Spanish ancestors. He and Irena, who was about the same age and of the same heritage, made a handsome pair. Both now had work papers, but had once worked as illegals, following the crops from Florida to the Midwest and back again. Even the smallest security had eluded them, and now their boy, Lolo, who was ten, was falling behind in school.

Clay had once warned Ainsley, "The best way to think about migrants is not to think about them at all," but who could listen to Clay?

"We had a place once in Texas," Emilio was telling her, "but when we got back, everything was rob." Ainsley had to wonder what a ransacked home might equal in terms of hours stooping and picking in the sun and wind and rain. That year, Emilio told her, they had spent most of what they earned on rent and food and then, when their truck had broken down, they had spent the rest fixing it so they could return to their vandalized home in Texas.

"All across Florida" said Jack, tomato pickers are making ten cents more than they did ten years ago, which actually amounts to less."

"How can we help?"

"Understand," said Jack, "workers don't have to live in crew bosses' houses, but rent deposits and short-term stays work against them." Typically, workers were picked up in the morning and dropped back at night, sometimes an hour's ride or longer to the fields. Jack housed a few year-'round workers in cottages, and during harvesting, in the men's bunkhouse, "But migrant work is migrant work," he told her. "By nature it's risky, low-pay and back-breaking."

Ainsley didn't want to think that her family's business harmed such hard-working defenseless people, but she also didn't believe that even Clay, with all his wealth, would be so callous either. Lolo had come outside and was standing next to Ainsley eating one of the cookies she had brought from home, and she wondered what his future held.

"I'm sure if there's a problem at Clay's groves he would fix it if he knew," said Ainsley, who wasn't really sure of anything at all. "I'll talk to him."

"Please, don't make no trouble, Señora," said Emilio.

"Of course not. Never."

"Gracias." He looked with uncertainty at Irena, who still hadn't said a word.

"I wonder," Ainsley said to Emilio, "wouldn't it be better to make a different, settled life for Irena and Lolo?"

Emilio looked as if she had struck him. "No," he said. "We work hard and my family is good. I want no different life, so my children can be ashame and grow away from me." Jack turned to him, "Nobody could be anything but proud of you, Emilio," and he gave Ainsley such a hard look it made her drop her head.

They'd left it that Jack would continue as he thought best. In that, at least, she credited him for doing the right thing. When school ended in summer, she resolved to look into things on her own.

It was almost dark when she returned to her parents' home. Grace was sitting on the patio swirling a glass of red wine and offering advice to Parker who was monitoring a rack of lamb, roasting on the grill. "At these prices you don't dare take your eyes away," he said, "especially when you only have one eye working." Grace went inside to look after the rolls, putting Ainsley in charge of the vegetable kebabs, threaded on rosemary branches and prepared earlier. "Try to find some spots where the coals aren't as hot," she called over her shoulder.

Parker closed the grill and sat beside Ainsley on a low wall edging the herb garden. She ran her hand lightly through the thick branches of basil, inhaling the heavy fragrance, and then felt the weight of her father's arm across her shoulder. "It's good to have my girl home," he said, "but me – well, surprises, even nice ones, make me uneasy." In that respect, he was just like her mother. He took her hand, examining it. "Is everything okay with you and Bear?"

"Ainsley!" her mother was calling from the kitchen, saving her. "Ainsley, telephone!" She sounded distressed. Squeezing her father's hand as she got up to answer the phone, she told him, "I never could hide anything from you, Daddy, but please don't worry."

Grace was standing in the doorway, her eyes narrowed. "My God! It's *him* calling," and her daughter knew just who *"him"* must be: Billy. And she could not hide her flush of happiness.

CHAPTER 26

BEAR HAD BEEN STARING AT the book, reading the same page again and again. He looked up at Ainsley, seated by the window in the last of the afternoon light, her head in a book as well. Two months since she had gone to St. Christie's and he had been left blissfully on his own. It seemed much longer ago than that. Their breathing and a ticking clock were the only sounds. How pleased with herself she looked, with finals behind her, and him with three still to go.

"Listen to this," she was saying, and he jumped, as if she had read his mind. He closed his book with a loud snap. Even her brow, furrowed in concentration, annoyed him. Everything did, and it was unfair, but he expelled an irritated sigh nonetheless. "I've got work. Can't you see that?" Then he sailed his book across the room where it landed face-down at her feet, the pages splayed, accusing her of something, he wasn't sure what, except he was irritated further when she picked it up, smoothed the pages and closed it. The proper parent, chastising him.

"I didn't mean to disturb you." Sarcasm. So much of that lately.

"All you think about," he told her, "is yourself, your classes and experiments. What do you need all that for?" almost feeling misled.

She threw the book back at him, just missing his soda can on the floor. "It's why I'm here. Maybe I'm smarter than you think, maybe just as smart as her – your old Miss Scholarship." It was the first time she had ever referred, even indirectly, to Dance.

"Why bring her up?" his voice squeaking like an old man's, and unnerved, he tossed a dismissive wave, hoping that would end it.

"I just wanted to read you something Professor Price wrote."
"Who?"
"You never listen. The department head."

He shrugged. "Who cares?"

"I do," she said. "You know I want to continue my father's work. Professor Price is encouraging me."

"When it comes to stupid ideas, your family needs no encouragement." As soon as the words were out, he felt ashamed because he had always admired Ainsley's family.

"At least we don't rob people, like the DeWitts." Bear surprised her with a laugh. "I just meant," and her voice had softened, "I wish you showed more interest in me, and the responsibilities facing us some day." Again that lecturing tone, like he didn't face his responsibilities, when in his mind he did, every day. Her family's groves, the shrimper, the marina: they were small potatoes compared to the DeWitt companies, but she didn't seem to see any differences. "You think *your* family is the only one with problems?"

She said, "So now we argue about whose family has more problems? Is there any subject that's safe for us?"

He knew that in a moment he would storm out of the house as he often did, the only way he could think to stop everything from blowing apart, and he always hoped that when he returned home she wouldn't be there.

❧

When Bear slammed out minutes later, as Ainsley thought he would, she was grateful she'd been invited that night for dinner at Beth's. Ever since Beth had married Nick, their group of girlfriends had seen each other less often, even though they lived only blocks apart. Tonight would be like old times. "Nick has a class, thank God," she'd told them. They were aware that Nick had grown possessive and now resented the friends he had once seemed to like so much. The couple had a one-bedroom place in a two-story converted garage which they'd furnished with repainted cast-offs, Beth's artwork, bed sheets and antiques from Nick's mother. His car was gone, Vickie's parked in its spot when Ainsley arrived. Her friends were waiting for her on a small porch and they all went inside.

Over Christmas, Charlie Portman had given Vickie an engagement ring, which she now polished on her shirt. Holding her arm out straight to admire it under the light, she looked at Ainsley, "You better stay married, Ainsley. I have no intention of giving him back."

"Vickie..."

Vickie shook her long hair. "Just kidding, but I know you were his first love."

"No..."

"Ainsley's still half in love with Billy," said Beth, trying to help, but quickly realizing her blunder.

"That's a terrible thing to say!" said Vickie.

"And not true!" said Ainsley. She already felt disloyal to Bear, but nobody else needed to know it, not even her best friends.

"I'm sorry," said Beth. "Of course not!"

It took a few minutes for the tension to ease, but Billy was now on everyone's mind. "Do you ever bump into him?" asked Vickie.

Ainsley hesitated. "He called me once." Both girls lifted their heads expectantly. "When I was home two months ago, he'd seen me in town, that's all. Just called to say hello." She was remembering it now, the weekend she had gone home, ostensibly to talk to Jack but hoping to see Billy. She pictured her mother frowning when Billy called, handing her the phone, then hearing his voice, the familiar warmth of it, telling her he had to see her. "Meet me here," he had said.

"I can't." Her parents had drifted off, not knowing what else to do, thank God, except maybe snatch the phone away. "Billy, I'm married," she whispered.

"I saw you waiting in your car for me downtown, Ainsley. Don't tell me you weren't."

"It was a mistake. I have to go now," and she'd hung up, torn.

The girls were waiting to hear what Billy had wanted, "That's it, a phone call," and telling them nothing at all about how she had felt or how much she had wanted to see him. Vickie, not sensing what Ainsley was hiding, told them, "I heard Billy's serious about Lorraine Rivera," but when the name didn't register, she explained: "The girl who's decorating yachts at the City Marina." If that was so, Ainsley wondered, what had Billy's call been about, a goodbye, or the hope of a last hurrah?

"I've been wondering," said Vickie, "how are things going between you and Lady these days?"

"I thought you'd never ask!"

Vickie smirked. "Me, I *love* my future mother-in-law!"

"I may have to kill you."

"Can it wait a minute? Hand me that," said Vickie, pointing to a bottle of French Chardonnay which she had brought, now chilling in a silver bucket. Glancing at Ainsley she asked, "Well?" and began opening the wine while Ainsley set out silverware.

"Here's the latest thing from Lady," said Ainsley. "The last time I talked to her, she said she would like it if I called her Mother! My God, I nearly fell over!"

"Mother! What did you tell her?" asked Beth, who had just come in from the kitchen carrying a casserole, her hands stuffed inside floral mitts. Ainsley set a hot plate on the table for her. "I didn't want to hurt her feelings, but I can't call her Mother, or even Mom, or Lady Mom, or Mom DeWitt. I just can't."

Beth lit the candles. "So how did you leave it?"

"I said, 'I've called you Lady all my life, and it's such a perfect name for you, I just couldn't change it.' "

"Did she buy it?"

"Of course not."

For Ainsley, the word Mother belonged only to Grace in all of its variations: Crazy Mother, Impossible Mother, Working Mother, Terrible Mother, Talented Mother, the Why Did God Let You Be a Mother? mother, and The Mother I Will Always Adore mother.

Beth raised her wine glass. "To mothers, and to my best friends." Ainsley, having long sensed something wrong between Beth and Nick, turned to Vickie and blurted, "Marriage isn't all roses, you know."

"Or even daisies," Beth said. Her head dropped, and her friends waited for her to finish something else she had started to say. "I love him," she said finally, "but he has a temper."

CHAPTER 27

AS SHE DROVE HOME AFTER dinner, Ainsley wondered if Beth believed Nick's promises never to hurt her again. "I know I'm not perfect either," she had told them, sharing blame which she didn't deserve. The evening hadn't been as enjoyable as she'd hoped.

The house was dark and Bear's car still gone. A relief, but he'd left no note, no messages either. The ornate mantel clock that Lady had given them ticked away the minutes. After changing into pajamas and slippers, she sat down with a cup of tea to re-read a letter from the Captain. Finally an hour had passed, and her earlier resentful mood returned, as she imagined that every car slowing down would turn into their driveway, but none did. When at last his car door slammed, relief gave way to anger. She stood in the doorway, arms folded across her chest.

"Where have you been?" He didn't answer, just dropped his gym bag with a thud, stomped to the bathroom and slammed the door. Following him, she shouted, "Don't you dare walk away from me!" and heard the bathroom lock click into place.

"You're not my keeper. If this is how you're going to be, I'll *never* come home!"

"Good!" The locked door was a further insult. "Open this up!" and she pounded on it until her hands throbbed. "How dare you threaten me!" A moment later, she heard water running in the shower and pictured him standing under the spray, oblivious, maybe laughing at her. "Let me in!" She pounded again until her fists buckled. Steam was escaping over the top of the door, and the shower was still running hard.

She felt helpless and furious, and raced to the kitchen, searching for something to pound with. Her eyes fell on the heavy oak chair. Lifting it like a battering ram, its four blunt legs aimed toward the bathroom door, she rushed forward, and with all her strength slammed the chair legs into the wood, past the hollow space in the center, and finally, through the soft wood on the other side. Her arms felt stunned and broken. The door splintered, as if a gun had gone off, and steam rushed out as the door broke from its top hinge and hung lopsided. The chair held there, suspended in mid-air.

She stared in amazement as Bear flung the door open. The chair crashed to the floor, its varnished oak and paisley swirls blocking his passage. He shoved it aside and his face was red with disbelief. "Are you nuts?" gesturing and spraying like a crazy, living fountain, he advanced toward her as she backed away. Water and suds leaped from his hair, his fingertips, his penis as he came toward her, leaving wet exclamation marks on the polished wood floor.

Then she stopped moving and leaned into him. "Where were you?" Lately her imagination had been getting the better of her. She stepped toward him, pounding his chest, but he grabbed her wrists and held her at bay. "Let me go!" When he continued to hold her, she stomped on his instep. Instinctively he bent over, releasing his grip, and she stumbled back. They stared at one another, and then he turned and walked quietly into the bathroom and picked up his towel.

Hours later, alone in bed and just having fallen asleep, the telephone woke her. "Now don't get upset," someone was saying. She recognized Sam's voice. "The Captain…" Fully awake now, she began to understand. Her grandfather had collapsed on the deck of his shrimper. "They didn't want to call you," he said, "but I knew you'd want to know." When she woke Bear, sleeping on the sofa, he tried to comfort her. "He'll be okay, he's a strong guy." It was as if their earlier fight had never happened.

Minutes later, she was dressed and packing – gathering things without thinking, not knowing when she'd be back. Her finals were over but Bear's weren't, and he would be staying on for summer school regardless. "I'm so sorry," he said as he rushed up and down the front stairs, loading the car.

It sat with its doors and trunk flung open, packed tight with suitcases, boxes and plastic bags. "If you need anything else, I'll send it or bring it." The neighbors' terrier was barking as she made the final trip, and stood beside Bear holding the last small box. "You should have waited for me to get that," taking it from her. They walked to the car and a shadow fell across the lawn as fast-moving clouds bore down from the west. As she buckled herself in, the concern on Bear's face reminded her of what she loved about him.

He leaned against the jamb. "Take care, hear?"

"I will. I'm sorry about last night."

"It's okay. I'll fix the door," grinning.

"Thanks." She started the engine and he leaned inside the open window to kiss her on the cheek. Then he watched her drive away – worried about the Captain, but grateful an empty house was waiting for him.

As she turned onto the main highway, Ainsley half-wished Bear had insisted on coming with her, but if he had tried, she would have discouraged him. Another sign their marriage was coming apart. A streak of lighting raced across the sky, followed by a boom of thunder, then nickel-size drops of rain splashed on the window, washing everything away. If only.

CHAPTER 28

WHEN AINSLEY WALKED INTO HIS hospital room, the Captain seemed to be sleeping, but as she stood beside his bed, he whispered, "I told them not to bother you," then opened his eyes. "Lavender soap," he explained. "I could tell it was you."

Days later, despite the urging of Parker and Grace to stay with them, the Captain returned to his old house, the one he'd given Ainsley. "Your parents would be too much trouble for me," he joked.

The doctors were optimistic for a full recovery, but prescribed a far less strenuous regimen. Over the next several weeks, Ainsley would tell him, "I'm only following doctor's orders," when she monitored his diet or insisted he take short walks on the beach. Now, awakening ashen and weak, he told her, "Father Time is catching up with me."

She marked the page in her book and came to his side. "Then you'll have to run faster," but her words were as false as the smile he returned. Sam had moved the Captain's favorite chair to the shabby, glassed-in porch overlooking the ocean, but even on this mild day, he had tucked a blanket over his knees. "Pretty soon, you're going to feel like sixty again, Grandpa." Her joke brought the quick nod she had counted on, but what they couldn't count on was seeing him at the wheel of his shrimper again, not at seventy-two, not like this. She erased the thought, and then remembered the flowers. "I have a surprise," she told him. From the kitchen she brought a basket filled with tiny pink and white roses. "They're from Phoebe's garden, with a card." She cleared her throat dramatically and began to read: "Get out of bed, you old thing. There's no time to be wasting."

"That's her all right."

"She'll be by later."

He thought of Phoebe in her youth – one of those wild girls people liked to whisper about. Even now, some part of the young Phoebe he had once known kept coming back, like beach daisies, unexpectedly.

"Yep, that's Phoebe," he said, admiring the roses. The room was filled with bouquets from his friends, and from all of Grace's and Ainsley's. When or where the custom of sending flowers to men had begun, he wasn't sure, but he approved of it highly.

"And Bear called last night," said Ainsley, smiling as if trying to make a sale. "I told him you'll be out surfing by spring."

His eyes lifted, remembering. Back Then. And Now. It was impossible, really, for young people to imagine that a *then* had ever existed for old people, or that their elders' strong, young selves still survived inside them somewhere. All they saw was the *now*. But Ainsley was different, he thought. She knew he wasn't some old has-been; he was still a man, with a history and maybe a future.

Surfing? Not anymore, but he had once been legendary for it, surfing before anyone had imagined beach boys, or bikinis, either. As a boy, he had seen photographs of South Sea islanders riding waves and had been inspired to build a board of his own and do the same. "Did I ever tell you about that time and that school of sharks?" he asked.

"Maybe…," sensing he wouldn't mind being humored.

"Well, schools of sharks, migrating and mating, was nothing new around here," he began, "but that day was different. I was a young man with a new bride to show off for.

"You, show off?"

"Only once." Waiting for an objection before he continued. "Anyways, I seen the mullet swimming thick close to shore, but I ignored the signs and paddled out." He sat up a bit. "Then here they come – a cloud of sharks, heading straight for me and the bait fish schooling in the surf."

"Yum, Yum."

"That's what them sharks was thinking: dorsal fins up, mouths down and open wide. There was tigers, hammerheads, black tips. If I'd reached out, I'd have cut my hand off on their sandpaper backs."

"You must've done a lot of praying."

"I never hung onto a board tighter. There was sharks behind me, below me, and to the sides." He shook his head, picturing it. "Them sharks was after mullet, and they headed right for the beach. A thousand sharks in a couple feet of water!" His voice seemed to shut down. "And then they was gone, and all the bait fish was gone. I still got the newspaper story."

He was breathing deeply, and when he closed his eyes, she drew the blanket across his chest. Coming home was the right thing to do.

By June, the stand of Spanish bayonets had flowered and faded, leaving behind dry, brittle pods, reminders of how fast time was passing. Bear spent every second weekend in St. Christie's, for appearances was the way he saw it.

"Even the doves are too hot to sing," he told Ainsley. With his bare foot, he pushed on the faded strings of the hammock where Ainsley lay working a crossword puzzle. "I give up," she said, "It's too hot to think."

He didn't bother to answer, but kept reading instructions for the new cordless drill, hoping she'd take the hint.

She said, "You look tired."

Useless. He put the instructions aside. "Yeah." Her sympathetic remark surprised him, and he felt a sudden warmth between them, noticing just then the way her flowered dress hugged the curve of her thighs, the outline of her breasts. When she told him she needed a nap, it was as if she had read his thoughts. "Wait," he said, and padded over to the hammock, lifting her to her feet as she laced her fingers behind his neck. Maybe everything could be fixed between them after all.

Upstairs, the bed was made up for summer with only white sheets and a thin cotton blanket. The scent of honeysuckle drifted into the room on a soft breeze. Ainsley threw herself down among the pillows while Bear turned on the overhead fans and drew the gauzy curtains closed. She held her arms open and he lay beside her, wrapping her in his arms.

Afterward, heart pounding, he rolled away and lay on his back, arms flung to the sides, and what he felt most was guilt.

∽

While Ainsley prepared an early dinner and Bear watched TV baseball, the Captain and Phoebe sat on the porch playing gin, cards snapping, voices soft. A long evening lay ahead, and Ainsley was feeling a sense of – what? Balance. For now, that would do. "All right!" she called, ushering them to a table set with salads, cold roast beef and ham, a disc of cheese and a bowl filled with strawberries and mint from the garden.

"Just the thing on a hot day," said the Captain, helping himself. Ainsley thought, you'd never know he had been so sick, the way he pretends, yet he had little of his old energy. They ate quietly, but when the Captain cleared his throat and looked at her expectantly, she knew he was about to say something that wasn't easy.

"Bear and me been talking," he said at last, and then he looked to the younger man for confirmation. Ainsley took her grandfather's hand. He said, "I think I've just been kidding myself…" his voice sounding shaky.

"About what, Grandpa?"

"Kidding myself about ever getting back to shrimping."

Ainsley kept quiet. To deny it would be cruel and false. "Bear could help you, Grandpa," and turning to her husband, "Couldn't you, Bear?" She wondered later how she could have measured the critical silence before Bear answered, his face flushed in embarrassment.

"Of course I'll help."

"Appreciate it, Bear, but you got your own life, enough responsibilities." Bear exhaled, his relief palpable, and Ainsley wished she could hide her shame.

"Nope," said the Captain, "it's time to let the boat go. I asked Jack to help find me a buyer. He'll be around tomorrow to talk about it." His heart was breaking, she knew, but he held his voice steady.

"I'll clean up here," Ainsley said after dinner, and her grandfather and Phoebe looked relieved to escape to the porch as was their custom, taking note that Bear, after his lapse at dinner, had jumped in to help out.

While Phoebe settled herself in the wicker rocker, the Captain fixed her a glass of tonic and gin.

"Frank, you know just what I like."

"I suppose I do." When he looked at Phoebe, he saw all the other Phoebes he had known throughout his life, not just the one sitting beside him. "I like that we go 'way back," he said.

"So do I."

They are among the few people who remembered either of them as teens – a mutual link unlike any other. Friendship from youth though adulthood added layers of memory to what existed in the present, coloring it, changing it.

"I still picture you back then, Phoebe."

"Please don't, or I'll be embarrassed."

"You're still a looker," he assured her. Not in the usual way but in a Phoebe way. If he had just met Phoebe today, he wouldn't be able to recall the girl who had worked at the Boones' fish camp, wouldn't know the Phoebe who had filled so many boys' fantasies, or the Phoebe who gave in to the impulses that had both condemned and endeared her.

"I remember you, too, Frank, how proud you were of that little fishing boat you fixed up, how you were the only boy around with his own earned money in his pocket. Everybody admired that. And how handsome you were in that striped baseball shirt."

"Wish I'd known you thought that."

"Long friendships are good," she said, "but when you meet someone later in life, they don't know all your mistakes. You can start fresh."

"Don't you like it that some of us remember you from the schoolyard, running around in your little gym bloomers?"

"No!"

"Or how you and your Dad would round up bums on cold nights, feed them and put them up?"

"They weren't all bums; they just didn't have places to stay." Poking him in the ribs she added: "Besides, most of them were family."

He could still picture her driving the Nash Victoria though town, and all those hungry, cold men jumping on the running boards. Back then, folks criticized: a kid helping the down-and-out, but nowadays they knew it was a good thing, that it could just as easy have been them.

"You were something, Phoebe."

"Stop it, Frank."

"Still can't take a compliment.

"That's right."

During the Depression, while her classmates were sitting in Jerry's drinking sodas, Phoebe, fourteen years old, was barreling down dirt roads and through the palmettos, by then driving a Model T, running rum. The Boones knew and loved cars, especially fast ones.

"All those memories," he said, "are part of us."

"Us?"

"Why not?"

CHAPTER 29

UNEXPECTED GUESTS CAN AROUSE SPECULATION of all sorts. At least that was the case when Jack arrived the next morning to talk about the shrimper, and brought with him a tall, blonde woman. He re-introduced her as Ilse, a friend passing through, but Ainsley, the Captain and Phoebe all remembered her, the same girl from a few times before, and wondered, could this be serious? About Jack's age, she spoke with a European accent, and her full lips and pale eyes made Ainsley think of some place northern and cold, except for the way she looked at Jack with a warm, sideways smile. Baggy khaki shorts and a man's sleeveless tee shirt, bare underneath, were both innocent and provocative, as was her hair, piled up as if she had pinned it there before stepping into the shower. She sat close to Jack, their fingers threaded, Jack brimming with confidence and clearly proud when he told them he had found two potential buyers for the shrimper. Every time there was a disaster, thought Ainsley, Jack showed up, or was it that when Jack showed up, a disaster was sure to follow?

"And I brought something for you," he told Ainsley, signaling them to follow him to his pickup, where he pointed to five orange trees in twenty-gallon plastic pots.

"Since you're a serious citrus student now, I thought you'd like these, from the original Quinn."

"Jack. Well." Not everyone brought you trees, thank God. "Thanks." He lightly tapped her arm, a kind of "you're welcome" gesture. "Bear would help but he already went back."

"That's okay. I brought my hand truck, if you'll show me where you want them."

Ilse was standing on the porch with Phoebe. "I'll wait here," she called, tilting her head, grinning sideways, obviously the woman who mattered around here. Jack unloaded the trees and rolled them into the greenhouse at the back of the compound, the Captain and Ainsley following after him on the last trip. He turned to Ainsley in surprise. "That's a fine nursery, more than I expected."

Row upon row of orange trees grew in straight lines, fifty in all, with plastic labels filled with writing, like patients in a clinic. "My professor at school drew up the plan for me."

"What happened to the orchids?"

"I sold them to a nursery in Orlando."

"Just as well," said Jack; "too much plundering in the orchid business."

"She was ahead of her time," said the Captain, who had joined them on the tail-end of things and was coming to her defense. "Now, instead of the orchid thing, she's got her driftwood thing," he said. "Tourists like it."

"A driftwood thing is good," said Jack. Being sarcastic, just like him, she thought.

"Exactly." said the Captain.

The greenhouse was thirty-by-fifteen feet, with a sprinkling system, humidifier, and screened windows that cranked open. "This must have cost you," said Jack.

"Just the glass; the building was here; heaven knows we've got enough extra buildings, but Sam did a lot of work," she said. "And some day, when I'm not ahead of my time anymore, I might go back into the orchid business." Putting him in his place.

"And maybe expand into the old packing house?" he asked, pointing to a wood-frame building attached to the south side of the greenhouse.

"Not any time soon."

"Now *that* is something," said the Captain, jumping in. "You ever been inside?" Jack shook his head, but looked anxiously back toward the house where Ilse was waiting. "Come on, if you got a minute. That old citrus packing house and jam factory is worth seeing." They followed him into a ramshackle building with random additions, now used mainly for storage. He stood in the center of the room, hands on hips, looking proud. "In the old days, quite a few people grew citrus on the island and on the mainland, and my parents packed and shipped for everybody hereabouts. Rich folks especially, they'd send fancy wood boxes up north for Christmas presents and for selling in stores. Oranges were a treat back then."

"The O'Rourkes are certainly enterprising," said Jack. Ainsley wondered if he were being sarcastic, and decided this time he wasn't.

"Just scraping by's more like it," said the Captain. He walked ahead, motioning them to follow. "Extra fruit, or what was blemished, got made into marmalade, right here. All our friends helped out." Jack was reading an old production schedule written on a chalk board still hanging on the wall. "That told us what was to be processed, how much, and for who," said the Captain. "Can't get myself to erase it." The room looked out over the river and seemed like a home-kitchen, but with big porcelain sinks, two stoves, a pantry, and a storage room for jars, lids and other supplies.

"All it needs," said Jack, "are a couple of refrigerators and sterilizers and it could be up and running again."

"Could be," agreed the Captain.

Ainsley shook her head. "Absolutely not!"

"Of course not," said the Captain, who was now part way into the room.

"Look here," he said, his voice flushed with pride. "After the jellies were cooked, we filled the jars here." He blew dust off a metal container. "This funnel fed right into them." He walked farther down the line, and they followed, Ainsley refusing to get caught up in their enthusiasm. "The lids dropped down from this tube and got screwed on automatic."

Jack looked at Ainsley. "Ahead of its time."

"It was," said the Captain. "And most of the machinery was built right here. It was running good up until my wife Sarah passed."

Ainsley, apparently forgetting the threat of a new business, now looked interested too. "I remember this!" She touched the frayed conveyor belt. "As the jars moved along on this belt, a girl would pull labels off a spool and stick them on." She climbed onto a high stool next to the conveyor. "I wonder if this thing is still working." She pressed a button, and they all looked at it expectantly as the conveyor began humming, then lurched forward, sending up clouds of dust. "Look at that! When I was little, I gave my dolls a ride on that belt."

"Built to last," said Jack.

"It was," said the Captain, determined now to show them everything. "My Ma, and later Sarah, would inspect every jar to make sure it was right – lids on straight, no spills. They even wore gloves so there wasn't no fingerprints on the glass." Jack walked ahead a few steps, nodding approval. "Where you're at," called the Captain, pointing, "that's packing and shipping." Jack turned around to listen. "We put a rubber stamp on the boxes, telling what was inside, and the date."

"Nice," said Jack. In spite of herself, Ainsley had to smile at him.

"We can't take all the credit," said the Captain. "Friends down the way shipped honey, orange blossom and saw palmetto. Couldn't stand the way we was doing things and showed us the ropes." The Captain dusted his hands together. "So that done it," he said. "We stacked the boxes over there until the truck showed up."

"That's it?" asked Jack.

"Pretty much." Trying to remember. "Except the person in charge would typewrite this report, telling what we done that day, and who for. We had a carbon copy for when we sent out the bills."

"Seems a shame this plant's been sitting idle," said Jack, confirming what the Captain may have been thinking for a long time.

"It's not a shame," said Ainsley.

"After Sarah, nobody was interested," said the Captain, "and following that, a big freeze took most Islanders out of the citrus business. Parker was hit hard, for one. And of course Grace wouldn't have nothing to do with it." He laughed, remembering what Grace had told him when he suggested she take it up.

Jack turned to Ainsley. "Imagine what this could mean for the migrants: a steady, safe place to work. I wonder what Irena would think of this…" But before he could finish his thought, a door opened, and a pie-shaped slice of light grew bigger on the floor.

They looked back to see Ilse silhouetted there. "I thought you forgot about me." No sideways grin now.

And it was starting to rain.

When they got back to the house, Ainsley found a note with her name on it, written in Phoebe's hand, with a telephone number Ainsley knew. Alone upstairs, with the bedroom door closed, she read the note again. It said a woman had called, but the number was Billy's. Almost without thinking, she was showering and changing clothes, still arguing with herself, and then rushing out the door without a word to anyone.

Billy still lived in the same house on the River Road. She could see it in the distance as she parked up the street and got out of the car. The rain was falling softly. Everything felt familiar, and yet it didn't. She was married, after all. Everything was changed, and yet it wasn't. She tried to see through the thick leaves of bay trees blocking the view as she walked toward Billy's house. There stood the old roadster, parked in the driveway, those same leather seats where they'd sat holding hands. She stood in the center of the sidewalk one house away, and a dog barked. Agnes? Could it be?

The front door opened and a dog ran out. Agnes, still full of life, came to Ainsley and brushed against her legs. Ainsley bent down, one knee on the sidewalk. "Hello, girl." Agnes, warm and trusting beneath her hands. Ainsley, burying her hands in the soft fur, fought something inside that felt like glass breaking. A shadow moved closer, and Billy was standing beside her. Placing a hand under her elbow, he helped her to her feet, and she felt like someone who had returned home, safe.

"I hoped you'd come." Putting his arm around her, he led her to the house, pulling her in close, Agnes at their heels. It was pouring rain.

❧

On the road outside Billy's house, a car was speeding up, trying to make a light.

"Slow down, slow down!"

"Stop braying," yelled Clay, pushing Lady's arm away as she grabbed at the steering wheel. "They should bottle that voice and sell it just to annoy people." He braked, but speeded up again; no place to pull over, not now.

"My God," said Lady. "That's Ainsley's car, I'm sure. Back up!"

"I can't. Are you crazy?" Clay looked in the rearview mirror, wondering the same thing Lady was: What was Ainsley's car doing parked just up from Billy Fiske's place?

CHAPTER 30

WHEN SHE AWOKE THE NEXT morning, Ainsley felt as if guilt were a physical presence, visible and smothering. Even if he suspected nothing, she dreaded seeing her grandfather. Any innocent remark, even "I heard you come in last night," would be too much to bear or hide from. So later, when Sam needed something from the hardware store, she volunteered for the errand, happy to escape the compound.

She liked the store's carefully arranged aisles, the shelves fanning in all directions, filled with solutions to problems she didn't know existed. In the paint department, she selected several color strips for the sun porch, which badly needed painting. A photo of a model room illustrated the possibilities of Calypso Green and Bahama Yellow. While the clerk helped another customer, Ainsley studied the photos and had almost forced out any thoughts of Billy and the night before, until she heard a familiar voice booming. Turning, she turned saw Clay and his foreman, Quentin Nash, pushing through the front door. Clay was someone else she didn't want to see that morning, but there was nowhere to hide. When had the world become so crowded with people she needed to avoid? While she stood there, immobile Clay looked up and she forced a smile. He signaled her to come over and what choice was there? Her legs began moving just the way she was telling them to, and her lips were obeying too, smiling, but she felt as if someone had written "guilty" on her forehead in Bahama Yellow .

He gave her the usual kiss on the cheek, but she wasn't prepared when, with hardly a pause, he held her stiffly at arm's length and told her, "I saw your car down on the River Road last night." Looking at her hard, his mouth set in a nasty line. Her face froze, knowing he expected an explanation. As she searched for one, a certainty flashed in Clay's eyes and she had to look away.

"My car broke down," she told him finally, her voice faltering.

"Sorry to hear it," he said, pursing his lips and shaking his head. "Why didn't you call me?" His voice oily with kindness, making her afraid.

"I called the auto club, the way I always do."

He was looking at some kind of hasp, rocking it from one hand to the other, studying it, as if their conversation were incidental. "It never occurred to me to call family," she added, filling the silent gap, then wishing she could stay quiet. Her mind was still running ahead, knowing he would ask what the trouble had been. What could she tell him? If she named something major, the car would be in the shop, towed away. It had to be something little, fixed on the spot. When he finally asked, she told him it was just a flat tire.

"Well, give me your keys," holding out his hand, calm and expectant. She stepped back, not meaning to, and he told her, "Let me get that bad tire out of your trunk right now and have it fixed. Don't want you driving without a spare."

She drew a deep breath and moved away from him, turning her head so he couldn't read her frightened expression. Was she good at lying? She didn't know. "The flat is already taken care of," she said finally.

"That's good, real good." He tossed the hasp back in its bin, where it clanked against the others. Putting things to rest?

No, not yet. He shook a Camel out of his pack and lit up. "Who fixed it for you?" His eyes were small and dark, burrowing into her, his suspicious and relentless nature asserting itself.

If she lied, he'd check. She pretended not to hear, and walked away a little, calling to the clerk, who was now free, concentrating on the rolls of screening she'd come to buy, and leaving Clay standing there. Sweat was starting to trickle down the back of her neck. With tiny steps she continued moving away, doing everything she could not to run.

He followed her down the aisle. "Usually the auto club tells you to stay with your car, and we didn't see you."

"We?"

"Lady and me. She was worried. Not the best neighborhood, as you know." His eyes had grown small and flat as nail heads.

"I did stay, except when I went to find a phone." The lies – she couldn't think fast enough anymore.

"Hey, boss. Gotta go, we're late." Quentin interrupting them. He'd found the part he wanted. Clay grimaced, enjoying himself too much to leave, but when Quentin goaded him again, Clay reluctantly turned to go. and they walked toward the door, heads together, a curl of cigarette smoke rising above them. Ainsley was about to take a breath when Clay turned back. "Next time, you call me, hear?" She nodded, and felt her stomach sink as he tipped his hat and finally hurried out the door. Her car keys, still in her hand, were shaking.

Thinking about Billy then, she trembled at the risk she had taken, a betrayal of everything that meant anything. And for what? Billy was already out of town again, and who knew what he was thinking?

At home and in the greenhouse again, she tried to concentrate on the trees, on the sun piercing through the glass, the work ahead, but nothing could calm the fear in her bones following her encounter with Clay. Even if Billy loved her as he had claimed, she couldn't see him again. What kind of woman am I, she wondered, to let myself hear such words from a man who isn't my husband?

From the greenhouse, she could see the trees that Jack had given her, already in the ground thanks to Sam, their dark leaves shaped into tiny canopies that foretold their future. The glass house and adjacent jam factory had seen many schemes and projects come and go. Along the north wall, were supplies for her driftwood projects, the key chains and other souvenirs made from her mother's stencils, many embellished with the lighthouse image seen on everything from T-shirts to books of poetry in St. Christie's. She began rearranging the dusty tools and paints, but knew it was useless. Her work was cut out for her: trying to forget the night before and make it through the day.

❧

It had been settled that a man named Dom LiBassi would buy the shrimper: a small down payment and the balance out of profits. He was a man in his early thirties, with a wife and a daughter four years old. He knew all about shrimping, he had assured them when he came up to re-inspect the boat. "Wouldn't want you to think you won't get paid on time."

"Nobody's worried," said the Captain

Two days later, the Captain and Ainsley waited, arms linked, as Captain Dom LiBassi prepared to take The Sarah out through the channel. She was seventy-five feet long and twenty-four-feet wide, a tough old boat with a heavy diesel, ready to stand up against the sea. Funny, the Captain thought, that he'd named her The Sarah, considering what the real Sarah had felt about his boat and his work. Just trying to win her over with the naming, that was all. He remembered dragging his young wife down to the marina to show her the glossy black lettering, the way she'd rolled her eyes and turned heel, not saying a word, and the way his heart had fallen, not for the first time or the last. In the end, he knew you couldn't make somebody love you, but he had never stopped trying.

As the boat's engine stood running, and last-minute details were checked, a stream of familiar faces moved toward them on the dock. They came in two's and three's, people seen over the years at the marina, old friends of the Captain who sat around the bait store passing time, and Parker and Grace, whose face looked puffy and red, as if she'd been crying. The Captain patted her on the back, and Grace's shoulders started to shake. Someone had brought a camera, as if this were an occasion they'd want to remember. It was too fine a day in which to say goodbye, he thought, with the sun glancing off the bright-work, and the newly painted hull glistening white. It should be raining.

They watched as The Sarah drew away, growing smaller, following it until they could barely discern LiBassi's wave as the boat disappeared around a bend, heading south.

"I'll never forget the first time you let me take her through the inlet by myself, Grandpa."

"Me neither," he said. "So much for that," dusting his hands off against his trousers.

"Part of us just slipped away," said Ainsley.

"Don't be gettin' blubbery, else I might, too."

As they turned to go, friends came one-by-one to shake his hand. "Best captain there ever was," one man said, and several others said something like it. Some who had worked as crew on The Sarah, said they would always love the sea because of him, clapping him on the back. Parker and Grace stood apart, her face moist.

On the walk back to the house, Ainsley tried to cheer him, "At least you've still got the marina to keep you busy."

Small consolation, he thought. Despite the importance of the marina and bait shack, it was The Sarah that had put most of the food on the table and given his life purpose. A doubtful look crossed his face. "I don't know. Bear's worried about the marina, too."

"Worried?" She stopped walking.

"No way I can keep it up. Bear thinks we ought to sell it all."

Bear hadn't said anything like that to her. Letting the shrimper go was bad enough, but sell the marina? "You can't sell, Grandpa. We'll find some other way." He took her hand and got themselves moving again. Up ahead, Sam had already reached the compound, and was leaning his lanky frame against Ainsley's screen door. The Captain turned down Ainsley's offer of coffee, and she watched as he waved to Sam and walked on toward the marina cottage where he lived.

"Miss Ainsley?"

"Sam?" Something was up.

CHAPTER 31

SAM SEEMED TO HAVE SOMETHING to tell her. "Quite a morning," she said.

"Yes ma'am."

They'd known each other for years, yet Ainsley could not remember when they'd ever had a real talk, just the two of them. His ties to her family went back a long way. As a young man, he had worked with her father in the groves, and she vaguely remembered stories that he had run away from home when his mother had remarried. After working for Parker, he had disappeared for a few years, and of course Vietnam had come along too. Then he'd drifted back, one of several times, and they'd come to accept his restless comings and goings just as they did the tides. He was good with citrus, a talented handyman and a hard worker. Because his mother married and moved often, Ainsley guessed he'd never had a chance to make lasting friends.

Whatever it was, she'd have to be patient. Sam always needed time to get started. Tall and slim, his face worn, his eyes so light blue they looked almost faded from his years working outdoors. His straight brown hair and closely-trimmed beard were sun-bleached too. Someone said he had come into a small bit of money lately, but the way he dressed was still the same and hadn't changed in years – thrift-store shirt tucked into blue jeans, a peeling brown leather belt, and ankle-high work boots of suede leather, everything clean and neat. His one possession, and only extravagance, was a red 1957 Thunderbird Convertible which he washed every week, and covered with a tarp every night to keep the dew and rust away. "It's like on TV, Dan Tanna's in Vegas," always mentioning that, in case someone didn't know it.

"We need a treat," she told him, "and you're just in time for my famous corn bread." He followed her into the kitchen. "Baking on a day like this, I must be crazy."

"Yes ma'am," a joke, and he squeezed out a laugh as he pulled up a chair to the table. She cut a thick slice from the yellow loaf and placed it on a napkin in front of him. Unconsciously he nudged it aside. "I don't know how to start."

"Is this about the Captain?" she asked after a while. "I barely made it through this morning."

"I know. And yes, it is." He scraped his chair back over the tiles. "I came by to say I'd like to stay on here steady and help out with the marina, Miss Ainsley."

"You already do. You know we need you."

"I can see that."

"You're kind, Sam, and even though I want so much for you to help the Captain, it wouldn't be fair to tie you down steady. You've never wanted to be settled; you have to think of yourself, too." He stayed in a small block building near the marina, one room plus a bathroom and a small kitchen, outfitted when it became clear that Sam would be returning from time to time. If she walked by at night she could always hear country music playing on his portable radio and imagined him inside reading one of his paperback Westerns. As far as anyone knew, he had never married, but there was a woman he'd been seeing over the years, a telephone operator at the dealership where he had bought his car. Sometimes they walked on the beach holding hands, and once in while they'd cook dinner on the oil-drum grill – eggs from a couple of chickens that roamed the property, fish and shrimp, greens from his garden, which he sometimes abandoned before the harvest if he got an itch to travel.

She brought a cube of butter and a knife and set it in front of him. Maybe that's what he had been waiting for.

"I always come back here," he put in. "There must be a reason."

"We're always glad when you do."

"I'm here to ask you something."

She tried to encourage him with a smile, whatever it might take.

"I'd like to stay on here permanent."

"Permanent?"

151

"I could fix up the storage house where I stay now, and no cost to you." He looked hopeful. "I've thought about it a lot and I'm ready. I'm just wanting a place to *be*. Home. With folks who know me."

"Family."

When he nodded, she got up, stood behind his chair and wrapped her arms around his neck. "Nobody can ever have too much family."

His face relaxed and he came to his feet, folding the corn bread in his napkin as he shambled to the door. "You can count on me," tossed over his shoulder.

Ainsley called after him. "And you can count on me." A few steps down the walk he turned back, and she read his lips and the word "home."

❧

Throughout that summer, Ainsley and Bear told everyone their separation was necessary because of the Captain's health, and during his weekend visits, he welcomed Ainsley's increasing occupation with her citrus nursery. Less time together, less conflict.

Even now, as he tossed his weekend bag on the sunroom floor, Ainsley made no effort to hide her annoyance. "You arrive and expect me to just drop everything," looking at the bag as if it were a second intruder, "You're making a mess."

"I just drove four hours to see you…" and wished he hadn't, but forced himself to kiss her on the forehead. "I'm sorry."

"Sorry you came home?"

"This isn't home." The under-size wicker love seat was another irritant, an uncomfortable place to sit while he riffled through the sports section, crumpling the pages. This is how it always began between them – badly. A period of adjustment he supposed, walking on glass. "I'm tired," he said at last. Lately he was sick of working so hard for things he didn't even want.

Ainsley met his eyes. "I'm sorry. I'm mad when you're away, and I get madder when you come home. I can't explain it."

152

"I know," throwing the newspaper on the floor in disarray, "but I feel a duty to come."

Startled, she looked up. "Duty?" Her face flushed. "Is it my fault you're unhappy?"

Was it? No, he thought, it was his, and the reason for his unhappiness was simple: choosing her over Dance. So there it was, a thought and a name he'd kept at bay all this time. Dormant memories and feelings long-denied came swiftly: Dance's hand in his, the way she smiled, sighed. He had caught glimpses of her on campus, but they had not spoken since that day when she had stumbled away sobbing, predicting he would some day try to see her again, and warning, "I won't let you." Was it too late to fix his mistake?

"Bear!" He had drifted off, and Ainsley was saying. "I am not to blame." Gently, he took her in his arms as he prepared to hurt her once again. In his softest voice he began, "It's not your fault, of course not. All the same, I need to tell you something I didn't admit to myself until now, wouldn't even let the thought into my head." Ainsley stiffened. "The truth is, I can't do this anymore. I've felt bad almost the whole time."

She stood up, knocking over a glass of water that splintered on the tile. "No. I don't care if you feel bad or bored or scared or whatever!" The water was spreading into a tiny river, and Bear was feeling small and mean as he sank back into the sofa. "Bear!" Her voice, full of resentment, stunned him. "It's not easy for anyone."

A sudden exhaustion overcame him, and Ainsley, noticing how contrite he seemed, sat beside him, leaning her head on his shoulder. "Why are you so nice, Bear? Don't you know it's what keeps me hoping for us?"

The truth about Dance – that's what he wanted to tell her, but how? In a sense, he loved Ainsley too, and with that thought, his courage slipped away. As if reading his mind she told him, "You can say whatever it is that's bothering you."

Reassured, he began. "I want us to admit our mistake and end our marriage." Then he waited, each word seeming to echo off the plaster, the glass, the tiles, until finally she took his hands. "We can't end it," she told him, and the hopeful look on his face disappeared. "We're having a baby."

CHAPTER 32

LIFE WAS ALL ABOUT WAITING, it seemed to Ainsley, Waiting for loved ones to mend; for trees to fruit; and now, for her baby to be born. November, and four months more to go.

Twice a week Jack came by to talk about the groves, a break in the routine, telling her about the continuing disputes with Clay, and about his idea of getting the jam works running again, a notion which she always rejected. "I have my driftwood souvenirs, I have my trees and I have a baby on the way," she reminded him. Despite misgivings, she agreed to let him and Emilio fix the old jam works up a little – the results of which, he was there to show her this morning. Accompanying him were Emilio, Irena and Lolo, still a boy without much to say, but whose heavy-lidded eyes took in everything. They were all on Ainsley's porch eating biscuits. "Taste this," said Ainsley, placing a spoonful of jam onto Lolo's plate. He dipped the tip of his finger in and tasted it, but gave no hint of either liking or disliking it.

She looked at him expectantly. "Well?"

He asked, "What is it?"

"My grandmother's recipe. Guess."

"Pineapple?"

"It's sea grape, from plants like those right there." She pointed to a spreading, woody bush with tough, plate-size leaves.

Lolo shook his head. "We picked grapes. That's not grapes."

Irena said, "The berries look like grapes," and gave him a hug, holding on tight when he tried to get away. "That sea grape is strong like you. It grows in salt and wind, and digs its feet in hard." And then she let him break free to join the men, who had begun walking ahead.

Ainsley glanced up. "Jack thinks we can make money with these jams."

"I know. Mr. Jack says for me to come here today, but Emilio he don't like it," and Irena was expecting a baby too.

She stopped talking because Jack had turned back and was bearing down on them. "C'mon, we want to show off for you!" and taking Irena and Ainsley by the elbows, nudged them along. At the door, he made Ainsley close her eyes while he counted: "One... two..." She knew he expected her to be amazed. "Three!" And she was.

The walls had been white-washed, the pine floor scraped and varnished, broken windows replaced, old ones cleaned, and all the equipment either painted or scrubbed. "It's beyond wonderful!" throwing her arms around Jack's neck.

"Don't go away," he said. "Your tummy got here before you did." In her pregnancy, Ainsley had gained just enough weight to remind him of the way she'd looked in her teenage years, when she had just discovered her charms and tested them on any male who wandered into range – a whole string of lanky boys with new Adam's apples, and occasionally even choosing him as a victim when no others were available. "So, what do you think?"

"It's hardly the same place." She was touching walls, counters, everything within reach. "Jack, it's so grand for my little endeavors."

"Just a little elbow grease, but for what I envision we'd need to do more."

"Don't envision!" she warned. Jack was walking ahead now, looking even more pleased with himself than usual, calling back to make sure she didn't miss anything. But Emilio was hunkered down near the door, seeming to ignore them, talking to Lolo and Irena.

She whispered to Jack, "Is something wrong?"

"He doesn't want Irena involved here, afraid she'll cut his cojones off, so to speak."

She started to say, "Fine. The male ego," but she didn't think that way about Emilio, who was as good a husband and father as he knew how to be. She had seen him picking fruit in the cold and in the sun, climbing thirty-foot ladders, bent over with the heavy, fruit-filled sacks. It was hard to find fault with someone so good, who might be feeling threatened.

She walked over to Emilio and took him aside. "If Irena wanted to help me here a little, would it make you unhappy?"

He shrugged. "Why would it?"

"I don't know. Maybe you think it's not right."

"Maybe I don't." He reached in his pocket for a pack of cheap cigarettes.

"I understand," and hearing those words, he looked relieved as the oddly pleasant sulfur smell of the match filled the space between them. Then he turned away to join his wife and son, who were already outside. Ainsley walked back to Jack, who seemed to be waiting for her. "You're kind Jack, and I love what you've done, but please — even though I may sell some jams at the marina, I'm not going into the jam business and neither is Irena."

"Okay. Not another word."

"Thank you Jack." Not every man gave you trees — or paint, either.

As she neared the main house, Jack's truck was pulling out, with Emilio and his family following behind in theirs. The November sun was burning hot. Even the asphalt driveway looked weary, its edges bleeding into the sand. She went up to the house to wait for her mother, who had called earlier, almost insisting on coming over. The coffee was just ready when the doorbell rang and Grace let herself in, kissed Ainsley on the cheek, and began to set out a bowl of strawberries she'd brought.

"These are so delicious! Try one." Although it was late morning, Grace had already put in several hours in her studio and was dressed in her usual long skirt and bright top, big brass earrings framing her face and an armful of bracelets jingling, yet she didn't seem herself.

Ainsley brought two cups to the table and poured coffee.

"You're looking good," said Grace, patting her stomach. Ainsley's weight had jumped overnight it seemed, and she was wearing a loose shirt of Bear's.

"I have to get a few new clothes."

"Have a strawberry."

"Mom, what is this about? Strawberries?"

"Can't a mother visit her daughter?

"No." Ainsley knew her parents worried. With a baby on the way, her grandfather still recovering, and Bear away at school, her parents were hard to fend off. Her mother had guessed the truth about that, she was sure, and her next question confirmed it.

"How's Bear?"

"Fine." More than fine, she thought. His life went on as before in Gainesville. "Mom, you said this was important."

Grace plunged ahead but needed a preamble. "I know you're a married woman, but feelings can sometimes take us to unexpected places."

"What places would those be?"

"I'm getting there."

"In a horse and buggy, Mom." She put one of the strawberries whole in her mouth. "There, I ate one. Now you can go home."

"I'm not finished."

"Do I have to eat them *all*?"

Grace wouldn't be rushed. "I wanted you to hear this from me, not some gossip."

Ainsley sat up. "Hear what?"

Touching Ainsley's arm, she said, "It's about Billy."

"Billy. Why am I not surprised?"

"I thought you should know. It's this, and I have it on good information: Billy's about to get married."

If there had been some lingering hope for her and Billy, it was buried now, but it took a moment for the words to sink in, and even longer for her to say anything. "Mom, it's wrong, and after all this time, you wouldn't think I'd take it this way," and she knew she was going to cry.

"I would."

"I feel disloyal."

"You shouldn't." Grace knew the way first love took hold, not only because it's new, but because *you* are, too.

"Why can't we ever get past high school?" said Ainsley.

"I don't know. Maybe because that's when we're our true selves, before life changes us."

"High school was my true self?"

"Why else can people pick up right where they left off at reunions? The years disappear, and for a while, they rediscover their authentic selves."

"Maybe," sounding doubtful, "but Mom, I want you to know this: I may love the memory, but I'm not in love with Billy anymore."

CHAPTER 33

LATELY, THE QUINNS AND DEWITTS were spending more time conferring and planning than either side would have liked. All because of the baby, due in a month. Earlier that day, Lady had called to announce a special surprise for Ainsley and Bear, and since they were visiting at the Quinns', Lady insisted on bringing it over so everyone could see it. Grace had barely enough time to put things straight – a visit from Lady being akin to a military inspection.

"How do I look?"

"Same as five minutes ago," said Parker, tilting his head toward the ringing doorbell.

"Thank you."

"I'm answering the bell now."

It rang again, and as soon as Parker opened the door, Grace saw she had misjudged once more. Lady and Clay looked as if they had been to their club for lunch, Lady in a mink jacket over a burgundy sheath dress, Clay in a sport jacket and slacks – the Quinns, Ainsley and Bear dressed for cleaning the garage. Well, thought Grace, it was either the house or me that got spruced up, and I'm glad I chose the house, since Lady will not be offended if I look awful.

Bear gave a hand, helping to carry inside a heavy, sheet-draped bundle from the back seat of the car. No secret to him what it was. They set it down and waited for Lady to remove the sheet, which she did with a flourish, her face lighting up expectantly. A bentwood bassinet, still gently rocking, sat in the middle of the floor with its tiers of hand-embroidered pillows and skirts spilling over the sides. "It's been in the Forneau family for generations," she was telling Ainsley. "My great-great grandfather had it made, and of course it's still in pristine condition."

"Prissy condition's more like it," said Clay. "All those mama's boys in your family must have loved it."

"Your own babies loved it," said Lady, "not that you were around much to notice." A scowl crossed her face but was immediately replaced with a tight smile, and what she obviously considered an indulgent, Southern-lady forbearance. "Isn't he the one?" she said, and everyone laughed self-consciously. He definitely was the one.

Clay was pacing, as if the space were too small for him, kicking absently at the base of the bassinet each time he passed it, setting it rocking and clearly delighting in Lady's suppressed fury. He crossed the room to join Bear who was standing off by himself, clasped him around the shoulder, patting him too hard. "A baby. Didn't think you had it in you, son. No, I didn't." Bear tensed, shoving his father's arm away. Clay leaned closer, saying in a whisper, "Are you sure you *did* have it in you? You haven't been around much lately." Ha. Ha.

Bear blanched. "Thanks for that thought, Dad. If you have something more to say in that vein, I'd think twice." When laughter started on the far side of the room, Bear, grateful for the diversion, turned his back on his father in a way he had never done before.

"Bear, over here," called Grace, waving her slim, pretty arms. Already, she was silly on a few sips of Champagne, and leaning into his shoulder, said: "I was just telling Ainsley that she will never draw another peaceful breath. Once you have children, you can't, you know. You're worried and miserable for the rest of your life."

Lady helped Parker roll closer in his wheelchair, which he seemed to need more often now. He was telling Bear, "I love children., but you'll discover it's hard to love and want them *all the time!*" and he laughed too loudly.

"What I'm worried about," said Lady, "are baby names." Everybody turned toward her. "Not that I'm suggesting anything, but the Forneau name always stood for something in the South."

"It stood for crap!" said Clay, heading in their direction. "It stood for pantywaists and deadbeats. No more about Forneau. For No! that's what I say."

Under her breath Lady whispered to him, "You liked it well enough at one time, back when you saw dollar signs in it!"

"When I *thought* I saw dollar signs," he hissed under his breath, "like everything else For Naught."

Poor Lady, thought Ainsley, who couldn't help overhearing. Usually, it was hard to feel sorry for her, but today she did. The more Clay picked on her, the more Lady seemed to shrink inside her pretty dress. Their voices were louder than they knew.

"Hey, cut him off," joked Parker, coming to the rescue. "Don't ruin the kids' day. We can always ruin it later."

But that was not the end of it. "You've been ruining *my* day," Clay told him, slurring now, after his head-start at the club. "Letting Jack Henderson pay those migrants like money's going out of style." He tossed back the rest of his Wild Turkey. "And you!" pointing his finger at Ainsley, "My own family, inviting those wetbacks right into her home."

"Dad, shut up," said Bear. Everyone went quiet. Clay grimaced. "We're going," he said, and put his hand on Lady's back, shoving his wife toward the door, Lady making nervous goodbyes and Parker and Grace calling unconvincingly, "Don't rush off!"

Ainsley followed, but Clay stopped unexpectedly and pulled her aside, kissing her on the cheek and whispering, "I'm real proud about the baby, but I want to remind you, I saw your car parked over at Billy's. So before I get excited about this new little baggage I want to know if it's mine."

Ainsley felt the wind go out of her. "I assure you, Clay, it's not yours." Clay drew himself up, and looming above her warned, "The little bastard better have the DeWitt chin."

CHAPTER 34

IN THE FINAL DAYS OF her pregnancy, a false good will on both sides had brought a measure of peace, as well as a special effort on Bear's part to spend more time on the island.

"If you think the baby's coming in the next couple days, I'll stay on here," he was saying.

"Go back to school. If you stay, I'll feel pressured to go into labor right away." His attentiveness was a change from their times in Gainesville, or even more recently, but Ainsley was afraid to think that life was getting better, afraid to jinx it. Now, after a day of working at the marina, Bear was staying on to dry dishes, even though he faced a four-hour drive back to school. He was banging cupboard doors, rattling crockery as he hurried to finish the task.

"My God, Ainsley, what's going on here? Where am I supposed to put the plates?"

"All the jars?"

"Looks like a jelly store in here."

"Blame Jack. Ever since he painted the factory, I feel obligated to use it some." The cupboards were filled with preserves – guava, sea grape, kumquat, and orange. "Take some with you."

"I will."

"They're from Grandma Kate's recipes."

"Who?"

It showed how little attention he paid, no matter what she tried to tell herself. "Never mind."

"The Captain's mother?"

"Yes. I've even sold a few jars at Tupper's store downtown. That's Jack's doing; it's impossible to discourage him."

"You holding out on me?" he joked.

"My private gold mine. Beth calls it market testing; you know how she gets carried away."

"Unlike you, of course."

"Absolutely." She walked to the high cupboard and pulled out a laurel-wood box made with dovetailed corners and a lid hinged in brass. Inside, neat labels separated the chowders from the seafoods, the meats and vegetables from the sweets, with recipes written in Kate O'Rourke's script. Bear was pacing, impatient.

"Listen to some of Grandma Kate's recipes." One by one, she began pulling out cards and reading the titles, "Indian Hush Puppies. Chayote Salad. And here's one for you... Bear Stew." She grinned at him. "Oh, and Pounded Green Turtle Steak with Hot Peppers."

He took the stack of cards and continued reading aloud where Ainsley had left off. "Frog Legs sautéed in Corn Meal. Crawfish Casserole with Lima Beans." He looked up. "Aren't these the newlywed recipes you tried out on me?"

"Family history," and taking the cards back she continued reading, but when she looked up, Bear was at the window staring into the darkness.

He saw the movement of her reflection and turned around. "You sure it's okay to go?" .

"Absolutely," she assured him. "I have another week."

Then, free to decide, he changed his mind. "I'm tired. I'll leave in the morning."

A few hours later, the first spasms pulled Ainsley out of a restless sleep. It's time, she thought, and reached over to tap Bear's shoulder.

"Attention! Attention!" Tupper was striking a knife against his Champagne glass. "A toast to Ainsley and Bear — and to many repeat performances!"

Their friends were gathered for the Christening celebration on the front porch at the compound, where Ainsley had set a table decorated with sprays of blue lobelia and white baby's breath. In a far corner, the baby slept in his bassinet. They'd already had breakfast with their parents, and this lunch with friends had been dragging on longer than either Ainsley or Bear had intended. The cake, with David's name and birth date, and the table, so pretty a few hours before, was in disarray. Exhausted from nights up with the baby and days of cooking and preparation, Ainsley was looking forward to a nap and a change out of the dress she had squeezed into.

When the applause died down after Tupper's toast, Bear rose to speak. "At this celebration for our son, David – named for nobody in particular, so as to offend both sides – I want to thank all of you for coming. And I hope that some of you will get busy so David has some buddies to play with and some pretty girls to chase after!"

"We'll be glad to help you out with that," said Charlie, placing his arm around Vickie's shoulders. "My bride-to-be has finally set a date."

"Vickie joked, "My dad wanted me to make sure Charlie got early acceptance to law school first."

"We can't wait 'til you to finish law school," said Bear. "Any other candidates for parenthood? Father Jimmy excepted, of course." They all laughed. Nick rose, steadying himself with one hand on Beth's shoulder. "I'm an old-fashioned man, living in a world of women's lib."

Beth shrugged his hand away, whispering, "Sit down, Nick. You're drunk."

"See?" said Nick. "No respect." A nervous twitter arced across the table, but before anyone knew what was happening, Nick grabbed Beth's arm and dragged her to her feet. She stumbled back into the table, but caught off balance, went sprawling on the floor, taking with her the tablecloth, silverware and dishes, crashing and shattering on the tile. Ainsley rushed to help while Bear held Nick at bay, and everyone else stood at the table, ready for what, they didn't know. Ainsley pulled Beth into the house. "I want to die, I want to kill him," she said.

"I know." Ainsley hugged her, patting her the way she did her new baby. Vickie and Anne Wilson hovered outside the bathroom, then came in and closed the door. Anne told her, "Don't go home with him, Beth. Stay here, or come with me."

"He'd kill me." Ainsley wet a washcloth and dabbed Beth's forehead while her crying eased. The door banged open.

"You ready?" Nick teetered there.

"You shouldn't drive," said Anne.

"Shut up!" He grabbed Beth's arm and dragged her away, but when Bear tried to intervene, Beth shook her head, and they all stood back helplessly as Nick pulled her toward their car and shoved her inside. Everyone watched them drive away.

"Sorry about your christening party," said Tupper, when finally they had swept up the broken glass and all sat down again. "Usually you can count on me to be the one gets drunk."

"At least you have the good manners to fall asleep in a corner," said Karl, and they all laughed. Ainsley put her arm around Anne Wilson, who was sitting next to her. Father Jimmy rose and extended his hand across the table to Bear. "Maybe I ought to leave so you can all talk without inhibition."

"Do we seem inhibited?" asked Bear, getting a big laugh. "Stay. You might learn something useful for confession."

"We've all known about Nick, and ignored it," said Anne.

"This is the south, wake up, honey," said Tupper. "We do what we damn please and folks look the other way, 'mindin their own bidness'." Baby noises rose from the bassinet.

"Father Jimmy," said Ainsley, "I think we could use a prayer."

After everyone had gone home and Bear had fallen asleep on the sofa, Ainsley stole over to the bassinet, where David had somehow slept through everything. She thought of the first time she had seen him, when the doctor placed him naked on her belly, and the first time she had held him, his heart racing against hers. That first look: ears, as translucent as periwinkles; the pale moons of his fingernails shining, everything intact, perfect. And a little while after that first look, dressed in his tasseled hat, he was comical and heartbreaking all at once, lashes casting shadows on his cheeks, knees jutting left and right. Next to her hospital bed, Bear, the Captain and both sets of grandparents had hovered, joy in all their faces. Looking at her son now, Ainsley felt the same emotions she had felt then. Without a bit of irony she whispered, "You picked the right parents," and lifted him from the soft bedding.

CHAPTER 35

DAVID'S LIFE WOULD BE COMPLETELY laid out for him if the grandparents had their say. Parker was sure he was cut out to be a grower. "Look at that physique," he would say, lifting a matchstick arm with his finger. Clay kept saying he'd be the perfect businessman, "Happy one minute, shitting himself the next."

This particular weekend had been blessedly quiet, no parents dropping in, and David, six months old, was at last sleeping through the night. Although Bear had just started classes again, he now came back to the island every weekend. "I'll finish up in here," Ainsley told him, folding yet another basket of newly laundered baby clothes.

"Thank you," rewarding her with a smile.

Bear headed down to the marina to work with the Captain, whom he found inspecting the hull of a small boat. A two-foot hole gaped in the side. Bear whistled. "Sea worms been busy."

"Had to rip out more than I thought."

An understanding had developed between them despite their differences, and by late afternoon they'd almost finished. The Captain stood up, bracing himself and bending backwards to relieve his stiffness.

"Good as new," said Bear, running his hand over the neat, unpainted repair they'd made.

"You stayin' on?" the Captain asked.

The old man's way of changing the subject and being so direct always threw him. "For a while."

"I know it's not my business, but I got something to say and I hope you'll let me." Without a pause, he went on, "This comin' and goin' ain't good. Not for Ainsley or the baby either."

"I'm not sure the baby knows." Actually, he'd wondered about that very thing.

"Six months. Don't you think it's time to settle under one roof?" Not looking up, the Captain was packing his tools neatly into a handmade box. "A woman needs a husband, especially when she's got a son to raise."

The old man's intentions were good, but Bear didn't welcome his advice. "I mean to talk to Ainsley about it." The Captain was dusting his hands together, as if that were the end of that. Hoping to avoid anything more, Bear picked up the toolbox and they headed toward the shed.

That night, a seemingly contented group sat down for dinner together: Ainsley and Bear, the Captain, Phoebe and even Sam, with David sleeping in his basket in the corner, away from the light. Phoebe had fixed dinner, a carry-over menu from her fish-camp days – peel-'em-yourself shrimp boiled in beer, fried potatoes, sliced tomato salad and chocolate cake.

"Couldn't ask for better," said Bear afterward. He put David to bed upstairs while Ainsley cleared the dishes. Sam went out on the porch to light up, followed by the Captain, chiding him about a habit that he himself, until recently, had indulged in most of his life. "I can't abide you health nuts," they heard Sam complain.

"They'll be at their gin game soon," said Bear when he returned. "How about a walk down to the beach?" wondering if he sounded anxious, but relieved when Ainsley gave no sign he had. Already he had a blanket in one hand and in the other, the portable Sony, which the Captain had condemned as a harbinger of trouble for America. "If we lose manufacturing, we've lost it all," he'd say. "You can't run a country on fast food and rock 'n' roll."

At the beach, an early dew was already settling on the sand, and a three-quarter moon was rising unobstructed by clouds. Ainsley was wearing a long, white dress, and with the moon behind her, he could see the shadow of her legs as they walked to the water's edge.

Then came a burst of panicked cries, a child's voice rising over the sound of the sea, and they began running toward it, the calls fading in and out. A boy of about twelve was standing in the shallow surf waving to them, and a dark shape, like a boulder, was moving slowly beside him, making its way to the soft upper sand. "In all my years living along the beach, I never saw a sea turtle laying her eggs," said Bear. The turtle had left a track in the sand, and when she reached a place above the high-water mark, she began scooping with her flipper a shallow pit to lie in. The trio sat a few feet away, watching the sand mound up at her sides. Ainsley whispered to the boy, "I was so scared when I heard you calling. I thought something bad had happened."

Once settled, the turtle began digging a conical nest about a foot deep. "I think she's about to drop them now," said Bear. They pressed their cheeks into the sand to watch. The first egg appeared, the size of a ping pong ball, glistening and dropping to the bottom of the nest. "It seems like it's made of rubber," whispered the boy. Tears streamed down the turtle's furrowed face. The boy was counting to himself, but concerned. "Is she crying?"

"I don't know," said Ainsley. "Maybe she's just happy to be home." Instinct brought the turtles back to the beach where they were born to lay their eggs, she told him. After a while, Bear started picking up seashells nearby, impatient for the egg-laying to end. He spread the blanket and tuned the radio to an oldies station.

"I have a tortoise shell bracelet," Ainsley was saying. "It's old, from before our people lived here, when raccoons, even bears, came here sniffing out nests, and settlers would hunt the eggs for cooking."

"Uuuggg."

"Imagine settlers sitting right here with their guns loaded for bear," watching the turtle closely, unaware of Bear's impatience.

"Eighty-nine… ninety!" counted the boy.

At last the turtle began covering the nest and smoothing the sand as if to hide it. "She seems so tired," said Ainsley. The animal turned to face the breaking waves, the whitecaps her beacon. Then she dragged herself into the sea and was borne aloft. They watched until she was only a spec on the water. A few minutes later, both the turtle and the boy were gone.

"Time to turn in," said Ainsley.

"Let's stay a minute."

"If you want to," but she was already yawning. He dialed the radio low as they settled onto the blanket, but something in Bear's mood made her feel anxious. "Is there a reason we're here that I don't know about?"

His face, always easy to read, looked stricken.

"What is it?"

Wanting to put it as gently as he could, he said. "I can't do this anymore."

She let it sink in. "*This,* meaning us?"

How could he find the words that would make everything unmistakably clear? "I want free, Ainsley."

But still she didn't seem to understand. "Free of me?"

"It's not like that." A romantic song came on the radio.

Shaking her head no, she looked as if he had stuck her, but right behind the hurt came anger. "If you don't care about *me,* care about David!"

"I do," and he placed his hands on her arms, holding her there.

She said, "Please don't do this to us," her voice a whisper, and the music kept playing as if nothing had changed.

"I didn't mean to hurt you. I didn't."

She managed to break free of his hold. "Why didn't you tell me before, instead of letting me have a baby?" shouting now. "Every hurtful thing you've done, I've tried to overlook."

He was running his hands through his hair, trying to find a way to explain. "I tried to tell you a long time ago, you know I did. But it was already too late." Immediately, he regretted giving what sounded like a pathetic excuse.

"Maybe you did try to tell me, but some things are too important to just cast aside. You're supposed to know what those things are." Ainsley wondered whether she had known all along where things might end up.

"It was a mistake." Now he was coughing hoarsely, looking away.

"Mistake is too soft a word, too blameless." She didn't say anything else until he looked at her again. "I loved you," she said. "I still do."

"But you're not *in* love with me. Maybe you were once, for a short time, but not now," daring her to deny it. "Don't you want more?"

"I don't have to be in love," she said, and couldn't hold back her tears any longer.

"No," he said quietly, "but I do."

Ainsley sat down on the blanket again, and Bear settled beside her, watching the moon travel its appointed path, wondering what to do next. Finally he was able to go on. "We have a son," he said. "I'll never let him down, or you either, never again."

She's stopped crying and touched his hand. "It's not all your fault. That wasn't fair." Her heart couldn't deny the tenderness she felt for him. The moon still hung on above. It seemed a miracle that it still could.

"We have so much to decide," she said, "and I can't even think."

"Whatever you want. First, I'll support David. You know that. And as for any dividing, I guess the only important things are the house and the groves."

"Yes."

"I don't want 'em. They're not mine."

Of course he'd say that. "Thank you."

He leaned toward her. "But I'll put it on record, my ma will be wanting that Forneau bassinet back." She had to smile, but just as quickly, she grew somber again. "There's one more thing I have to ask."

One more thing. That would be the question he had anticipated and was braced for.

"Is it Dance?"

The truth. He owed her that, and reaching out, drew her close, her heart beating fast against his. "Yes," he whispered. "It's Dance."

After all the discussions, threats, warnings and tears had been issued by both sides of the family, Ainsley finally felt a kind of peace. She was on the sun porch, David sleeping upstairs. This, at least, was honest. Bear had decided to finish school, and she, to remain at the compound. He could see the baby and take him for visits whenever he wanted to. As simple as that, it was settled.

She was alone now. The men she had loved had all left her – Bear, Billy, Charlie too. And she couldn't help thinking again of that day long ago that still seemed to be haunting Clay, the day he and Lady had seen her car parked outside Billy's house. The day she had read Billy's note and had taken off wildly in the rain, racing to the River Road, Agnes rushing out the door remembering her, then going down on one knee holding Agnes and feeling Billy's hand under her elbow, lifting her up, holding her again. She still remembered every moment.

He'd come running from his house, splashing through puddles, holding a newspaper over her head, but she was soaking wet by the time they were inside. Agnes shook herself off, and he'd said, "Oh! nothing sweeter than a wet dog." They toweled Agnes off, and then, as if time had collapsed, they went outside again, and it was still softly raining. Less than fifty feet away, the river was empty of boats. Billy had an outdoor shower where he cleaned up after working on his car, and because they were soaked-through and full of Agnes's spray, he started to take her clothes off, kissing her wet skin as each piece fell away. No need to pull the curtain closed over the rusty rod. Ainsley looked up at the sky, gray from end to end, and then he turned on the tap – cold only, as was often the case in old Florida homes, even inside. A shock, and she threw herself naked into his arms.

Then Billy was stripping and she couldn't take her eyes away: his scarred and battered hands, his buttocks, his penis:

fine, every part of him. He stepped close beside her under the spray and lifted his face to the sky, falling rain and shower water mixing together, swirling down the drain, and then he pulled her tight against him. Lightning flashed in the distance, followed by a soft boom. Holding her close, he rubbed the bar of soap into a lather, and with his hands, covered her body with translucent foam that glided across her shoulders and breasts, nested between her legs. Water flowed down their arms, their legs, their hips, merging into a stream, and it felt as if a drought of a hundred years had ended. He said he wanted to be with her always, said he had never stopped loving her. But then, ridden with guilt she had pushed away, forced herself to leave, ran off before being with him completely, the way they both had wanted. One more thing to regret.

BOOK III

CHAPTER 36

December, 1985, Captain's Park

GROUND FOG HOVERED OVER THE frozen grass, licking the hems of parkas and hiding innocent children from sight. It smoked against the bunting on the platform where Ainsley sat shivering. Jack Henderson adjusted the microphone and addressed the crowd. "This is one helluva day, what with this weather." His breath visible in the air.

"I know you growers are worried about your citrus, like I am, and the rest of you about your gardens. So, yes… better cover up your bushes with bed sheets tonight. Another hard freeze is coming." In the oceanfront park, metal chairs glazed with frost had been set in tidy rows. He paused.

"Now that I've cheered you up, let's get to the business of the day. First, I'm proud to see so many of you here on this cold morning so close to Christmas. It's a tribute to Captain Frank O'Rourke, who gave us this land so long ago." Enthusiastic clapping was muted by gloved hands, but everyone now gave their attention to the Captain, who sat in the front row with Phoebe Hunter and a little boy of about five. "We're here to officially name this park for the Captain and to give you a preview of Speed Weeks, coming up in February.

"This naming has been a long time in the making since we like to go slow here in St. Christie's Island." He smiled at the Captain. "This gift was especially generous, because as you know, life hasn't always been easy for the Captain or his family." He threw up his arms in a gesture of helplessness. "But Captain, it's done, and we're not giving it back." The old man laughed, and pulled out a handkerchief, just in case.

"After this program, we're going to have some music by the St. Christie's High School Band, which we all enjoy. We have some Speed Weeks beauty queens, whom we also enjoy, and some of our favorite race car drivers here this morning." More applause. "You're invited to meet them in that big white tent, after the music." Heads turned to look at the tent, whose sides were slapping in the wind.

"If the tent blows down, you can meet them right here," said Jack. "But first, on behalf of the Captain, I'd like to present his granddaughter, Ainsley, who you all know..."

Ainsley, bundled in a long black coat, white knit hat and scarf, stepped to the microphone and smiled at her grandfather. She took a deep breath and began speaking in that honey-smoked voice, her eyes sweeping the park, thanking everyone for coming, and recalling town events that had been held in the park over the years.

In the first row, signs reading "Reserved for Billy Fiske," had been hung with ribbon on two empty chairs, and Jack, his eyes on Ainsley, thought, She's looking for that stray ol' stud. He took a sip of coffee from a cardboard cup just as the wind gusted and the crowd hunched its shoulders in a collective shiver. Ainsley was now recalling the Captain shrimping right offshore of the park, and how comforting it was that the land would always remain just as it was. In the distance, a group of farm hands stood stoically, as if the crowd had arranged itself in social and economic layers. Jack thought of their hard days ahead working in the freezing cold. He would have sat them right up front. Ainsley went on, telling them a bit more about the Captain, and finished up by thanking everyone again and calling her grandfather to the platform.

As the Captain spoke, his little tribe listened with respectful pride – Ainsley standing nearby; Grace, Parker, David, Phoebe and Sam – the people he loved most, sitting down front. "Thank you all for this," he ended up, "and welcome, everyone to your park." The band started playing as Ainsley returned to her seat, biting her lip. Jack pulled out her chair and patted her on the back. "I hadn't expected to feel all this," she said, her voice breaking.

"I know." The lambskin coat weighed on Jack's shoulders, an unaccustomed burden. Overhead, clouds were swagged purple and low. He wondered how the Speed Weeks beauty contestants were faring in their thin sequined dresses, and thought of a time, not that long ago, when Ainsley had been one of them. The girls began giggling then, and pointing toward the pathway.

Jack turned to see an unmistakable shape silhouetted against the cold sunlight, the race car driver they had all been waiting for, moving slowly down the aisle.

Billy stopped midway and looked up at Ainsley, who had already turned away after catching sight of him. He continued making his way down the aisle, clasping hands on either side. With the park being named for the Captain, he knew Ainsley would be there, and his indecision about coming had made him late. After finding his row, he was surprised to see where they'd put him. People pulled their knees sideways and tucked their feet under to let Billy squeeze by and take his seat next to Ainsley's grandfather and son. The boy, who was clutching a stuffed bear, smiled when Billy sat down, but the old man just lifted his wild eyebrows. Not exactly a greeting, but all that Billy figured he deserved.

Ainsley was just as he remembered her. Time had streaked by but little had changed, in the town or in her. Still the auburn hair, or what he could see of it poking out from under her knit hat, the pale skin, the long legs hidden beneath her coat, imagined. He couldn't help thinking of the girl with the rhinestone tiara or the woman he had last seen, who'd come running to be with him, to hold him naked in the pouring rain. Maybe he shouldn't have come today.

Ainsley felt his gaze, but didn't glance away this time. Billy looked older, used up, better. They hadn't spoken since that night almost six years ago.

The band stopped playing, the momentary silence giving way to a sharp rustling wind in the palmettos, like a nest of rattlers in the freezing park. She turned away from Billy then, noticing how forlorn the park looked under the steely sky, the battered Christmas garlands competing with bunting and checkered race flags. Even her friends looked worn: Tupper, unusually quiet; huddled next to him, Beth and Nick and their napping daughter; and nearby, Charlie and Vickie sharing a tartan blanket.

Off by themselves were Clay and Lady, Clay looking half-frozen, slumped in his chair and nodding as if still listening to a speaker. He often complained that speeches everywhere grew longer and more boring every year. Lady, nestled deep in her mink coat, clung to his arm, drawing attention as she always did with her drama and excess. Ainsley knew they'd take a moment to say hello. Keeping peace. Everyone put a lot of energy into keeping the peace, even Clay sometimes.

Now the mayor, Karl Schweitzer, was standing in line to greet the well-wishers. Who could have imagined one of their own, the youngest Mayor ever? It was twenty minutes before the platform was cleared, but as the park emptied, Ainsley saw Billy still standing next to his seat, and Lorraine Rivera, who had since arrived, leaning in close to talk. It seemed their marriage was fine, but no children yet. Ainsley kept up with Billy in the newspaper, couldn't help it if she had tried. Close by, Clay and Lady had left their seats and were talking with the Captain when Ainsley joined them.

Clay was saying, "Bet you'd have thought twice back then knowing what this land is worth today."

David was stamping his feet to keep warm. "Mom, can we go now?"

"Hey, fella." Clay bent over to tweak his grandson's chin.

"We'll go in a minute." She pulled him inside her coat, wrapping it around him like a tent, and waited for Jack, who was coming their way. The DeWitts made hasty goodbyes, likely to avoid the issues still burning between them and Jack.

Out of breath from hurrying over, Jack clapped the Captain on the shoulder. "I was hoping we could talk for a few minutes about this weather."

"Our place is closest. We'll fix you breakfast."

"Hoping you'd say that." Same old Jack, Ainsley thought, always polite, but with that attitude. Nonetheless, he was a blessing at times like this. Out of the corner of her eye, she saw Lorraine slip her arm around Billy.

CHAPTER 37

THEY ALL PITCHED IN WITH breakfast. David setting the table, the Captain breaking eggs into a big yellow bowl, Ainsley measuring flour, baking soda and salt for pancakes, and Jack laying a fire. Ainsley brought the electric griddle to the table so they could have their hot cakes straight off the heat. The Captain had finished mixing the eggs and was melting butter in the skillet when he had a sudden change in thought. "Where's that pretty gal you had with you a while back?" he asked. "Haven't seen her lately."

"Grandpa, really."

"It's okay," said Jack. "She's a traveling kind of girl, comes and goes. Now she's off to the next thing."

"What kind of thing?" asked Ainsley, envy overtaking restraint and getting the better of her. She didn't know Ilse, and had always been curious about her.

"She rarely writes, just shows up. Said something about Brazil. Time before that, I don't even remember."

"An adventurer," said the Captain, and Ainsley felt an unexplainable betrayal, comparing Ilse's large world with her own small one. She checked the bacon, and began adding milk to the pancake batter.

"Too bad," said the Captain. "Bet you miss her."

"She'll come back, always does." Ainsley must have groaned because everyone turned to look at her.

"Time to start the hot cakes?" asked Jack, all innocence.

"Let's see." She wet her fingers and shook a few drops of water onto the griddle, where they bounced and sizzled. "It's ready."

'No eggs, please," said David.

"This batter's lumpy," complained Jack.

"Like it's supposed to be."

He looked doubtful, but poured four neat little rounds, while Ainsley stirred the eggs and kept an eye on the bacon. The Captain had long-since abandoned his cooking tasks and was reading the newspaper, making comments. "They say here the temperature's heading down in the low thirties. Maybe lower."

"I hope it lets up before Christmas," said Ainsley.

"Everybody's worried," said Jack, "not just citrus growers." He flipped the pancakes, which were bubbling on top. "Up in the panhandle, it's in the 20s, livestock folks are hurting." With his free hand, Jack picked up part of the newspaper and began reading aloud, "Pasture grasses are killed and eighty percent of the wheat crop is gone."

The Captain nodded. "It's bad clear down to Miami." Jack lifted the browned edge of a pancake to peek underneath. Satisfied, he began stacking them on the platter with the scrambled eggs and bacon which Ainsley had set in the center of the table. The Captain helped himself and David. "No eggs," he confirmed.

"We're irrigating our fields now," said Jack. Well water, at 72°, would release heat into the groves at night. Ainsley thought of Professor Price, the patient way he had explained evaporative cooling, the way water gives off heat as it freezes.

"I remember when my parents put in overhead sprinklers, all that work and expense for nothing." The layer of ice that formed on the branches acted as a protective blanket against temperatures below thirty-two degrees. Thirty-two was nothing to a citrus tree, but overheads had drawbacks.

"Back in '62," said Jack, "growers with overheads killed their groves dead. The weight of the ice split trees right down the middle, sounded like rifle fire all night long."

"Any more eggs?" Ainsley asked. "Come on, finish them up." She hated thinking about freezes. In the 1970s, freezes had put many growers out of business. They hadn't the money or heart to re-plant and wait for their new trees to bear again. In fact, their own were among the few large groves still remaining in Halifax County, thanks mainly to Jack's ideas about micro irrigation and close-plantings.

Jack was pouring circles of batter again. "How did you like those lumpy pancakes?" she asked.

"Delicious, I like 'em lumpy." They heard a car door slam, then someone knocking.

"I'll get it," said Jack, who was closest. Cold air rushed in, and Billy Fiske was standing there in the doorway.

"David left this at the park," said Billy, holding out a stuffed bear. David saw the teddy, which he hadn't yet missed, and ran to the door.

"Binky! It's Binky, Mom!"

Now Ainsley was standing there too. Nobody could think of what to say until the wind banged the screen door against the house, "Can you come in?"

"Nah." He smiled at her. "Saw the teddy laying on the ground and thought I'd run it by, that's all." David was clutching Binky. "Wife's waiting in the car."

"Wife – well, then… Okay…"

"Okay…" She started to close the door when he turned back.

"See ya," and this time, he did go.

"Time for me to head out too," said Jack, folding the newspaper, carrying his dishes to the sink. Ainsley walked him to the door. "Call if you need us," but she knew she wouldn't hear from him until the freeze was over, one way or the other.

CHAPTER 38

THE ROAD BACK TO THE ranch was almost empty, the weather keeping the usual Saturday shoppers at home. Jack set the heater on high, but it was no match for the cold. Ainsley's groves were on his mind, and worries about what another freeze might do. Rumor was she didn't take much help from Bear, just a token sum for David. Migrants were another worry. It wasn't like summer when they might have other places to find work. And he thought of his parents, his father and his Seminole mother; no one had ever been caught or punished for what was done to them.

As a boy, he had often tagged along to the groves with his uncle, but he had been too young to remember much of what had been told him about his parents. It wasn't until he was older, poring over scorched diaries his father had left behind, that he really came to know him.

Jack's grandparents, Lowell and Helen, had started out with a small house and a big, ruined grove, purchased after the hurricane of 1926 had forced many settlers to give up on Florida. Because the house was so small, Lowell decided they would have a chickee, a thatch-roofed shelter where they could rest at mid-day, and a place to string a hammock. As it turned out, this was a decision with unforeseen effects. "We'll have the best," Lowell had said, "authentic, like the Seminoles build for the rich down in Palm Beach."

Their son, James, would be sent to a Seminole camp near Lake Okeechobee, where chickees had become by then the traditional Seminole dwelling, replacing their former log houses. At 18, James would be making his first long journey alone. With his mother's provisions of dried beef, biscuits and fruit in a small knapsack he set out, catching rides at first where there were roads, then going by river, and finally taking overland trails into the 'glades. It was the wet season and he knew the camp would be a savannah surrounded by saw grass swamp and islets.

When his food was exhausted he lived off the land – gigging frogs and roasting the legs over an open fire, boiling hearts of palm and picking black-haw fruit from the bush. As foraging grew more difficult, the trail also became harder, infested with snakes and insects. He kept an eye out for wild hogs with their deadly tusks, and alligator tracks wherever there was water. In the suffocating heat, he doubted the trip could be worth the effort just for a chickee.

After three days, exhausted and sun-burned, he came upon a cleared path which was as his father had described it, leading to a camp on the crest of a knoll. Two Seminole women were sitting on the platform of a chickee, about three-feet above ground, open on all sides, with palm logs holding up a roof thatched in palmetto fronds, One woman was sewing an intricate patchwork skirt for which the Seminoles had become known, the other, making a doll from palmetto fiber. Three other chickees crowded the camp, each having its own purpose: storage, sleeping, or cooking, as he would later learn.

"Tommy Wildcat?" called James, directing his question to the eldest woman. It was the name his father had given him, but the woman cast her eyes away shyly and shook her head. They seemed to be alone and he didn't want to frighten them. "I'm James Henderson," he called, patting his chest, then thinking how stupid he must look. Few Seminoles spoke English, and this time he pointed his words to the second woman, who continued sewing on an antique, foot-pedal machine. She gestured toward a bucket hanging from a nearby tree, and he understood that he was to help himself to water. Grateful, he drank several cupsful, and then not knowing what else to do, picked a spot under a guava tree and lowered his body to the spongy earth.

A scent of roasting meat awoke him. He had not eaten since morning, and by the sun's low-slanting rays knew it was late afternoon. Near the cooking chickee, a young girl stood over the open fire stirring a small, hanging kettle. She could not have been more than fifteen. Her gaily colored skirt and ruffled capelet were reminiscent of mid-Victorian fashion. Her hair was deep brown, full and held with a beaded band. Around her neck, she wore dozens of strands of tiny beads extending down to her collarbone, giving her neck a long, elegant appearance. From her hair to the sand-covered toes showing at the hem of her long skirt, she seemed a creature apart. Then she turned, looked directly at him, and without showing the least bit of interest, turned back again to the cook pot.

Her face was an oval, delicate and sensual, although she was little more than a girl. He closed his eyes, wondering what to do next, when a boom of thunder, followed by the sound of men's voices, brought him to his feet. Stretching his legs, he walked cautiously toward the laughter rising from the pathway calling, "Hello, hello!" not wanting to surprise anyone. Four men appeared at the head of a cassava patch, one of them older, and James rightly guessed this was Tommy Wildcat.

Tommy, because of his work for developers on the coast, had learned a considerable amount of English, and greeted James as an old friend at the mention of his father's name. Another clap of thunder and a dry rustling in the trees warned of an afternoon storm. Minutes later, wind whipped through the palms, and quarter-size drops of cold rain pelted them, followed by a cloudburst that sent a narrow stream coursing through the camp. Then, as fast as it had begun, the downpour ended, leaving the trees washed clean, the sky drenched blue, the air cooled.

James learned, when they sat in a circle to eat, that the two older women were sisters, and both were wives of Tommy Wildcat. The three young men were his sons.

"There was a girl," said James.

"My daughter Anne," Tommy volunteered. Tommy said nothing more, but continued eating, dipping the thick fry bread into the venison stew. When Anne failed to appear, he asked about her again.

"Anne flows," said Tommy, "She cannot cook for men or eat with men when she is not clean." James felt the heat rise in his face, but the others didn't seem to notice, and continued eating until all the stew and swamp cabbage was gone. That night, lying in a hammock, he fell asleep thinking of the barefoot girl.

He had hoped to see her in the morning, but she was nowhere in sight when they left camp at daybreak.

༄

The Henderson chickee went up quickly. Tommy Wildcat and his sons spent two days preparing the site and felling the palm trees to be used as its frame. Once begun, construction would take only a few days more. James had learned nothing more about the girl. Now, eight palmetto logs were standing upright, ready for the rafters which would support the chickee's thatch roof. As work was drawing to a close, James found the courage to ask Tommy about the girl, ready to be disappointed.

Tommy clapped him on the back, and before the day ended, was answering James's questions not only about Seminole courtship but marriage: that marriages where usually arranged by the men of the family, but could take place only if the woman approved, in keeping, he said, with Seminole autonomy for every person.

Even though James had not spoken a single word to the girl, his mind was leaping ahead making plans, outrageous plans. He would return to the camp with Tommy, and if Anne agreed, they would declare themselves married and he would bring her back to St. Christie's. Except what could he promise her? A decrepit grove, not even a decent home. It was madness to have such hope, but James could imagine nothing else.

On hearing his plan, Lowell and Helen were dumbfounded. James had never before pursued a girl, and this was one they had never met, someone so different from themselves. But James could not be discouraged. He only wondered, would Anne agree? In Seminole families, it was customary for a husband to live in the wife's home, so he would have a further challenge, persuading her to return to his. Despite all logic and every argument, he convinced himself he would succeed.

As the tiny group disappeared from sight on its trek back to the Everglades, James on his momentous quest, Lowell and

Helen watched with apprehension. Intermarriage was not looked upon kindly in Halifax County.

When the men were at last mounting the familiar knoll, a woman's scream cut through the air. James prepared to defend himself and ran forward with the others. A figure came flying in their direction, wielding a machete overhead, yelling and laughing. James watched in astonishment. It was Anne, with three small children trailing behind. She held her long skirts and a basket dripping blood with one hand, the machete in the other and raced past, nearly knocking him down.

The object of her pursuit was a just-sighted gopher turtle. With a leap she caught the animal, threw her machete aside, and grasping it by the carapace flipped it on its back. The helpless turtle flailed the air with its flippers. Then she picked up her weapon and severed its head with one pass of her great knife, jumping back as bright red blood soaked the ground; the children watched soberly, as did the men.

Immediately hacking and pulling, she removed the carapace. Then she butchered the animal on the spot, reserving the eggs and the liver in a large leaf, and adding the meat to the basket, which was nearly filled with meat from several other butchered animals. A turtle stew would follow that night. The children carried the basket and the shell away, and Anne turned to reward James with a smile. Exhausted from their long trip, the men bathed, napped, then later sat down to a meal of spicy turtle stew and the eggs, which were served separately. They ate squash and the corn gruel called sofki, and by the time they finished their meal, the setting sun had painted the savannah gold. As if by design, Tommy Wildcat and the others disappeared after eating, leaving James to sit alone in the chickee. The night came and went, then a full day, followed by another. What was expected? He had no idea what had been said to Anne but sensed she knew of his intentions. Each time she passed him in the camp she would look his way, then lower her eyes, never giving a sign of any kind.

At dusk on the third day, Anne came again, her bare feet clinging to the limestone outcropping and wearing a dress emblazoned with orange and purple and yellow embroidery. He rose to his feet, wanting to reach out, but could only stand there, still as a totem. "Anne." It was a name he had repeated silently numberless times. He extended his hand, and she clasped it in hers. Then, stepping closer and wondering if she understood, he asked her to marry him.

Answering him in English she said, "I wish it." And so it was done. Still holding his hand, she began leading him away; night was falling and he followed her down across the limestone shelf to the bridal chickee that had been prepared for them. In the trees, panthers were dreaming, and high above, stars blazed with light. Frogs sighed in the distant brush, and crickets were calling in the tall grass, singing a wedding song for the boy and girl who slept in each others' arms, the world far away.

After they returned to Halifax County, they were married in a small Catholic church, but James knew his true marriage had been under the stars in that distant hammock. Over the first few months, the couple lived in the chickee, then in an old caretaker's cottage some distance away in the grove, which Lowell and James had cleaned and repaired. Anne planted a garden, sewed a Seminole dress for Helen, and curtains for her new home, and accompanied James when he fished in the tributaries of the St. Johns River. To Helen and Lowell, so skeptical at the start, Anne was their hoped-for daughter, but to others in Halifax County – kind people in most other ways – Anne was forever the half-breed, drawing stares and whispers wherever she went. Before the year was out, a baby was on its way.

Outsiders, men and women alike, said she was too independent for a woman – especially an Indian – and told James he ought to put her in her God-intended place. James listened, but when he followed their advice, Anne would tell him, "We are equal," and he didn't know what he was supposed to say next.

The baby came on a warm March night, a dark-haired boy with eyes the color of Blue Spring. They named him Jack. When the cord that had bound the baby to Anne dried and fell away, she buried it for luck under an oak tree at the edge of the grove. In four months she would cut Jack's hair and trim his fingernails, which would be saved and given to him when he was grown. When this had been done, Anne would return to her husband's bed. She would never have the chance to give Jack his lock of hair.

CHAPTER 39

THROUGH THE YEARS, JACK HAD replayed his parents' stories again and again, but now as he drew near his groves, he forced himself to think of the problems at hand. The weather. The trees. The migrants. All of it was bearing down, but the truth was, seeing Billy Fiske standing in Ainsley's doorway holding a teddy bear seemed as unsettling as anything else. Crazy. Even though Billy was married, he wondered if something was still there between him and Ainsley. In the years since her split with Bear, Jack had sometimes made teasing advances to her, but she had always rejected him, as if by some prior agreement.

He turned onto an unpaved road that ran through the groves and back toward a group of weathered out-buildings – a small storehouse, a barn, cottages, and a long, narrow field house with white smoke spiraling from the chimney. A horse barn stood where the drive curved away, and further along in the distance, the main house sprawled atop a low rise. He parked next to the field house porch where a yellow dog, asleep on the steps, lifted her head.

On either side of the dirt road, men hunched inside their worn jackets were picking oranges, stooped with the weight of the fruit in their canvas sacks. It was body-wracking work, climbing the 30-foot ladders, reaching, picking the fruit, which always held on tight to the tree. Then climbing back down with a loaded sack and moving the ladder to a new spot. Jack jumped from the truck and hurried inside the field house. The warm, moist air held a heavy, lingering scent of bacon from the breakfast served hours earlier. The single large room was deserted, but rows of slatted wooden tables held paper plates, cups and cutlery for the coming noon meal. In the background, a radio crackled. He poured himself a cup of coffee. Outside the window, where a large thermometer had been hung at eye level, he took a reading, then another. Thirty-three degrees both times. He swore he could feel it every time the thermometer dropped a single notch.

"Morning, Mr. Jack," Leola squeezed past him – the cook, cleaning woman, and sometime nurse for the ranch. Only five-three, and weighing just over a hundred pounds, she had energy enough for two, and attitude enough for three, based in the knowledge that she could out-cook, out-manage and out-smart any of those around her. Most people guessed her age as forty, but she was almost ten years older than that, with skin as dark and glossy as an eggplant, and hair which she tamed with a turban, her trademark look. Thanks to her Dominican parents, she spoke fluent Spanish, which some men discovered to their surprise and embarrassment. She headed to the porch, leaving the door open to a rush of cold air, and tugged on a thick rope that set the bell in motion, a deep bong! calling the field hands to lunch. The day had run away from him.

The men stopped their work, and turned expectantly toward the sound, straightening up slowly, working the stiffness out. They filed in quietly, a few bowed their heads by way of greeting. Some had been working all night. "Sit before it gets cold," said Leola, like a bossy aunt as she set out platters of fried potatoes and slabs of ham with red-eye gravy. A girl ladled bowls of bean soup, smoking in a kettle at the stove. Hot meals were another of Clay DeWitt's complaints about the way Jack ran things, though even Clay knew people worked better when they weren't hungry. Two girls had come before dawn to help prepare food that would be served in shifts that day and for days to come. They were about fourteen, he guessed, and seemed shyly aware of their graceful young bodies, averting their eyes when they approached the tables filled with rough-looking men.

Travis Gates, the foreman, sat alone in a corner, his head resting against the wall, a Stetson tilted to shade his eyes. He often seemed as if he wanted something and was likely to get it: in his early thirties, good-looking in a hard-living way, with a sharp jaw and straight blond hair that he wore longer than most. His chest rose and fell softly. A third girl appeared from the kitchen and began clearing away coffee cups and dishes, but as she reached for the mug at Travis's elbow, his hand shot out, fast as a diamondback, and grabbed her wrist. "Leave that," he said, as the startled girl jumped back in surprise.

She twisted her arm free. "I thought you were sleeping."

He was thin and wiry, with eyes that seemed to dare people. "Hard to catch me sleeping, Miss," and he held out his cup. "Sweet thing, get me a refill, if you please." Travis watched as she walked slowly away and back again, carrying the coffee pot. About seventeen, white and scrawny.

She poured the cup too full. "Anything else?" Her voice was challenging, yet she averted her eyes.

"Nope," sizing her up as she moved away: uneven, dirty-blonde hair and a face surprising in its fineness. Travis looked around the room. As tired as they were, the other men were also watching. Then they hunched over their plates again, still dressed in their jackets, ready to work.

Jack had come up beside the table. Travis nodded toward the girl. "I wouldn't mind having a go at what's inside them blue jeans – a sweet little jump to brighten my day." Jack let himself down onto the wooden bench. Travis was talented at stirring up trouble. "What do you think?" Travis asked, gesturing toward the groves.

Jack shook his head. "Hope for the best. Today I'm worried about saving the crop. Tomorrow I might be worried about saving the trees." The thermometer had dropped another half-degree.

CHAPTER 40

THE ARCHED WINDOWS OF CLAY DeWitt's dining room looked out past the dunes to the sea beyond. The sky was one-dimensional and gray, the cold almost visible. He turned again to the lead story in The Island News, an idea buzzing at the back of his head. In St. Christie's, weather stories always played a big role, but panic was in today's report. That's what the locals found interesting – the moon, the tides, who was catching what fish, and where.

What a place. Even its name. St. Christie's Island. Did such a saint ever exist? No. The story was that the naming could be traced to the late 1700s, when a certain T. D. Roth, an Englishman, received a land grant from the crown, as though the bloody crown had a right to grant anything. Because nobody had thought to tell the Seminole Indians about the grant, they burned Roth and his sugar mill to the ground. Some said Roth had named the island for St. Christopher, the patron of travelers, which fit nicely with the modern touristy, souvenir and T-shirt side of things. The most popular opinion, however, held that the island was named for a West Indian girl who had been Roth's mistress, and this being the most satisfying notion, was widely accepted. People did not like being vexed by uncertainty in matters of such importance.

Clay, still reading, concluded that this freeze probably did merit alarm. The day's photos showed dirty, exhausted men working to save the crops, accompanied by brave statements from growers. Jack Henderson was quoted as saying: "I don't intend to give up no matter what." They all said that. Finally, the idea he'd been trying for surfaced – if it worked out, he'd have the weather to thank for it.

"More coffee, Mister Clay?" He shook his head, annoyed at the interruption, and returned to the newspaper. The maid removed the expensive dishes and refilled his coffee cup anyway.

Pearl had been with the DeWitts since their marriage and Clay thought she enjoyed riling him. She was a big woman, about sixty, but her size didn't slow her down, nor did her sex or her race. From her small house in the Negro part of town, she arrived at the DeWitts' every morning by bus, dressed in a starched white uniform. "I can't abide them maids what dress any which way," she would say. Pearl thought of herself as a professional, and from her earnings, and those of her husband, a short-order cook, both of their children had graduated from college."We's proud of them, and they's proud of us," she would say.

Clay turned to the back page and Pearl leaned in closer. "Looks bad for them growers, *ummm, ummm,*" shaking her head. She had the annoying habit of reading over Clay's shoulder, but today he didn't mind. In fact, her remark made him happy. Screw the growers, even though he was one of them. So what if he lost some trees, when his plans were so much bigger than that? He folded the paper carelessly, threw it on the floor, and thought about his idea of dropping in on Jack Henderson – a friendly visit. On the pretext of offering help, burying the hatchet even, he'd feel Jack out. Besides, with Lady off shopping in Palm Beach, it gave him something to do.

Before leaving, he checked himself in the mirror, satisfied with what he saw: a man of fifty-three, with a full head of graying hair and a compact build. Scuffed, handmade leather boots. Faded, alpaca-lined coat. No jewelry. Nothing for the locals to either envy or snigger at. All his life he'd played it conservatively, the good ol' boy, going by the rules, and it had paid off. He had power and respect, this almost-mansion on the ocean, and a striking wife. A good beginning.

A pale ray of sunlight glanced off his wife's portrait, hanging above the mantel. Provocative and romantic, the full-length painting showed her in costume of the 19th Century. Conceived partly as a joke, it nonetheless fit perfectly the dramatic interior of the room. Lady was a true southern belle, and there was the portrait to prove it. As he closed the door behind himself, he could almost feel her eyes following him, chastising. Next time he saw her, he'd make her go down on him for that.

The engine on his ten-year-old Porsche had to be coaxed to start, and the cracked leather seats were cold and uncomfortable. The car was a relic, but it suited the image Clay had contrived for himself – a man who fit in with the unpretentious life of St. Christie's. Their house was passed off as a whim to humor Lady, which was partly true. But nobody objected to it so much that they turned down invitations to dinner, or, for that matter, weekends in the Bahamas aboard the seventy-five footer. Nobody knew that starting out, he'd been stretched to the limit, nuts hanging in the breeze. Thank God, there was always credit to be had if you acted arrogant enough. He flipped on the radio, relishing the forecast of colder weather yet to come. The car, warm at last, glided over the white highway. Florida had good-looking roads.

Every time he drove the car, he thought about the plans, safe in the trunk; they stood for life on a scale unheard of in St. Christie's. The radio hummed and he snapped it off, caterwauling aimed at the locals.

After about twenty minutes, he saw the wooden sign, white with gray letters, marking the entrance to Henderson Groves. The grove was alive with men on ladders, picking fruit, packing crates. Even the air had a citrusy bite. He felt a grudging admiration. When Jack had finished with the war and college and came back to run the place, it had been on the verge of going under. As for Jack's parents, well – too bad, but no sense thinking back on that. A group of men working on oil heaters broke apart, and from the center, Jack stepped out. He stood hands on hips, looking at Clay's car, then began walking over with his long, lazy stride. You never knew how things stood with Jack, a good poker player, well to remember that.

"What brings you out on a day like this?" Jack said, stopping short of handshake distance. At his side stood a short-haired dog, bracing its legs. "Easy, girl," said Jack, running his hand along the dark yellow coat. "Don't worry about Boots. She's just saying hello." He appraised Clay, waiting for him to say something.

Clay knew his visit seemed odd; they'd been at each other for years, and Clay had never before come by.

"Had breakfast?"

"Just."

"Coffee? It's the only warm thing between here and San Juan." They walked toward the field house, heads down in the cold, keeping a space in between. Jack walked with a swaying gait, making headway on an easy tack, but Clay saw the slump in his shoulders, and the suggestion of a limp, which he had noticed before.

"We'll have a cup over there," Jack said. "I haven't been up home since this damn front moved in." The building was deserted except for the cook and her helpers, who were laughing and washing dishes in back. Steam from the kitchen clouded the windows, etched with frost around the edges. Jack filled two mugs and carried them back to the pine table just as a sliver of warm light found a rip in the clouds. Jack looked up. "Stick around. Don't go away." Then, just as unexpectedly, the clouds closed and the sun disappeared, taking Jack's smile with it. "What brings you by?" he asked. The swiftness of the question took Clay by surprise. Sometimes he forgot that Jack wasn't exactly one of the locals. He'd been away to college, and served in the war. Didn't always spend time inquiring after your health and your children before getting to the point. So Clay decided to plunge ahead, see what happened. "It's no secret us growers got troubles," liking the way he had included himself in it.

Jack shook his head. "Thanks for reminding me."

His laugh hit Clay wrong, but he let it pass. "I came to talk some business, help out," he said, "or maybe talk later, when things have settled."

Jack stirred another spoon of sugar into his coffee. "Business?"

"Land."

"Don't waste time, do you?" He laughed again, but this time, seeming a little bothered. "I'm not ready to give up on my groves yet." Another spoonful of sugar went in.

"It's not your groves I meant," said Clay. "That piece down at the beach. I could take it off your hands if you find yourself strapped for cash."

Jack took another sip. "I sure as hell hate to sell things when I'm hard up for cash and everybody knows it."

"I'd give you more than a fair price," said Clay, lifting his famous chin. The words were out before he could stop himself.

"What would you want it for? Not that it's any of my business."

"A project, nothing much." Clay thought he'd struck just the right balance between politeness and unconcern.

"I'll keep it in mind." Jack set his cup down with a noisy finality, a signal their meeting had ended, and the two men rose and walked to Clay's car. The sky looked like a smothering pillow of gray. Jack turned back toward the groves, Boots nuzzling at his heels.

❦

The house was quiet with Lady away, no calls, no lunches going on, nobody to show off for or boss around, and Clay wondered how much of his money she was dumping on Worth Avenue. Today, though, he welcomed the quiet. He'd brought the plans in from the car, tucking them under his arm as he walked into his office. This space was his alone, and the guest house out back, too. Well, not exactly. Lady owned the house, because he had sensed when they built it with her only remaining money that he should not put his name on the deed. It was a gambit that had won her trust. He'd seen too many spouses raise the warning flag by grabbing up assets, feathering their nests for a future flight from the coop. That wasn't what Clay had in mind. Despite his taunts, the Forneau name had meant something, and with Lady's good looks, and his cajones, Clay had eventually made a fortune with the decrepit paper and pulp business he'd inherited. The house was the least of it now.

He unrolled the plans, which curled back of their own accord until he weighted the corners with books. The paper felt glossy, expensive, and the artist's renderings of the future St. Christie's Island Resort and Club left no doubt that it would also be the most eye-popping, glossy and expensive development in all of

Central Florida, his flagship. Few people, other than Lady, knew about it, and they were sworn to secrecy. Sunlight falling across the plans lit the white sand, the shimmering water, the waving grass of the golf courses depicted there.

Clay thought again about his meeting with Jack Henderson, certain Jack would need cash, if only for his bleeding-heart causes. Only two pieces of land had yet to be acquired: Jack's and Ainsley's, and no problem with hers. Too bad those two parcels would likely cost more than the six others he had secretly optioned combined. With everything in place, a little under the table in Tallahassee, and with enough support in the right places, gambling was a sure thing for the future. Maybe it would come in increments, but it would come, and then wealth beyond imagination. He could almost hear the clink of the slots, the fall of the chips, the rattle of dice. Only a question of time, and after that, everything money could buy, at the highest levels of influence, not just in Florida. Nobody knew *that* plan, even Lady.

CHAPTER 41

THERE WAS NOTHING LIKE A freeze to put you in your place, thought Ainsley. All your work, your bravado, added up to nothing when Mother Nature decided to bring you to your knees. At the compound, she and the Captain had been keeping a vigil, watching the thermometer move in its relentless downward track. Two degrees in less than an hour, and likely it was colder in the groves, away from the ocean. Every degree and every hour could mean the difference between survival and bankruptcy. And there she was, at home doing nothing.

"Grandpa, I'm going to the groves. I can't stand by helpless."

"Good idea," he said, coming to his feet. "I'll get my coat."

"Maybe you'd better stay. It's going to be a long night."

"Don't try to make me out a helpless old man." He was already struggling into his fleece-lined jacket, and it was pointless to argue.

"Where we going, Mom?"

"To the groves. Get your big jacket, and your hat." She headed for the closet, pulling on a large cardboard box. "I wanted to go yesterday," she called from inside, her voice muffled.

"I figured as much."

"I should have, too. I don't know why I let Jack Henderson intimidate me."

"I'm sure I don't, either." The box was out in the room, open now, and she was sorting through boots and hats and gloves, handing a scarf to her grandfather and smiling at the sight of him, wider by half than usual in his fleecy jacket.

"Mom, do I have to wear these?" David held up old-fashioned galoshes with metal buckles that were clinking as he waved them at her.

"You do. They'll be irrigating and you'll be happy for dry feet." Resigned, he sat on the floor to finish dressing. A small mountain of clothes had risen on the floor.

"These boots smell funny."

"They're rubber; they're supposed to."

At last she found the sweater she had been looking for. "And he acts as if they're *his* groves, not ours, like I'm meddling."

She quickly took inventory as she began gathering pillows and extra blankets. "Let's go," checking everything one last time, she ushered the two ahead of herself into the dusk .

Jack Henderson spotted Ainsley's pickup as it turned in from the highway and called Travis over to the window. "I knew she'd come, can't stand to miss anything." They watched as the odd trio made its way to the field house, loaded down with blankets and pillows. "The amazing Mrs. DeWitt," Travis said. "Come to help us with our trouble, or make some."

"If we're lucky." They went out on the porch to meet their newest crew.

"Taking it easy, I see," called Ainsley.

"Oh, yeah," said Jack. "C.E.O. privileges. Just waiting for fresh replacements." They all went inside. Some of her friends and Sam were already working, he said. "Your mom and dad called; they'll be by any time, carrying Phoebe with them." David headed to the kitchen, where Leola was holding up a cookie. The Captain wanted to get started and put himself in charge of heaters. Ainsley watched him disappear down the sandy path, bundled like a moon creature on the Florida landscape. "Leola and the girls are in the kitchen," said Jack.

"Good."

When she didn't move, he seemed confused. "Leola —"

She cut him off. "I hope you don't think I came out here to work in the kitchen."

"No offense, but working in the kitchen is important duty here."

"Sounds like something for a C.E.O. then."

He looked at her, suppressing a laugh. Tasseled knit hat pulled down to her eyes. Hand-knit Irish sweater that once knew some larger owner. Baggy wool pants tucked inside rubber galoshes. How could she move? "I hate to see you ruin those nice clothes, so remember, it was your idea." He handed her a shovel and pointed to a line of high-school boys and girls who had been recruited to hill up the young trees, banking them with a waist-high cover of earth that would be removed when the danger of frost was past. She walked away pumping her shovel in the air.

Two hours later, she no longer felt the pain in her back. Her arms were numb and her fingers seemed permanently shaped to the shovel's handle. From where he was banking nearby, Jack watched with mixed feelings of regard and pity. He walked over and saw that she was perspiring, her bulky cap and sweater lying rolled in the trench beside her feet. "Hey! you can't expect to pull this soft duty all night," he said, giving her a hand up. She looked wobbly on her feet.

"Well, look what you've accomplished!" Two rows of small trees were banked, standing like soldiers in the field, ready for whatever might come their way. "C'mon," he said, picking up her discarded clothing and leading her back to the field house. The lights had been turned low and it was almost cozy inside. David lay in a nest of blankets in the corner sleeping, his arms curled around Binky. The Captain was still in the groves.

Parker poked his head out of the kitchen. "Look who's here!" signaling Grace and telling Ainsley: We've got fresh coffee, gumbo, and your mother's oatmeal cookies."

"Coffee," said Ainsley, and Grace poured a cup. "I take it back," she told Jack. "Working in the kitchen is too important for a mere C.E.O."

Parker wheeled over beside her. "Keeping my fingers crossed for the Quinn," he said. He looked worn. "This is the real test, back-to-back freezes."

"I know, Daddy."

"I'm not looking for miracles," he assured her, "just a good showing."

She patted his shoulder. "Me too, Daddy. I'm praying."

They worked until ten o'clock. The more work Jack piled on, the more determined she was not to give in. Finally it was time to rest. Jack had insisted. Men were sleeping all over the field house floor, humming in their sleep, coughing, snoring, whistling. A progressive-music ensemble. Ainsley stretched out in a corner and must have dozed off. When she opened her eyes, she saw Jack come in the front door, head for the kitchen tip-toeing in his boots, then cross back her way, carrying a mug. He sat on his haunches beside her whispering, "Here. Drink this," circling her waist, helping her sit up. Every muscle and every bone throbbed, as if she would never again move as a normal person. She closed her eyes, grateful for the gumbo steaming in its mug, almost too hot to hold.

"Phoebe took David home, and your grandpa's resting in back on a cot."

"Good."

"When you go back out, I think you've had enough shovel work."

Go back out again? "I have?"

"Yes, and no arguments." Mocking her now. "What I want you to do now is put sleeves on the young trees, like little foam sweaters."

"Chanel?"

"Exactly," he assured her.

Nothing in life was simple. The Styrofoam sleeves were slit and came in bundles that had to be separated, like paper plates, then fitted around the trunk of each tree. She tried to work fast, bending and adjusting each one, hoping some of the trees were Quinns, hoping they'd make it, but the night was growing colder. Throughout the grove, thermometers had been set in place, some in wooden boxes atop poles. In the low ground, air settled in frosty pockets, while near the lakes, it was warmer.

No thermometer was needed to tell her they were in trouble. The cold seeped into her clothes, froze her fingers so stiff she could hardly move them, and turned her breath to fog. She tried to work faster, to do as much as possible. The radiant heaters were going strong, but were no match for the cold. Sprinklers, irrigation, nothing really worked well enough, or else it cost too much.

"How you doin' ?" The Captain's voice startled her.

"Grandpa, I'm fine. How are *you*?" She got to her feet, and clasped his arms. "I thought you were resting," trying not to show concern.

"I was, then I wasn't. Headin' back in," he said. "Rest up a bit. C'mon."

Barely able to set one foot ahead of the other, she was amazed at her own weakness. It felt like a kind of loss. "Still working on the stacks, Grandpa?"

"Yep. A hopeless job."

"Too windy."

"Oil's costing too much anyway."

Over the years, nothing they had ever tried was a sure thing, not overheads, not the old smudge pots. She remembered her parents trucking the smoke-producing pans into their fields and trying to keep them filled with fuel oil. Other growers burned old tires and anything else that would create an inversion layer of smoke and heat. But it only worked on still nights when there was no wind to blow the heat away. That was before anybody knew about the environmental side of it, and people started building their homes near the groves and objecting to the smoke. The government had long since put a stop to smudge pots, and if growers wanted heat, they brought in radiant stack heaters and diesel fuel, but when the price of #2 diesel hit 22 cents a gallon in '72, up from 16 cents in '62, most growers couldn't afford to heat their groves at all. Jack still did it some, but relied mainly on micro-irrigation. The Captain had been tending the heaters, knowing there weren't enough to make a difference. It was 1 a.m. and the temperature had fallen to 27 degrees. The critical hours lay just ahead.

In the field house, more men were stretched out, catching a few hours' sleep before going out again at dawn. The Captain and Ainsley crept inside. Most people had no idea, she thought, what others had to do just to get by, how hard they had it. A tiny light still burned in the kitchen, but the cook and her helpers had gone home and would be back in the morning. Grace and Parker had gone home too.

"I'm so exhausted, Grandpa," whispered Ainsley. "I don't know if I can be any more use."

"Why don't you go on home then?"

"I couldn't. Look at these men. Bone tired. I can't do less." Travis looked like he was coming over, wearing his usual smirk.

He clapped her on the back, almost toppling her. "I gotta tell you," he said, "you are some worker, Miss Ainsley. Don't let nobody tell you you're just a pretty face." Under the caked grime, she could feel her color rising. "I don't think I'm in any danger of that."

∽

She woke to the smell of coffee and a chorus of morning noises. It was still dark outside, but Leola and the girls were working and talking softly as they prepared breakfast. Paper plates had already been set out, she noticed, and her mother was back, rolling out biscuit dough on the long counter, which must mean her father was there, too, outside. Slowly, the men were waking. No need for bells when there was biscuits and sausage gravy. She sat up and stretched, surprisingly rested, even though her muscles ached.

There was only one restroom in the field house, so even though she considered most men a sub-species in matters of hygiene, she had no choice but to dash in, wash her face in a shock of cold water and brush her teeth. Out in the groves after eating a quick breakfast, she felt an even greater sense of desperation than the day before, a clear struggle for survival.

Jack was in a nearby field leaning on a shovel and talking with her father and grandfather. He signaled to her and her heart fell, hoping he wasn't about to hand the shovel to her. "We dodged the bullet last night," he told her, "but another one's aimed our way tonight."

Two days before, in a measure of desperation, some of the trees had been sprayed with a chemical to loosen the stems of the fruit. Now mechanical arms were shaking the limbs, causing the fruit to fall into catch frames, but it wasn't working well. Most of the fruit was still in place, clinging, and would have to be hand-picked with clippers anyway.

"Your dad and me'll be working with the tubs today," said the Captain. Ainsley wanted to protest, but his raised eyebrows stopped her. Two determined men, one old, the other in a wheelchair, could accomplish a lot. She watched as oranges dropped into the catch frames, and then moved by belt into field collection boxes, each holding ninety pounds, one and three/fifths bushels. Her grandfather was overseer. Ten such boxes, nine-hundred pounds, comprised a tub. The tubs were filled with both mechanical and human precision, and then each was kicked off to a truck and taken to the processing plant.

"I've never seen so much activity in the grove so early," said Ainsley.

"Taking a chance," said Jack.

Normally, the workers came from camps by bus or truck and began harvesting after nine o'clock, when the night dew had dried off, protecting against spoilage. "We got to get it in, and hope for the best," said Jack. "They're already stacked up at the plant, and if this fruit waits too long, we'll lose it anyway." Hurried or mechanical harvesting was hard on the fruits' appearance. "I guess we can write the fresh fruit market off," said Ainsley. Their most profitable outlet.

"Looks like it."

"What do you want me to do?"

"Tend to the sprinklers. Turn 'em on and off in sequence, give each block a good soak, starting with the farthest groves." She started to object. "Just do it, okay? Take the golf cart." and he turned and headed to where the limb shakers were working.

Micro irrigation pipes had been installed to replace the old overhead rainbirds, and by three in the afternoon, all the fields had been watered. The sun had come out, with temperatures peaking at 45 degrees at 3:30 p.m. She'd been useful and planned to return to St. Christie's with her Grandfather, check on David, who was at Lady's, rest, and come back to work that night.

"The thought of it makes me want to collapse," she told the Captain.

"Then stay home some."

"Sure."

Driving back to the island, they saw frantic activity in all the groves. Some growers had installed wind machines to keep the air moving and keep it from settling in the cold hollows.

"We're lucky with high ground, Grandpa."

"Lucky with lakes, too."

"Yep, we're the luckiest!" And they couldn't help laughing.

By late that night, they'd harvested all the fruit they had strength for, and it sat there wet, in tubs. The processing plant was working three shifts. The temperature dropped into the mid-twenties. They could hardly take their eyes away from the thermometer.

"We did our best," said Jack, resigned. "At least we can say that." He kept watch over the window-mounted thermometer through the remaining night, seeing the temperature plummet from 25 to 20, and finally to 16 just after midnight. Even with a hard freeze, harvesting would go on for days, because some of the fruit, if it passed inspection, could still be saved for juice, though the yields would be low.

It would be five or six months before they knew if the trees had survived. Five or six months! Jack, his arm around her, walked Ainsley to her truck. Boots followed, looking happy for all the attention she'd been getting. As Ainsley turned the key in the ignition, Jack leaned inside the open window and put his hand on her shoulder, giving it a squeeze. "You did good."

CHAPTER 42

CARS AND TRUCKS PARKED ANY which way filled the lot, the swale and the lawn at Herb Foley's processing plant. Most showed plenty of wear, rusted on top from years of Florida dew. These were locals' and migrants' cars, never garaged, lucky to be running. Jack tucked into a spot near a dumpster, hopped down and let Boots out. She was a sociable dog who liked riding in cars. Herb was outside talking with one of his foremen, his head bobbing like a sparrow's. Seeing Jack, he signaled him to wait in the office. Jack settled Boots in the entry.

Through the glass partition that separated the office from the plant, Jack watched the workers sorting and inspecting fruit and running the washing conveyors, the juicers and vats, as yet another truck backed up to the dock. The office had only an electric portable that wasn't working right. Jack could see his breath on the glass.

Herb came in balancing two mugs of coffee. "Sorry. Got a lot of greenhorns on the line, working 'round the clock. We already lost a lot of fruit – rotting in tubs, on the trees. I'm processing your stuff first, when I can."

"Thanks."

The situation was as Jack had thought. He told Herb, "Don't forget, "any good fruit that can't be processed, I might be able to take off your hands."

"What for?"

"I have major plans!" and they both laughed.

Unconsciously, Herb reached into the shirt pocket where he had kept his Kools for thirty years before he quit smoking. "We're not gonna' do half what I expected this year," he said. "You know I got my life savings in this plant." Herb's family had been long-time Florida ranchers and stable owners, but when Herb inherited the family holdings at age 25, it took him only a few years to run through almost everything. "Fast cars, fast horses and fast women whenever I could catch one," was how Herb recalled it. With the funds he had left, and the luck of a horse that ended up in syndication, he had managed to put together another small stake, and bought a grove and an old processing plant, still gambling.

What Jack saw was a man in his late fifties, crumpled inside his red plaid shirt, maybe fighting for his last chance. "Anything I can do," Jack said, "give a holler. I owe you."

Herb offered a calloused hand Jack had known since boyhood. When he came back home after 'Nam and college to take over his parents' groves, Herb had helped get the business back on its feet. He was telling Jack now, "I guess you know, you're not as popular with some folks as you are with me."

"I'm sure."

"Some growers say you took advantage, workers deserting them to help you. Worse, there's talk about them organizing, and you'll likely be blamed. Watch your back."

"Thanks for the heads up."

"Ainsley and her folks doing okay?"

"They all have a lot riding here."

"That Grace..." shaking his head "She's still something ain't she?" The foreman opened the door and the noise of the factory rumbled into the small office, vibrating through the soles of their shoes. In the entry, Boots was soundly sleeping.

Except for the family of cats that lived under the dock, the marina was deserted, and Ainsley was trying to convince her grandfather to call it a day. Harvey, a gray, ring-tailed tom prowled the pilings, missing the bait fish that normally could be had from soft-hearted fishermen. Along with the cold, a ten-knot wind had made captives of pleasure boaters, and even commercial shrimpers and charter captains wouldn't chance the inlet.

"You might as well lock up," said Ainsley.

"Nah, You never know when some fool will want something. I'll keep her open a while." He busied himself straightening supplies his customers most needed: line, reels, nets, hooks. "I think I'll head back," said Ainsley, shivering. A potbellied stove stood in the corner, but it was no match for the weather.

"Are you going to crank up your jam business?" he asked. "I thought you and Jack had some scheme. With the oranges. That's what he said."

"Oh that Jack!" Taking over. It had been a good five years since he and Emilio had refurbished the factory, but now she had to admit that starting it up again might be their best option. She had a vague plan, and Jack had a very definite one, apparently. The Captain made a point of arranging Ainsley's jams and jelly jars. What her grandfather arranged, she rearranged. "Beth thinks we could do more too."

"Like what?"

"Not just marmalade and jams, but candied citrus peel, spiced in flavors like cinnamon, or jalapeno even, and selling in other places besides St. Christie's." She winked at him, teasing. "Not that you don't do a superb job of selling here in the bait shop."

"Beth?"

"And maybe Irena, too."

He frowned, remembering her other failed big ideas. He blew some dust from the shelf.

"Did you have to do that?"

"What?"

"Blow dust!" Then she told him about Beth's ideas for distribution, the tiny booklets telling Grandma Kate's story, attached to each jar with an elastic cord, and about Jack's plans for eventual automation. It had not been his intention to spur her on to this degree, because her optimism often kept her from seeing the pitfalls in life. Finally, it seemed she had finished rearranging everything. "Maybe I'll be a tycoon yet."

"I guess there's worse things could happen to a woman."

Despite himself, he had been caught up with the idea, even though she was not always practical, and too good looking – considerable drawbacks in a woman. But the men in his family had always had a weakness for beauty, and trying out new things.

Whatever happened, he had an eye on the future too, and meant to keep on keeping on – just like that old tomcat, Harvey. He watched Ainsley as she ran home over the dunes, kicking up sand that lifted into the wind and vanished.

∽

"That's my plan," said Jack when they met at the Jam Works a few days later. He crossed his arms over his chest. Ainsley did the same. Everyone else, seated on old orange crates, seemed to go along with Jack's idea to start up production with the windfall of oranges that couldn't be processed to juice. Beth, Irena, Tupper and Leo Johnson were nodding in agreement, Emilio at a distance watching. Even the Captain and Phoebe were smiling. Leo and Tupper were the key guests: Leo, because he headed up marketing at a supermarket chain, Tupper, because his father headed up a bank.

Jack said, "What do you think, Tupper?"

Tupper set his beer on the floor. "I like the products. We've been selling some at our store downtown, but this is bigger. The bank can make the loan if you have the orders to back it up. With all the costs up front – fruit, sugar, jars, cartons, and not to mention labor – it's a big nut."

A crate scraped on the floorboards and Leo was standing. "Tupper and I have already talked this over. Our stores are in, but we'll be starting small, two outlets, testing," and everyone stared in surprise. "In Spring, we can do a three-way promotion with English muffins and Irish butter, set up a toaster and free samples in a couple stores, coupon it, see how it goes. It will fit in with our British Isles promotion."

"Really, Leo?" said Ainsley. His ideas were grander than anything they'd hoped for. Beth was hopping up and down. "Oh my God!"

For hours after Tupper and Leo had left, everyone stayed to talk, while Jack laid out a plan. "Emilio, what do you say?" Emilio stood up, resting his hand on Irena's shoulder. "I am change my mind. This plan give us a chance. There is no other work."

"Okay then." Jack outlined the setup: Beth in charge of marketing; Emilio, the factory; Irena, training and running the line; Jack and Ainsley, everything else. They'd start right away. Jack offered to drive Phoebe home, but before leaving, she took Ainsley aside. "I just want to tell you, dear, you could be a little nicer to Jack. He's sticking his neck out for you."

"I'll try."

"He has your interests at heart."

"I know."

"I also want you to know I've bought one of your mother's thingamajigs, bells or chimes or whatever they are. I have an idea."

"Thank you, Aunt Phoebe."

"You're welcome, dear. And remember what I told you."

After they'd locked up, Ainsley and the Captain sat on the porch, exhausted. "Grandpa," she whispered, "I'm afraid I'm going to be the marmalade princess after all."

CHAPTER 43

AINSLEY GLANCED OUT THE WINDOW just as Clay's old Porsche came into view, high-beams blazing in the rain. Just like him to show up unannounced, assuming every door was open to him, anywhere, any time, but she had to smile despite herself. Clay leaped from the car before it had quite stopped, his favorite trick, then slammed the door onto the dangling, frayed seat belt. An impatient man, not known for making social calls.

He was almost handsome. An abundance of gray hair on a leonine head. A short, muscular neck suited to the college football he once played. A not-quite-tall body. And charm. All on the surface, but no one could deny it. It was hard to think of him as family, but despite her divorce he was, and although still a mean father, she had to admit, an attentive grandfather.

She cracked the upstairs window, and was pelted by rain. "Good morning!" He looked up in the direction of her voice, which was barely audible above the wind and the crash of the distant surf. "Got a cup of coffee?" The rain was coming down harder, but he didn't seem to care, just stood near a clump of Spanish bayonets, the water running fast over his stained canvas shoes.

"Of course. "I'll be right down." Quickly she slipped out of her jeans and into a pair of pressed slacks, a habit formed years before of wanting to look her best for Clay and Lady, always feeling judged. A fire was burning on the hearth in the kitchen alcove where she found him seated, feet propped on a low oak table. His appraising look didn't escape her. Same old critical Clay.

She hadn't recovered fully from her weeks in the groves, the vigils that followed the freeze, or their fledgling enterprise at the factory. She poured the coffee, and silently forgave Clay for stopping in so early. The warmth of the fire, the scent of pinewood, the tattoo of rain on the old tin roof, all made it seem that life was returning to normal.

The house had been built over a period of years, with some of the additions prompted by necessity, others by spurts of creativity. Now, like a woman who no longer expects to be noticed, the house had relaxed into a quiet state of worn comfort. Linen cottage curtains hung from rings, letting in filtered light. In the kitchen, the flooring of glazed red brick was still glowing after years of wear. In most of the other rooms, the floors were of broad, pine planks, bright with wax and protected with cotton rugs. The plump sofas, in their faded florals, seemed from another time and place.

"How is the proprietor of the St. Christie's Grove and Jam Works?"

"Are you making fun of me?" She leaned back and swung her legs onto the sofa, asking sweetly, trying to discomfit him.

"Of course not. I just couldn't help noticing there's been a lot of activity around here lately, half-breeds, all kind of people in and out."

"We saw a chance to salvage something from the freeze, that's all."

"Glad to hear it. You always were a doer." He finished his coffee and set the mug on the floor. "You wouldn't want to let your little jam business collapse, like your little orchid business, or your little driftwood souvenir business." Ha. Ha.

She flushed. "No, I wouldn't, and my little driftwood business is on life support, not dead." Would he ever let her live down her past defeats, even the small ones? She picked up his cup and her own, pausing in the doorway to the kitchen, appraising him. Clay could be so transparent, and he didn't even know it. "But I don't think you're interested in my little jam business, as you call it."

A smile that was too big lit his face. He saw he had overstepped, and now she was upset. "Oh, come on. Where's your sense of humor?" he chided.

She cocked her head. "Why is it when people insult you, they insist on questioning your sense of humor as well?"

213

"I'm sorry!" deciding then to come to the point. "I'm here about some land, that's all."

She set the cups down, plumped a pillow and sat on the sofa again. "Ah, some land."

"Yes." Her attitude irked him. "Maybe I'd better come back when your grandfather is here, or your manager." He shifted coolly, gazing over the top of his glasses, the way he did to intimidate people. "Jack does come around from time to time, doesn't he?"

She rose from the sofa, and picked up a wrought-iron poker from the fireplace. "Not in the way you're implying." She prodded the logs, sending hot coals onto the hearth. "If you want to talk about my land, go ahead. If you want to talk about my grandfather's land, then you should speak to him, but the Captain lives at the marina now, as you know."

"It's you I came to talk to," knowing she could talk the Captain into almost anything, if it came to that.

"About some land," still poking at the logs, wood flaring and crackling.

He nodded, heartened by her apparent curiosity. "I know somebody who might be interested in buying your beachfront property – the compound and all the way to the inlet." He paused, waiting for a reaction, but when there was none, he went on. "It must be costing you plenty in taxes every year. The way things are going, you could lose it."

"When you have a prosperous jam business such as mine, you don't worry about taxes." He didn't know how to react until she laughed. The logs were popping, shooting coals at her feet, which she began stomping. "What would you give me for it?"

"I didn't say it was for *me*."

"But it is," challenging him to lie.

"Does that mean it's for sale?"

She gave the logs another prod. "I've never thought of such a thing."

"Hear me out. For you, I could go maybe twenty thousand a front foot on the ocean, and fifteen on the river." He said nothing more, the practiced salesman waiting for a yes.

"Hmmm." She tilted her head, but he couldn't tell what she was thinking.

"So, can we talk?"

She set the poker back in its stand. "Even talking about selling feels wrong." She smiled as if to say she was sorry. "I'd have to talk it over with Grandfather anyway."

"You're the owner, aren't you?" Now his friendliness was fading and he knew it. Those Quinn women. Maybe Bear had been wise to run off. "Well?"

"Since Grandfather gave me the land, I owe it to him to discuss it, and much of it still belongs to him, you know."

"But you *do* want to sell, right?" He knew how to put pressure on people, a kind of gift.

"I was curious what your 'interested party' would offer, that's all. It's only natural, isn't it?"

"Sure." Coming to his feet now, he was ready to back off and fight another day. Eventually, he always got what he wanted. "Maybe we could talk about it some other time."

She didn't answer, which seemed like telling him to leave, but he wasn't quite finished. "First," he said, "I want to show you something." Before she could stop him, he was at the front door, letting the rain blow inside while he ran to his car.

Ainsley glanced at the morning paper which Clay had brought in earlier. He'd set it on a chair in front of the fire to dry, and as she turned the damp pages she saw Billy's face, staring back from the sports page. The local hero was still looking for his first win at the Daytona 500. Even now, she felt unsettled when she saw his picture unexpectedly. The front door slammed and she put the paper aside. Neither rain nor cold nor doors can stop Clay, she thought, and tried to steel herself against his persistence, his overwhelming presence.

A long cardboard tube was tucked under his arm. "Are you curious to see what I have to show you?" leaning forward, smiling like a TV preacher.

"Do I have a choice?" she said sweetly. She followed him into the dining room where he removed a plastic cap from one end of the tube and carefully extracted a rolled set of drawings

215

on heavy paper. "Clay…" her fingers rested on his arm as if to prevent something from going further. "This property has been in our family for generations, and some day, it will belong to your grandson. Wouldn't you like that?"

"I have something better for David," and then he was unrolling a brightly colored artist's rendering that encompassed the entire south island. With that, he turned toward her, a spring wound tight. "This property is ideal for a deep-water harbor – cruise ships, tourists, condo buyers…" and his voice trailed off.

Why did she feel guilty and responsible? She studied the plans while mustering strength to be honest. "Clay, this sort of development belongs in Miami or Boca." Huge sections colored green indicated a 36-hole golf course. Her property, and several other parcels adjoining it, were shown as a hotel and condominium complex with buildings reminiscent of Aztec pyramids, with bougainvillea spilling from stepped-back terraces. Next to it was Jack Henderson's property and two large adjacent plots, now transformed into beach cabanas, pools, tennis courts and a domed clubhouse.

He was so absorbed, it seemed he hadn't heard her remark. "What do you think?" he asked, his famous DeWitt chin lifted and proud. "Of course I'll build in phases, and hold onto part of it. I knew if you saw it…" Her intention had been to praise the project, no matter what it was, to be polite, but now, she couldn't. "This kind of development is destroying every wild, natural thing we love."

Now he was listening, and his hands were clenched. The table jumped when he pounded it, and so did she, stepping back. "You'll never get over that small-time Quinn mentality, will you?" He smoothed the drawings as if to affix them permanently to her table. "Do you know who drew these plans, what I paid for them?" Without waiting for an answer, he told her. "Thomas Berlin!" as if to threaten her with the name alone. Then his voice softened. A sudden idea had come to him. "If it's uprooting you're against, we could work it out. A life estate, something like that. Where there's a will there's a way." He paused to consider his own genius, the way he'd made such a bold concession without being asked.

"That's not it." She began rolling the plans up again, but it was clear he didn't like anyone touching them. He took them from her and placed them back in the cardboard tube.

She said, "Have you thought what a development like that would do to St. Christie's?"

"Put it on the map like you said: Miami, Boca."

Clay could be obtuse without even trying. "That's not what I meant. It would deplete every resource we have."

He looked at her with contempt. "Like you care!"

Naked insults were always a surprise, even from Clay. "What does *that* mean? If I have to sell, it won't be for something like this – thousands more people, golf courses draining our wells, dumping poisons into the river," and she turned away.

"Miss high and mighty! Miss hypocrite!" She spun around and he was looming over her. "*You* are so righteous, you and your whole family, taking and destroying, and donating parks to soothe your dirty consciences!"

"What are you talking about?" She could hardly speak.

"Every damn thing your family ever did helped destroy your precious environment."

"That's ridiculous! We've done no such thing."

"Sure!" His tone was cynical. "Everyone gets respectable *after* they take what they want. Dredging for your precious marina. Fertilizing your groves and helping kill off every damn lake in Central Florida with run-off."

"Not anymore. We know better now. Everybody does."

"My point exactly." He was leaning in close, "I did it too, but I admit it."

"Yes, you did." She couldn't seem to stop herself. "Your paper mills poisoned the air and the rivers with stink and chemicals, and lobbyists bought you a way out in Tallahassee." And then she stopped talking, put her hand on his arm, sorry for what she'd said, and how she'd said it. "Clay, we're family, but you need to leave now."

"If *I* can't convince you, maybe your dear townspeople can."

"Really!"

"Eminent domain."

Her jaw dropped. "You're ridiculous!" but doubt instantly set in. Could town pressure force a sale in the public interest? It had happened in other places, to bring in jobs, boost the tax base and benefit private parties who had connections. In fact, the law upheld it. He was tucking the tube under his arm. Not so charming now.

"By the way…" she said, and he turned to face her. "While my little jam business may not seem worth much to you, it means a job for me and a few other people too."

"Yeah…"

"*And–*" her voice rose above his. "*And* my grandmother's jam recipes paid for this land you seem to want so badly." Without a goodbye, he turned to leave. Just as he was about to get into his car, she called to him from the open door: "Clay!" He stopped and looked back, the rain driving against his chest. She was signaling him back, and with a faint but hopeful look, he bounded toward the porch, splashing through puddles. He was soaked through and breathing hard when he got there.

"I want to tell you, I'm stronger than you know. Don't ever patronize me again," and she closed the door quietly as he stood there, a pool of water collecting at his feet. Inside, Ainsley leaned against the jamb, knowing this was not the end of it.

CHAPTER 44

"ABOUT TIME YOU GOT YOUR ass here." After his disappointing scrap with Ainsley, Clay had driven home and called his son, a different scheme in mind. He was standing in the foyer doorway now, looking with disgust at Bear's oil-stained jeans, tapping his foot, clearly upset.

"Got here quick as I could," said Bear. "Busy."

"Busy screwing your egghead wife? Oh, excuse me, she's not your wife, is she?" He turned away before Bear could answer. "We'll go out back," nodding toward the door as he pushed past Bear, opened his umbrella and left his son standing in the rain. Out back, as he called it, was Clay's favorite place, a guest house where he was the only guest allowed in, away from Lady and all the other braying women.

Inside, Clay sat down and began kicking off his boots. Then Bear was pounding on the window, his head tucked low in his thin, tan jacket, water streaming down. "Hold your horses." Clay hobbled to the door and Bear stomped inside, tracking water. "Stupid door locks behind you. And take your damn shoes off."

"I can't stay."

"As usual. Here, give me a hand with these boots." He sat back in his chair, and Bear watched him struggle, ignoring the order to help, shifting back and forth, impatient. "What's up?" He couldn't get used to the sound of his own voice, the tough way he'd been trying to talk to his father lately. Dance's influence.

"My project."

"I don't want anything to do with it."

Then mocking him: "I don't want anything to do with it! Tough titty. I need your wife's land."

"Ex-wife. Time you got these things straight."

"Ex, yeah. Couldn't hang on to *her.*" He tossed his boots aside, walked to the wet-bar, and began pitching ice into a glass.

"Thanks, Dad."

"Ex-doesn't matter. She's David's mom. This is for his eventual good, yours too."

Bear left a wet trail as he clomped to the bed, absently sitting on the silk comforter, ignoring the look Clay gave him. "I can't help you, knowing how Ainsley feels about that property." He looked at Clay and then, as if deciding something, he sat up. "And I wouldn't help if I could," amazed how calm he felt telling him that.

Clay walked over to the bed, grabbed Bear by his jacket and yanked him to his feet. His son was looking down at him, but nobody was smarter or tougher than Clay DeWitt. "You wouldn't help me?" keeping his voice quiet but mean.

Bear rocked from one foot to the other, his breathing shallow. He'd seldom defied his father, more from upbringing than fear, but Clay in a rage was bad news. Everybody knew that, Clay especially. Yet the outburst Bear expected didn't come. Instead, his father walked to the bar and poured himself a Wild Turkey. "You could've had some of that property when you divorced if you'd had any balls."

"Didn't want it. It wasn't mine."

"Moral superiority? It will get you nothing. If you fight me, you'll lose."

"I'm not fighting you."

"Funny. Seems like you are. But I hold all the cards, and don't forget it." He was pacing now, his voice deeper, rising in volume. "I own more land than anybody. I own more politicians than anybody. And son, I own you. Why I'd want to own something so worthless is beyond me."

Bear stepped closer to his father, took a breath. "There was a time when words like that would have felt like a gut-punch, but not now." Bear took his father's glass, walked to the wet-bar and poured the whiskey down the sink as Clay watched, seeming amused. "And Dad, I don't need to brace myself with liquor. You know why? Because you can't get to me anymore," yet he felt his hands shaking.

Clay sneered. "Tough guy. We'll see how tough you are when I cut you off, when you come begging some day for *my* help, when they read my will and you get one big, fat dollar bill."

"When your will is read, I'll be hearing that you can't make life miserable for anybody anymore." The minute the words were out, he regretted them, his true nature asserting itself even now, but it was too late.

Clay's eyes narrowed. "You've had it so hard!"

Bear walked to the window, where water was streaming in thick sheets. "I did have it hard, but not in the way you mean it." Clay started to say something, but Bear took him by the shoulder.

"Shut up, Dad." Clay stepped back.

"This is how I had it hard: I was raised by a mean, unloving father, who mistreated me, my mother and sister. You were that father. I knew no matter what I did, in your eyes I wouldn't ever measure up." Clay started to say something, but Bear cut him off: "There's more. I'm almost done. I tried to make you love me, make you proud of me, but because of something I don't understand, being cruel made you happier."

With a grimace Clay asked, "Is that all?"

"No . Tell me, in what way did I let you down so bad?"

"You are your mother's boy. That's enough. You two can have each other."

"We already do."

"And you'll never have anything more from me. Nothing!"

"That's what I want, nothing. Because 'nothing' sets me free." And with the last tie between them broken, Bear expected to feel some kind of loss, but instead he felt a freedom that he had already claimed, but never truly felt.

"You're set free?"

"I was partly free when I no longer wanted or expected your help. Now I don't expect anything at all – not your help, your approval, not your love. Especially not love." A shadow had settled somewhere near his heart, but his voice was steady. He unlocked the door and the rain blew inside. Then he turned back, and true to his nature, left the future partly open, just like the door. "Unless you apologize to me and Mother and Tessie for every mean and heartless thing, naming them one by one, I'm done with you." And he closed the door quietly.

Clay sat on the bed, hearing Bear's car pull away, listening for him to come back, and then he smoothed away his son's damp imprint on the comforter.

CHAPTER 45

AINSLEY STOOD AT THE WINDOW long after Clay's car had disappeared from view, thinking about everything he'd said. The land meant more than security, and Clay knew that. It held her family's history, and its beauty, once gone, could never be recovered. Yet Clay had planted a seed. Could the town force a sale as he had threatened?

The rain was easing. She opened the door to let in the cold morning air and sat on the sun porch, pulling a blanket around her. Surf fishermen were making their way to the beach now, dressed in parkas and knit hats, struggling under their burdens of rods and chairs and coolers. She tried to concentrate on them, to shake the fear Clay had planted. Some of what he'd accused her family of was true. They'd hurt the land, if only through ignorance. She pushed her foot against the upright post: rocking, thinking, fighting against a sudden exhaustion.

Time to get going regardless. As hard as it might be, she'd have to confide in Jack, ask him to unite in stopping Clay. Unluckily, the camaraderie they'd had in the groves had vanished over a trivial disagreement at the Jam Works, and they were back to their scrapping ways. She walked to the closet and reached into the far corner for her grandmother's fox jacket. Once nestled inside it, she could almost feel her Grandma Sarah's spirit giving her strength.

Jack watched as the trainer took the trotters through their morning workout. The sky was clearing, the air soft and fresh. His view from the top of the fence where he was sitting encompassed the entire track and the trio of horses pulling their lightweight buggies. He had bought them the year before, not knowing a thing about horses. Anybody with sense wouldn't have done it, but since the owner had needed to get rid of them at any price,

Jack had bought them and built a track with a three-board white fence. He tapped his boot against the railing, berating himself for indulging in an enterprise that would be so short-lived.

The new owner would be there to pick them up any day. Too many people needed his help to hang onto an expensive hobby. Boots suddenly stood up, ears pricked and placed her forelegs on the lowest board. Jack bent down to scratch her neck, almost losing his balance. "What's up?" Boots backed away barking. Jack jumped down and sat on his heels, patting her head. "You run just as nice as those trotters, I mean it." The horses drew near again, but the sound was muffled by an approaching four-wheel drive. Boots shot down the road, legs flying, the most ungraceful animal he had ever seen. At the sight of Ainsley's pickup, she began trotting alongside, head up, tongue out. .

Ainsley parked next to the track and jumped from the truck waving her hand in a big half-circle. Just like a damn prime minister, he thought, wondering what she wanted, but he softened when, walking at half-tilt, she bent to feed Boots a treat she'd thought to bring along. Showing up just as if they were the best of friends again. Lots of people showing up lately. He had boosted himself back up, and from atop the fence she looked tiny. "Didn't recognize you at first," he said. "That is you hiding in there, isn't it?"

Even knowing she looked as puffed-up as a blowfish inside the fox jacket, she wouldn't let Jack get the upper hand. "Don't try to make me feel ridiculous; I'm onto you."

"Your fur jacket could make some people mad," he chided.

"It's a family heirloom."

"Heirloom, nice." He reached down, offering her a hand and she hitched herself up beside him, their heels hooked below, their eyes fixed on the trotters, beating a rhythm on the newly-turned earth. "I suppose," said Jack, finally, "you came to deliver some insult that slipped your mind at the Jam Works?"

She laughed, but her lips were pursed. Then he surprised her by putting his arm around her shoulder. "I'm easy, you were right."

Shrugging his arm away, she drew herself up within the bundle of fur. "I'm here under a flag of truce."

"Ah. In that case, let's go to the conference room." He jumped to the ground and swung around to help her down, but she was already beside him, striding toward the field house, looking pleased with herself. Most of the breakfast dishes had been cleared away, but the coffee pot was still half full. He poured two mugsful, added cream and sugar, and stirred ceremoniously, as if he were being judged. His carefulness seemed to please her.

"How do you know I like cream and sugar?"

"I am an observant man," and he added two more teaspoons to his own cup.

He was one of those men that people called interesting looking, more because they liked him than anything having to do with appearance. Somewhere beyond six-feet, he was slim but not someone you'd want to pick a fight with. His hair sprouted in ambitious outcroppings, but his eyes held a certain caution. He looked at her expectantly. "I know, since it's ten in the morning, this isn't a social call."

"I don't know where to begin…"

"Is it about the hole in the ozone, the fact one-third of American women wear size 16 or better? Is it…"

"It's about your beach property, the piece Grandpa sold you down by the compound."

Regardless of what she had to say, he could listen to that low, musical voice all day. "*Everybody* wants to talk about that lately. What about it?" He drained his cup and started to pour another, but the pot was filled with grounds.

"People say you were talking with Clay the other day."

"And?"

"Clay needs our property. Without it, I doubt he can build what he wants." It seemed evident to her that this would be good.

"That's a shame!" Taunting her. It was hard to be serious, talking to a big, furry ball.

"Jack! He wants to build a resort and a city, almost, with walls and gates, making people who have lived here all their lives feel small and locked out." She described the plans she'd

225

seen. In the distance, the horses had come around again, seeming to float in a low morning fog that hadn't yet burned off.

"This town is dying for the kind of project Clay wants to build," he said. "They'll figure, let DeWitt build it here or we'll lose out to some other place." Development was pushing east from Orlando and south from Daytona, and one day, the western groves would likely be solid houses and shopping centers, the beach stacked with condos. Ainsley had seemed to retreat inside the jacket, as if hibernating. Jack's voice softened. "Don't take it so hard. Think what you can do with the money."

"I don't care about the money."

He looked at her, doubtful. "I know what the freeze cost you, what trouble you're in. With a little money, maybe you could get into something exciting."

"Like what?"

"Like a tourist attraction."

"A what?"

"Drive people around in one of those fancy golf carts, wear a short skirt and that little fur coat…"

"I see you don't want to talk seriously," and she started to gather up her things. "I guess I'd better go." She picked up both cups and Jack followed her to the kitchen, then outside toward the track, Boots trailing along. They both knew that many people would like to have the tax base a big development would bring, the money for construction and jobs, and everything that would continue into the future. If the right people wanted it badly enough, they would find a way. Private investors had built hotels and condos all along Florida beaches, taking land under the guise of public interest.

"If we hold out," she ventured, "maybe it won't happen for a long time, if ever." They stopped walking for a moment and he rested his hand on her shoulder. "I don't want to sell either. I got a good price for my trotters."

"I didn't know…" Her head swung around as the horses pounded down the track in front them again, the earth shaking, mud flying.

"I'll be fine," said Jack. "But if I ever decide to sell the beachfront, I'll sell it back to you over Clay. Of course it would be nice if you had some money to buy it, which you don't."

"Money again!" Back at her truck, Jack opened the door while Ainsley bent to give Boots one last pat. She was driving slowly away when she saw Jack running after her, waving his arms, Boots at his heels. She stopped and backed up, rolling down the window. Gasping, he leaned on the door frame to help catch his breath.

"What is it?"

"I just want you to know, you don't have to make up these excuses to see me!" She laughed, and he started jogging back toward the track. Travis Gates had been watching and walked toward him with that rocking amble women always fell for. "You better stay away from them dangerous-type women," he advised.

"Unfortunately, they seem to stay away from me," said Jack. They hunched their shoulders against the cold, walking back. "Amazing she's on the loose so long," said Travis. "Four years? Five?"

"Yeah. Amazing."

"Some folks say she never got over Billy Fiske."

"Don't believe everything you hear." Wishful thinking?

The field house was overly warm, the windows steamed. "She is one broad," said Travis. "'Course sex ain't what it used to be no matter who." He nudged Jack. "Remember the good ol' days when a shot of penicillin cured anything ailed you?"

Jack said, "I read even Koala bears have some kind of venereal disease."

"Everybody needs rubbers."

"Condoms, Travis. You got to talk polite."

"I'm just thinking about lost chances. Makes me horny. Women like her do that to you."

CHAPTER 46

AINSLEY HAD TO ADMIT HER knack for underestimating problems. Trying to increase operations at the Jam Works hadn't been as simple as she had led herself to believe. After their first full week, with workers other than just herself on hand, she felt exhausted. Nothing had gone smoothly, despite what she thought were their realistic hopes. The men, helping out temporarily, resented Irena's authority, and Ainsley had to laugh, thinking how boss-like Irena had become. Bossing must be something that came naturally, a thing lots of people liked to do. She locked up for the day and decided to look in on her grandfather, hoping it wouldn't seem she was checking on him.

The bell over the marina door chimed when she opened it, startling the napping Captain. "Just resting my eyes," he told her.

"I'm going home, Grandpa. Tomorrow is going to come too early. And the sitter is waiting."

He stretched his arms, yawning. "Maybe you just don't need to be working so hard now that Clay is wanting to make you a rich woman."

Nothing got by him. "Who told you that?"

"There's no secrets when it's got to do with money or land."

He'd caught her in a sin of omission. "I'm sorry I didn't tell you, Grandpa." She kissed his forehead. "I didn't want to upset you, and I never gave it a minute's thought afterward."

He got up from his chair and started counting the money in the day's cash box, which didn't take long. "I knew you wouldn't do it without telling me." He turned away, looking embarrassed.

"Right," she chided, with all the sarcasm she could muster. "Grandpa, with the money from this store and the Jam Works, they're going to have to open another bank around here." She lifted the cash box as if weighing it, raising her eyebrows in approval. "Not bad."

"Right," doing it back at her.

She laid her arm across his shoulder. "Besides, I have bigger things to think about. What am I going to wear to the Speed Weeks dance? How should I fix my hair?" Then, turning serious, she told him, "Don't think I'm not worried: taxes up, and the groves…"

He wasn't sure whether he wanted her to worry or not. With the shrimper sold and the orange crop half gone, there was only the marina and Ainsley's driftwood souvenirs to pay the bills. Land poor. Just a few years ago, even with the shrimp business thriving, he'd been forced to sell off beachfront to Jack just to keep up. "You get on home now. It's getting dark," he told her. "We'll figure it out tomorrow." She grabbed a chocolate bar from the display and waved it at him so he'd notice. He said, "Keep that up and you won't fit into your Speed Weeks dress. And don't think you can come by eating up my profits and checking on me all the time either."

After he saw lights go on in Ainsley's kitchen, he sat down in his easy chair again, to watch the sun as it began to set over the river. Winter sunsets, 'way south on the horizon, were the most vivid, sunsets he'd been watching all his life. Beyond the mullioned windows of the bait shop, the stand of cabbage palms was still going strong. They were poor relations to the coconut palms of Miami, and the Royal Palms lining the boulevards of Palm Beach, but he loved them. His father used to compare the O'Rourkes to cabbage palms – durable, determined, and plain. Now, he wondered about the durable part.

Soon after arriving in St. Christie's, his family had begun clearing cabbage palms and scrub palmetto to make a place for their new house. "Just enough so as not to be a disturbance," his father had cautioned, wanting to fit into the scheme of things, like an uninvited relative who hopes to go unnoticed. In the long-ago, the island had been a volcanic mountain where saber-toothed tigers had hunted. The wildness of Florida was what he loved best, the part most people didn't know existed.

His parents had moved to Florida from Michigan in 1915, lured by the building and land boom. He was Little Frank then, just seven years old, but he remembered it still. Back North, his father had been a finish carpenter and had worked on some of the famous homes in Detroit, mansions owned by the industrialists and auto magnates. His father had told them that Mr. Henry Ford and his gang were no more special than anybody else, as far he could tell, and that he, Patrick O'Rourke, had just as much chance to make a fortune as they did. Relying on that notion, he had packed their few belongings and his carpenter tools, and he and Kate and Frank had set out for Palm Beach on Mr. Henry Flagler's railroad train. There was plenty of work for skilled craftsmen in those days. The Mellons, the Rockefellers and all their rich society cronies were determined to drain the Florida swamps, conquer the mosquito, and multiply their millions of dollars like the loaves and fishes.

Patrick worked on one hotel and private mansion after another, and the future seemed to hold all the promise they'd dreamed of. Each week, his father and mother would sit at the kitchen table and, by the light of a kerosene lamp, divide the week's earnings into small piles, the largest of which was their savings. Kate had a kitchen garden, with a patch of rhubarb and cabbages to remind her of her girlhood home in Mayo County, Ireland. What clothes they had, she made on the White sewing machine, carried with pride from Michigan.

In no time, they saw their riches stacked high, little mountains of wealth that grew taller each month. Young Frank watched as they counted out the money each week, and his mother would enter the amounts into her ledger. She liked telling her dreams to her young son, not thinking he truly understood or would remember. In her daydreams, Kate imagined herself in a dress of pale blue silk, her husband and son beside her as they walked down the center aisle of St. Agatha's Church, everyone's eyes upon them. What would Father Donnely say of such sinful pride? And yes, she wished for a bit of luxury in the present too. "Could we not buy fabric for new curtains?" she every so often asked her husband.

"Aye. You can have your new curtains, Love. But not yet," he would tell her. As Kate had discovered, Patrick had a sweet Irish way of saying no. As their money grew, hiding places within the rented cottage became scarce. Kate loved knowing the money was nearby as she worked, feeling a stab of joy when she reached under the linens and struck the thick stacks of bills, bound together with string. When she placed the freshly laundered pillow slips in the linen press, she always paused to let her fingers hunt beneath the heavy rows of fabric for the treasure she and Patrick had buried there.

At night, while eating their potatoes and boiled ham, Patrick would describe the homes he was helping to build for the ladies and gentlemen who would arrive to inspect them, dressed in their fine clothes and driving their new automobiles. "That's us one day," he told her.

"You're getting too big for your britches," Kate cautioned.

"Then it's new britches I'll be needin'," he joked. "Some day, Kate, *you'll* be ridin' in one of those automobiles, and everyone in the county will be staring at you and Frank."

"Get on with you." She slapped him lightly with her apron, dreaming along.

It was 1925, and there was a fever, a land fever. Henry Flagler's grand railroad to Key West had only been the beginning. Florida was booming with railroads crisscrossing east to west, a state highway system, and even a radio broadcasting station. In Miami, Carl Fisher had dredged sand from the bottom of Biscayne Bay and created a tropical paradise. George Merrick was building a fantasy city in Coral Gables, and everywhere, men were turning themselves into millionaires overnight.

Kate knew it was only a matter time until she would set her table with the strawberries and racks of lamb pictured in magazines instead of their usual fare of potatoes and cabbage, a time when Patrick would never again wear mended socks. Even young Frank, now seventeen, was bringing in money, working on boats at the marina and contributing to the household funds and to their savings. Kate's dreams were as fragile, but real, as the eggs she gathered in her apron each morning. It was with these thoughts that she went about her tasks that day: weeding the garden, putting the ham bones on the stove to simmer, boiling the linens, setting Frank to his reading.

Afterward, she could not explain what had prompted it, but as she drank her afternoon tea, an impulse drove her from her chair to the linen press, their finest piece. The mahogany wood, with its brass fittings, showed not one fingerprint as the light glanced over its face. It was as it always had been, when Kate slid open the heavy, top drawer. In neat stacks, tablecloths and lace-edged pillow slips handed down by her's and Patrick's mother and aunts, pressed down on all the others stacked below.

She felt guilty, like a miser about to count his riches as she slid her hand under the bottom-most fold. Then her hands froze. Her fingers found only smooth, varnished wood, not the usual stacks of money, counted, bundled, and tied with white string in a bow. Droplets of sweat rose at the back of her neck and her spine stiffened as if someone had plunged a long, thin pick into it. Now frantic, her hands were marauding through the linens, uncovering, sifting and re-sifting, and finally, casting the table linens, napkins, sheets and pillow slips on the floor, first shaking each one and finding nothing.

Their money was gone.

Ten years were gone and it seemed her life was gone with them. "Mary Mother of God," she murmured. Frank heard his mother weeping, went to her side, and placed a son's loving hand on her shoulder.

CHAPTER 47

WHEN THE COTTAGE CAME INTO Patrick's view that evening, he sensed something was wrong. Why wasn't Kate standing in the doorway as she always was, urging him to hurry over the bit that separated them? He quickened his pace, the flimsy trousers flapping about his thin legs, his black hair falling into his eyes. "Kate! Frank!"

He found her sitting in the chair rocking, her arms crossed tightly in front of her waist, a low, keening moan rising in the air. "Kate, my God. What's wrong?" No sooner were the words on his lips, but he saw the open cupboard, the scattered linens. "Kate!" And he knelt beside her. "It's all right!" taking her in his arms, whispering as if she were a child. "Don't worry, darlin', don't." Then, as she began to understand what her husband was saying, her grief turned to disbelief. "You did this?"

Sheepish, he hung his head, the thin neck forlorn within a collar meant for a man of more size. "I was meanin to tell you." He tightened his hold. "It's wonderful news, Kate. We're going to be rich, I swear it!" Frank tried to make himself small in the corner. His mother's voice had a tone he had never heard before. "You took the money and you didn't ask me? You didn't even *tell* me?" Her voice sounded big in the little room, like an echo.

Patrick laughed nervously. "Kate, I only meant it for a surprise."

"A surprise? How could you dare surprise me when it was *my* money, too?"

"*Your* money?" He could not believe what he was hearing. How could it be *her* money? Was it not he, Patrick O'Rourke, who reached his fist into the back pocket of his trousers every Friday and produced the dollars to pay for their food and shelter? And was it not *she*, Kate O'Rourke, who praised him and thanked the saints for sending her such a good provider? "You've gone daft."

"Daft am I?" She was standing with her fists in tight balls on her hips, her arms in wings, as if to fly at him.

"Darlin'," he joked nervously, "don't get your Irish up until I explain."

"If it's not my money too, you needn't explain." And she stomped out the door and didn't return until morning. Morning! Nor would she allow him to explain his actions in the months and years that followed. Each time he tried to tell her about the investments, she walked away. Each time he exclaimed how much more their money was worth, she turned her back and left the room. A distant politeness had crept into her, like dampness on a fog.

When Patrick heaped his wages in the center of the table, she refused to touch them, even with her eyes. She would not allow the money in her linen closets, under her pillows or in her cupboards. And so he put it in the bank as he had always wanted to do, together with the neat pile of stock certificates, which grew thicker each month. Patrick truly possessed the luck of the Irish. Hurricanes slashed through Florida in 1926, and again in 1928, destroying lives and property, but Patrick's holdings went unscathed. Now, he had money for the car and the home they had always wanted. Kate could not stop him from buying what he wanted. If only Mr. Henry Ford could see him now! His happiness was contagious, and their love for each other and their son so real, that in time a truce was made between them. Again and again, Patrick had tried to justify, with the stock market rising daily, what he had done, but Kate refused to listen.

"Your stubbornness is sinful," he warned.

She feared he was right. It was a sin because Frank, now grown to a man himself, listened and understood, and also because Patrick deserved to be forgiven. And so, over time, she relented, but Patrick knew she didn't believe herself the full partner she once had been in their marriage. "I have my *own* financial affairs," she would say, and he never knew if she were serious, so he tried not to laugh. There was a bit of money from the garden, eggs and jams, which he was sure she saved, but there could be little beyond that. He thought better than to tease her, or to go near the linen press, but he wondered.

When the banks failed. When stock market and land millionaires made bonfires of their paper profits. When the Depression came rolling in like a fast freighter on Mr. Flagler's railway, Kate O'Rourke continued tending to her family and her garden as she always had, but Frank knew her heart was filled with sadness as she watched him and his father trudge off daily to find work, any work.

1930. As fast as they had become rich, they were poor again. Fifteen years gone. Patrick counted up the losses. Frank was 21 years old and ready for a life of his own. Kate 40, and he was 42. Everything he had worked for and saved for was gone. The house. The car. For food, they relied on their garden, the ocean and the river. He looked at his worn shoes, the empty cupboards, his wife's thin body and blamed himself. God knows, he and Frank had tried to find work at any wage, but there was none to be had. Kate had taken in sewing and paid washing, and it shamed him to see the wicker baskets standing in the corner, filled with freshly laundered and folded clothes meant for homes with better providers. It was time to go back north and throw themselves on the mercy of family, like flotsam left behind on a Florida tide. "I need to talk to you," he told her one night.

After the kitchen was swept and the dishes washed, she found him sitting on the porch swing, his feet pushing off against the rail, the rusted chain squeaking, Patrick lost in thought. It was night, but the heat still burned like a hot mosquito bite. Patrick patted the spot beside himself, and she sat down, resting her head on his shoulder. He spoke softly. "I decided, Kate, we're going back to Detroit. Family will take us in for a while."

She studied his face, the lines etched from nose to mouth, the clenched jaw, his dark hair now streaked with gray. "I'm not going back. Florida is my home."

He didn't seem to hear her. "I wanted too much. I'm sorry for that."

"I'm not going back," she said again.

He stopped swinging. First a man loses his money, then his pride, but he had never thought to lose his family. Nor would he. "You're my wife, Kate, and being as you are, you'll do what I tell you." The words didn't match the look in his eyes.

"You never learn, do you, Patrick?"

"God made the rules, not me, Kate. If you want to complain, talk to Him." Patrick knew God would back him up.

"I talked to God, Patrick." She took his hand. "God says stay in Florida."

Blustering now, Patrick got to his feet. "Did God say how we're going to live, and what we're going to eat?"

"Sit down and I'll tell you." She reached up and pulled him beside her. "God said this: 'Kate and Patrick O'Rourke are going to live in St. Christie's Island.' "

"Did He now?"

"Aye. On their own land, purchased for next to nothing by Kate O'Rourke, with her own money." He thought it must be a joke, but her expression told him otherwise. His head dropped in shame, but Kate put her arms around him and rested her cheek on his back. "God warned me about this, Patrick. He said to tell you that a woman has pride too – but to know, in the end, all blessings come from Him. And He reminded me, that whatever you did before, it was never with a mind to hurt me."

He could hardly believe any of it. First shame. Now this: St. Christie's, a place for her, and him, and Frank, and any and all O'Rourkes to come. Yet, he hung his head.

"God also reminded me that it's been you, Patrick, working whether sick or well every day in the heat and cold, putting food on the table all these years, putting clothes on our backs, and protecting and loving us as well as any man ever could. The rest is up to you now, Patrick." They put their arms around each other, and in the distance, the bullfrogs sang.

❧

Their land curved to the north in a sheltering arc. The southernmost point marked the tip of the barrier island that was St. Christie's, situated at the inlet that led from the river to the open sea. Stands of sea oats anchored the dunes and the fine white sand that held together so tightly it could be driven on by automobiles.

Kate walked barefoot over the dune, keeping an eye out for the round sand spurs that could embed themselves and cut like a razor. A one-room cottage sat there now, but their permanent home would hug the top of the rise. Patrick, Frank and she would build it with their own hands, from coquina rock, palmetto logs, Florida pine and ocean salvage. It would be what people called a cracker house, the kind built by the first settlers, with wide doorways and verandas and big, low windows double hung to let cool air in at the bottom and hot air out at the top.

"Every room is going to have cross ventilation," said Patrick. "That's how the rich people do it, and God knows I've built enough of their houses to know." A broad roof overhang would allow the windows to remain open even in heavy rainstorms. In time, a reflective tin roof would shield the porches east and west, but their first roof would be made of overlapping palmetto fans. "This is a natural Florida house," said Patrick. "The air flows right through it like a chimney." With a stick, he sketched his plan in the sand so they could see how the center hall and stairway would draw air up through the house. An inside room on the second floor would be a refuge from floods and storms.

This is the room I want," said Frank, his finger pointing to the sand picture. It was the space at the top of the house, high-ceilinged like all the others, but directly under the roof.. Frank, twenty-two, wouldn't live there for long. He had his heart set on someone and had already picked out a clearing nearer to the river where he could build a place of his own some day, and a small marina. Kate was planning a house that would resemble the Greek Revival homes that were popular near Pensacola, true plantation houses over there, some with tall, fluted columns. "And we'll plant more trees," she said, hardwoods to shelter and cool the west side in summer and allow it to heat up in winter when the leaves dropped. Inside, the house would be warm and plain.

237

Patrick wanted a room "big enough to hold everyone we know," an open hearth, high and timbered ceilings, a kitchen floor of red glazed brick. And it would be theirs forever.

Forever… A dog was barking somewhere, barking and startling the Captain who sat dozing in his chair, stirring him from his dream of the past, and for a moment he didn't know where he was. He woke just in time to see the sun's after-light silhouetting the cabbage palms as it faded from the sky.

CHAPTER 48

"ARE YOU TRYING TO KILL us again?"

"When did I try to kill you before?"

Clay was driving too fast, showing his childish frustration. "For God's sake, slow down!" cried Lady. Already, the evening was going badly. She closed her eyes as he sped around a corner, throwing her hard against the door. By the time they got to the Speed Weeks Dance she'd be a wreck. When he finally let up on the gas, she sat motionless and silent, punishing him. "I'm not doing your dirty work with Jack Henderson," she said. "I'm not."

"C'mon, honey. You're much more persuasive than I am. Dance with him, rub those tits up against him."

"Clay! Besides, Jack and Ainsley both said no, they're not going to sell you their land."

"Do you know how many "no's" it takes before you get to a "yes"? That was just one try, one no. Of course, sweetheart, you never said no to me the first time, did you?"

"Because you are so irresistible."

"Now, about Jack: I'd do it for *you*." Even to his own ears, it sounded like a lie. He placed his hand between her legs. "You can soften him up." Lady smoothed her dress, and breathed deeply. Long ago, she had realized her husband would use anyone to get what he wanted, especially herself. When he wanted to, Clay could be charming.

"All right," giving in as she knew she would.

He looked at her approvingly and inched his hand higher. On the outside, his wife was still a seductive package at fifty-one, with her slim figure, her silky blonde hair twisted in a bun. She wore a dress brought back from Palm Beach, ivory satin on top with long, tight sleeves, fastened with emerald and diamond links he had bought for her in Bogota. The top was cut low, with patch pockets over each breast, the satin giving off highlights that danced up and down as she breathed. The skirt was emerald green satin, tight and deeply slit. "You look very fuckable tonight," he told her "Every man will want to spread these legs," and he tucked his fingers inside her panties. Lady was a fool for compliments, even crude ones, and her expression brightened. Clay relaxed into the leather seat, smiling. He'd talk with Ainsley again too, the perfect time to re-open that door.

The parking lot was almost full when they arrived. The valet attendant's nose was red from the cold and already he looked tired. As the front door was opened and closed, they heard a hum of conversation from the main ballroom, underscored by Latin music. Lady braced herself for another evening among the social elite of St. Christie's Island. Doubtless, she was the social leader, but she always wished she had a larger arena – not Palm Beach, that was too high up and she'd go unnoticed there – but perhaps Charleston, her family home, which she still thought of nostalgically.

If there were a hub to the town's social life, The Westbrook Country Club was it, even though, technically, it was situated on the outskirts and not in St. Christie's at all. Its membership was comprised not only of the affluent, but the powerful, if local people could even be viewed in such terms. At times, Lady was tempted to show her contempt for such nonsense, but wisely refrained. There were two other clubs in Halifax County, the newest of which was the Beach Club, mainly comprised of young families. The oldest and best-established was simply called The Country Club, and numbered among its members the older, more wealthy residents of the county. But it was much farther away and the men, although richer there, were not nearly as handsome, nor were the women as young or charming as those at the Westbrook. The DeWitts belonged to both.

The building had once been the mansion of Wesley Westbrook, whose family had made its money in railroads and banking. Later, he set his sights on other goals, and being pragmatic, had then decided to become respectable and loved. Old Westbrook had built the mansion as his winter home, and then bequeathed it to the town that had never truly accepted him. Even yet, old-timers liked to brag that the strange New Yorker, with his sharp accent and funny knickerbockers, had never made the social grade locally, never mind that he was listed in The Social Register. Imagine, looking down upon the mighty!

Later, when the town tried to sell the mansion, litigation was brought by Westbrook's heirs, who rightly claimed that the club wasn't even situated in St. Christie's. Eventually, the county won permission to dispose of the property, and sold it under questionable terms to a group of businessmen who promptly converted it: first into a speakeasy, and then into a tennis club, in 1935. Various other groups had owned it since, but it seemed secure in its present incarnation, prospering because of its membership, and also because no other local club could claim a golf course designed by Robert Trent Jones II.

Over the years, Halifax County had grown with an influx of retirees from the smokestack cities of the east and Midwest, land developers and drifters, retail business owners, and the usual number of competent but undistinguished professionals: doctors, attorneys, dentists, and college professors. Some, from all strata, had settled in St. Christie's and were considered intellectuals, including those who seldom thought about anything more taxing than taxes, or their golf scores.

Lady recalled her first introduction to the local social scene: not like Charleston in the old days, when her family had entertained Washington bigwigs, industrialists, and world-acclaimed artists and writers. Clay had warned her not to be patronizing. In St. Christie's you played by the rules or you didn't play at all. Wesley Westbrook was a prime example. His triumphs may have been chronicled in The New York Times, but he had seldom been mentioned in The Island News. Nor was he ever invited to become a member of The Country Club, the only club existing in his day. Lady DeWitt had no intention of learning the social lesson taught so vividly to Mr. Westbrook, to punish him for being from New York, and being 'way beyond comfortable.

Clay and Lady entered the club just as the Captain and Ainsley were arriving, but after quick greetings they broke apart and went their separate ways. Whenever Ainsley was a guest there, The Westbrook never failed to invoke a sense of history, rooted in everything from its soaring arches and thick, stucco walls, to the ornate floor, set with red, gold and black Moorish tiles. Even the menu, which remained the same year after year, was somehow comforting in its staid reliability. As a former Speed Weeks Queen, she treasured the invitation she and her family received every year. Her mother also received a yearly invitation, but often tossed it in the trash unopened.

The building was a replica of a castle in Barcelona. When it was built in 1917, it had cost an unheard of five million dollars. Inside, it was a kaleidoscope of color, sound, and the mingling fragrance of flowers and expensive perfumes. The Captain nudged Ainsley and said he was going to find Phoebe, first saying hello to Jack Henderson, who was coming around the corner, looking debonair in his tuxedo.

"Hey," was his greeting, and he left it to his expression to say the rest.

"Hey yourself."

She knew she looked her best, with her hair pulled high in the back, caught in a clip of confederate jasmine, her dress a white shimmer, close fitting and dipping low in back. Even so, he always made her feel self-conscious. "I was hoping you'd be here," she said. "I need to talk to you for just a minute if you don't mind mixing business with pleasure."

"With you, it's always a pleasure."

Could he ever be serious? "Now?" she asked.

"Fine." He took her hand, and she didn't know what to do about it.

They circled the perimeter of the candlelit ballroom, nodding to friends on both sides, Ainsley taking social inventory as they went. It seemed almost everyone had somehow managed an invitation. The Buelles were there, down from Augusta with their niece. Nearby and looking happy were Joe and Helen Todd, reconciled after their split, but everyone knew his girlfriend still drove by the house at all hours.

Jack stopped to let a waiter pass.

Nick and Beth were slow dancing, looking glamorous and happy. Who would ever guess the truth? She'd lost five pounds. Tim Avery and Cora McKennack were showing off her engagement ring, even though everyone said the romance had already cooled. "Ainsley Quinn!" Debbie Mack caught her in an embrace. People still remembered that Debbie had had to drop out her senior year, even though she had since married and had a sweet little girl. And over there were the Vitantonios, back on the island to stay this time. Vickie and Charlie Portman were at a long table near the dance floor, with places saved for Ainsley, the Captain and Phoebe. Tupper was with them, being extra-attentive to his new girl, who he said had posed for Playboy.

In one corner, the boys from Duke clustered together – Tim and Erica Cornell (who was a Byron from Atlanta), Wood and Holly Skinner, just back from Gstaad, and her with a terrible cold, and Paddy and Kitt Hepler who were building that house with the towers. Ainsley's parents were sitting next to the Heplers, and Grace blew a kiss their way. Jack picked off two flutes from the server and held them overhead as they squeezed around the perimeter of the dance floor.

"Hey, watch where you're goin', you big elephant!" Tupper and his girl were on the floor now, but when Tupper dropped her hand, the un-moored beauty pressed her breast against his arm, making a claim. He rewarded her with a kiss on the lips, and whirled her away, his hand at the small of her back, making her skirt ride up high on her pretty thighs. Something for everyone to remember tomorrow.

Jack led the way to a small vacant room adjoining the lobby. He nudged the door closed with his foot and a blissful quiet enveloped them. He handed her a glass and they each took a long drink of Champagne. "Now I know how a salmon feels fighting upstream," said Ainsley, sinking into the old leather sofa. The room had high, coffered ceilings of hand-carved walnut, and dentil molding that framed a gilded painting of cherubs in the center. Three of the walls were paneled, and the fourth was dominated by a fireplace with a marble surround, where a small fire of fragrant cedar had been lit, its flames reflected on the walls.

Jack reached across Ainsley to set his glass next to hers on a small table at the far side of the sofa, and as he did, he was poised directly over her, attracted as always by the blaze of indigo in her eyes. He bent down, and as if he'd done it a hundred times before, because in his mind he had, he kissed her. When she tried gently to push him away, he drew her closer, the jasmine in her hair perfuming everything, and then she was kissing him back, parting her lips.

It didn't last. The next moment, she was shoving him away. "Stop it, Jack!"

He let go, half smiling. "Okay."

"You caught me off guard."

"Seemed like you participated some." He was leaning back in the soft cushions, annoyingly confident. "After you got to liking it, that is."

"I didn't." She struggled to rise, but the sofa was low and soft, the cherrywood floor waxed, her shoes new, and she slipped back beside him.

"Oooh!" he yelled, faking. "I think I'm injured here." He tried to help her up but she slapped his hand away.

"If you don't want to be kissed, you've got to stop throwing yourself at me."

She struggled to her feet. "They should outlaw these sofas."

Jack folded his arms behind his head. "I'll take care of it." As she turned away, he called: "What about our little talk?" Ainsley tried to slam the door behind her, but instead of banging shut as she had intended, it closed slowly, politely, on its heavy brass hinges.

In the ballroom, she smoothed her dress. That Jack! He thought himself irresistible, and had probably had a few drinks. She joined Beth at their table, happy that Nick had wandered off to find a waiter.

When Billy and his wife entered the ballroom, there was no way Ainsley could avoid looking at them. They were on the second-floor landing overlooking the ballroom where the twin staircases joined. A Waterford chandelier was centered there, shooting light, making the pink beads of Lorraine's dress sparkle, and her dark hair look like a ribbon of silk. Her earrings swung invitingly, nearly brushing her olive shoulders, and that was all Ainsley saw, as the crowd closed in around them. She thought, After all this time, I ought to be over it. Over *him*. It always surprised her that she wasn't, not quite.

CHAPTER 49

FROM THE START, AINSLEY'S AND Billy's romance had achieved a minor folk status – two young people with so much promise, then her broken heart, then Billy's disappointments as a driver – and then whatever people chose to think, a love story with a sad ending, the kind that most liked best, and remembered.

Seeing Billy and his wife now, Ainsley wondered, Is he happy? He'd never won the Daytona 500, and although he was a talented driver, he was becoming one of the pack. Lights were shining on new, younger men, but in St. Christie's, Billy was still king. He certainly had changed her life, had sent her rushing into Bear's arms, and now Bear was gone too, but she didn't blame Billy for that. Was it chance or was it fate that had brought them together under a big white tent after a day of racing? Ainsley would have said chance, because she couldn't believe some unseen force controlled her life, or agree when people said, "It was meant to be." If so, God was the world's foremost meddler, everything pre-ordained, with people having no control over their own lives. To choose chance, however, was to believe that life's most important events were meaningless accidents. Neither theory was acceptable. Was it chance that at this very moment Lorraine and Billy were dancing in her direction? and that even now, heads turned, first to look at him, then to glance furtively at her? Memories were long on the island.

"May I?" Startled, Ainsley looked up to see Clay extending a hand, inviting her to dance, a surprise, considering their last encounter. She stepped forward, and he led her to the center of the floor. For a man of apparent sophistication, his dancing was always self-conscious and awkward, making her wonder if this, too, were some sort of ruse. In contrast, Jack was on the floor too, smiling confidently at a girl she didn't recognize.

"I've been meaning to stop back to see you," Clay told her. "Sorry about our little tussle."

Rather than make it easy, she'd let him take the lead. After all, Clay never made things easy for anyone else. Despite that, people always seemed to fall for his ways, forgive and forget.

"About the land, have you had a chance to re-think it?" He was smiling, inflicting more than enough charm for one night, but when she failed to answer fast enough, he pressed on, impatient as ever. "Did you think to talk it over with your grandfather?" Feeling power over Clay was new to her, his pushy confidence so intimidating, but in this moment, she felt surprisingly at ease. Let him chafe a little.

"I know this will disappoint you," she began, and a chilly detachment crept into his eyes as he anticipated what was coming. "I'm sorry, Clay, but I thought my feelings were clear. I'm not going to sell, I can't." She almost felt bad for him, but he only shrugged, as if it didn't matter. By the time the music ended, the cold and abusive Clay she had seen so often in his dealings with Bear was there again, just below the surface.

A succession of partners presented themselves, and now Billy and Lorraine were dancing nearby, her hand draped across his back, her rings catching the light. In that huge ballroom, there was not one empty space to accommodate Ainsley's gaze. She wished she were dancing with a husband of her own instead of the stranger who held her. Billy didn't seem aware that she was close enough to touch. He was compact and muscular, and like the cars he drove around the track, there was not one unnecessary part to him. His sandy hair was abundant but unremarkable. His features went to no extra trouble to be either handsome or plain. His movements were direct and purposeful, unchanged since she had first known him, and all of it was appealing still. Billy spun away without a glance.

Her mood changed then, and the evening ahead looked endless, with all the traditional and party dances to come: the Conga, the Hokey Pokey, and all the tedious others still to be endured. But then her glance fell on the people sitting along the walls, the old and crippled with their walkers and oxygen; the no-longer young in their frumpy dresses, not even making an effort anymore; the alone, and worst of all, the forgotten men and women, pretending they mattered to someone still. She smiled at her partner, ashamed. "It's a lovely party," she told him, and he squeezed her hand. At nine o'clock a rock band took the stage, the sound system blasting louder than ever. Busboys were dismantling the buffet table, which was a shambles of wilted lettuce, half-empty serving trays and an ice sculpture of a race car partly melted, as if it had been in a wreck.

At the far end of the room, Lady could not wait to get home, but she still hadn't talked to Jack Henderson, who seemed to have disappeared.

On the staircase landing above the ballroom floor, a sudden commotion drew her attention and everyone else's to a man, quite drunk, who sat precariously on the railing singing off-key but loudly, as if to compensate. Someone equally drunk called out: "Tupper, you celebrating' getting your wick dipped, or what?" The onlookers gasped, giggling. Tupper was drunk, but they always overlooked it, because of his family you know, but such language! Another heckler responded: "Tupper ain't got a wick, he wore it out."

Tupper looked down, pointing. "Hey, it's our hero!" Billy Fiske was standing where Tupper aimed his gaze on the floor below, between the curving staircases. Billy, an arm's length away from Ainsley, called out: "Let it rest, okay?" Tupper waved, nodded and started to climb down and everyone took a deep breath. Billy looked past Ainsley, then back again, and for the first time, acknowledged seeing her. He shook his head in disbelief of Tupper and smiled. Lorraine was nowhere in sight.

He took a few steps closer. "May I?" opening his arms.

His formality and politeness, his lack of presumption or hint of previous intimacy, filled her with an unwanted warmth. She hesitated, but when he lowered his head and lifted only his eyes to meet hers, she let him take her hand. A slow dance, at last. He pulled her close, and his body felt just as familiar as it once had been – his calloused hand, the touch of his faintly whiskered cheek against hers, the scent of his cologne, as they barely moved to some unknown song. It was as if the universe was spinning in perfect synchrony. She thought, fate is too important a word for ordinary people like us, and I don't believe in fate anyway, but what other word was there? And she knew no good could come of it.

Lady found Jack talking with a group on the glassed-in terrace, where candles glowed inside cut-crystal hurricane lamps, casting starry shafts of light. The circle opened to include her and she joined in easily, the way attractive women usually do: her opinions sought after and carefully considered. Skillfully, she soon drew Jack aside, talking first about the party, then about the freeze, nodding, making her voice sympathetic.

"I thought we were here to have a good time," he joked.

"I'm interested, that's all." She feigned hurt, knowing her status and beauty made it difficult for men, even younger men like Jack, to object to anything she might do. Except Clay. "It amazes me sometimes that you growers can keep on," saying it in her most caring, Southern lady way.

"Clay knows. Sometimes we can't." From his expression, it was apparent that her interest was having an effect; every man wanted a woman to be concerned about him.

She pressed his arm gently. "If there's anything Clay or I can do, you let us know."

"Thank you. I appreciate that." She wondered, would that be enough effort to satisfy Clay? Of course not, so she pressed on. "Clay's keen on a piece of property you own. Did he tell you that?" — as if she and Clay hadn't discussed it, who would believe that?

He looked surprised. "He did. But I'm going to hold on long as I can." She nodded and looked away, too exhausted to persist, yet knowing that Clay would make her repeat every word, describe every gesture, every nuance in Jack's voice and manner, and she would have to endure it. She kissed his cheek. "You should, Jack." Lady patted his arm as she turned to leave, and the circle of guests opened again to include him.

The musicians had stopped playing and were loading their equipment out through the rear doors. Lights were up bright to discourage people from lingering, and the club manager seemed to be cursing as he toed the carved Oriental carpet where the skeleton of a cigarette ash lay. Over the door, a drooping paper sign read, "Welcome Speed Weeks Boosters," put up by the ladies' committee. Everything about the room looked suddenly shabby. The Captain had just said goodbye to Phoebe, whose ride was waiting, and now he stood at Ainsley's side. "Hon. Let's go." Only a handful of guests remained, plus a small cleaning crew: a wizened man, pushing a long-handled broom around the carpet's perimeter, and a few busboys pulling down decorations. They had already stacked most of the chairs upside-down on the tables, making the room look as if it were inhabited by rows of giant palmetto bugs on their backs. She and the Captain were walking to the cloak room when he said, "I seen you dancing with Billy."

"Don't worry, Grandpa," reading his mind. She helped him into his coat, holding it low as if it were shrugging, maybe mirroring her grandfather's fears that something might start up again with Billy.

It was midnight when Lady kicked off her shoes inside her bedroom door. The party had been exhausting, but she knew Clay would be stimulated as he always was after a night out. Quickly she undressed and stepped into the shower, turning the water to cool in order to wake up for him. In the adjoining dressing room, Clay was noisily opening and closing drawers in his usual careless way.

"How do you think it went?" he called.

She leaned her head against the tile, exhausted. "Wonderful. I think everyone had a good time."

"Did *you*?" he yelled.

"Of course." He didn't like it when she belittled St. Christie's. Like other men she knew, he considered it a personal affront if she didn't enjoy herself when she was with him. Not that he cared, not really. A draft of cold air hit her as Clay opened the shower door and stepped in beside her.

"God, that water's cold!" he cried, and immediately turned it up hot. Chin raised, he closed his eyes and stood motionless beneath the pulsing jets that spouted from six directions. The steam rose in a cloud, and the scent of Lady's freesia soap surrounded them. She opened the door to leave, but he caught her arm, pulling her back inside. "Not so fast," and she felt his softness pressing against her body. How old he seemed, his skin loose and sallow, his penis vulnerable and foolish in its impatience. In the growing heaviness of the air, she raised her hips as he grasped her buttocks in that mean way of his, and Lady did what she knew she must. In a few minutes, her head would be cradled on her pillow.

Clay woke first to a bright morning, sunny but freezing. All the out-of-town yo-yos would be at the races for the time-trials, half-dressed in their T-shirts and cut-offs. Lady was asleep in a curl, her arms flung toward the headboard, as if she were thirty years younger and a cheerleader caught mid-leap. He pulled back the covers, her chest rising and falling against her lace gown. He'd often seen men's open envy of him when they looked at her, but all he felt was irritated. Her eyes slit open. "What are you doing? pulling the blanket up tight to her chin.

"Time to wake up." When Clay was up, everyone was up. He had things to do, since neither Jack nor Ainsley was open to his offers.

CHAPTER 50

SOMEWHERE BETWEEN SLEEPING AND WAKING, Ainsley was dancing with Billy, then being pulled away by someone else. And bells were ringing… bells… and in a moment she was fully awake, putting on her terry cloth robe as she rushed downstairs. Beth was shivering on the landing and carrying a flat white box and her leather portfolio.

"I come bearing gifts," she said, handing a box of donuts to Ainsley.

"Thank you. Inside, quick, it's freezing."

"All our favorites," said Beth. "It's the least I could do, showing up the morning after," emphasizing *after*. Ainsley put on a pot of coffee while Beth re-arranged the donuts telling her, "I am only eating one, maybe two."

Ainsley brought up a chair: "About Billy…" They both laughed.

"Did I see what I think I saw?"

"No. Is that why you're here, to torment me?"

"Yes, and to show you something," nodding toward her portfolio.

"It was just a dance. He's married after all."

"Not for long, from what people were saying."

Ainsley took this in. "Should I be happy or sad? I guess I'll be sad. It's the right thing to do." She laughed and picked up a jelly donut, blowing some of the sugar in Beth's direction.

"Will you not do that?" shaking her head. "Nick humiliated me with that girl, Clarice."

Ainsley poured the coffee. "Once again, why do you stay with him?" Since her own divorce, she wondered that about a lot of people, not that she advocated mass divorce. Beth held up her hand and started ticking off reasons on her fingers. "I stay because One, money… Two, my kids… Three, noises in the night and spiders…" Throwing up her hands, she said: "I could run out of fingers, but mostly I'm afraid I'll end up like so many women we both know – oooh, excuse me!" She put her hand on Ainsley's shoulder.

"No pity, please."

Beth added more cream and stirred her coffee. "When I see groups of women out everywhere together, I wonder whether they're happy, and I don't want that to be me."

"I know, but why do surveys show that men are happier being married than women are, and that women leave their spouses far more often than men do?"

"Because," said Beth, "men want to have a guaranteed screw within arm's reach at all times. And I wonder," she said, "don't you miss things, like having someone to eat donuts with in the morning?"

"I have you," said Ainsley, "but yes… I miss a lot of things."

"Someone to cut your grass…"

"To hold my hand…"

"To change your oil…"

"To *sleep* with me, Beth, to sleep with me!" The telephone rang and it was Grace, sounding so frantic Ainsley could hardly understand what she was saying. Her mother seemed to be choking back tears. "Ainsley," she said, "I just picked up yesterday's mail, and you'll never guess what happened…!" Crying now.

"Mom! What's wrong?"

"My chimes, Ainsley! Oh, my God! My chimes!"

"What happened to them, Mom?" Ainsley shrugged at Beth, who had no idea what was going on.

"My bells – chimes!" said Grace, a little calmer now, "have been accepted for a show at the American Craft Museum in New York City!"

"Oh, my God, Mom! That's wonderful!" grinning at Beth to let her know it was okay to relax, then turning back to the phone, listening. "That's the best news, Mom!"… and listening again.

"She did what? Wait, Mom. Beth's here and I have to tell her, too." Everything Grace said, Ainsley repeated: "Phoebe had purchased one of my mother's bells, had it packed up and shipped to a museum in New York City." Nodding her head, she covered the mouthpiece and whispered to Beth: "Phoebe read about an art show open for submissions, so she sent some slides, then one of mom's thingamajigs, which is what Phoebe calls them." Then back to her mother. "Phoebe knows art, Mom, you always said so. She's seen the world's best."

"I know."

"Mom, you're an amazing artist. Did you need someone else to tell you what you've always known?" When they were about to hang up, Ainsley said, "Promise you won't get uppity now. You still have to help me with my driftwood." Then she repeated all the details to Beth, the person who would best understand what it meant.

After the cups were cleared, Beth set her portfolio on the table, pulled the heavy zipper and looked at Ainsley to make sure she had her full attention. Then she began turning pages filled with sketches of new jars, labels, packaging and displays for the Jam Works. Ainsley, after paying close attention, looked into Beth's expectant face. "I love them. I don't know what else to say." She pointed to a squat, pressed-glass jar. "It gives you a true sense of Old Florida." They looked at everything a second time, before Beth zipped the case closed.

"Come on," said Ainsley. "Now I want to show *you* something you haven't seen in a long time." She took a coat from the hook, slung it over her robe and handed Beth her jacket. Barefooted, she ran ahead to the greenhouse, where the glass was fogged and streaming. Inside, she waved her arm over rows of orange trees growing in plastic pots. "My father's work continues. Look how well these trees came through the freezes."

Beth looked dubious. "Didn't these have help, being in here?" Ignoring Ainsley's frown, she persisted: "How are the actual groves doing?"

"We won't know for sure until summer," she admitted, "but in fact, I'm going to look things over with Jack tomorrow, afraid of what we might find, of course." They arrived back at the house just as a florist was walking up the drive carrying a long white box.

"It's an epidemic of big, white boxes," said Beth. They broke into a run.

The vertical handwriting on the card was familiar: its big capital A, the deeply curved Y. Billy must have ordered the flowers in person that morning, their names, linked together once again.

Billy was lying on the sofa waiting for the telephone to ring, waiting to hear that low voice singing over the wire. And then, there it was, but he made himself wait before answering.

"Thank you for the roses." Neither knew what to say next. "Ainsley…" Just saying her name, and knowing she was hearing it, was almost enough. "I need to see you."

"Why?"

"You know why."

"I can't, Billy. You're married." Her voice caught, and he could picture her struggling to do the right thing, but it was her voice, not her words, that gave her away.

"I'm hanging up now," she said.

Then he heard the dial tone. Agnes came to his side and he closed his eyes, recalling the night before, the scent of jasmine, her skirt swaying as she moved. After all this time, it was Ainsley Quinn, still.

CHAPTER 51

ON HER WAY TO THE groves to meet Jack the next morning, Ainsley was dropping David off at Irena's cottage to play with Tina. The children, both five years old, rushed off with their tin buckets swinging to pick up acorns from the live oak trees. Jack fed them to his hogs and Ainsley to the squirrels, paying the children for their efforts. Irena, sitting on the steps, had turned on the garden hose just as Lolo came around the side of the house.

"You want a shower?" asked Irena. Playfully, she aimed the hose toward her son, but Lolo shook his head. At 16, he didn't want to be seen as his sister's playmate, but he smiled at Ainsley.

"I am cleaning up in the groves for Mr. Jack," he told her.

"Thank you; you're a good worker." He rinsed his hands, then sprayed his mother as he shook them dry.

"Stop!" she said, and rose to unpin a towel from the clothes line. "Go now. We have things to do."

Lolo had recently quit school and Ainsley knew it was no use to talk about it. The family needed the money, but more than that, Emilio wanted his son to follow in his footsteps. Long ago she had mentioned school, and remembered Emilio telling her, "I take care of my family. Is my son too good to work like me? Is he ashame?" His voice had quaked, and Ainsley wanted to take it back, meaning well, but it had turned out badly.

"Of course not," she had said. "You know I don't think that," and she had promised herself never to meddle again.

Irena had once told her that ever since childhood Emilio had known only the crops, traveling from Texas to Michigan, Wisconsin to Maine, Ohio to Florida, a never-ending cycle year after year to this day. Sometimes crops failed and there was no work. Sometimes they made only enough money to keep their truck moving from one state to the next. They had lived in shacks and sometimes in open fields. Worse, to Ainsley, they had lived without hope of anything better. It sometimes hurt Emilio,

Ainsley knew, to see his wife heading in new directions at the Jam Works. Her heart went out to him. Perhaps sensing what was on Ainsley's mind, Irena said, "Emilio and the men are meeting tonight about the work next year. They are going to join together. Organize. So things will be better. They are decide."

Like a union? That could be dangerous, but she didn't want to say it. "I'm glad, Irena. Some good might come of it." Jack had arrived, driving the old field cart.

Irena was unconsciously gathering her skirt into a knot. "I am afraid."

"I know."

"The boss at Coller Ranch, he say every penny workers want is money out of his family." Her eyes were cast down. "He say Mr. Clay will put a stop. He blame you and Mr. Jack," and she looked away, afraid at having said too much.

In the grove, the smell of rotting fruit hung in the air. Ainsley rode next to Jack in the field cart, hardly moving, her eyes sweeping the rows of trees. "All this waste, this hoping, all for nothing," she said. The trees were freeze-blackened, and a carpet of curled, brown leaves covered the ground, crunching under the cart's wheels. Six weeks had passed since their frantic efforts to save the crop, and it would be four months more before they knew the fate of the trees.

"Lolo's working and a crew will be here in the morning to help with the cleanup." He saw her brow furrow, no doubt thinking of yet more expense. "Hope for the best," he said.

"I do." She put her scuffed boots up on the faded dashboard, closed her eyes and leaned her head against the backrest. Only 10 a.m. and the sun was already hot, pouring through the open top and sides of the cart. The weather had changed overnight. Boots had been let out and was running ahead through the groves. Clumps of grass stood in brittle spikes. Spoiled, cracked fruit lay everywhere, brown spheres amid fallen, dead leaves. Flies buzzed crazily.

The buggy jerked and Ainsley opened her eyes. Jack was bending forward, his hand searching for something under the seat. "Water," he explained. She leaned back again, but could feel his eyes on her, and the drops of sweat gathering on her forehead. "Better watch out or you'll have an outbreak of freckles," he warned, still searching for the bottle, the cart still bumping along the sandy ruts.

"I wish I could still worry about things like freckles," she said. "I wonder how I arranged such a life for myself, always worried about things I have no control over."

He'd found what he wanted, and pulled out a dust-covered bottle. "Too much worry will add wrinkles to your freckles." He tried then to make his voice sound encouraging. "I like to think this freeze is just a little setback." He unscrewed the top of the water bottled and held it toward her. "Drink?"

Ainsley reached out, then pushed it away. "It's warm!"

"It's wet." He took a long drink. "Aah!" a big, satisfied sound, meant to annoy her. Again he held the bottle out to her, and she shook her head. "Suit yourself, but you're missing out on some fine germs." On a leaf-littered rise he stopped the cart and vaulted over the low door. Neither door opened since a rollover a while back, and he came around to her side, arms open to help her over the top of the frame.

"Aren't you ever going to fix these?"

"And miss my chance to assist Miss Ainsley and earn her endless gratitude?" She stood up, he took her hand, and as she stepped on top of the door frame, he leaned forward and bent her over his shoulder.

"Hey!" She pounded his back, but he held her legs tight, stumbling down a row of wasted trees, through leaves crunching underfoot, bees and flies buzzing. Finally he stopped. "You are a lot of woman. I mean that in the best way." He was panting and laughing.

"Let me down!"

He flung his arms out to his side, and she could only hold on or fall. Tightening her arms around his neck, she could feel his chest heaving, see the sweat running down his face. When the tips of her boots touched ground, she was still clinging to him. He put one hand around her waist and with his other, touched her face, running his thumb over her brow, and down across her cheek to her lips. Then he let her go, but she held onto his neck, surprising herself, and pulled his head forward and raised her mouth to his. His lips were salty from sweat, rough from the sun, and he kissed her softly, finishing something. That's what it felt like to her. They walked back to the cart, fingertips touching, not saying anything. Was it the heat, was it his kiss at the dance, or was it that she was just going a little crazy? In the cart, she reached for his hand just as he was reaching for hers, but then Boots was there, leaping into their laps, barking, ending it.

BOOK IV

CHAPTER 52

THE SUMMER AIR WAS HEAVY with thunderstorms every afternoon, signaling early stirrings in the Caribbean to worry about. Jack turned the truck's air-conditioner on high, then dialed the radio up a notch. Boots put her nose closer to the pickup's cooling vents.

He patted her head. "You're hogging all the air, kiddo." Should he turn around and go home, or continue on to the compound? Ever since that day in the groves, more than three months ago already, he couldn't decide how to act around Ainsley. It would be easy to want more than friendship. Not love, which he'd managed to avoid ever since Julia, but something else maybe. He could have put the month-end figures in the mail as usual, but here he was, and already parking.

Before he reached the door, Ainsley and David were standing on the porch waiting. Boots ran ahead and joined them. They liked to come out to greet you, never let you get to the door and collect yourself first. She was dressed in shorts and a white shirt tied above the waist. David was dressed the same, without the tied-up part. At five, he was energetic and always full of questions. Jack was relieved the Captain's truck wasn't there.

David called his name and ran across the sandy drive. Jack crouched down, lifting him up as he came hurtling into his outstretched arms. Jack held him overhead, David's legs pumping air, then set the boy on his feet. He raced back toward his mother as Jack lunged after him, ending in a roll on the scrubby grass. And then pain. Jack cried out, but Ainsley and David, thinking it was a mock injury, started laughing. Only when Jack began cursing did she run to his side.

Jack was sitting up swearing, a patch of sandspurs digging into his flesh – hundreds of pain-inflicting hooked arrowheads. Ainsley crouched next to him, cooing in her low voice, "I'm so sorry. I thought I'd gotten rid of all of them!" and led him by the elbow into the kitchen, pulling up a chair next to the window where she could see better. "Sit, and take your shirt off," she told him, but every time Jack breathed, the barbs dug deeper.

"Here, let me help," and she held the shirt away from his back while he struggled out of it. Then she collected scissors, a magnifying glass, tweezers, alcohol, and cotton swabs. David watched quietly while his mother arranged her supplies as if it were a clinic, and aimed a gooseneck lamp at Jack's back, sighing.

"Doesn't sound promising."

Methodically, she dipped the tweezers in alcohol and began pulling the sandspurs out, one by one; even the heat from the lamp was painful. "Sorry…" she said it over and over as she continued plucking and dabbing his back with alcohol. It looked as if he had been stung by a nest of fire ants. When she leaned in close, he could smell lavender soap, even felt a stray lock of hair brushing against his cheek, but it didn't help.

"How many more?"

"Not a thousand, definitely not that many."

"Very funny."

"If you stop being cranky, I'll invite you for lunch."

The smell of food had been wafting from the oven. "You notice," he said, "with the mention of lunch I've stopped complaining."

"It's meatloaf," piped David.

"What else? Smells like hoecake."

"Sweet cornbread," said Ainsley.

"Hoecake?" asked David.

"Hoecake is like cornbread but not fancied up for company. You never had it?"

"Uh-uh." David looked to be waiting for an explanation and Jack continued: "Okay, hoecake. First thing you need is a hoe or shovel," he said, "because that's what you bake it on."

Ainsley looked doubtful. "You do?"

261

"Yep. Suppose you're working in the field. You mix up your batter: corn meal, water, salt, get a good fire going, pour the corn batter on the back of a cleaned-off hoe and let 'er bake. Nothin' like it."

"Could *we*?" David asked, liking the idea.

"I don't see why not. In the old days, field hands made it, and soldiers – they used to bake it on the blades of their swords, nice, skinny little hoecakes, but you could bake it in a pan, I suppose, if you didn't have a sword handy." They were so intent on the story, they didn't hear the car drive up, and as Jack finished telling it, Billy Fiske was standing there, filling up the screen door. Not again.

"Mornin'," called Billy. "'Scuse me for eavesdropping, but I didn't want to break in on your story."

"Billy!" David ran to the door, and Billy was lifting him up high. Stealing my thing, thought Jack, minus the sandspurs.

"You must have gained ten pounds," said Billy. "How's Binky?"

"I'll go get him," and David ran up the stairs.

Jack continued to sit bare-chested as Ainsley fussed with tweezers and swabs. Billy tried to put everyone, including himself, at ease. "I see you got a mess of sandspurs."

"Teach an old hand like me to go rolling in the grass, or non-grass." David had come back, and handed Binky to Billy to hold.

"That was the last one," said Ainsley.

Jack began putting his shirt on. "I'll just get going," he said.

"Don't rush on my account," said Billy.

"Duty calls," said Jack, and he extended his hand. "Best of luck next Sunday. You ran good in the qualifying."

"Thanks," said Billy, appraising him. "We're still tinkering." He looked at Ainsley. "I just came by to talk to the Captain about my boat. Guess he's not here."

"At the marina."

"I'll head on down," but he didn't leave.

Ainsley, forgetting her promise of lunch to Jack, now seemed anxious to be rid of him. "Thanks for bringing the statement," she said, and it sounded as if she might be explaining his presence to Billy.

"And thank *you* for the torture treatment,"

Neither Jack nor Billy moved. If they were waiting each other out, it was up to Ainsley to break the standoff. "I have things to do, so – good seeing both of you."

And nobody gets meatloaf, thought Jack.

CHAPTER 53

AFTER SEEING BILLY AND AINSLEY together at the Speed Weeks dance, the Captain wasn't surprised when Billy showed up at the marina, and was glad for a reason to hurry off after just a few minutes. The hurrying was legitimate, a promise to stop by Phoebe's with some photos from the dance, including a nice one of the two of them. And he wanted to thank her in person for being so thoughtful toward Grace, sending her thingamajig off to that museum. Must've weighed a ton and cost a bundle just to ship it.

Phoebe was clipping roses when he got there and he launched right in telling her about Billy's visit. "He'll be back. Those two might still get together," he said, "especially with talk his marriage is over."

Phoebe laughed. "It would be convenient if nothing else."

"Hope not, but I'd be happy if Ainsley found somebody."

"When you're young, you think it's easy, but it's not."

He said, "Look at us, on our own so long. Of course, we've got all the time in the world." Phoebe was 73 now, he knew that, and he had her by a few extra.

"We do," she agreed, and nodded for him to follow her indoors. "What about Jack?" she asked. "I always thought they might be a match, but I guess not."

"You'd think so, but Jack and Ainsley keep their distance, and he's never made a try, not even to see a movie together." Phoebe was hunting through her cupboard for a vase.

His voice getting quiet, he asked, "Do you miss it? Being married I mean."

After just a few moments, she answered. "Yes, sometimes. You?" Having found a vase, she began filling it with water.

"Yes, but Sarah and I weren't really suited."

"I know. Don't take offense, but more than once, I wanted to tell her to wake up to what a good man she had."

He felt his color rising, the Irish curse. "You thought that?"

"Of course." She set the vase on the table, and brought glasses and a pitcher of tea, while the Captain took a seat.

"You and Mr. Moffitt were suited."

"We were."

"Never heard a word against him."

"He was good. Gave me everything, and it broke his heart he couldn't give me what I wanted most." Phoebe glanced down at her lap where her hands were clasped. "We can't have everything can we?" smiling that crooked smile. "You have a good family, Frank."

True, he thought. Sometimes family made everything else worthwhile. Other times, family made you feel swallowed up, and then guilty for thinking it. "It's the best thing ever happened to me," he told her. That, too, was true.

"Not marriage," a statement.

"No, but crazy enough, I miss it, even though I was mostly miserable." Laughing.

"You hid it well."

"No point in not. Sarah couldn't change, only a scrap of warmth in her, even for little Grace." He'd never said that to anyone before, and worried that Phoebe would think less of him, but instead, she reached over and lay her hand on top of his. A hand with tapering fingers and oval-shaped nails finished in bright pink polish. Her wedding ring, which she'd continued wearing for a number of years after being widowed, now circled the ring finger on her right hand, a wide platinum band set with small diamonds. He could imagine Phoebe telling Mr. Moffitt, "Nothing big and fancy, or I won't like it."

Her hand was still there, and he didn't know what to do. If he moved, she might think it was a signal for her to let go, or think that he didn't like it. Maybe if he put his other hand on top of hers, then let go right away, they could break apart like boxers do, no harm done. Just as he was perfecting his plan, Phoebe gave him a light pat, removed her hand and stood up. "I know it's early, but how about a real drink?" That usually meant a glass of wine, a habit Phoebe had picked up in Europe, and a custom that had lately caught on in St. Christie's. Who'd have thought it?

He followed her into the kitchen, fetched two glasses from the cupboard and set them on the table while Phoebe reached into the bottom shelf of the refrigerator. She was wearing a white cotton skirt and when she bent over, her hips seemed to bloom, as the fabric fell to the front and lifted in back, showing two good, tanned legs. She had a bottle by the neck, and still bending over, turned to raise it in the air for him to inspect, glancing back over her shoulder.

"Is this okay?" fanning it back and forth like a pendulum.

"Looks good to me," and knowing she had caught him studying her, added: "The wine, I mean."

'That's all, just the wine?" A teasing look on her face.

"Everything looks good, Phoebe." Emphasizing "everything." Good God. What must she think? She shut the refrigerator door, put the wine on the table and began rummaging for the corkscrew. It felt like some kind of chance had just passed him by.

When they had long since finished the wine, and the glasses were rinsed and drying on the rack, the Captain knew it was time to leave. Phoebe had said something about playing cards that night. He rose, slid his chair back in and plumped up the small pillow. "Time to go."

"I'll walk you out, Frank." Taking his arm, they moved toward his truck, and all of a sudden he stopped, turned to her, and placed a hand on her shoulder. "When I told you everything looks good, I meant it. Everything." She was waiting, he knew, to see if he could cross that great, empty space, vault into the unknown, and he knew that if he could just bend forward a little, if he could only remember how easily it could be done... but he couldn't, and kissed her on the cheek. Wouldn't want to risk a friendship.

Driving home, he kept rewinding that tape. Pictured Phoebe's face, the light blue eyes, the lips that he had almost kissed. And what if he had?

Chapter 54

THAT NIGHT, JACK AND TRAVIS were sitting in a far corner of the Last Chance bar. "Get a better view from here," said Travis. "Better pickin' and choosin'." The country-western band had just begun its second set. The musicians looked ready to call it a night, although it was still early and the bar was just starting to fill up. "You notice," said Travis, "how quiet it was the first set? Everybody sitting around, planning their moves?"

"I'm planning mine, right out the door," joked Jack.

"Nah. See them girls?" asked Travis. "We better say hi soon or else forget it for tonight."

"I suppose," said Jack, but he felt indifferent. He'd beat a path away from Ainsley when Billy showed up, so what was he doing here, he wondered.

One of the local men two-stepped by, giving Travis hope. "This place could prove that even God is not infallible," he said. The man's sleeveless shirt was unbuttoned all the way and flapped open to reveal a hairy belly that bobbed up and down over tight blue jeans. He wore a bola tie and a battered straw cowboy hat pushed back.

"We might have a chance after all," said Jack.

"The gals that come here, they're all right," said Travis. Jack chugged the last of the beer. "So tell me, what was the princess DeWitt doing this morning besides giving you a hard time or a hard-on?"

"A little of both."

"Brother, if you have ideas, you need to make a move. I hear Billy Fiske is split up with his wife and on the prowl again."

"I heard too. He was there. Came by."

"Oh, my man." Travis clapped Jack on the shoulder.

"Ouch, damn!"

"Sorry. You shoulda moved on her when you had the chance. Five years of chances," he reminded him. Jack nodded. That day in the groves, that was his chance, and right afterward. But taking chances had consequences.

"Hey, hey!" Travis elbowed him. "Get a loada them maracas. I am about to die!" A girl approached the dance floor alone, every man's eyes trailing her. She was about twenty, wearing scuffed white cowboy boots and a white fringed skirt that fluttered back and forth on her thighs. But what Travis liked most was her vest, brown suede and too small for the sides to meet in front, held together by leather laces that stretched across the middle, and nothing underneath.

Travis got to his feet, moving toward the girl, who was swinging her hips from side to side. Her eyes were closed and her head thrown back, long brown ringlets tumbling out of her cowboy hat. Travis drew up beside her and, without a word, circled her waist and turned her out, catching her on his other side. A nervous laugh ripped along the bar. Then he pulled her in tight, hardly moving on the tiny dance floor. "Darlin', I want to marry you," he whispered.

She looked at him with bright blue eyes. "You mean it?" letting her tongue dart out in an endearing way.

"What's your name?"

"Rickey Anne," and then she placed her hand on the back of his jeans, drawing him in closer.

"Rickey Anne, I love you more every minute." She smiled and lifted her little-girl mouth up to meet his. They danced, tongues teasing, through the end of the long number, while Travis worked his fingers up through the leather laces.

"You are so nice, Rickey Anne." Her fingers crept down his thigh, finding his crotch. When the music ended, his mind had leaped ahead. "How about you and me headin' someplace else?"

"Nah. I come to dance, hon."

Jack was watching, when suddenly Travis seemed upset and some kind of disagreement was going on. Travis was standing there, hands on hips, talking fast, his head bent forward, bobbing over the girl. She stood looking out over the room, not listening, her feet planted in her boots. Then Travis turned and stalked off the floor. He sat down in the booth shaking his head. "You are not gonna believe this, 'cause I don't." He told how Rickey Anne had refused to leave with him, and how he'd tried to grab her for the next dance. "And then, listen to this, she says, 'I don't dance with nobody for more than *one time.*' One time! Do you believe that? I didn't think I was hearing her right, not after the way we were going at it. You saw. But I sure as hell *was* hearing right."

He signaled the waitress. Now Rickey Anne was dancing with an older man, shorter than she was. Travis took in the details: one of those hicks in a plaid shirt and a bolo made of feathers. "Looks like some fuckin' reject from the chicken coop," he said. The man's hips were pushing hard against hers, making her swaybacked, but her head was bent forward the opposite way, stretching down low so their lips locked together, and the man's fingers were poking up under her vest.

"She looks real happy," said Jack, laughing.

Travis could hardly wait to see what happened when the music ended. He nudged Jack. "Catch this. Soon as the music ends, she gives him the heave-ho." They watched. First the man said something, then Rickey Anne said something back. Then the man looked confused. They could almost lip-read the conversation: The man: "What'd you say?" And Rickey Anne: "I don't dance with nobody more than one time." The two men roared and the people at the next table looked over, annoyed.

"Hot shit. Them tits is gonna be all wore out before the next set," said Travis. He nudged Jack, "Go cop a feel," but Jack shook his head. "Why get worked up for nothing?" The bar was packed now, hot and stuffy, with a smell of sweat, beer, and frustration , a good ol' boys bar where Travis and his friends usually hung out on payday. Jack hadn't been there in years. Travis nudged him again. "Catch them two princesses, sighted at two o'clock. Sweet pussy! What your Uncle Travis's got for you!" He knocked back the rest of his drink. "What do you say?"

"Looks good to me," and they rose together and walked toward the girls' booth. All eyes at the bar followed, first watching the men, then the girls, whose sixth sense set them in motion — eyes fluttering, hands smoothing. Travis stepped up close to their booth, extending his arms to the edge of the table, and leaned forward on the heels of his hands. For a long moment he didn't say anything, just smiled in his lopsided way. Give the ladies a chance to size me up, he explained later. He loved the chase. "Evenin' ladies." Polite, that was the secret, he later added, don't come on strong, and don't talk dirty, at least not right away.

"Hi," the girls in unison.

"You ladies from around here, or you just don't know any better?"

"Vacation," they said, giggling.

"I'm Travis, and this here's my friend Jack."

Jack stepped forward. "Evenin' ladies." The girls were pretty. Tourists, he thought – don't know where the hell they are or what they might be getting into, just feeling horny and looking for excitement. "Where you girls from?" he asked.

"Valdosta, you know, Georgia," said the dark-haired one. "Where the peaches come from."

"Sweet and juicy I might add," said Travis. "Mind if we sit?"

The girls looked at each other, then slid over to make room. They were new school teachers just out of Georgia Southern in Statesboro. The dark haired one was named Via and the blonde was Charlene, and the way they seemed to be pairing up was Jack with Via and Travis with Charlene. The waitress brought their check from the other booth and they ordered drinks. The band had switched to one of those slow, done-me-wrong country songs. "Dance?" asked Jack. Via nodded and he rested his hand lightly on her slim hip as they walked to the floor. She was graceful, almost weightless, and he realized how long it had been since he had danced in a dark bar with a pretty new woman.

Via stayed distant, but when Jack pressed lightly along her spine she eased in closer and rested her cheek against his, soft and fragrant with hints of spice. Who knows, he thought, and drew back to study her young Georgia face, and a body that showed just a hint of curves. But what was the point, a one-night stand? After one more beer, and despite protests, he said goodnight to Travis, Charlene, and the young teacher from Valdosta. It was late, and he wished he had the nerve to drive back to the compound for a checkup by Nurse DeWitt.

CHAPTER 55

THE WORKERS HAD ALREADY GATHERED outside Emilio's cottage for what the men didn't want to call a union meeting, but it was as close as you could get to one, according to what Jack had told Ainsley. They meant to set work rules that all the growers would agree to for the next season.

On the lawn, Emilio had set up two tables made from sheets of plywood resting on saw horses, and Irena had covered them with starched white cloths. Ainsley had brought a sandwich tray with ham, roast beef and cheeses, and from Grace, two sheet cakes, chocolate and coconut. Jack, already waiting for her, helped carry the food from her pickup. "Leola will be over with beans and rice, fixings for tacos, and beer."

Ainsley was surprised to see so many people – at least thirty families with their children, about eighty in all. "It seems both festive and uneasy," said Ainsley.

"If there's anything Big Agri-business doesn't want," said Jack, "it's a migrant revolt, or a union. They won't agree to anything without a fight."

"A mis-matched fight."

Emilio was walking toward them, his hand extended to Jack. "We are going to begin now, this big day." He strode to the center of the crowd and raised both arms. "Hello, friends. Thank you for coming." Everyone quieted. "I am not accustom to speak, but I will do my best in English." His eyes rested for a moment on each of them. "The time has come to stand up for ourself and our families." A man in back began to clap, and others joined in.

Emilio raised his hand, again asking for quiet. "The law does not protect us. The growers do not. So we must protect ourself and each other!" With each statement, the crowd gathered courage, and by the time Emilio had finished speaking ten minutes later, they were on their feet. Emilio was smiling as he

271

sat down on the zigzag-patterned blanket. Irena threw her arms around his neck.

Jack joined Ainsley, who was sitting on a bench under a live oak. "Do they have a chance?" she asked. "Do growers and business owners even care?"

"We'll make them care. They care about getting the crop picked." She held her glass of ice water toward him, and he took a long drink.

"You're the exception, Jack."

"Thanks."

"But I guess in the scheme of things, you're small potatoes."

"You know how to flatter a man."

He leaned his head against the tree, thinking about how much courage it had taken for the workers who had shown up, risking what little they had. The sun had peaked and a chevron of birds was coasting by on a breeze – except, something was wrong. He sat up straight. Instead of a clear sky, a furling black funnel drifted along the horizon, gray near the top where the wind had stirred it, growing wider and darker below. He squinted to make sure of what he was seeing, but then he smelled it too, the acrid odor of burning wood. "Fire!" he shouted, and all heads turned toward the groves. Jack was on his feet. Trees must be ablaze, the remaining fallen leaves and dried grass perfect tinder. "Call for help!" he told Ainsley. He and the other men were running for their trucks, or scrambling into the beds of pickups already pulling away.

"Hoses and pumps are still at the lakes," he shouted. "Hurry!" The choking, dirty smoke was blowing their way now, just as it had when he was a boy and he and his parents had been awakened by toxic smoke, and flames racing through their upstairs bedrooms, blocking their escape to the staircase. He could still hear his father calling: "Jump, Jack! The window!" his words coming from a distant somewhere, and Jack, four years old, was afraid to move.

As his pickup sped toward the burning groves, Jack couldn't erase the memory of that long-ago blaze, the sound of wood and resins exploding, the white cloud seeping in around his bedroom door, flames lighting the night sky. "Jump now!" his father called, and he had padded barefoot in his pajamas to the window, its sash already raised, the screen giving way to his slight push, the sound it made when it landed in the bushes one story below. Again, he heard his father's dim voice calling… "Jump, Jack!" His fingers had clutched the rough wood on each side of the frame; he threw one leg over the sill, sensed the night air rushing past his bare foot, hoped his father and his mother would be there in a moment to scoop him up in their arms. He let go of one side of the frame, brought his other leg up and was teetering on the sill, dizzy, looking out at a sky of leaping yellows and orange. One finger at a time, he loosened his grip on the frame as the heat grew stronger behind him, pushing him forward, and then, heeding his father, he had closed his eyes, and stepped off into nothingness. He remembered muffled shouts, the words, "half-breed," and a young man's high voice growing fainter. Running feet seemed to stumble, and the sound of a car's engine faded as he lay on the ground, his leg jutting oddly, the house behind him a torch shooting flames, the distant blast of sirens and his parents nowhere in sight.

CHAPTER 56

FOUR HOURS AFTER THE FIRE began, the men straggled back to Emilio's cottage. Even though it had been relatively small for a brush fire, the exhausted men, covered with sweat and soot, had barely been able to contain it, even with the help of county firefighters who had arrived quickly to help. "We are lucky with so many people here," said Emilio. He looked at Jack for confirmation that the blaze had been caused by chance.

"That fire was set. This was just a warning," said Jack. "We all know it could have been far worse, and next time it might be."

Emilio couldn't help feeling responsible. The brave men of a few hours earlier looked beaten now, lying on the grass while Irena and the other women brought cups of ice water and fresh sandwiches. "I think we are finish," said Emilio "Now everyone will be afraid to be organize." He picked up one of the notebooks they'd been writing in earlier, recording the workers' stories, and lists of demands they had planned to make on the crew bosses. Irena brought a folding chair for her husband, and standing behind him, began massaging his neck.

After everyone else had gone home, Jack and Ainsley went to break the news to Parker.

Emilio and his family sat exhausted in their small sitting room, three of them squeezed together on the sofa, Tina lying on the floor. He took Irena's hand and put his arm around Lolo, who was on his other side. "I have come to a decision today," he told them. "To be a migrant worker is my life. It is a hard life, and because of what happen today, I am more determine than ever to make it better."

Irena was trying not to cry and tucked her head into his shoulder. "I am proud," she told him.

"I am proud of you," he said, and kissed her on the forehead. "You do new things now, Irena, and are not afraid." He told them that starting the next day, Lolo would return to school, and would only work with his father in the summers. "After you have your official paper from high school, you can decide what to do."

Lolo looked up. "Me?"

"You. Then if you want to be a worker like me, okay. If you don't, okay too, and I will help you if I can." With his bare toe, he nudged Tina, stretched out in front of him. "You will get your high school paper also. I will put it high up on the wall for everyone to see it." Tears were welling in Irena's eyes, and he brushed them away with the back of his hand. "I am a lucky man, Irena, and a determine man. And I am not afraid no more."

Long after Ainsley and Jack had gone, Grace sat thinking about what they had told her and Parker. She knew what crew bosses were capable of. Violence was commonplace, and murder not unheard of. Now the threat loomed close to home. Next time, the compound or Jack's house might be set on fire, or their own. She poured herself a glass of wine, and after coming to a decision, made a phone call, took out her car keys and kissed Parker on the cheek. "I'm going out to run those errands. I'll pick something up for dinner."

For years, she had kept a guilty secret, rationalizing everything, and knowing that in the beginning, selfishness had prompted her silence. That was long over and whatever the costs or fallout, the threats to her daughter outweighed everything, and perhaps today, she could also partly re-pay a debt she owed to Jack. She had a bargaining chip and was about to play it.

Grace was the first to arrive at the darkening park. She backed the car behind a shed where the grounds-keeper stored his tools. The park was seldom visited, not now or as far back as she could remember. I want a cigarette, she thought.

Clay pulled his old Porsche alongside Grace's car and jumped out before it stopped, that same stunt perfected over the years. He tapped on her window, waited for her to roll it down, and leaned inside. His after-shave was the one he'd always worn, and triggered something deep in her brain. Clay's presence was as overpowering as it had ever been.

"What's up?" Drumming his fingers on the roof.

"I think you know."

"I don't know. "I – Do – Not – Have – A – Clue." He opened the door and started to slide inside. "Scoot over." She moved to the passenger's side and he sat beside her. "Calling me, making demands to drop everything. Lady listens in, not that I give a damn."

She fumbled for a cigarette, then changed her mind and came to the point. "Someone set fire to Jack's and Ainsley's groves today. Lucky it didn't amount to much."

He looked away, "Fires start… lightening, lots of reasons."

"You knew about the workers' meeting."

Shrugging his shoulders. "I heard something, yeah."

"That fire was no accident."

"Why tell me?" His voice, defensive and mean. "What can I do?"

His hip was pressing on hers, and she moved away. "Put a stop to it. The others will listen to you, even the crew bosses."

"Not my business. Anyhow, why get all riled about a bunch of wetbacks? Most of 'em aren't even worth killing." His voice became loud and threatening – his way of intimidating people. "They're not my employees. Get that straight." That cold tone she'd heard so often over the years, now directed at her. "Talk to the crew bosses," he said. "That's who they work for."

She pushed his shoulder. "Get out."

He looked at her as if she were joking.

"Get out. I mean it!" Still he didn't move.

"My daughter was out there, and your grandson."

He grabbed her wrist. "She should have been *our* daughter."

She wrested her arm away. "And whose fault was that?" The ache, the humiliation he'd put her through so long ago was welling up, as fresh as if it were yesterday. "When you deserted me for Lady, I knew what mattered to you: money and power."

For an instant, he looked like the boy she had loved so many years ago, shaking his head, denying everything, typical Clay, a liar then and now.

"That's not true. If I could have undone things, I would have, a million times over."

"Stop it!" Once, long ago, she would have believed him. She'd known for years what his marriage was like, how much he regretted what he'd done, but only after he'd become successful, when money was something he knew he could get on his own.

"Everything turned out just the way it was supposed to," she said. "You have what matters to you, and I do, too."

"You're lying." He took her by the shoulders, expecting her to give in to him – he bragged that he always got what he went after, but she pushed him away. "You know I'm not lying, Clay, and that's what eats away at you."

"I know." He took her hand, a way of asking forgiveness maybe. She pulled away, but could still feel his torment. For a long time, neither of them spoke and then he touched his forehead to hers, whispering, "There's still time for us, time to make up for everything." She knew people did things like that, did it all the time, shaking their lives like a kaleidoscope, and making a brand new picture of it. "No," she said, "It *is* too late, and it's not a question of time."

He pulled her close, his chest heaving. "I've always loved you, Grace. You know that." His face was buried in her neck, his words muffled. "Whenever I see you, I'm punished all over again." She cradled his head in her hands; he wasn't telling her anything she didn't know. "I was young, a stupid man who made the worst mistake he could." He pulled back, looking at her hard and she saw the real Clay again, the man she had escaped.

"Don't, Clay… please."

" I didn't live my life right, Grace, I admit it."

She took his hands away. "I want you to make a promise, Clay, and it's this: Everything that ever happened between us, and everything said here today, will be forgotten. It's for your own good."

"We have a chance."

"Listen to me. I don't want a chance," her voice was solemn and dark.

"Grace…"

"This is a threat."

"A what?"

She ran her finger lightly across his chin. "A threat." He looked up, puzzled. "It's about the night Jack's parents' house was set afire." Everything went still then and a long-buried fear came back to life. "That fire is the reason I'm here." She pressed a hand to the side of his face, forcing him to look at her. "I know you did it, Clay. I have proof." Until that instant, she had never seen him look afraid. Several moments passed before he could speak. "It was an accident, a prank," he said. "I was drinking, never meant it to go that far! For God's sake!"

"I know. That's partly why I never told anyone." His face was ashen and he turned away. "Clay, as long as you promise to let everything between us stay in the past… as long as you stop trying to hurt Parker, and as long as you stop scheming to get Ainsley's land – I'll never tell anyone what you did to Jack's family. That's my promise. Now it's up to you."

"That's blackmail."

"Yes, it is." He sat staring into the distance, and she knew he could scarcely wait to escape her.

"Fine." And he was gone.

"I know you were with her," stormed Lady. "Calling you here, as if she can order you around anytime she wants, just says 'jump' and you jump."

"Shut up!"

"Where did you go? What was so urgent?"

"It was business."

"Business! Oh, business!" Lady's voice loud and mocking. "Whenever a man trots out that word we're supposed to genuflect; let the bastard hide behind his most holy word, 'business'."

"I'm warning you."

"Warning me? Warn all you want! Warn away!"

He took a step toward her, "I told you to shut up!"

She stood fast, trembling in anger. "I know everything about you. I've seen you disgusting, bloated and drunk. I've fixed your meals, listened to your lies, laughed at your jokes, let you inside me any time you felt like it." She was crying, wailing, as if she wanted to turn the world upside down. "I've had your children, let you mock me and use me, seen you wanting other women, looked the other way when you went out of town, on 'business'." Her eyes were puffed and streaming, her body shaking.

Then everything went quiet. "When I see you look at her, your eyes filled with lust, you look like the fool you are, because she'd never have you, and you know it. She escaped!"

With a contemptuous sneer, he turned his back and started to walk away.

"What makes it bearable for me," she said softly, "is your never-ending agony. There can be no greater joy, every single day, than watching you suffer."

CHAPTER 57

THE PHONE WAS RINGING AND Ainsley shook herself awake on the sofa. Jack's voice, a not-so-bad voice to hear when you're not sure where you are. She must have sounded sleepy when she answered.

"Napping in the middle of the day?"

"I wasn't napping," she lied. The fire two days before had taken its toll.

"Slip on a suit and meet me at the marina. It's a nice day."

"No."

"Hurry. Snook are biting," and he hung up. Jack kept a runabout at the city-run marina on the mainland side of the river. It *was* a nice day. Clay had telephoned her that morning to say that everything was taken care of, not to worry about the workers or any more fires. Not like him at all, but a blessing nonetheless. Maybe family did mean something to him. She pulled on a faded black bikini, and in five minutes was out the door.

Jack spotted her sitting on a piling next to his boat and sprinted toward her, a cooler banging against his leg. Two brown pelicans perched nearby, a slight breeze ruffling their feathers. Just in case, he was wearing what he thought of as his can't-miss blue shirt. "Couldn't resist, huh?" throwing her a smile. "I thought you turned me down."

"I felt sorry for you."

"Works for me." He set the cooler, rods and tackle box on the dock and jumped aboard. The pelicans had moved to the other side and took off noisily. Jack tugged the line to draw the boat in. He couldn't believe how happy he was that she had come, and realized how disappointed he would have been if she hadn't. She handed him the turquoise and pink cooler, looking at it suspiciously. "Isn't there a rule these things have to be red, or blue and white?"

"Let's break all the rules today," he said, and wondered if he meant it. He gave her a hand aboard, and she began rearranging things, taking a moment to look inside the cooler. He'd stopped for a six-pack and two deli sandwiches, packaged under clear plastic domes.

"I was afraid it was only bait... I see you were expecting me."

"They're both for me," he told her. Then, "Just hoping," he admitted. After fumbling under the seat for the key, which he stored there, they were ready. "OK," he said finally, and started the engine. They headed north on the river, staying in the channel instead of venturing toward the mangroves where snook might be hiding. The air felt heavy. "Last time I was out here was March," he said, "going for cobia with Seth Martin."

Ainsley's face lit up. "Me, too. Every year I get cobia fever."

"Ever catch one?"

"Once, and certainly not in a boat this size."

"Whoa!"

She could recall every detail of that cobia, looking like a shark when swimming, with a treacherous personality when caught. In spring, when the manta rays moved north, the cobia swam in the shade beneath the rays' giant wings.

"Seth and I saw this dark blotch on the water," said Jack. "That ray's span must have been twenty feet. I pulled my boat up easy, didn't want to spook her and have her dive to the bottom. Her back was so filled with lures and tackle it sparkled like a Christmas tree. I tossed my jig out and reeled in, jerky, and zap! That cobia hit!"

"You boarded a cobia in this boat?" Jack put on a hurt expression.

"No offense."

"I boarded her after considerable disagreement on her part. I didn't realize what that cobia could do, since I'd never taken one before," and he shook his head. "It slipped off my gaff and damn near tore my boat up." Cobia that didn't like their

281

accommodations had been known to sink small boats just with the fighting and commotion they caused. "Finally Seth comes with this club, called it his cobia domesticator. Said that's what it takes when it's him or you."

"I'm glad your boat survived. You, too, of course!" Ainsley dug out her sunglasses, looking at the sky. "Think that storm will get this far north?" A tropical depression had been brewing in the islands.

"We're due."

They spent an hour on the river, hardly talking, not fishing either, something unsaid passing between them. Ainsley had closed her eyes, dozing, and when she opened them, saw they were heading back. "What about the snook?"

"Snook was the bait. You are the catch." She didn't seem to mind. Jack wondered at himself, being so cheeky lately. Time was running out, that must be it, but running out on what? Bear was in the distant past, and nobody since had mattered to her, as far as he knew. Except Billy maybe. All the while, he'd let time slip away, as Travis liked to point out, but wasn't that where he was comfortable, on the sidelines? Maybe not.

He turned the boat south in the channel, staying close to the bends where the water ran deep, heading toward a cove. Ainsley stood up, feet spread apart for balance, and started to take off her terry-cloth cover-up, glancing back as she folded it up, and him taking a long look as she teetered there in the bow. They were near a spot where a pod of dolphins made their home. Locals called it Vanishing Island, a huge sandbar that came into view and vanished with the tides. He pulled the engine back, almost to idle, with just enough speed to steer to the lee side of the bar.

"Watch the prop," warned Ainsley, looking into the light-colored sandy bottom where the water was shallow. Jack vaulted over the side and pulled the boat up while Ainsley set the anchor. She handed chairs over the side, then the cooler, before jumping in the water with him. They set the cooler between two low-slung sand chairs, sat down, closed their eyes and let the sun seep in. Gulls cawed overhead, the only sound, a weekday afternoon and no other living thing in sight. After a while, he reached over and took her hand. "Some people feel horny being in the sun like this."

"*Some* people?."

"So I've heard."

"Some people don't." Her long legs were stretched out, her head tilted back, shaded by a floppy straw hat rippling in the breeze.

"C'mon, let's cool off," wondering to himself what he really meant by that. He pulled her to her feet, and she let her hat blow into the dune, caught by sea oats. Close to shore, the water was almost as warm as the air, but as the current took them out, it became deeper and cooler. She lay on her back and the small current carried her hair downstream and Jack, beside her, took her hand, as if they were on a huge raft, kicking lightly, gently rocking and floating away together. He squeezed her hand. "Take your top off," he told her.

"Are you crazy?"

It seemed to him that lately he and Ainsley were having some kind of – not a romance certainly, but something that had been long hidden, simmering. It wasn't his imagination, of that he was certain, but would she take the next step? Maybe, or had she been thinking only of Billy, ever since that day he had busted in on them, looking for the Captain, he said.

They'd drifted into shallows near the boat again and Jack stood up, still holding her hand. Water flowed between them as he pulled her close, kissing her. Reaching behind her back, he unhooked her top, slipped it off, and tossed it into the boat. Her naked breasts pressed against him, and her arms were locked around his waist, holding him close. Then he was tugging at her suit bottom, and she was helping him, pushing it down, until it fell to her ankles, finally kicking it off, and then she was easing him out of his shorts. Somehow, the suits got pitched into the boat.

Currents lapped at their sides, and Ainsley hoisted herself up, wrapping her arms around his neck, her legs around his hips. The water buoyed them effortlessly, and then she felt him there, in that warm and perfectly made space, intended just for this. Nothing could ever change what was happening, erase it, or make anything the same as it had been before.

She leaned back, connected, floating, her fingers lightly holding onto his hips, everything moving fast, the sky spinning, the sun blazing, and life as complicated as it could be.

CHAPTER 58

WHAT HAD SHE DONE? ALL Ainsley could think about was Jack Henderson and what had happened the day before; it didn't mean a thing, a mistake. The irony was, a few hours after she left Jack at the marina, Billy had called, and a few hours from now, she'd be with him again. She tried to wish all her guilt away.

At five, she drew a bath, added lavender oil to the water and let its scent fill the room as she undressed, studying her naked body, imagining it through Billy's eyes. She had no way of gauging how much she might have changed since they were last together, and she had no doubt that he would later have an opportunity to judge for himself.

The hot water soothed muscles strained from a day of lifting and digging in the greenhouse. She let it rise to her chin and closed her eyes, submerging her head and feeling it close above her. But the water reminded her of Jack, being with him on Vanishing Island, wrapping her legs around him, and everything that came afterward. What was she thinking? She picked up the pumice stone and smoothed her elbows and feet, slicked her legs with a new razor, and with a nail brush, drove out every grain of greenhouse sand. Then she pulled the plug and stood under a cool spray, trying to rinse away every troubling thought.

On the bed, she laid out the clothes she would wear, a pale blue sun dress with a low back and high-heeled sandals. Dressing slowly and carefully, she finally inserted the pearl studs in her ears and she was ready. Billy had likely known many women since her, but it didn't matter. She sprayed perfume and looked at herself in the long mirror, and what she saw reflected back was happiness and doubt.

His tap on the car horn was light but insistent. She picked up her bag and dashed outside in time to see Billy leaning over to push her door open. Same old Billy. A piano concerto was playing, filling the car, and every part of the universe it seemed, with joy.

They rode for miles without talking, and when he reached for her hand, it seemed he had never stopped doing just that, his palm rough and warm, with cuts and callouses, just as she remembered. He seemed to be reading her thoughts. "You can't imagine how many times I've thought of being with you like this," he said, "your same perfume, everything."

Ainsley knew she had changed. Her younger self might have wanted to punish Billy, might have withheld something, but now, all that mattered was being there, holding hands. "We'll go to my place," he said, confident that's what she would want. People said Billy and Lorraine had never lived on the River Road together, preferring their place on the ocean, and she was glad of that. At the stop sign, he leaned over and kissed her lightly on the lips. How had she survived, not knowing that this might ever happen again?

Having Ainsley sitting beside him was something Billy had pictured numberless times – over how many years was it now? almost ten since they had first met? So much had happened since: marriages come and gone, a child, losses of all kinds, a few gains, and still lots of hoping and striving. Without knowing when it happened, he had changed, and doubtless Ainsley had, too. You couldn't live ten of the biggest years of your life without being affected, and when you looked back, you knew this wasn't how you had planned it. When they had first met, their timing could not have been worse: he, at an important threshold in racing; she, still a kid. Maybe it could be different for them now. Billy had always put a lot of stock in timing.

The morning had been spent preparing for her, something he'd never done for Ainsley in the old days, not for Lorraine, and not for anyone else. He wasn't sure what he expected, but what he hoped for, he had thought about for years. They were on the River Road. "Your house looks so different," she told him. "I saw the changes, the second floor you added."

"The whole street is changing," he said. "Getting ritzy." He parked in the drive, and when they went inside the house, Agnes was waiting at the door, lying with her head on her paws, tail flicking slowly.

"Agnes, Oh, Agnes! I hoped I would see you." Ainsley dropped to her knees next to the old black lab, nuzzling her fur, every emotion flooding back, but Agnes was waiting for Billy's touch. "Agnes, good girl," running his fingers along her flank, patting her head. "I still take her on the road with me sometimes."

Ainsley set her purse on a chair, and studied the changes in a place she had once known so well. "It's good, Billy."

"The second story's even nicer, better view of the river." Agnes, content now, had settled back onto the tile.

Ainsley said, "I don't know which of us was happier to see you today, Agnes or me."

"Nobody is happier today than me," he said, taking her in his arms, holding her along the length of his body, absorbing everything about her.

"Why doesn't this seem strange?" she asked.

"Because, in my mind at least, we've been together like this a thousand times." He buried his face in her hair, breathing deeply. "You knew, same as I did, this had to happen someday." He led her to the staircase that curved up to the second level. When she reached the landing, she stood still, taking it all in. "Hard to believe, how changed it is." Through banks of floor-to-ceiling windows, they could see for miles north and south on the river, and to the east, beyond the island, the ocean.

"I wanted to stay on here. It's my good luck house, so I went ahead and fixed it up," and turning to her he added, "and it's lucky again." The great room stretched forty feet along the river, and twenty feet on the north and south ends. Heart pine flooring from an old barn, Billy told her, was laid with wood pegs. The ceiling was twelve feet high, and on the north end, a coquina fireplace was flanked with shelves filled with trophies and pictures of Billy with his family and friends. The furniture was covered in beige cotton with big, soft cushions.

"It's just right in every way: the room, the water, the boats."

"I only wish I was around to enjoy it more." All his time lately was taken with getting ready for the Daytona 400 race July 4 weekend, only a month away, and two other races in-between. They walked into the kitchen, where a wall of glass windows and sliding doors faced west over a broad deck, planned for watching sunsets. "Back here is the bedroom," he said, sweeping her up in his arms, just like that. "Saving the best for last," he told her.

"I think we've done this before."

"This is the very first time again."

In the bedroom, a bottle of Champagne was chilling in a bucket on a long table, and two flutes rested on a starched napkin. Under a glass dome, a round of Brie, now at room temperature, sat next to a small knife. A baguette had been cut into thin slices, toasted, and placed in a basket. "Uptown," he said, winking at her. He uncorked the Champagne and filled their glasses half full. Far different from the first time she had visited his home and they had drunk sodas in the room downstairs. The glasses rang like bells when they touched them together. "To fresh starts," said Billy.

"Fresh starts."

He pulled back the pale comforter, they kicked off their shoes and sat cross-legged on the bed. When he had called her the day before, he wondered if his thoughts over so many years had been nothing more than daydreams, but in her voice he had heard something of the past, as alive and real as it had ever been. "That's enough of that," he said, taking a last sip of his drink and setting both their glasses aside. He slid his arm around her waist and eased her down onto a pillow, gathering her hair to one side, as his hands moved down along her breasts, her legs, following some never-forgotten path. "I know you so well," and he wanted to believe it.

He lifted the skirt of her sun dress, and without hesitation or second thoughts, they were together just as they had been so long ago, and all the empty years disappeared. How many times had he imagined this: her face, her parted lips, her hips rising beneath him, how many times?

CHAPTER 59

A MONTH LATER, ANOTHER FIRECRACKER 400 was being written in the history books of racing, with Billy's name in seventh place, a good showing, but not the win he had hoped for. While Billy talked to a reporter, Ainsley waited with Wendell Jablonski, still his crew chief, showing some wear now, but quick as ever. Little had changed in the years since Ainsley had first stood in a victory tent following a race: not the atmosphere or the fervor of the fans.

For Billy, the 400, which took place over the July 4 holidays, was second only to the elusive Daytona 500, the win he wanted most, like everybody else; some of the best drivers had never won it and never would. When the crowd cleared and she and Billy were about to leave, Wendell clapped him on the shoulder. "Don't let her get away this time."

There was only one place Billy wanted to be that evening: right there at home, and after a quick shower, he threw himself on the sofa, exhausted. For weeks, the 400 had been all-consuming. Ainsley sat on the edge of the cushion massaging his shoulders.

"My neck is in knots."

"Turn over again and stop complaining."

"I want to look at you." He drew her head down on his chest and closed his eyes. In a few minutes, his rhythmic breathing told her he had fallen asleep, and soon after, she was sleeping too. When she awoke, Billy was in the kitchen fixing dinner, whisking the dressing for their salad, and she found herself thinking: This could work, but right on its heels came doubt.

"I always admire a man who can cook."

"You got one. On my own too long, I guess," and he stepped out on the balcony, carrying glasses and silverware. A few rogue firecrackers were popping nearby, and now and then something bright rocketed across the sky, but Billy, pre-occupied still, didn't seem to notice. When he came back inside, she said, "You've changed," not in an unkind way, but as an observation.

"A little." He looked up. "That's okay, I hope."

She blinked, surprised. "Of course." Like everyone, he'd been scarred, simply from living; nobody escaped that, the years piling things on – his failed marriage, his career not quite what he wanted it to be. If racing had been important to him before, it had become clear to her over the past month that it was even more-so now that time might be running out.

From the balcony they had a good view of the fireworks people were setting off on the banks of the river, a prelude to the official July 4 show the following night.

"You're rested now?" she asked.

"I'm fine. Nap did me good." Racing was harder these days, more competitive than when he'd started out, big business trying to hang onto a good-ol'-boy notion for the public.

Dinner was almost ready. In a red pottery bowl, he tossed fettuccine with ribbons of pancetta, fresh tomatoes, toasted walnuts, then shavings of cheese on top. They carried the plates and salads to the balcony, but Billy was quiet, thinking about the race, she could see that. A home rocket whistled past, the sky flaming with blues and whites, with curls and streaks that bloomed and faded, Billy seeing none of it.

"Billy…" It took a few seconds for his name to register. He looked at her sheepishly. "I wonder," she asked, "do you ever think you've missed out on other things?"

"Other?"

She hesitated. Where might this lead? "Like family?"

His brow furrowed. "I've got Agnes. I've got racing. And now I've got you, so I guess I have family," but this last was a question.

"Of course." The fireworks seemed to be tapering off, and she was glad for Agnes, who was cowering under a chair. But then someone launched a half-dozen rockets all at once, blazing and then waning, lasting only moments, and then they were gone.

CHAPTER 60

JACK WAS WAITING NEAR THE field house, signaling her to park alongside his truck. It was July 10, six months since the freeze, their agreed-upon date for a careful survey of the trees. Earlier inspections had proved inconclusive and disheartening.

"Sorry to bring you out on such a hot, miserable day," he said.

"It's okay. Hurricane weather. I'm more worried about a storm than I am about the heat." A hurricane could take the year's crop and the trees. She looked tired and thinner too, and he wondered why, when everyone was talking about her rekindled romance with Billy Fiske. Almost two months had passed since they had supposedly gone fishing for snook, and right afterward, Billy had showed up again. Travis had been right.

They walked a little way into the groves, sun beating down, inspecting the trees closely. Those growing near the road, where traffic and fumes took their toll, were blackened and dead. None had survived. Some of the untilled grass had greened up, but the trees were dry and bare. "Jack, about…"

"Stop right there." For emphasis, he stopped walking, and so did she. Instinct told him she was about to bring up that day at Vanishing Island. "You don't need to say anything. It just happened, so no need for us to explain anything away."

"That day… I don't *want* to explain it away." She stooped to pick up a branch that had broken from one of the trees. "No matter what you might think, and despite everything said and done over the years, that day mattered to me."

Those last words had been chosen with considerable care, he noticed. "It mattered to me, too," and then they fell silent and continued walking, rounding a bend into a newer grove. Again she stopped walking, not quite finished. "Afterward, Jack, I admitted I had been thinking of you that way for a long time. I'm not sorry."

If that was true, he thought, she certainly had kept it a secret. "Is that all?"

"That's all."

"I'm not sorry either," And there was something else he wanted her to know, but just then, a rabbit dived across the furrowed path just ahead and disappeared into the grove.

"Wait!" She put her arm out, and they both looked where she was pointing, but not at the rabbit, and just as he had expected, Ainsley started walking faster, then running, with Jack following on her heels. She turned to face him. "You knew, didn't you?"

"Thought I'd wait until I was absolutely sure."

She continued to gaze at the trees and at the leaves beginning to unfurl, small and reflective in the sun, like a million trembling, mirrors. Throwing her arms around his shoulders, she began trembling too. The groves were coming back. Unlike trees that had sprung back early and died again in a false start, six months was the test. Their trees were greening, new growth sprouting, branches that had looked dead, now strong and alive. Ainsley began running among them, bending branches to test their suppleness, calling to him, and finally running back to where he was still waiting.

Jack told her, "None of the other groves came through the way ours did, except those close-planted in the Quinn."

"He did it, Jack. My father did it." Tears were falling faster than she could rub them away, tears for the trees, and for her father.

CHAPTER 61

FROM THE GROVES, THEY DROVE to Jack's house, which sat on a small rise, "a true Florida mountain," according to him, located at the edge of the property. It was a good size, with lap siding painted white, one story with a high roof that made it look like two, and a covered porch twelve feet wide across the front, with half-columns resting on a broad railing. A magenta bougainvillea climbed up one side, and a yellow allamanda up the other. In between, Leola had hung baskets of trailing ivy and white petunias, drooping in the heat.

Inside, the house was friendly and unpretentious: one big room, with beamed ceilings and oak floors: an open kitchen with a curving bar; a dining area with a cherrywood table and six chairs; and a living room with the usual furnishings. "Early Comfortable," as Jack described it, a room that made you feel as if you'd been there before.

They'd driven up the hill to talk about the next step, but first, to fix sandwiches, which they were eating at the kitchen bar. Something, he wasn't sure what, made him reach over, take her by the shoulders, and bring her to her feet. Not easy to do when you're sitting on bar stools, and on the way up, he kissed her, and that was the end of his resolve. Despite everything he had been telling himself, despite trying to forget what had happened between him and Ainsley weeks ago, today's shared happiness had overtaken him, and Ainsley made no effort to stop it.

When he let her go, she asked, "What is this about, Jack?"

"I don't know."

Then she began kissing him the way she had once before, but this wasn't a game without consequences anymore. Over the years, she had always rejected him so firmly that playful exchanges had come to seem harmless, until lately, when everything had changed. Gently, he took her hands away and she stood there, as chastened and baffled as a child.

"You invite me here," she said, "take advantage of my feelings, then this," but when he touched her arm, she pushed him away. "Leave me alone!" She stalked into the bathroom and he heard hiccupping and water running, and she came back drinking from the far side of a glass, her hiccup remedy, dripping water and leaving dark blotches on her shirt. An insult was apparently in order. "Today," she said, "being as happy as I am, I guess I wasn't thinking straight," and she sat on the sofa, far away from him.

"If that's the case, take advantage all you like. A man has his principles."

"Why are you joking?" There were no tears now, just indignation. "You do it all the time, to push people away."

He sat up, surprised. "Who'd have an ornery thing like me?"

"See? You're joking again. Where is Ilse, what happened to her?"

"Ilse? What's she got to do with it?"

"Where is she, pushed away?"

"In Guadalajara, married to a rancher." He wanted this to be over.

"Why aren't *you* married again? You *were*."

Taking time to think. "I was married," he said at last. "A long time ago."

Her tone softened to match his. "I want to know about it."

He looked away, considering, and felt the sofa give as she moved closer, hemming him in. She leaned against his shoulder, and after a while he began telling her the story he had hidden for so long, thankful for someone he wanted to tell it to.

"I was living in Michigan then, sent home from 'Nam in '71 after taking a hit. Limped a little, still do some days." He laughed quietly, "Got a lot of sympathy from the ladies," and he nudged her playfully. "I wasn't ready to come back to Florida, and a buddy got me a job working the line at the Ford plant where the Mustangs rolled out. When they accepted me into college at Ann Arbor, I was surprised. I forgot all about my ruined groves down here and thought I'd find out how the rich folks live, take up business or law."

"I thought you might be smarter than you seem."

"Thank you." He took a sip of her water while he considered the next part of it. "I met Julia at an anti-war rally. I was there just for the hell of it, a veteran wanting to hear what those do-gooders and draft dodgers had to say. Julia was standing on this makeshift platform, the wind fierce and cold as hell, and she had this long, red scarf blowing out around her in a comical, crazy kind of way. Here's this real serious girl, and she reminded me of Snoopy, with that scarf of his. Anyway, I worked my way up close and liked her in spite of myself."

"But you didn't agree."

"Not then, but she talked with so much sense I found myself clapping for her. When the rally ended, I hung around and made sure I met her, walked her back to the dorm." He took a breath. "That's how it started."

"What was she studying?"

"Theater, wanted to be an actress, and could have been."

"Was she attractive?"

"Not in the way models are, but better than that, at least that's what people said. Big eyes, brown and wide-set, a body that was lanky and agile like a dancer, and long blonde hair hanging down straight, the way girls had it back then." And he was picturing his wife's face, the Snoopy scarf, her gentleness. Julia wasn't as strong as he had first thought.

"So the war veteran and the anti-war activist fall in love?"

"Not quite that simple, but yes, and then she got pregnant, and you can guess the rest. We were in love so we went ahead and got married," and he stopped talking. She waited quietly for him to continue, and before long he did. "Her family wasn't happy. They were society people from Grosse Point, high up in investment banking. They decided to punish her, or us. Said if we were old enough to get married it wasn't right to give her money for school."

"And that was it?"

He thought back through the sadness and about the ways he'd seen people use money to punish, to reward, to bribe. "No.

Pretty soon they changed their mind, but it was too late. Julia had dropped out, because there were problems with the pregnancy."

"You don't have to tell me."

"I want to." They settled deeper into the cushions and he drew her close beside him. "Julia never was well again after Tommy came. Her kidneys. It scared us both. So to forget, or as an excuse, we got heavy into weed for a while. After that, Julia took up booze."

"And you felt responsible?"

"In some way I was. She'd always had everything, an easy life, and then she was married, a mother, college gone, her health gone." He leaned his head back and closed his eyes. "One night I came home after a late class and the house was dark. I called out, but there was no answer. Then I heard my little boy crying, and I realized Julia had gone out and left him. He was only two." The telling slowed, but he went on. "At first I was furious. Then I calmed down. Maybe she got sick, had to go to the hospital and wasn't thinking straight. We only had one old car and I was driving it, so I called around to friends. Finally I picked up my boy, put him in the car and went out looking."

He sat up. "I found her at a bar a couple of blocks away, dancing, this guy's hands all over her. I walked in carrying my son, shoved the bastard away and grabbed Julia. The guy started swinging. I was still holding Tommy and somebody must have taken him out of my arms. I could hear Julia, her words slurred, and people were yelling, and the band never stopped playing. Finally a couple of cops showed and broke it up, threatened to haul us in. I got myself together, but when I looked around for Julia and my boy they were gone. I went outside and the car was gone, too."

"Home?"

"No. I got a call from the hospital, a car accident. Julia had died on the way."

"Oh, Jack…"

"Tommy died two days later." So now he had told someone. Julia was the drunk driver who'd killed his family. Ainsley moved closer, but couldn't find a single word she thought would help.

"Tommy woke up just once and called for his mom, and wrapped his skinny little arms around my neck… so light, I could hardly feel them, his breath on my cheek and smelling so sweet, the way kids do." He took a long drink of water. "I'm always stopping to figure out exactly how old he would be, thinking what he'd be like." It was midnight when they awoke, propped up against each other on the sofa for support.

BOOK V

CHAPTER 62

TWO WEEKS LATER, JACK WAS driving into the compound just as dawn was lifting from below the horizon, a dawn that had hurricane written all over it. Upstairs, a faint light warmed the windows near where David would be sleeping. He closed the truck door quietly hoping he wouldn't wake him, but when he looked up at Ainsley's window, he saw a curtain moving. His muffler, probably. To let himself be seen better, although she certainly would recognize his truck, he stepped out of the shadows and waved. He felt ridiculous.

Downstairs, Ainsley opened the door a crack against the wind and whispered through the narrow opening. "Good God, Jack, do you know what time it is?" Since that day in the groves and at his house afterward, she had felt some kind of change between them, not sure of its direction.

"Can I come in?"

"What if I said no?" sighing louder than needed to make her point, she stepped aside to let him squeeze past. "We're in for a big one," he said. "Governor gave the evacuation order down at the Cape."

"I know, the Captain and Sam were hauling boats all day yesterday," moving sleepily into the kitchen. She was wearing shorts and a T-shirt but looked as if she had just woken up.

"I was worried," he said, hoping to overcome his cool reception, and followed her inside. They had just sat down to coffee when they heard a light knock, the Captain's distinctive tap.

"Is this Grand Central? It's open!" she called. Already dressed in baggy pants and a windbreaker, the Captain was ready for work. She complained, "Isn't anyone allowed to

299

sleep around here?" unhappy that another fourteen-hour day was starting so early.

Jack explained, "Thought I'd stop by, see if I could be of any use. With the evacuation, the roads are already backing up. Storm could come ashore near here."

The Captain turned to Ainsley. "We all set?"

"Set as we can be." The day before, she had carried their emergency supplies upstairs in case of flooding. They had enough to get by for several days: water, canned food, cans of Sterno, matches in metal boxes, a battery radio, lanterns, flashlights, extra clothing and blankets, and a laundry-list of other post-hurricane essentials.

Jack looked concerned. "You wouldn't stay out here with a hurricane heading up the coast, would you?"

"'Course not," said the Captain. "All that stuff is for afterwards. Sam will finish boarding up and we'll get going soon as we're packed. Boats are keeping us busy."

"Better get out soon."

The Captain ignored him, just kept setting cups and plates on the table while Jack tended the toaster, right at home. "I been through dozens of these storms," said the Captain, like he'd been thinking it over, "so don't go nagging me, like Ainsley. Owners'll be cluckin' around their boats before the morning even starts." Ainsley went to search the pantry for more English muffins.

"What can I do to help you?" asked Jack.

"We're in good shape. Go by the Bentons. They could use a hand."

"You sure?"

The old man patted Jack's arm. "Go where you're needed, and we'll catch up with you later. I'm good as new, you know," and he was thinking: after this storm was all done with, he had plans. That is, if Phoebe would say yes.

By the time Jack left the Bentons' it was close to five in the afternoon, and almost dark. He'd hurt his shoulder when a sheet of boarding plywood cut loose, and now he tried to ignore the throbbing pain. Driving west toward the shelter, the sky was heavy with clouds. People had been evacuating the island since morning, but the roads were still clogged. Usually you saw one person to a car, but today it was two or more, plus cats and dogs, TVS and racks of clothing.

Huddled and shaking in the archway of a motel, he spotted a young man thumbing a ride but standing too far back to be seen. Jack tapped the horn, and the woman in the car ahead turned around, shaking her fist. Jack tapped it again and the boy looked up. He pointed to himself, Me?, and started splashing toward the truck, leaving a rooster-tail of water behind him. The boy could hardly open the door against the force of the wind.

"Oh, man, thanks! I been trying to catch a ride for an hour. Didn't know where to go or how to get there." Water ran off every part of him, making little rivers that melted into pools on the seat and on the floor. "Oh, gee, I'm sorry," he said, eyeing the puddles.

"Don't worry about it. There's a couple of towels and an old blanket behind the seat." His name was Andy Hall, nineteen, and down from Michigan looking for work. He told Jack, "They've closed 'most everything back home. The Japanese got it all, or the Koreans or somebody… not us." Jack was happy he drove a Chevy. "We got too uppity," said Andy. "Now everybody's flipping burgers or typing into computers for minimum wage and wondering what hit 'em."

"Here, too."

"We had a good life in the factory," said Andy. "We used to be in the middle class."

At the high school shelter, cars filled the parking lot, and another lot at the nearby city marina. It was past seven, two hours to make a fifteen-minute trip. He left Andy with a group of young people and began searching for Ainsley, finally catching sight of her as she struggled through the chaos of sleeping bags, playpens and luggage – apparently searching for him, it looked like, and dressed in jeans and a sweat shirt with a map of Florida on it.

"Jack, thank God!" a welcome that made him happy, but not for long.

"Been on the road two hours," he explained. "You settled in?"

"No. Yes. I mean, the Captain isn't here yet." She noticed his arm, and touched it lightly. "You're hurt."

"Never mind that. Didn't you come together?"

"No," her voice faltered. "He was supposed to leave right after Sam and David and I did. He convinced me to go ahead and find us all a place."

"Why in hell…"

"He *insisted*, Jack. You know how stubborn he is, and he wanted to drive his truck over, get it on higher ground."

"Where's David?"

"Over there, with my parents."

He was calculating all the things that could have happened, none of them good. "You're sure he's not here?"

Her patience was running out. "He's not, I'm positive."

"Maybe he went to a different shelter." Ainsley kept shaking her head. "It was none of those things." She took hold of his jacket. "I'm sure something happened."

"You should have insisted he come with you, stubborn or not!"

"I have to find him." Jack stood there stunned when she turned and started running toward the red exit sign.

"Hold on! Ainsley!" His shouts drew alarmed stares as he followed her into the storm, giving a reassuring wave to her family on the way out, before finally catching up and taking hold of her. "Where do you think you're *going?*"

"Back to the compound to get my grandfather!" but she couldn't shake herself free. "Let go!" She should never have let her grandfather stay behind, should have insisted they all leave together.

"Listen to me," Jack said. "They'll never let you through. All the roads east are barricaded, everything is one way, west."

They stood in the downpour arguing. He yanked her with his good arm and pinned her against the wall. "A1A was about under water an hour ago, and the causeway may be totally washed out!"

As she struggled against him, tears welled up. "This isn't for *you* to decide."

No, it wasn't his decision, he knew, but even if he couldn't stop her, he could reason with her. "You've been listening to the radio. There's no way back to the island."

"There is, by boat."

"Boat? What boat?"

She stared at him defiantly. "Your boat. I know it's here at City Marina."

"No way! Do you think I'm going to let you kill yourself?" With only one good arm to hold her, she broke free. There was nothing he could do to stop her. His injured arm hung at his side as streams of water ran off his fingertips. "Look, my shoulder's busted. I don't know how much help I can be."

"Who said anything about help?" She looked at him, expressionless. "I'm going now. Are you coming?"

"It's too damn dangerous. You'll get swamped, the motor'll die. You'll never make it!" He stood there, soaked through. In the driving rain he could hardly see her face. "Tides are eight feet above normal, you know?"

"I know. And the river is six feet." Breaking free, she waded down the road toward the marina, Jack splashing after her.

CHAPTER 63

JACK'S BOAT WASN'T BUILT FOR speed, she was strong and slow, but their headway against the wind was so slight they could hardly measure it. It's worse, thought Ainsley, than I knew, worse than I ever imagined, but she kept bailing, exhausting work, and almost futile. Long before, she had lost track of time. They were only a quarter of the way to the island, and already her strength was giving out, her arms unfeeling. They would never make it. The rain was mixed with driven sea water, but instead of falling, it came at them sideways, continually pushing them back toward shore.

"Hold on!" yelled Jack. "Here comes one!" They both crouched as an avalanche of water collapsed over the bow, currents striking from so many angles that steering was nearly impossible. Then another wave took them almost broadside, Jack trying to head into it so they wouldn't capsize, but he couldn't hold it, and another sheet of water swept over them.

We're going to die, thought Ainsley. She was numb with cold, her hands cut and bleeding, smarting in the brackish water, and she could hardly lift her arms. For just a moment she stopped to rest, praying.

"Keep bailing!" Jack shouted.

"I am!" her voice dazed and weak.

"Keep bailing! You said you could do it, now *do* it!" and from his expression, she knew he was cursing himself, thinking that somehow he should have prevented this. Full moon, high tide, the worst possible combination, and with only one good arm, he needed her. But she felt herself slipping in and out, as if in a dream, picturing David, his face in front of her, and then she was dipping the bucket again, filling it, lifting, dumping, feeling nothing. How long had they been in the boat? She had no idea, but from somewhere she had gained a second strength;

she breathed, she bailed, her hands were raw, but she couldn't feel anything.

The channel markers were gone and Jack prayed they would not run aground, would not bend the prop. The storm had brought havoc to the channel, and in the roiling waters, debris of every sort swept by: planking, a roof truss, small animals driven from their burrows, uprooted trees. With nearly all the vegetation on St. Christie's blown away, the wind had gained an unobstructed sweep at them, and the boat moved forward only between gusts. The wind whistled by, sounding like an orchestra tuning up.

Yet inch by inch the far shore grew closer, and at moments, between the sheets of driving rain, she recognized the contour of the compound and the outline of their house, still standing, and hope took hold. Jack saw it too, but the look he gave her said, "Keep going."

Nearer to the compound, he could scarcely believe what they were looking at. What had once been land was now a lake. Trees were stripped naked of their leaves, and the shallow-rooted palm trees were bent flat to the ground. He dreaded what they would find once on shore, but didn't dare let up. A few familiar landmarks came into view: a shed, the Jam Works, Ainsley's nursery. He headed the boat into a sheltered space behind the marina, dropped anchor, and tied up as best he could. A moment of peace. Using an extra line, he tied knots to give them a hand-hold, then wrapped it around their bodies so they would not become separated. Whatever happened would happen to both of them. They jumped overboard together, gasping as they hit the chest-deep icy water and began wading toward the house.

Clouds obstructed the moon, but Ainsley could distinguish the lines of her grandfather's truck. Instinctively she tried running toward it, stumbling over unseen debris, each step a battle of luck and will. Jack waded ahead, taking the brunt of the wind. "Hold onto my jacket, and don't let go." Although she tried, the jacket billowed like a sail, blowing him backward. She stumbled after him, running into his feet, struggling to stand, but as she tried to push herself harder, she fell face-first into the water.

Something hard, moving fast struck her side, and she let go of the jacket as water closed above her.

"Ainsley!" The rope had slipped down around her legs and he groped beneath the waves, then dove into the water and found the line. He pulled her to the surface with almost the last of his strength, and she collapsed against his chest before being able to move forward again. "I'm all right," she gasped. She squinted against the rain, searching for her grandfather. All at once she stopped moving. "There!" and let go of the jacket with one hand and pointed with the other. In the darkness she discerned a shape pinned motionless to the pickup.

"Grandpa!" She tried to run, but fell again, "Grandpa!" Jack gripped her around the waist and they fought their way toward the old man and saw that a fallen cabbage palm had trapped the Captain's body against the door of the truck. Shoulder-deep water washed over him.

He lay motionless, his head cocked at an angle. Jack reached him first, cradling his head. The Captain opened his eyes and closed them again, but there was no light in them. The tree must have fallen just as he was preparing to leave; inside, the truck was tightly packed with boxes and tools, and Harvey, the ring-tailed cat, sat atop a bundle of clothes, safe inside looking at them, one paw raised against the glass.

Jack was trying to find the Captain's pulse, but couldn't detect one. Finally, his numb fingers felt a faint something. Maybe, if they were lucky... but how could they free him? If they didn't do it quickly, the Captain would drown or die of hypothermia, or they would, and he didn't know how seriously the Captain might be hurt. Ainsley would be thinking the same thoughts. Barely within reach, a thick piece of lumber was rushing by. Jack stretched to reach it, and managed to grasp one end. He fought to pull the plank toward him, and then he was falling, getting up, but still holding on.

Feeling with his feet, he found a solid spot beneath the tree. The fulcrum. He put all his weight behind it, and managed to wedge the plank into place. Tenth grade physics class. Maybe he'd learned something after all. He might be able to use the plank as a lever and lift the tree enough to pull the Captain free.

"Get hold of your grandfather," he yelled, and Ainsley dived forward through the surge, grasping him under his arms.

"Be ready to drag him out!" The wood cut into his hands as he threw his weight against it, leaning at the very edge, hoping it wouldn't break. It was bending dangerously, and Ainsley was battling to hold the Captain up, ready to pull him out.

Then the plank lost its purchase, slipped in the mud, and threw Jack back into the water, flailing. Ainsley was still holding on desperately to her grandfather. Jack fought his way back to the surface and tried to position the board again, but it wouldn't hold. Luckily, his shoulder had gone numb and the pain had gone with it.

Ainsley prayed out loud.

Jack shoved the plank in place again, this time gaining a slight hold. With half his weight he leaned on it, closer to the middle. "Now!" he yelled, and threw all his weight on the board. The cabbage palm rose – one inch, two inches.

"Higher!" yelled Ainsley.

Jack moved closer to the end of the board, when a gust of wind caught him. If he was blown off now, the palm would crush the Captain's chest. He leaned into the wind, hardly able to breathe. Ainsley felt her arms slipping; she could barely hold her grandfather's head above water, her strength nearly gone. "Again! Try again!" Jack shook his head, and leaned on the plank, inching closer to the end, bending it into a dangerous arc. Another gust caught the board at an angle, giving it a slight thrust… a lift, and the board was holding, the palm was rising, just a bit, just enough, and for a single moment, all resistance stopped, and the Captain was floating free.

As best they could, they carried and floated the old man in his drenched parka toward the house. There was no choice but to lift him onto Jack's good shoulder. Water was two-feet deep on the lower level of the house, and chairs and tables floated around as if on some strange planet. Ainsley had shut off the electricity and water before leaving that day, so they waded through to the stairway with a degree of confidence, but hoping no snakes would be there.

"We'll have to make it upstairs," said Jack, stumbling as he carried the old man up the dark and slippery steps, with Ainsley in back taking hold of the Captain's legs. The wind was so great that water pulsed through the lap of the siding. Still, as they ascended, it was dry inside.

At last they took the thirteenth step and gained the landing. "We'll be safe here," said Ainsley, as if to convince herself. They laid the Captain on the floor and collapsed beside him. After a few minutes, Ainsley forced herself to get up, found the candles and dry matches and lit them. The room seemed almost cheerful. "If I sit, I'll never get up again," she said, gathering blankets and feeling something like hope.

Wind beat against the boarded up windows, ringing like music. Jack dressed the Captain in a dry flannel shirt and pajama bottoms, his breath still so faint they could hardly detect it. They managed to lift him onto a bed. Ainsley covered him with blankets, but still he shivered beneath her touch. Then she heated water on the camp stove, still praying, and feeling more frightened than she had since that day her parents had come home after their car accident.

They both changed into dry sweaters, pants and socks and Ainsley sat on the floor next to the Captain's bed. In the light of the kerosene lamp, the lines in his face were etched deeper than she had ever seen them, each ridge casting its own dark shadow. Jack threw a blanket over her shoulders, and she held the Captain's hands; after a long while she felt them slowly warming.

Jack made tea and brought her a cup, laced with honey to soothe noses and throats that still burned from sea water. He sat on the floor nearby, his head against the wall, eyes closed, feeling the vibrations of the storm, a counterpoint to the eerie country music still being broadcast on the radio. Ainsley fell asleep sitting on the floor with her head resting against the mattress where the Captain lay sleeping. Jack listened to them breathing in unison, the Captain's harsh, rasping gasps; hers, quiet and even. He wrapped another bedspread around her, tucking it in at her feet and around her head, which was covered with leaves and sand and twigs.

When the western edge of the hurricane rolled onshore, it roared like a hundred cars on the speedway. Ainsley woke and sat up peering into the dark, listening to her grandfather's breathing, which was now reassuringly even, his hand warm in hers. Overhead, the tin roof rattled like a thousand tympanies. She whispered, "Jack?"

"I wondered what it would take to wake you." His voice was comforting and calm. "I turned the lamp off, sorry, don't want to start a fire. This is it, you all right?"

"I'm scared."

"I know," closer now, his breath on her cheek.

"Jack? Whatever happens, I want you to know how sorry I am I got you into this."

"I know."

"I'm grateful. I wouldn't have made it without you, and neither would he."

He slid his arm around her shoulder. "It's okay," and then he took her in his arms and they waited as the storm's intensity grew, beginning with a rumble, rocking the house gently, then shaking and vibrating it to the foundations. Studs and floorboards trembled, nails moaned and pulled, window boards downstairs were wrenched away. The sound was louder, more terrifying than anything she could ever have imagined. The house itself seemed alive, screaming. The storm went on, hour after hour, until gradually, the winds began to slow and Ainsley took a deep breath. Had she been breathing the whole time? Everyone else on St. Christie's must be feeling the same thing; if there was anyone else. They lit the lanterns again and Ainsley heated water while Jack searched the radio, looking for a signal. "We made it," she whispered.

"We did, and why are you whispering?" Hour by hour, the storm's fury lessened, and they fell asleep, Ainsley on the sofa, Jack sprawled in an easy chair, the Captain in his bed, breathing deeply and evenly. Not even the storm had wakened him.

They opened their eyes to light streaming through an east window where a strip of boarding had ripped away. They pressed their faces against the narrow slit and gazed out on a desolate landscape that stretched beneath a calm, gray sky. Where there had once been dunes, now there was a lake. Where there had been trees, none were standing. As far out to sea as their eyes would carry, waves mounted, capturing air beneath tons of water… then collapsing, carrying plumes of foam against the sky. And everywhere, the beach was littered with debris: a nurse shark, roof shingles, a child's doll.

"Jack…," she began, but he placed a scarred finger on her lips, drew her close and held her.

"You're brave," he told her. "Tough and brave." Hearing that, she sank into his shoulder, and Jack stroked her matted hair.

CHAPTER 64

THE SCENT OF INCENSE WAFTED through the church, clouds of white smoke rising. In front of the altar, banks of votive candles were burning, petitions for health, love, wealth, a child… all the things people most wish for. Ainsley sat with David, her parents, Phoebe, and Sam, all there for her grandfather's funeral. Every seat was taken and people were forced to stand in the aisles at St. Mary's little church. They must have loved him, she thought, to stand through a Catholic mass.

The Captain's death had been unexpected. After the storm, the doctor said he'd come through fine, no internal injuries, just a few bad scrapes. He'd returned home, seeing friends, tending the store, but two weeks later, Sam had found him slumped in a chair.

Now a soprano was singing "Ave Maria," one of her grandfather's favorite hymns, and Father Jimmy had even consented to "Danny Boy," another. For someone with such a big heart, it seemed fitting that the Captain had used his heart up completely. Father Jimmy invited anyone who wanted to say something to come up and not be shy. Many did, and their words painted a picture of his life, the choices her mother had talked to her about.

A Friend told them: "My family and me moved here when I was about twenty, and I figured if I was to fit in, I'd have to pick a fight with somebody, and Frank O'Rourke was the one I lit on. One day we was throwing some punches, both of us banged up pretty good, and Frank says: "Let's call it a draw, and go wet a line." So we did, and we been wettin a line neigh fifty years. I miss him."

A Young Father said: "I finally got me an old tub, a fourteen-footer. I never was more proud, and the Captain kept it running for me. It wasn't just about the boat, but that he wanted for me to have it."

An Older Woman: "When I was a kid, my restless side took me away to make my fortune. 'If you get to New York City," Frank said, "bring me back one of those big pretzels,' and when I came back, no matter how boring my stories were, he always listened, and he never asked about the fortune thing, or the pretzel either."

Another Old Man: "From our early days, I knew his dreams, and him mine, and we never made fun. I'm proud he called me friend."

And a Litany of Other Recollections... "No matter what he was going through himself, he was always rooting for you."... "He told me once he'd never made a mark in the world, and I'm proud I thought to tell him, 'Maybe not, but you made an impression, you old goat.' "... "He gave me a chance and I ain't been back to prison since."... "He took all morning to show my Jimmy how to surf cast, when I woulda killed the little bastard."... "Never reminded me of the money I owed, knew I'd pay when I could, which was a good while."... "That old checkered shirt, I thought he'd be mad as hell not being laid out in it."... "He had slowed up some, but everything was fine, fast or slow, when he took up a wrench."

Father Jimmy shook every person's hand as they stepped down from the alter. "A fine job," he told them. "And now," the pastor cleared his throat, "before the final blessing, I've asked Ainsley to read a few parts from letters her grandfather wrote to her when she was away at school."

Ainsley stood at the foot of the alter, looking out at the faces her grandfather had loved – his family and friends, and hers as well: Beth and Nick, Tupper, Anne and Leo, Charlie and Vickie, Bear and Dance and their two children. Seated in the back were Emilio and Irena, Lolo and Tina, other workers from the groves and from the jam factory, and Jack, Leola, the Bentons, Clay and Lady, small boat owners from the marina, fishermen and his cronies from the old days who still played gin together every week.

"Seeing all of you here today," she said, "tells me what a fine life my grandfather led. In ways I cannot know, each of you meant something to him and he meant something to you. And you know what he meant to his family," her voice faltering. "His kindness, his hard work, even his stubbornness touched our hearts." Then a breath, her only defense:

"He often gave me advice when I was growing up – I wish I'd taken more of it – and when I went away to school, he made sure to give me timely doses of St. Christie's wisdom. In his letters… I kept them all… I've marked a few passages, which I'll read for you now." In the front pew, Parker had one arm around Grace, the other around Phoebe. Ainsley glanced away, fumbled for the first letter and began reading.

"Dear Girl," he wrote, "Family is the greatest blessing God can give us… There when you need nursing. There when you need a few dollars. There when you need a comeuppance… Not that you need this last one. But if you ever do, you can count on us."

She looked up and knew they were all remembering his voice, his never-failing good intentions. "This next passage is about work."

She began: "Darling Girl, … Take time off from your studies, because there's too much work in the world, and not enough play. Work's a fine thing, of course, but don't work yourself so hard you disgrace the family."

She folded the paper, put it aside and picked up the final letter. "This last one has to do with love." She read: " 'We all want love, darling. It's a gift. We don't have to work for it, or barter for it. In fact, you can't, and that's the glory of it." When she looked up, heads were nodding, and she braced herself to go on. "If we're lucky, love finds us, and if it doesn't, we have to look inside, hope it's there, and give it away. That's what I think, anyway, because most of the things I've worried about in life and worked hard for, have never amounted to much of anything compared to love.' "

Later, everyone came back to the compound. Neighbors had brought their special dishes, and Ainsley and Grace were spared having to do anything at all. There were so many people she didn't know, so many events in her grandfather's life that she had not been a part of. He had been an open man, and yet he seemed to have had a life separate from all of them. "I'm…" and the strangers would tell her their names. Or they'd say, "I remember your grandfather from…" and tell her a story she knew nothing about.

And it became clear to Ainsley that no matter how close you were to someone, that person had his own friendships, loves, adventures, misfortunes and hopes that you couldn't even guess at. Jack, the last person in line, was talking to Grace and Parker, and now was turning toward Phoebe, patting her back. David stood at his side, too young to understand his loss. And Phoebe, she truly had been the one, almost.

It had been a long day and most friends had said their goodbyes when Ainsley noticed a small group gathering in a tight knot. Whispering, glancing her way. Then Jack began walking toward her, head down, and put his arm around her shoulder.

"I'm sorry. I have more bad news," he said, "It's about Billy," and something inside her gave way.

"An accident. He's asking for you."

CHAPTER 65

"YOU CAN ONLY STAY IN there a few minutes," said the nurse. "He's awake now." Ainsley pushed through the swinging door into the intensive care unit. Six beds were lined up against one wall; along the other, nurses and doctors sat in a glassed-in room staring at machines and filling out charts, the sound of ventilators and beeping monitors making an eerie background noise. Billy was in the first bed, curtained off, his eyes closed, his head bandaged.

She took his hand. "It's Ainsley," she whispered, and his eyes flicked open. He looked helpless, not Billy at all, and no words came when he tried to speak. With her face close to his, she said, "Billy, you're going to be fine, you are." He closed his eyes. A lie, he seemed to say, and again he tried to speak, but all she heard were gasps. Ainsley clung to his hand.

"You'll have to leave. Sorry." The nurse entered with two doctors, elbowing her aside as they surrounded Billy's bed. "Routine," she assured her. They'd only had a few minutes together. For hours afterward, she sat in the waiting room with his other visitors including Wendell Jablonski, but finally, told that she wouldn't be allowed to see Billy again that night, she left the hospital. It was dark outside, but she wasn't surprised to see Jack still waiting; he'd driven her over that afternoon and was sitting on the steps, ready to take her home.

News of Billy's accident was on television and radio, but there was no picture of the accident in the next day's Island News because it happened out of town during a practice run and no photographers had been there. Billy had insisted on being flown home. The story had quotes from Dr. Jose Vargas who was attending him, quotes from track officials and from Wendell. Had Billy Fiske run his last race?

A different article at the bottom of the front page reported that six crew bosses had been arrested at the Coller Groves on charges of fraud, aggravated battery, rape, false imprisonment and slavery. The grove owner said he was sorry, but those people didn't work for him.

"He's a tough man," said Dr. Vargas, being interviewed a week later for the local TV station. "Luckily, Billy was in excellent physical shape."

"Will he race again?" the question everyone asked.

"We have high hopes."

"A full recovery, Doctor?"

"It's been only a week," he said, letting them speculate, which they seemed to like doing.

Inside, Ainsley was sitting at Billy's bedside as she had each day. His mother was staying in town, and Lorraine visited too, so they made an effort to time their visits, both for Billy's sake and their own. Flowers and cards came every day, and he liked having Ainsley read them to him, but this day, even the fan mail didn't cheer him. Earlier, he'd been up and walking and seemed drained. "Put the letter down and look at me, Ainsley. I know my fans are there for me. What I want to know is this: Are you?"

He had taken her by surprise. "I've always been there for you," she said. Questions about their future had risen well before the accident, but the hopes she'd carried for so many years now seemed from a far-off place and time.

Although Billy sat up only for short periods at a time, he asked her to help him do it now. Just as she had many times before, she tucked the pillow behind his back, and adjusted the bed. Dr. Vargas and the physical therapist said his progress was remarkable, walking further each day but he still wasn't himself. Wendell was certain Billy would make it back all the way.

"I don't know what I'd have done without you," Billy told her. "Seeing you keeps me going."

"It's where I want to be…"

"Hush." He raised his arm in its cumbersome cast to quiet her. "Being in here has made it clear what matters."

"I think you always knew."

"What matters," he interrupted, "is you," but he stopped to add a smile, "and racing."

"At least you're honest."

Then he took her hand, pulled her close, and out of the blue whispered, "I want you to marry me," at last, the words she had waited so long to hear. "As soon as I get out of here," he said quickly, "I'll be the man you've always known."

"I know you will."

He signaled for a sip of water and she handed him the glass. He said, "I know things are changed with me like this, and with you being such a smart girl, I don't want you to think I wasn't planning to ask you before, because I was," and he took a long drink. "So... no need to answer right away. Nothing between us was ever easy, so why would it be any different now?"

"Okay..." Had he, she wondered, seen a fleeting concern in her face?

"Tomorrow? Is that too soon? You know how I feel."

All she could do was nod.

✎

Irena and Emilio had moved temporarily into the Captain's home at the marina after his death, helping Sam, who had taken over there, helping Ainsley not just at the Jam Works, but looking after David, the way the Captain had. Only now did she realize how much he had done. The empty space in David's life had to be almost as big as the one in her own.

After saying goodnight to Irena and tucking David in again, she sat in the dark on the sunroom porch, thinking about Billy, his proposal of marriage. He had wondered, as she had, too, whether his injury would cause her to turn away, and of this she was certain: It wouldn't. His being injured had always been a possibility, and in the years since she had first met him, loss and struggle had been a steady part of life for almost everyone she knew.

Billy had promised to be the man he had always been, but there was no such man; both of them had changed. At seventeen, she had hardly known herself, so how could she possibly have known him? Had he seen doubt? Did it exist? And then there was Jack, and what she didn't want to admit: feelings she had fought against for so long because of her dream of Billy. She lay down on the little sofa and the sounds of the sea lulled her to sleep.

CHAPTER 66

FOR THE FIRST TIME SINCE the day of the accident, Ainsley had asked Jack to drive her to the hospital, and unsure why, he was wary. It was dusk, and the summer sky was holding onto its last strokes of color as they rode together in silence. Finally she began: "I asked you to drive me because I have something to tell you, Jack – and I'm taking a taxi home, it's all arranged, so no arguments."

"I love bossy women."

"This is real, Jack, don't joke." That voice, husky and serious, said it all. "It's about us, and Billy." The parking lot was almost full, as usual.

"Excuse me, but forget Billy a minute. What *about* us?" He found a space and pulled in.

"He's asked me to marry him."

He clicked off the radio. What could he say? "Now? Now he's asked you to marry him?"

"Please, stop."

He rested his head on the steering wheel. "Don't do this, Ainsley." He knew he sounded like some dickhead, but he didn't care. "Let Billy get as well as he can get. Then we'll duke it out, mano-a-mano, whatever." Now he really *was* a dickhead. He turned off the engine and the air conditioner shut down. It felt instantly suffocating. Embarrassed, he lied a little: "I'm not putting myself in the picture, not at all. That's not my point."

"I'm going to tell him yes, Jack." And only then was her decision made.

"You know it's wrong. Don't make a second mistake."

She was picking up her handbag and a sports magazine she'd brought along. "Don't wait for me," and then she got out of the truck, and Jack did, too, coming around to her side, pinning her against the door. "You may have wanted Billy before, but not anymore; you know it and so do I." Without admitting it, he'd been picturing a life with her and David, seeing them in every part of his day. "You can't do this." He was holding her in his arms, not an embrace really, just keeping her there. And she took it in, all of it, and threw her arms around his neck, kissing him, imprinting it on her personal circuit board they sometimes joked about, so that whenever she chose, she could recall this moment. And then she was gone.

When the great doors opened and she came out of the hospital a while later, Jack was sitting on the granite steps outside, getting up when he saw her step out of the elevator and start toward him.

She called out, "I said not to wait."

"Sorry, boss."

"I ordered a taxi."

"I paid him. Told him to have a nice day." He was on the landing with her now, taking her by the arm as she tried to slip past him. "Sit down." He put his other hand on top of her head, as if she were under arrest, pressing down until she sat on the steps, and then he sat next to her. "Did you do it?"

Looking away, she dropped her head. He willed himself not to say or do anything, and then Ainsley turned to him, wrapping him in her arms, comforting him the same way he'd seen her consoling David.

Billy had been looking forward all day to seven o'clock, the time Ainsley was due to arrive. He'd had a late shave, changed into one of his shirts from home, and had asked the nurses to leave them alone. "Put up the 'Do Not Disturb' sign," he told them. "And don't come sneaking around in those funny rubber shoes." He had a private room, and earlier in the day, Wendell had brought a bottle of Champagne, two flutes, a wedge of Brie and sesame crackers for their celebration, a reprise of an earlier time.

Ainsley arrived at seven, as he knew she would, tired but lovely, wearing a short white sun dress he liked, her hair pulled up from the nape of her neck. She kissed him on the cheek. "I brought you a present," she said, and handed him the Sports Illustrated magazine. "You're in it." He flipped through the pages, saw his photo but wasn't really interested.

"How about something to drink?" he nodded toward the Champagne. "Opening it's a little out of my range, so why don't you do the honors?" The bottle sat chilling in a bucket of ice-water, and she wrapped it with the starched napkin that Wendell had brought, glancing at Billy for approval. Not necessary. Everything she did pleased him. That smoky voice of hers, the way she moved, the thoughtfulness that seemed to be part of her.

She looked at him as she cut the foil, then loosened the wire and twisted the cork, the way he'd taught her. He thought back to the first time she'd opened a bottle of Champagne, not that long ago. Things had seemed so perfect then – his career on a little rise again, a new start with Ainsley, and even after that, when she seemed different somehow, he'd loved her more, wanted her more.

But just now, when he had looked out the window of his room awaiting her visit, and saw her in Jack Henderson's arms, kissing him the way she had, he knew that what Ainsley felt for him now wasn't love. Not anymore.

Poof! A tiny explosion, then a small stream of Champagne cascading down the sides of the bottle. Ainsley laughing, trying to stop the impossible. "An almost perfect job!" she said, and began filling their glasses, pouring a little at a time into each one.

They touched them together in a toast.

"To you," he said.

"Thank you. To you, Billy." They drank their glasses empty.

"But not to us," he said.

She stared at him, not grasping it. "What do you mean?"

He took her hand. "I mean, Ainsley, we had our time together. I'll never forget it. Or you. But I tried to kid myself, something I don't usually do, into thinking we could go back, find whatever we once had. Some people can, but not us."

He turned away. "I'm sorry." Her eyes were brimming. And then he kissed her. He watched her leave, and afterward, held the pillow hard against his chest to keep everything inside from shaking loose.

❧

Sitting on the steps outside the hospital, Ainsley finished telling Jack what had happened. "What he'll never know, is that I was going to tell him no, I couldn't."

Jack stood up and gave her his hand. "C'mon. Let's go home."

"Home?" His smile was her answer.

"Don't think this has anything to do with you, Jack."

"Why would I?"

"And don't get any ideas about the future."

"Don't *you* get any ideas, either," he said. He put his arm around her waist as they walked to the truck, and she believed him when he told her, "Everything's going to be just fine."

ABOUT THE AUTHOR

 Because writers are required to have favorite topics, Ellie Osborne has chosen love – romantic and familial love, as well as love of grits, pets and place and all the other kinds of love that make us want to die or live forever – love squandered, love betrayed, love lost and found again – a subject worth thinking about, caring about and writing about. A journalist and editor, she has lived north, south, east and west, and has long been settled on the Atlantic coast of wild and wonderful Florida.

Acknowledgments

Just when I thought everyone would leave me in peace, a family member or friend (sometimes one and the same person), would ask: "What about your book?" After enough such prompts, and many visions and revisions, I finished writing it. For that, I must first thank Jack Goellner, who waded through several versions and provided insightful and gentle criticism each time. And then there was Jeri Grail, who read it first and never stopped encouraging me, and Kevin Grail, who may be waiting for the audio book, but has been supportive. Among the first readers were dear friends and fellow writers, Roz Silva and Gloria Lintermans, and later, the Tuesday Book Club – friends since our first meeting on Sept. 11, 2001 and friends to this day. Thank you, all of you, and each of you.